BODY LANGUAGE

A. K. Turner

ZAFFRE

First published in Great Britain in 2020 by
ZAFFRE
80–81 Wimpole St, London W1G 9RE

A CIP catalogue record for this book is
available from the British Library.

ISBN: 978-1-83877-004-4

Also available as an ebook

1 3 5 7 9 10 8 6 4 2

Typeset by IDSUK (Data Connection) Ltd
Printed and bound in Great Britain by Clays Ltd, Elcograf S.p.A.

Zaffre is an imprint of Bonnier Books UK
www.bonnierbooks.co.uk

For Katy
And in memory of Ann Edwards – the real 'Mrs E'

Chapter One

The zip of the body bag parted to reveal Cassie's first customer of the day. The woman's half-open eyes, a surprisingly vivid blue, gazed up at her, unseeing.

'Hello there, Mrs Connery.' Her voice became gentler than the one she used with the living. 'My name's Cassie Raven and I'll be looking after you while you're with us.' She had no doubt that the dead woman could hear her and hoped she took some comfort from the words.

The previous evening Kate Connery had collapsed while getting ready for bed and died, there on her bathroom floor one week short of her fiftieth birthday. Laughter lines latticed her open, no-nonsense face beneath hair too uniformly brunette to be natural.

Cassie glanced up at the clock and swore. There was a new pathologist coming in to do the day's post-mortem list and with Carl, the junior technician, off sick and three bodies to prep, it was shaping up to be the Monday from hell.

Still, she took her time working Mrs C's nightdress up over her head, registering the faint ammoniac smell of sweat or urine, before carefully folding it away in a plastic bag. The things somebody had been wearing when they died meant a lot to their loved ones, sometimes more than the body itself, which

1

grieving relatives could struggle to relate to. A dead body could feel like an empty suitcase.

'We need to find out what happened to you, Mrs C,' Cassie told her. 'So that we can get Declan and your boys some answers.'

From her first day in the mortuary five years ago it had felt totally natural to talk to the bodies in her care, to treat them as if they were still alive – still people. Occasionally they would even answer.

It wasn't like a live person talking – for a start, their lips didn't move – and the experience was always so fleeting that she might almost have imagined it. *Almost.* Usually they said something like '*Where am I?*' or '*What happened?*' – simple bewilderment at finding themselves in this strange place – but now and again she was convinced that their words contained a clue to how they'd died.

Cassie had never told a living soul about these 'conversations'; people thought she was weird enough already. But they didn't know what she knew deep in her gut: the dead could talk – if only you knew how to listen.

The only outward sign of anything wrong with Mrs Connery was a few red blotches on her cheeks and forehead and a fist-sized bruise on her sternum where either her husband or the paramedics had administered desperate CPR. Cassie looked through the notes. After a night out at the pub watching football, Declan Connery had come home to find his wife unconscious. An ambulance rushed her to the hospital, but she was declared dead on arrival.

Since Kate Connery had died unexpectedly – she'd apparently been in good health and hadn't seen her GP for months – a basic or 'routine' post-mortem to establish the cause of death was an automatic requirement.

Cassie put her hand on Mrs C's fridge-cold forearm and waited for her own warmth to expel the chill. 'Can you tell me what happened?' she murmured.

For a few seconds, nothing. Then she felt the familiar slip-sliding sensation, followed by a distracted dreaminess. At the same time, her senses became hyper-alert – the hum of the body-store fridge growing to a jet-engine roar, the overhead light suddenly achingly bright.

The air above Mrs Connery's body seemed to fizz with the last spark of the electricity that had animated her for five decades. And out of the static Cassie heard a low, hoarse whisper.

'I can't breathe!'

Chapter Two

As always, it was all over in an instant. It reminded Cassie of waking from an intense dream, your mind scrabbling to hold onto the details – only to feel them slipping away, like water through open fingers.

In any case, Mrs Connery's words weren't much help. Cassie could find no history of asthma or emphysema in the notes, and there was a whole bunch of other disorders that could affect breathing. She was still wondering what, if anything, to make of it when she heard the door from the clean area open. It was Doug, the mortuary manager, followed by a younger guy – tall, with a floppy fringe – who he introduced as Dr Archie Cuff, the new pathologist.

Stripping off a nitrile glove, she offered Cuff her hand.

'Cassie Raven is our senior mortuary technician,' beamed Doug. 'She's the one who makes everything run like clockwork round here.'

Although he wore cufflinks (*cufflinks*?!) and a tie, Cuff couldn't be much more than thirty, barely five years older than Cassie. A single glance told her that his navy waxed jacket was a genuine Barbour, not a knock-off – its metal zipper fob embossed with the brand name – and going by his tie, a dark blue silk with a slanting fat white stripe, he'd been schooled at

Harrow. Cassie noticed things like that, had done ever since she could remember.

'Looking forward to working with you, Cathy.' He spoke in the fake, demi-street accent favoured by the younger royals, his smile as glib as a cabinet minister's, but it was clear from the way his glance slid over her that she'd already been filed in a box labelled 'minion'.

Cassie didn't often take an instant dislike to someone, but in the case of Archie Cuff she decided to make an exception.

'Me too,' she said, 'especially if you get my name right.'

A flush rose from Cuff's striped shirt collar all the way to his gingery sideburns, but at least he looked at her properly this time. And from the flicker of distaste that crossed his face, he didn't much like what he saw – although it was hard to tell whether it was her dyed black hair with the shaved undercut, her facial piercings, or simply the way she held his gaze. She had to fight a juvenile impulse to lift the top half of her scrubs and flash her tattoos at him.

Doug's eyes flitted between the two of them like a rookie referee at a cage fight, his smile starting to sag. 'Right then, I'll leave you folks to it.' Cassie knew he would probably remind her later of his golden rule: *'Never forget, the pathologist can make your job a dream – or a nightmare.'*

After Cuff's brief external examination of Mrs Connery, during which they barely spoke beyond the essentials, he left Cassie to do the evisceration.

She placed her blade at the base of Mrs C's throat. This was the moment when she had to stop thinking of Kate Connery as a person and start viewing her as a puzzle to be unlocked, unmapped territory to explore. Without that shift of perspective, what normal person could slice open a fellow human being?

After the initial incision, a decisive sweep down the sternum laid open the tissue as easily as an old silk curtain. Reaching the soft gut area, she didn't pause but let up the pressure to avoid damage to the organs beneath, ending the cut just above the pubic bone.

Within five minutes, the bone shears had cracked open Mrs C's ribcage, exposing her heart and lungs, and Cassie was deftly detaching the organs from their moorings. Once that was done, she used both hands to lift out the entire viscera, from tongue down to urethra, before delivering them gently into the waiting plastic pail. This was a sombre moment, which always made her feel like a midwife of death.

Now for the brain. Going behind Mrs C's head, Cassie repositioned the block beneath her neck. The scalp incision would go from from ear to ear over the top of the head, so that once it was stitched up again the wound would be covered by her hair – especially important since the Connerys were having an open coffin funeral. Combing the front half of Mrs C's thick dark hair forward over her face, Cassie noticed a shiny red patch on the scalp. Eczema? It hadn't been mentioned in the medical notes, but in any case, eczema didn't kill people.

After peeling the bisected scalp forward and back to expose the skull, Cassie reached for the oscillating saw. Moments later she had eased off the skullcap and was coaxing the brain free. Cradling it in both hands for a moment, she imagined Kate Connery as she would have been in life – a down-to-earth matriarch with a ready laugh, surrounded by family and friends in a Camden Town boozer.

When Archie Cuff returned in his scrubs, the atmosphere between them stayed chilly: in the forty minutes it took him to dissect Mrs C's organs, he only spoke to Cassie once, to complain that the blade of his PM40 was blunt. That only confirmed her initial impression of him as the latest in a long line of arrogant posh boys who viewed mortuary technicians as one step up from abattoir workers. A more experienced pathologist would have asked her opinion on the cause of death, and not just to be polite: technicians spent far longer with the bodies and sometimes spotted clues that might otherwise be missed.

As Cuff moved along the dissection bench to rinse his bloodied gloved hands in the sink, Cassie started to collect Mrs C's organs into a plastic bag, ready to be reunited with her body.

'So, what's the verdict?' she asked him.

'There's nothing conclusive to account for her death.' He shrugged. 'We'll have to wait and see whether the lab finds anything useful.' Toxicology would test Mrs C's bodily fluids for drugs, while samples of her organs would undergo histopathology to look for any microscopic signs of disease.

'Did you find any petechiae in her lungs?' asked Cassie, keeping her voice casual.

Cuff turned to look at her. 'Why do you ask?'

So he had.

She lifted one shoulder 'I just thought her face looked quite congested.'

I can't breathe.

Petechiae – tiny burst blood vessels – could signal a lack of oxygen.

Cuff looked flustered. 'She was found face down. It's clear from the latest literature that a prone position post-mortem can cause petechial haemorrhage.' He managed a condescending smile. 'If you were hoping for a juicy murder, I'm afraid you're out of luck: there's absolutely no evidence of strangulation or suffocation.'

Cassie knew as well as Cuff did that asphyxia could just as easily have a medical cause, but she stifled a comeback. Dropping a nugget of kidney into a pot of preservative for the lab, she caught sight of Mrs C's body on the autopsy table – her ribcage butterflied like an open book, a dark void where her organs used to be. Above the ruined body, her shiny brunette hair looked out of place.

The light from the fluorescent tubes overhead flared, forcing Cassie to close her eyes, the ever-present reek of formalin suddenly harsh enough to claw at her throat. Behind her eyelids, images flickered: Mrs C's blotched face, the scaly patch on her scalp. She felt her throat start to close and in an instant, everything clicked into place.

'Just popping to the loo,' she told Cuff, before slipping into the corridor, where she pulled out her phone.

'Mr Connery? It's Cassie Raven from the mortuary.'

Ten minutes later she was back. 'Sorry I took so long,' she told Cuff. 'But I just had an interesting conversation with Mrs Connery's husband.'

'Husband . . . ?' He sounded confused at the idea of a body having a spouse.

'Yes. Before he went out last night, she told him she was going to colour her hair.'

'I don't see what . . .'

'He says that she had suffered allergic reactions to her hair dye twice before. Nothing too serious. But this time, it looks like it triggered a fatal anaphylactic shock.'

Chapter Three

'It's only me, Babcia!' Cassie had learned the hard way that it was a good idea to announce her arrival when letting herself in to her grandmother's place, which had become her childhood home, after her parents died. Once, when she was seventeen, she'd nearly got a rolling pin over the head, crashing in at three in the morning off her face on MDMA.

As a little girl, she'd always loved this moment of leaving the wind-lashed concrete walkway and stepping into the flat's toasty, cinnamon-smelling interior, as if the doorway was some kind of magic portal to another world.

'Cassandra, *tygrysek!*' Her grandmother turned from the stove to greet her. The top of her head barely reached Cassie's nose, but her hug was fierce enough to crack a rib. 'You've lost weight,' she observed, accusingly.

'No thanks to you.' Cassie sniffed the air. 'Mushrooms and sour cream. With . . . dumplings. And poppyseed cake for afters?'

Her grandmother looked up at her through narrowed eyes. 'The mushrooms of course you can smell, but what about the dumplings?'

Cassie ran a finger along the worktop edge and showed her grandmother the trace of white dust on its tip. 'You've either been making kopytka or bread – and I can't smell yeast.'

'And the poppyseed cake?'

'There's a new copy of that magazine you like in the hall. Which means you've been to the Polish shop in Islington – and you never go there without buying makowiec.'

'Go and sit down, clever-clogs.' Unable to suppress a smile, her grandmother shooed her out of the kitchen.

In the front room, Cassie sank into an armchair and felt the warmth settle over her like a duvet, the only noise the comforting *pop pop* of the gas fire. Hard to believe now that as a teenager she'd seen the place as an overheated prison cell, with her grandmother as the beady-eyed chief warder. By the age of sixteen Cassie had already had her tongue pierced, put a turquoise flash in her hair, and smoked her first skunk. As for school, '*Cassie prefers to question her teachers rather than learn from them*' went a typical report card. Back then, it had felt to her like the entire adult world was united in a single aim: to destroy her right to self-expression.

From the kitchen she heard 'I've got something for you!' – followed by the sound of the freezer door closing.

Babcia came in with her hands behind her back before holding out a long, rigid plastic-wrapped package. 'Can you guess?'

Inside, Cassie found a squirrel, frozen stiff. Laying it face-up in her lap, she examined it as gently as she would one of her human charges – already picturing it restored to a kind of life through taxidermy, which she'd recently taken up.

A dead squirrel would seem like a seriously weird gift to most people, but then they didn't know what Babcia knew – that ever since she was tiny, Cassie had been drawn to dead things. She could still remember the first time she'd seen a fox lying in the gutter, killed by a car. Bending to stroke the poor thing's bristly gingernut fur, she'd seen him transformed, just for a moment, restored to a frolicking cub.

'Aren't you beautiful?' She stroked the squirrel's pristine pelt – too perfect to be roadkill. 'Where did you find him?'

'I got it off the dustman. He owes me one.'

Cassie didn't like to ask what *that* meant: her grandmother waged a one-woman war in the tower block against graffiti, rubbish dumping, and other antisocial behaviour. A few weeks ago, she'd even confronted a drug dealer who was selling weed to schoolkids in the stairwell. But whenever Cassie tried to talk her out of such risky behaviour, the old lady raised her chin and said that she hadn't emigrated to a free country only to live in fear. Like Cassie, Weronika Janek had been a rebellious youth – with the difference that in 1950s Poland her involvement in protests against the communist regime had earned her six months in jail.

When the food was ready, Cassie folded out the old green baize card table her grandmother used for meals. As they ate, she mentioned the arrival of the new pathologist.

'And you don't like him.' Weronika's gaze was piercing.

'My opinion is irrelevant. I'm just one of the underlings.'

Except today, the underling had scored a small victory.

She told the story, leaving out the bit about hearing Mrs Connery say she couldn't breathe. Her conversations with the dead were too ... *sacred* to be shared with anyone, even her grandmother. In any case, whenever she examined these moments rationally she had to admit that they could simply be her subconscious putting two and two together: for instance, hadn't she noticed the blotches on Mrs C's face *before* hearing her speak?

'Her husband told me she'd had outbreaks of hives before, after dyeing her hair.'

'But she carried on using the same dye?'

'She probably thought a bit of skin irritation was worth putting up with.' The red patches on Mrs C's face and neck hadn't been eczema but the last traces of urticaria, an allergic rash. 'Maybe her GP didn't warn her that there was a serious risk her immune system would get more sensitised every time she coloured her hair. Yesterday it went into overdrive. Her airway swelled up so much she literally couldn't breathe.'

'Poor lady.' Weronika crossed herself. 'So, why didn't the smartypants body doctor work it out?'

Cassie pictured again Archie Cuff's astonished expression when he realised a lowly technician might have stumbled on the cause of Mrs Connery's death. A couple of minutes later he'd signed a form ordering the specialist blood test needed to confirm the theory – all without saying a word.

Twat.

'To be fair, they only get thirty to forty minutes for a routine post-mortem and anaphylaxis is notoriously difficult to diagnose after death.'

'But *you* noticed something. You pick up small things that other people miss – you always did, even as a little girl.' She pointed her fork at Cassie. 'You should be one of the body doctors, you have the brains for it!'

Cassie's shrug was sceptical – this was a well-worn argument between them. She knew she was a pretty good mortuary technician, but the idea of becoming a pathologist? It was laughable – like going from five-a-side knockabout in the park to playing for Arsenal. Medical school wasn't for girls like her – semi-educated and raised in a council tower block – it was for people like Archie

Cuff; posh and male, who seemed to float through life on a bubble of unshakeable self-confidence.

'What about those A levels you got at night school?' Her grandmother counted them off on her fingers. 'A's in biology and chemistry, a B in physics. *And* an A star in classics!'

'Which is about as much use as macramé.'

After leaving school with four poor GCSEs, Cassie had been consumed with the idea of escape: she loved her grandmother but back then, the near fifty-five-year age gap between them had felt like an unbridgeable chasm. Her ultimate dream had been to go abroad and live somewhere cool like Berlin, but when Mazz, her boyfriend at the time, told her about a room going begging in a squat in a disused office building in Chalk Farm, she decided it was better than nothing.

The day after her seventeenth birthday, bent under the weight of an overstuffed rucksack, Cassie had hugged her grandmother goodbye on the doorstep, both of them fighting back tears. But by the time Cassie reached the street her tears had dried, replaced by a rising sense of excitement: she was finally free, and starting adult life properly at last, answerable to no one.

After the relationship with Mazz fizzled out barely three months later, Cassie had stayed on at the squat, moving on to the next place after each inevitable eviction. You couldn't call it a comfortable life – everyone was skint, and they often had no water or electricity – but her shifting band of housemates were an exhilarating mix of the crazy and the creative. Fiercely loyal to each other, they shared everything from food to drugs, and she had revelled in the freedom of living beyond the margins – at least for a while.

After about eighteen months of this vagabond life, Cassie was selling the *Big Issue* outside M&S one day when she had the chance encounter that would change everything. A stylish woman in her late forties stopped to buy the magazine and stayed to chat. A science teacher from the local adult education college, she quickly became a regular visitor, always bringing Cassie a sandwich and a cup of coffee.

Their conversations had ranged thrillingly wide, from how the eye perceived colour via the discovery of water on Mars, to the finding that Europeans had as much as five per cent Neanderthal DNA – encounters that sent Cassie's brain firing off in all directions like a Catherine wheel. A few weeks later, she found herself signing up for science evening classes with Mrs Edwards – or Mrs E, as all her students called her. After a rocky start, Cassie had inhaled knowledge like a free diver coming up for air.

'Well, I know one thing,' Weronika was saying, 'your mama, God rest her soul, would be so proud of you.'

Cassie followed her look to the photograph on the mantelpiece that showed a pretty girl in her late teens wearing a ruffle-necked blouse, her smile shy beneath auburn hair. Her mum had been just twenty-five, her dad a couple of years older, when they were killed in a car crash, victims of a teenage driver in a stolen Porsche. Orphaned at the age of four, Cassie could barely remember her mother beyond a handful of impressions – a soft cheek at bedtime, the watermelon sweetness of her perfume, a dress bedecked with giant orange poppies. For some reason, her memories of her dad were more vivid. Being carried on his shoulders through woodland, her hands clutched tight in his dark curls, the funny faces he would pull, playing airplane with a forkful of some food she wouldn't eat – the same face that could stretch suddenly, thrillingly, into a scary monster.

'Babcia . . . how old was I when I started bringing home dead animals?'

Weronika looked up, startled. 'Oh, about four, or perhaps five. Our first house guest was a dead magpie you found in the walkway.'

'I remember! He had such beautiful plumage, I couldn't believe that something so perfect would never fly again.'

'It was the Devil's own job getting you to part with it,' chuckled Weronika. 'I told you that the dead body was just a wrapper – like an empty sweet packet – that its soul had already flown away. *Pfouff!*' She opened both hands in the air as if releasing a bird. 'In the end, I persuaded you that if we gave the poor thing a proper funeral, its body and soul would be reunited in heaven. I dug out a shoebox for a coffin, and you sprinkled some of my potpourri around the body.' She gave a hoot of laughter. 'We launched it in the canal like a dead Viking. It didn't stop you bringing dead things home, but at least they didn't turn into permanent lodgers.'

'Did you ever think of taking me to see a shrink?' Cassie took a sip of water, avoiding her grandmother's penetrating stare.

'Why do you say that?'– Babcia's tone sounding suddenly guarded.

'I don't know, a little kid collecting dead animals . . . it's not what most four-year-olds are into, is it?'

Not for the first time in her life, Cassie felt a distinct shift in the atmosphere. Something unspoken hung in the air, as if her grandmother was holding something back from her.

'You didn't need a head doctor,' said her grandmother reaching out to enfold Cassie's hands in her warm leathery grasp. 'I understood. You were a little girl who had lost her mama.'

Cassie unlocked the door to her own ninth floor flat in a dilapidated council estate north of the canal. A third of the block was boarded up, but she'd been lucky to get it – being bumped up the housing list was one of the few perks of working for the NHS.

Inside, a sinuous movement in the darkness made her jump.

'Macavity! Don't do that!' As the cat threaded himself through her legs, she imagined him laughing silently.

Stroking his silky head gave her a pang: he was the only one to greet her these days. It had been four months since the split with Rachel – about the same length of time they'd spent living together – but now that winter was starting to bite down, coming home to a cold and empty flat felt harder.

Cranking up the heating, she recalled what her grandmother had implied: that her childhood fascination with dead animals had been a way of dealing with the loss of her parents. Rachel – who was training to become a psychotherapist – would have agreed, having tried more than once to persuade Cassie that she might be suffering from something called 'unresolved grief'. According to Rachel, Cassie found relationships difficult because she'd never properly processed her parents' deaths.

Psychobabble.

For Cassie, her connection with the dead was a vocation, a gift that she'd been lucky enough to discover early in life. And if she had difficulty finding a partner who understood her, well, that wasn't exactly unusual, was it?

On impulse, she did something she'd been resisting for months and opened Rachel's Facebook page. Annoyingly, her stomach still did a flip at the sight of that laughing freckled face. Then she saw the three words.

In a relationship.

She instantly closed the window. Well, it had been bound to happen sometime. She didn't regret the split, she told herself, the time had been right to move on. A treacherous thought bubbled up: *you're* always *moving on.* It struck Cassie that she'd be twenty-six in a few weeks and her longest relationship to date hadn't even made the six-month mark.

Sometimes, in the middle of the night, her ex-lovers, male and female, would parade through her thoughts, repeating their complaints. *I can't reach you, Cassie . . . I never know what you're thinking . . . It's like you're behind glass.* All variations on a theme. Recently, they'd been joined by the memory of what Rachel said on the day she left. *I realise now that you're never going to let me in.* Her words sounded final, but her expression told Cassie that she was waiting for her to protest, to fight for her, to promise to change.

Maybe they were right, she thought. Maybe I'm just not cut out for relationships with the living.

Picking up the cat, she buried her face in his fur. When he objected, stiffening his legs against her chest, she put him back down. He stared up at her for a moment before looking away, the muscles of his back convulsing in a single, economical twitch of protest that made her smile. 'You and me are two of a kind, aren't we, Macavity? We're better off on our own.'

Chapter Four

There was no better way of putting your own crappy little problems into perspective than looking after a bereaved family. The thought sprang into Cassie's mind the next morning as she led Mr and Mrs Middleton towards the dead body of their nineteen-year-old son Jake.

Jake Middleton had collapsed during rugby practice the previous afternoon. Despite being airlifted to hospital, he'd died of a cardiac arrest an hour later, defeating all attempts to resuscitate him. His mum and dad were away on holiday in Barcelona when it happened and had come straight from the airport that morning to see their boy.

Mrs Middleton's swollen eyes and ruined face spoke of a night of unimaginable grief, while her husband was so rigid with repressed emotion that he looked like he might shatter at a touch.

My father loved me like that once, thought Cassie suddenly – seeing her dad's encouraging smile as he pushed her along on a scooter. She felt conflicted – wanting to hold on to the new memory but unsettled by it arriving at such an inappropriate moment.

Ushering Jake's parents into the viewing suite, she closed the door behind them, using the moment to focus. 'So, when I open the curtains you'll see Jake through the glass lying in a bed. He's got a coverlet over him, and a pillow under his head.' Preparing people for what they were about to see helped to dull the shock a little. And she had taken her time over Jake's appearance: combing his hair, cleaning the smears of mud from his face, and remembering to put a rolled-up towel under his neck – it tilted the head back, preventing the lower jaw from falling open.

'Just let me know when you're ready,' she said.

Mr Middleton nodded, impatient. The A&E staff nurse had mentioned that he was something big in the City and seeing the tidemark of dried shaving foam under one ear, Cassie felt a rush of pity: it must be hard for someone so used to being in control to come up against a problem that he couldn't fix.

She pulled on the cord that opened the curtains.

At the sight of her son's blade-clean profile, Jake's mum sagged, and might have crumpled without Cassie's steadying hand beneath her elbow. The father stayed dry-eyed, his face as immobile as a carved wooden mask: the type who in her experience might implode without warning.

'Can I . . . touch him?' Mrs Middleton's tear-wrecked face was hard to look at but Cassie held her gaze.

'Of course,' she said, opening the glass door for her.

After just a few minutes with his son, Jake's dad emerged alone, a strange half-smile on his face.

Here we go, thought Cassie.

'The doctor mentioned a . . . post-mortem.'

'Yes, Mr Middleton. The coroner has asked for one – to find out what caused Jake's death.'

He bent his head towards her. 'Listen to me,' his voice a low growl. 'You tell the coroner that if anyone lays a finger on that

19

boy – *my boy* – in there, I will make it my business to find him and to kill him.'

Cassie met his eyes. 'I'd feel the same if he was my son. He's such a beautiful boy, isn't he?'

Mr Middleton looked confused for a moment, before nodding wordlessly, the long-suppressed tears spilling down his cheeks.

When Cassie saw them out more than an hour later, Mr Middleton was no longer threatening blue murder against anyone who touched his son, and had even agreed that maybe it would help to know what had taken Jake from them.

In the loo, Cassie replaced her lip rings and eyebrow bolt and scooped the top layer of hair back into its usual topknot, exposing the shaved undercut arching above her right ear. She always toned down her look for a family viewing, knowing that some people, especially the older generation, found it off-putting. It was a bit of a chore, but she didn't mind: making the bereaved feel as comfortable as possible trumped everything.

Maybe it had become something more than that over the years, she realised: a ritual marking the borderline between her work with the living and the dead.

It was a relief to get back to the autopsy suite, where a body-bagged figure lay waiting on her table. Carl, the junior technician, back at work after his day off sick, had thoughtfully retrieved her customer from the fridge for the midday PM list.

'Heavy viewing?' He looked up from laying out the clean sample pots.

'Aren't they all?'

Carl nodded. Although only twenty-two and a relative newbie, he already knew the score: the toughest part of the job wasn't dealing with the dead, it was looking after their grieving relatives.

20

There was a crackle of heavy-duty plastic as Cassie unzipped the body bag. But she'd only got it open as far as the collarbone when she stepped back, her breath trapped in her throat.

She must have made some kind of noise, because the next thing she knew Carl was next to her, putting his hand under her elbow just like she'd done with Mrs Middleton.

'Cassie? What's up?'

'It's . . . this lady.' She pointed to the body-bag label, amazed at how calm her voice sounded. 'Geraldine Edwards. I know her.'

Chapter Five

Cassie leaned against the rear wall of the mortuary, head tipped back, barely aware of the cold rain strafing her cheeks, desperate for a cigarette.

Mrs Edwards, dead.

She heard again the crackle of the body bag opening, saw again that familiar face, and yet she still couldn't grasp the idea. For the first time she understood the bewilderment she saw in the bereaved every day, the sheer impossibility of connecting the person you loved – alive, warm to the touch, *animate* – with the shop-window dummy laid out in the mortuary.

Cassie's chance encounter with Geraldine Edwards while selling the *Big Issue* had changed her life. Mrs E hadn't just inspired her return to education; she'd been the first teacher to recognise the insecurity beneath her defiant facade. She had gone on to pilot Cassie through her A levels, giving her extra tuition outside class and convincing her that she *could* pass the exams, even the dreaded physics.

After she'd got her A levels and started work at the mortuary, they'd stayed friends, with Cassie dropping by Mrs E's house most Sundays for coffee. This comfortable tradition had gone on for five years – until a few months ago, when Cassie overreacted to some-thing Mrs E had said. They hadn't spoken since, although just the previous week Cassie had spotted her former teacher in the fruit and veg aisle of Sainsburys. With a stab of shame, she remembered ducking into the bakery aisle and loitering there until the coast was clear.

Now, a thought struck her with cruel force: that moment had been her last chance to make things right, to reconnect with someone who'd played such a huge role in her life. And she had screwed it up.

Well, there was one thing she *could* do for her old friend and teacher.

'It's really not a good idea, Cassie,' said Doug, anxiety creasing his brow after she told him who was waiting to be prepped for a post-mortem. 'You know the rules – we don't work on people we know. It's just . . . too personal.'

'They're not like cast-iron rules, though, are they?'

'Well, good practice, whatever you want to call it. You can't maintain the same professional distance working on someone you know.'

'I can handle it, Doug, honestly I can'– putting a briskness into her voice she didn't really feel.

His eyes flickered over her face. 'You say she was your teacher?'

'She taught me science A levels at evening classes.' Like it was no big deal.

A sudden flash of Mrs E's fiercely intelligent grey-green gaze, her aquiline nose, asking in her Welsh lilt as she bent over a dissected pig brain, '*Now, Cassandra, do you remember what this is called?*' And Cassie saying, '*Is it the* corpus callosum?' A surge of satisfaction when she received an approving smile.

Now she would never bask in the warmth of Mrs E's approval again.

'Look, Doug, it wouldn't feel right, Carl dealing with her.'

'I could call in one of the locums?'

'Or any stranger. I should be the one looking after her.'

The tiniest slackening of the extraocular muscles around Doug's eyes told her he was about to give in.

'Well . . . all right then. But if you have second thoughts at any stage, just shout.'

Back in the autopsy suite, Cassie noticed that Carl had turned off the radio – no doubt out of respect for her feelings. 'Put some music on, Carl,' she said. 'Let's keep everything as normal as possible.'

Taking a deep breath, she picked up the report on Mrs Edwards' death. Apparently, she had died suddenly at home while taking a bath, and since she lived alone, her body hadn't been found until the following day – by her cleaner. The cops had ruled out any suspicious circumstances, which would have triggered a full forensic post-mortem, but as in any unexplained death, the law still demanded a routine PM.

A note on the file said that Mrs E was a widow, as Cassie vaguely remembered, and her next of kin, her only son Owen, would be coming down from Rhyl in North Wales to view the body in the next day or two. In all the years she'd known her, Cassie could only recall Mrs E mentioning her son once – a rare snippet of personal history, delivered in a way that discouraged further questions.

She started gently extracting Mrs E from her body bag. 'I'd forgotten your name was Geraldine,' she murmured. 'It's a lovely name. But then you always were a bit of a dark horse.'

She replayed her chance sighting of Mrs E in the supermarket, searching her memory for signs of anything amiss – like a drooping eyelid or poor gait – but drew a blank. She had, perhaps, looked a bit preoccupied, but might just have been deciding what to cook for dinner.

As sometimes happened, death had given Mrs E the ultimate Botox, massaging away the crow's feet and laughter lines, leaving her face tranquil and younger-looking than her fifty-one years.

Cassie started to scour the body for any signs of bruising she might have sustained in a fall getting into or out of the bath, relieved to find herself able to turn her without calling on Carl. 'It's a good job you're so slim,' she murmured close to her ear, 'or this bit might do my back in.' More striking than conventionally pretty, Mrs Edwards had always cut a certain dash, wearing clothes that showed off a good figure, even if it was hidden under a lab coat much of the time, and with her dark hair always well cut and styled.

A sudden memory came back to Cassie: the major wobble she'd had a few weeks into night school. Struggling to keep up in a physics lesson that might have been in Mandarin for all the sense it made, she'd sneaked a sideways glance at her classmates. Seeing their untroubled expressions, something had dawned on her with terrible clarity: *I don't belong here.* Who had she been kidding, thinking she was smart enough? She should've knuckled down at school, instead of giving the teachers lip – but now it was too late. Her best hope was to get a job in a bar or working on a market stall, like her dad – try to save enough cash to go travelling.

Mrs E must have detected her panic because after the lesson she'd intercepted her before marching her to the nearest Starbucks, where she announced that she wasn't prepared to lose '*the best bloody science student I've ever taught'*. Cassie could still hear her saying it. An exaggeration, *obviously*, but the fierceness of Mrs E's belief in her had been enough to persuade her to stay on.

Now, under cover of feeling for any haematomas on the back of the dead woman's head, Cassie bent down and murmured, 'We're going to find out what happened to you, Mrs E.'

She hovered there, close enough to count the individual hairs of those dark eyebrows, awaiting the dreamlike state that foreshadowed a moment of connection. But all she heard was an echo of her own voice.

'Morning all!' A tall silver-haired man swept through the door from the clean area, a lunchbox tied with string dangling from one hand, a battered briefcase in the other. 'Ah, it's the ravishing Ms Raven.'

Cassie couldn't help but smile: anyone else greeting her that way would get a mouthful, but Professor Arculus was her favourite pathologist. And since he was also one of the best in the country, it was a relief to know that Mrs E would be in good hands.

'What cornucopia of exanimate delights do we have in store today, Cassandra?' he asked, peering at the list through the bottom of his bifocals, one arm of which she noticed was newly mended with a piece of duct tape.

'Three ladies and a gentleman, Prof. First up is Mrs Geraldine Edwards.'

'Anything I should know?' Perhaps picking up something in her voice, the Prof sent her an enquiring look.

'Mrs Edwards is . . . was my science teacher, Prof – and, well, a good friend. She got me through my A levels. I didn't want anyone else looking after her today.'

The Prof gave a brisk nod. 'A commendable attitude. Shall we begin?'

After formally checking Mrs E's identity, Prof. Arculus leafed through her medical summary. 'So our young lady had no chronic illnesses . . . no history of hospital admissions . . .'

Smiling at the old-school gallantry of that 'young lady', Cassie referred to the notes. 'She had slightly elevated cholesterol, but her blood pressure was normal for her age, and she wasn't on any long-term medication. Her son said she sounded fine when he last spoke to her, around a month ago' – further evidence to Cassie of a less than close relationship between mother and son.

The Prof turned to the coroner's report. '*The deceased was found by her cleaner in the bath, submerged under the water,*' he read out loud. '*Police found no sign of a struggle or obvious injury. No evidence of prescription or illegal drugs found, although a glass containing whisky was found nearby.*'

Half-turning Mrs E on to her side, he ran practised fingers over the back of her skull – Cassie noticing with gratitude that he was handling the body with particular gentleness, almost as if she were a living patient.

'Hmm. No obvious contusions to suggest a fall.' He looked at Cassie over the top of his specs. 'Unless those eagle eyes of yours have spotted anything germane to our enquiries?'

She felt herself flush: unlike that chinless muppet Cuff, the Prof wasn't too grand to ask her opinion, or to congratulate her when she spotted something he might otherwise overlook in the brief time allotted to a routine post-mortem.

'Nothing, Prof.'

'Right-ho.' His eyes met hers briefly yet incisively, no doubt assessing whether she really could handle eviscerating someone she had known, before he disappeared to check his email.

Cassie picked up her favourite blade, but as its bright point hovered over the notch at the base of Mrs Edwards' throat, she froze, pitched back to her very first evisceration. Now it came to it, could she really handle this?

Yes. It was the least she could do for Mrs E.

The initial incision was tough, but once that was done, she was relieved to find herself going into automatic, the muscle memory of thousands of eviscerations taking over.

Twenty minutes later, Prof. Arculus arrived at the dissecting bench and, delving into the pile of Mrs E's viscera, started to separate out the major organs.

He pulled the lungs, still attached to the windpipe, towards him and made a deft stroke through the bronchus at the point where it entered the right lung, releasing a small outrush of water. He cocked an eyebrow at Cassie. 'That'll be the bathwater. But our first question is, did it enter her airway post- or ante-mortem?'

Cassie nodded: they needed to establish whether the immediate cause of Mrs E's death had been drowning while also looking for the underlying cause, like a heart attack, that might have made her pass out and slip beneath the water. It was a common misconception that water in the lungs was proof of drowning. In fact, even if Mrs E had stopped breathing before she went under, water would still have found its way into her lungs.

The Prof made a series of swift downward incisions into the tissue of the right lung before turning and studying each slice as if they were the pages of a book, which Cassie always thought of as 'reading the organs'. He stood back, inviting her to take a look.

'So, what do you see on the cut surface?'

'Froth. Bloodstained froth.'

'Caused by . . . ?'

'Pulmonary oedema?'

'Correct.'

'So she was still breathing when she went under the water?'

Prof. Arculus grimaced. 'As you know, our old friend drowning is a tricky customer to diagnose with complete confidence. Whatever the television crime dramas would have us believe . . .' his eyes narrowed; this was a favourite hobby horse, '. . . conclusive proof is elusive.'

He paused, looking at Cassie enquiringly.

'Drowning is a diagnosis of exclusion,' she said, pressing a smile out of her lips. 'Based on ruling out all other causes of death.'

A nod. 'Quite so. Nonetheless, the circumstances in which she was found would appear reasonably to direct us to that conclusion. Now we must establish the *underlying* cause of death: why might an apparently healthy lady in early middle age suddenly lose consciousness for long enough to drown.'

He sliced open the stomach with another decisive stroke of his scalpel.

'The stomach is empty, so she hadn't eaten for a good four or five hours before death' – bending down, he sniffed – 'although I'd say she'd enjoyed a good dram of that whisky. No sign of any tablet residue but we must await the toxicology verdict for confirmation'

Next he turned to Mrs E's heart. Cassie knew he'd be looking for any furring in the arteries or other evidence to support a heart attack – but she couldn't hang around to watch: she needed to take samples of the major organs and bodily fluids and pot them up for analysis.

Later, seeing him go over to the sink to rinse the blood off his hands, she asked, 'What do you think, Prof? Do you have any idea what might have made her pass out?'

He gave a shake of his head. 'Nothing conclusive, I'm afraid. The heart and coronary vessels present no evidence of thrombus, atheroma or infarct, and the brain shows no sign of CVA.'

In other words, no narrowing of the arteries, nor signs of a clot, heart attack or stroke – the usual suspects for a sudden collapse in an apparently healthy person.

'I'm afraid I shall have to give the cause of death as "unascertained pending toxicology and histopathology",' he went on, sending her a kindly look over his specs.

Her eyes drifted to Mrs E's poor shell of a body. 'Off the record, what's your gut feeling?'

The Prof's eyes crinkled to two bright points, as they did whenever he was deep in thought. 'Personally, I should be surprised if the samples reveal any sign of underlying disease – the lady appears to have been in excellent health.' Looking at Cassie, he said kindly, 'You know, it's possible that she simply drank a little too much Scotch on an empty stomach. In combination with a hot bath, that could have caused quite dramatic vasodilation.'

Could it be something so terribly simple? A combination of alcohol and an over-hot bath causing a sudden widening of the blood vessels, making Mrs E's blood pressure plummet so that she passed out?

'So you think she . . . blacked out, and just slipped under the water?'

'I may yet be proved wrong, but I'd say it's the likeliest conclusion.' He gave her shoulder a rough pat. 'Well played today, Cassandra. It can't have been easy for you. I'll ask the laboratory to expedite the results.'

Cassie was the last person in the mortuary that evening. As she walked through the darkened body store, the headlights of a car leaving the car park swept across the expanse of polished steel, briefly illuminating the initials of the occupants scrawled on the surface – like hieroglyphs on the wall of some Ancient Egyptian tomb. Picturing her guests slumbering behind the doors of the giant fridge she murmured goodnight to each of them as she passed.

Reaching the door behind which Mrs E was stored, Cassie touched her fingers to the steel, assailed by a memory.

Mrs E stood at the blackboard, elegant and long-limbed. She was in full flow, sketching a diagram of the human respiratory system with sweeping gestures, her expression intent to the point of sternness. But when she stood back to view her handiwork, she hooted with laughter. 'It's a bloody good job I don't teach art!'

Suddenly dizzy, Cassie had to set a steadying palm against the wall – grasping something properly for the first time. If Mrs E hadn't sensed the thirst for knowledge behind her mutinous teenage posturing, hadn't steered her through the storms of self-doubt, her life might have turned out very differently. She'd probably still be living in a squat, selling the *Big Issue*, self-medicating with booze or gear. Pissing her life down the drain, in other words.

Opening the fridge door, Cassie pulled the drawer out on its rollers and unzipped the bag so she could look into Geraldine Edwards' face.

'I'm so sorry I didn't get back in touch in time, Mrs E. I suppose I just thought you'd always be around. I never even thanked you, not properly, for all the extra tuition, the times you supported me when I nearly gave up. Without you I wouldn't be doing a job that I love . . . I might not even be here at all.'

Resting her palm on Mrs E's shoulder, Cassie held her breath for a long moment, straining again for some shift in the atmosphere, any hint of communication.

Nothing. The dead woman remained mute, as cold and unreachable as a stone knight Cassie had once seen stretched out on top of a medieval tomb.

Chapter Six

On the way home, she dropped in to the Sainsbury's on Camden Road to get some cat food – the same store where she'd glimpsed Mrs E the previous week. After emerging, she hovered on the pavement for a moment, before striding out in the opposite direction of her flat.

Geraldine Edwards' house at number 12 Patna Road stood out from the long curve of the grand Victorian terrace, its traditional pale grey frontage a sober contrast to the Love Hearts shades her neighbours had chosen. Cassie remembered her old teacher eyeing one new candy-pink paint job, muttering 'stuff and nonsense' – the disapproving tone undercut by the twinkle that was never far from her eye.

Cassie remembered all the Sunday mornings she'd climbed the steps to the dark blue front door clutching a bag of fresh pastries. Mrs E had been one of the few people she could talk to properly about her job, and the only one to truly understand its fascination – the thrill of deciphering the clues written on the body.

There was only one subject they had disagreed on.

After passing her final exam, Cassie had mentioned how relieved she was to be done with education, at which Mrs E had set down her coffee cup and fixed her with a look. 'You're never *done* with education, Cassandra' – her North Wales accent making the words more emphatic. 'Your A level results were a fantastic achievement, but they're the beginning of a journey, not the destination. You could study medicine next, if you put your mind to it.'

The subject kept coming up, and Cassie kept ducking it – until *that* Saturday back in the Spring when Mrs E had handed her a university brochure with her mug of coffee. It was opened at a page that detailed the financial support available to students from disadvantaged backgrounds applying to study medicine.

As Mrs E rattled on about the grade A maths A level she would need, Cassie had to fight down a rising tide of panic.

'I know you're reluctant, Cassandra,' she said, fixing that hawk-like eye on her, 'but I really think you should consider it.'

Cassie had protested that she loved the job she already had, but Mrs E wouldn't let it go. 'You know, it's probably my greatest regret, not studying medicine. I would hate to think of you feeling the same way one day.'

Cassie felt cornered, angry – like she was sixteen again with her grandmother trying to talk her out of leaving school. *Why couldn't everyone just leave her alone*? The exchange with Mrs E had ended with Cassie storming out, but not before saying something that still had the power to make her cringe.

'You're not my mother, you know.'

When Mrs E left her a conciliatory voicemail the following day, Cassie had kept meaning to call back, straighten things out, but something – embarrassment, or stupid pride perhaps – always stopped her. She'd been living with Rachel by then and bit by bit the whole troublesome business had slipped down her agenda.

Now, catching a glimpse of someone moving about in Mrs E's living room she took the stairs up to the front door at a run. It was probably Imelda the cleaner, who she knew, which would allow her a last look inside before Mrs E's son Owen sold the place. She'd already rung the bell when it hit her: what if it was Owen himself who she'd seen, just down from Rhyl? She could think of no good reason to be here – and since they would inevitably meet when he came to view the body she couldn't even retreat with some excuse.

Cassie legged it, but she'd only gone thirty metres or so down the road when she heard the sound of a door opening behind her and a man's voice, Welsh-accented, call out, 'Can I help you?'

'Sorry! Wrong house,' she threw over her shoulder, praying that she was far enough away for him not to recognise her again. Heard his angry mutter, followed by the slam of a door.

The rest of the walk home she spent trying to understand what it was that had stopped her getting back in touch with Mrs E: why she had been content to walk away from someone who'd been so important to her? Someone who, she realised now, really had been a surrogate mother of sorts. What was it all about, this tendency of hers to push away the people she loved?

Cassie suddenly remembered sitting on the sofa in front of the pop-popping gas fire, the day that Babcia told her that the angels had taken her mama and papa to heaven. And a thought sprung out at her: *look what happens when you let yourself love someone.*

Back home, she fed Macavity before logging in to Facebook. She was surprised to find that Geraldine Edwards, always an avowed Luddite, had set up a profile page in the summer, although she'd only been active for a few weeks. Her profile pic was an outdoor table set with a bottle of wine and two glasses, taken somewhere sunny. Scrolling through the handful of posts, Cassie found a picture of a cake iced with the message *Good Luck!* and snaps of Mrs E's college leaving party – clearly she'd finally followed through on her frequently mentioned plan to retire early. So her stupid pride had even made her miss Mrs E's retirement.

One pic showed Mrs E aboard the London Eye, all dressed up with a sharp new haircut and holding a glass of champagne, the night-time backdrop of the city's lights echoing the sparkle in her eyes. The expression she wore clutched at Cassie's heart: it was a look that said to the world *I'm not done yet.*

She went to the fridge for a bottle of beer before reaching for her phone. Without allowing herself time to reconsider, she hit speed dial.

'Rachel? Hi, it's me.'

'Cassie? Wow. It's been what . . .'

'Four months next week. Not that I'm counting.' *FFS.* She pulled her 'madwoman in the attic' face at the phone to relieve her feelings.

'So . . . what's up? How's life at the mortuary?'

Did Cassie detect a flicker of distaste at the word? When they were together, she sometimes thought of her job as a dead body she'd brought home: a corpse propped between them on the sofa while they watched telly, ever present but never mentioned. Maybe working with the dead would always be an unbridgeable barrier, making relationships with 'civilians' impossible.

After a bit more pointless small talk, she took a courage-inducing swig of beer. 'Listen, Rach. Can I ask you something?'

'Sure. Ask away' – but sounding cautious.

36

'Was I a rubbish girlfriend?'

'No! Of course not. You were funny and super-smart and . . . you could be loving.'

'"Could be"?' – trying not to sound offended.

'Well, yes, when the mood took you.'

Cassie tried to think of a smart comeback but knew she couldn't really argue: showing affection had never come easy to her.

'My turn to ask you something,' said Rachel. 'Those times you didn't come home, when you said you'd got drunk and didn't want to wake me up?'

Oh Christ.

'Did you really just fall asleep on Carl's sofa?'

'No, I was actually having a threesome with Carl and his flat-mate . . . *Yes,* I slept on the couch.' Cassie could hear how unconvincing she sounded, but what else could she say? 'Look, Rachel, I was never unfaithful to you, if that's what you're getting at.'

She stopped then, suddenly remembering the first time she'd seen that wide freckled face, walking into the reception at the tattoo studio where Cassie was waiting to have a sleeve done. And the punch-the-air feeling she'd got when Rachel had agreed to go for a drink afterwards. Things had accelerated at breakneck pace, and barely a couple of months later Rachel had moved into Cassie's place. Too soon, in hindsight, but at the time it had just felt right.

Rachel sighed down the line. 'I've thought a lot about what went wrong between us. Do you know what I really think?'

'Was it my tofu Bolognese?' Silence. 'Sorry.'

'When you talked about your job, it used to make me . . . envious.'

'*Envious?*'

'Yes. You gave so much of yourself to the dead, I sometimes felt like there wasn't much left over for the living.'

Cassie heard a murmured query, a female voice, in the background. 'Look, I've got to go,' said Rachel. 'It's been good to chat, you know? We should have coffee some time.'

Cassie sat on the sofa as darkness congealed in the corners of the room, wondering why she'd called Rachel in the first place, giving into a momentary urge to hear her voice. What the fuck had she been thinking, letting her guard down like that?

Maybe Mrs E's death had stirred up feelings about the past; feelings that were best left alone. What she needed was to stop wallowing, get out of the flat and have some fun.

Chapter Seven

As Cassie pushed open the door of the Vibe bar, a middle-aged couple spilled out as if carried aloft on a wave of music and raucous cheering from inside – their expressions suggesting they'd chosen the wrong pub. Inside, the air pressed itself, hot and damp, against her face while on stage a flame-haired drag queen in a slinky white gown murdered a Donna Summer track to the approval of the gyrating crowd.

She'd been trying to cut out drinking on a 'school' night, but after the Rachel conversation this was exactly what she needed.

After her first beer, she decided she felt fine. Better than fine. She and Rachel weren't meant to be. The important thing was to put it behind her and move on. As for Mrs Edwards dying: that had come as a massive shock, of course it had, but once the cause of death was established, she would just need a bit of time to get over it.

Three or four beers later, Cassie was tucked into a darkened corner of the bar, getting cosy with a twenty-year-old drama student called Tish. Or was it Tash? A fashion student at Central Saint Martins, she wasn't the sharpest scalpel in the box but she made up for it with thick dark eyelashes and buzzcut white-blonde hair that showed off a skull as elegantly sculpted as Nefertiti's.

'So what is it you do?' Tish-Tash asked.

Cassie took a swig from her bottle, wondering whether to fudge her answer.

'I work in a mortuary, helping to find out why people died.'

'No way! That's amazing.'

The girl's interest seemed genuine, with none of the shrinking away Cassie was used to getting when she told people about her job. If anything, she was leaning in closer now, the length of her bare upper arm warm against Cassie's, her plush lips rounded into an admiring 'O'.

'Did you like, always want to work with the dead?'

'Maybe,' Cassie shrugged. 'I used to bring dead animals home when I was a kid.' An image came to her of the magpie she'd found, its once-keen little eyes cloudy, its downy white underside so soft, so vulnerable-looking. 'And when I was eleven I asked for a copy of *Gray's Anatomy* for Christmas.'

Tish-Tash nodded knowledgeably. 'My mum has the box set.'

'No, dingbat, the medical book!' She nudged the girl's warm arm, enjoying the old familiar thrill at the possibilities the night held.

The girl laughed, her gaze admiring. 'Do you believe the soul survives death?'

Cassie shook her head. 'But I have heard the dead speak.' The words slipped out, startling her.

'Oh my days! Are you like, psychic then?'

'No, death is the end.' She picked at the label on her beer bottle, already regretting her slip-up. She had never talked to anyone about her moments of communion before: the intense feeling of connection she got with people who logically, she knew were dead. 'I suppose, if every thought we have is a bunch of electrical impulses, it's not impossible that people's dying

40

thoughts hang around for a bit.' Pseudo-scientific crap, but the best she could come up with.

'Yeah, I get that.' Tish-Tash sucked on her straw, making her cheekbones pop.

'Maybe it's just my way of giving the bodies back their humanity.' Cassie waggled her beer. 'Or maybe I've had a few too many of these.'

'I love hearing you talk,' said Tish-Tash, her face so close now that Cassie could smell the mint in the mojito she'd been drinking. Her voice fell to a murmur. 'So, what's like, the most gruesome thing you've seen in the morgue?' – her lovely lips parted.

A rubbernecker, thought Cassie, with a little stab of disappointment.

'Sorry, I never talk about stuff like that.'

'OK.' Tish-Tash gave a micro shrug, before offering Cassie the straw of her drink. 'Have some. It's delish.'

Rubbernecker or not, she *was* drop-dead gorgeous. Reaching out her hand Cassie drew it over the curve at the back of the girl's head, the bristles of the buzzcut hard-soft against her palm.

'Has anyone ever told you that you have a beautiful skull?'

Chapter Eight

Cassie woke the next day with a jangling head and a dry mouth, unable to recall how the night had ended. Then she turned over and smelt mint on the pillow.

The silence in the flat told her Tish-Tash had already left – which brought a tiny stab of regret, before she imagined the ordeal of breakfast small talk with someone she had no intention of seeing again.

After levering herself upright she felt worse – a booming head and a gnawing hunger in her gut she hadn't felt since ... *Oh shit.* A flash frame image: her reflection in the mirror of the club loos, bending down to a line of white powder, Tish-Tash draped over her shoulder. *But where ... ?* Then she remembered scoring it off one of the Somali kids who hung around outside the club.

The most Cassie ever did these days was the occasional joint. She hadn't touched coke, her one-time drug of choice, for years – had managed to stay away from Class A's since she'd left the squatting life. She still saw some of the old crew now and again around Camden but she never hung out with them – better to avoid temptation.

Now it felt like she'd blown it – and for what? A bit of one-night-stand Dutch courage.

The canal towpath that took her into work was almost deserted at this hour. The air clung to her face like damp cotton and a sullen sky turned the water near-black, reflecting her mood.

In the body store, her coke-and-beer hangover mollified by ibuprofen and a triple espresso, she tried not to let herself dwell on the thought of Mrs E stretched out behind the stainless steel. Her first task: to retrieve a gent called Harry Hardwick who the undertakers were coming to collect that morning, and do a routine 'stockcheck' of their guests.

A couple of minutes later she went to find Carl in the staffroom, where he was having a cuppa, still wearing his motorcycle leathers and smelling of the cold outdoors.

'It was you who put Mr Hardwick back in drawer sixteen, right?' She consulted the paperwork again.

'Yes?'

'Well, he's not there now.'

'Maybe he's done a runner.'

Cassie batted him on the head with her sheaf of papers. 'You must have written it down wrong, Einstein.' But beneath the banter she felt a tiny wingbeat of fear.

Carl joined her in the body store having hastily pulled on his scrubs. Opening one of the doors, he pulled drawer sixteen out on its runners, releasing a frosty gust of air. They stood peering into the emptiness within.

'When did you last see him?' asked Cassie.

'On Friday, when I put him back here.' Carl's face grew a frown. 'He was the last one I put to bed before I left.'

Closing the door, he pointed out the initials 'H.A.H.' and his date of birth scrawled in marker pen on the polished steel surface: their at-a-glance reminder of who was stored where. 'See?'

Cassie remembered checking Mr Hardwick in when the porters had brought him over from the hospital the previous Friday – five days earlier. A skinny old gentleman with shaggy silver eyebrows and a wry half-smile that had survived death, he had reminded Cassie of her own granddad, who'd died just a few months after her parents.

She started to work her way along the body store, opening each drawer and checking the names on the body bags against her list. As she bent her head to read each nametag she murmured a few words to each occupant – '*So sorry to trouble you, Mrs S*' . . .'*Hello, Mr J, I hope you're feeling more settled today*' – speaking under her breath as usual so that Carl couldn't hear.

As she greeted each of her charges and checked off their names, her uneasy feeling ticked up another notch. She shut the last fridge door with a thunk that echoed doomily off the low ceiling.

'Carl.' Her voice a raw whisper. 'He's not here.'

They stared at each other, before repeating the process, this time with an edge of panic: they both knew that Cassie didn't make silly mistakes. But the count remained stubbornly unchanged: there were twelve names on the list and only eleven guests in the body store.

Harold Albert Hardwick, deceased, was missing.

Hoping against hope, Cassie even went to check the forensic body store, located at the rear of the mortuary, but its only occupant was a nineteen-year-old Asian kid called Hanif, victim of a drug-related stabbing. Panic clamouring in her head like a broken fire alarm, she started a ring round. But it only confirmed what she already knew. Since Friday, the hospital porters hadn't been over to drop off any bodies, and no undertakers had attended to pick anyone up.

Back in the body store, Cassie stared at the wall of steel as if it might deliver the answer. A squall of November rain had blown up, hissing against the skylights and clattering on the flat roof overhead.

It was only then that the full enormity of it hit her. It was her responsibility to look after the dead, to ease their journey out of this world as best she could. Losing an elderly gent entrusted to her care felt like the betrayal of a sacred bond.

Her next job was to break the news to Doug.

'When was the post-mortem?'

Since he'd arrived at work, Doug's pacing had practically worn a groove in his office lino. Cassie eyed his face, pale and sweat-slicked, suddenly looking a lot older than his forty-three years.

'Around three on Friday afternoon,' she said. 'Mr Hardwick was one of four on the routine list.'

'Cause of death?'

Cassie checked her notes. 'Pulmonary embolism following a routine hip replacement. He was eighty-one and in pretty poor shape according to the PM report. He had diabetes and angina.'

'So when was the last stocktake?'

Cassie hesitated, before Carl saved her from having to drop him in it.

'I was supposed to do it Monday and Tuesday,' he admitted. 'But we hadn't had any new arrivals or pick-ups, so...'

Doug blew out a breath.

'Darrell confirmed that Harry was the last body they brought over,' said Cassie. 'He also said that they don't make a habit of taking dead bodies *back* to the hospital.' Doug and Cassie exchanged a look. Chief Porter Darrell Fairweather was notorious for his thin-skinned belligerence.

'And you' – Doug aimed his index finger at Carl, who sat fidgeting in one of the swivel chairs – 'you're *100 per cent sure* he went back in the fridge after the PM?'

'Yes.' Carl was a young man of few words but Cassie trusted them all.

'I just can't understand it.' Doug threw Cassie a desperate look. 'I suppose . . . he might still turn up?'

'He's not going to turn up, Doug' – speaking as gently as she could.

His face crumpled. 'I can't believe it. Mortuaries don't just *lose* bodies. It's unheard of.' Cassie noticed that he was swallowing more than usual – a sure sign that the news had brought on one of his acid attacks. Before doing anything else, she'd dig out some antacid liquid for him.

The rest of the morning disappeared in a flurry of phone calls. The coroner alerted the cops who told Doug they'd send forensics over straight away and that a detective would attend later that day.

Cassie managed to get hold of the sister on Harry Hardwick's ward, who took the news in her stride – her distracted tone and the hubbub in the background suggesting she had more pressing issues involving the living.

'I don't know what I can tell you that might help.' The shrug audible in her voice.

'According to the notes he didn't have any close family,' said Cassie.

'That's right. He lived alone after his wife died last year, and they didn't have any kids.'

'Small mercies, I suppose. Did you have any inkling that he might not survive the hip replacement?'

'No. But honestly? It wasn't a huge shock when he didn't come back from theatre – he had hypertension and diabetes. We already had to delay his op once after he had a hypo.'

A hypoglycaemic episode – a drop in blood sugar, in other words – caused by a surge in insulin levels.

'He was such a nice friendly old chap usually, no trouble at all, but he started shouting his head off, accusing us of trying to starve him. It was a good job he did lose his rag though – when we ran bloods, his glucose levels were through the floor.' Cassie heard an urgent mutter cut through the background noise. 'Sorry, but I really do have to go now.'

When the forensics team turned up to take prints in the body store, Cassie and Carl took a walk over to the coffee van in the hospital car park.

'So what do you think happened to Mr Hardwick?' asked Carl as the espresso machine hissed.

Turning away from the counter she lowered her voice. 'Somebody must have taken him. I can't see any other explanation. Nobody has access other than us and the porters.'

'How do you think they got in?'

'No idea. There's no obvious sign of a break-in.'

They took their coffees to the plastic table beside the van. Cassie could see the mortuary a hundred metres away over Carl's shoulder, its 1970s brown PVC fascia peeling on the sunny side, hunkered down behind its screen of tatty conifers. There was nothing about the single-storey structure to give any clue to its function – an indication of the way the living shunned the dead, protecting themselves from any reminder of their own mortality.

'What could anyone possibly want with an old gent like Harry?' she said.

'Could someone have taken him to harvest his organs?'

She pulled a sceptical face. 'Organs have a short shelf life, and even if someone took him on Friday night, he would have been dead at least twenty-four hours.'

'Don't some body parts survive for longer? Remember that scandal in America, those undertakers who were flogging bits of dead people?'

Carl was right. A few years back somewhere in the US, the cops had uncovered a lucrative trade in body parts, with criminals paying funeral homes to harvest bones, ligaments, tendons – even heart valves – from the bodies in their care, then selling them on for use in operations. To avoid detection, they'd even replaced leg bones with lengths of plastic pipe – a desecration of the dead that made Cassie's skin crawl.

But she also remembered that the younger the victim, the more money their body parts fetched. 'There were half a dozen people younger than Harry in the body store. Why would a body snatcher choose an eighty-one-year-old with a heart murmur and diabetes?'

Carl's stared gloomily into his paper cup, shoulders slumped. He seemed to be taking it hard.

Picturing Mrs E lying in her mortuary drawer, Cassie shuddered at the thought that the thieves might have taken her body instead.

She drained the rest of her coffee. 'The whole thing is a clusterfuck, especially when the HTA find out.'

The Human Tissue Authority, which regulated the handling of human remains, had a fearsome reputation – and the power to close down a mortuary for losing a single tissue sample, never mind an entire body.

She noticed Carl's fingers worrying at the edges of his cup, peeling the plastic film from the cardboard.

'What's up, Carl?'

'Should I start looking at job sites?' he asked. 'I was the last one to deal with him, wasn't I?'

Carl had become a mortuary technician after being made redundant from the garage where he'd worked as a mechanic. If he was found to be at fault, his job would be on the line.

'You didn't do anything wrong, Carl.' She sought his eyes. 'None of us did. And Doug sticks up for his staff.'

'True.' He shot her a mischievous look. 'But maybe I'll do a few extra lines on the lottery this week just in case.'

'Good idea. Throw your money down the bog. You can afford it.'

Despite being just a few years older than Carl, Cassie sometimes felt like his auntie.

Chapter Nine

They got back to the mortuary to find a uniformed PC buzzing at the front door. In his early twenties, his cheeks were stippled with razor rash. 'I'm here for your missing person,' he said with a grin that told Cassie how seriously he was taking the crisis.

He said there was a detective sergeant on the way and accepted her offer of a cup of tea while he waited.

'My money's on a paperwork cock-up somewhere along the line,' he told her, leaning wide-legged against the staff kitchen worktop like he owned the place. 'I mean, stiffs don't just go walkabout, do they? Pop out for a pint.' He grinned at her over the lip of his mug.

Cassie had to repress the urge to throw her tea in his groin. 'I don't see how that's possible. And we prefer to call them bodies, by the way.'

His eyes flickered over her body beneath the scrubs. 'It's a funny kind of job, this – especially for a girl. Do you actually cut up the bodies and . . . everything?'

'Uh huh.'

He mimed an elaborate shiver. 'Doesn't it give you the heebie jeebies?'

Same old same old. No one ever asked her even a halfway interesting question about her job.

'You get used to it,' she said – the response she handed stupid people.

'Yeah? Some people get a buzz out of death and skulls and all that, don't they?' His gaze, speculative, drifted from her eyebrow bolt to her lip piercings. 'You're a bit of a Goth, right? I bet you've slept on a gravestone or two in your time.'

Some people seemed to think that her look gave them licence to get personal. Unable to stop herself, she stepped closer. 'Never slept on one, no,' she breathed in his ear. 'But I've had sex on a few – with boys *and* girls. You should try it.'

'Ha ha!' Eyes wide with alarm, his mug went down with a clunk. 'Yeah. Right then. I'll just go call the nick.' And he was out of the door.

His sudden departure amused Cassie, but her smile faded as she remembered her first run-in with the police, during the eviction from the squat in Hawley Road. A red-faced male cop in his forties had manhandled her into a police van, before using his body to pin her to the floor for the journey to the nick, despite her repeated protests that she wasn't even struggling.

She could still remember what he'd murmured, his breath hot against her ear, 'You know, you wouldn't be bad-looking if you took all that metalwork out of your face.' Worse, the horrible realisation that the thing pressing into her thigh wasn't his radio. Twisting her head to meet his eye she had said quietly, 'If you don't take your tiny fucking dick off me right now, I'll scream so loud it'll stop the traffic'. It had worked, but the episode left bruises on her upper arms that had taken a week to fade. Her distrust of the police never had.

Coming out of the kitchen she found Deborah, the admin assistant, ushering a visitor down the corridor: a tall, upright

51

woman so unmistakably a cop she might as well have worn a blue flashing light strapped to her head.

After introducing herself as DS Flyte – no first name and no smile – she told Cassie, 'I'd like a tour of the place, and I'm told you're the best person to explain how the various systems work.'

Flyte wore her wheat-blonde hair scraped into a tight bun and as she stood on one leg to pull on plastic shoe covers, the hem of her trouser leg rode up to reveal nice ankles. Cassie might even have fancied her, if she hadn't been a cop.

As they crossed the threshold to the autopsy suite, Cassie sensed Flyte recoiling and remembered the first time she'd smelt it: the unholy mix of bleach, blood, and bodily fluids, like a butcher's shop crossed with a urinal, topped off with a dash of sweaty joggers.

'Give it ten minutes,' Cassie told her. 'Believe it or not, you get used to it.'

In spite of Flyte's tight smile, it was clear the place made her seriously uncomfortable – a response Cassie might have expected from a civilian, but which seemed odd coming from a cop.

Ten minutes later, Flyte was frowning down at her notebook. 'You and your colleague Carl say that all the windows were closed and locked when you arrived. The office staff report the same on the other side of the building. That only leaves the main entrance and the door to the hospital side, and they both have security keypads, correct?'

Flyte's eyes were an unusually pale blue – the colour of a midwinter sky. How old was she? Her immaculately applied makeup made it hard to tell, but Cassie decided she was probably only in her mid-thirties.

'That's right. We all have our own individual codes that get changed every few weeks.'

'And nobody has seen the body in question since Friday afternoon? Is that normal?' – an accusing edge to Flyte's voice.

'Opening the drawers unnecessarily only raises the fridge temperature,' Cassie told her. *Horseshit.* But sharing Carl's slip-up with a cop wasn't going to help find Mr Hardwick.

Flyte made a note in handwriting that Cassie noticed was neat but schoolgirlish, possibly because she held her pen stiffly and at an odd angle.

'How many people have access to these codes?'

Her vowels, like everything else about her, were precise – a bit over-precise – like she'd been coached to speak 'nicely'. Not born posh, like Archie Cuff.

'I think it's five altogether, but it might be less.'

'Fewer,' murmured Flyte, half to herself, writing it down.

Cassie stared at her.

'You're not just a hospital mortuary, though, are you?' Flyte frowned. 'So what about bodies who've been declared life extinct elsewhere?'

'If it's outside working hours, whoever's on call will come in to check them in.'

'And as far as you are aware, nobody has set foot in here outside normal hours since Friday?'

'That's right.'

DS Flyte studied the room, making Cassie suddenly aware of the rust streaks down the painted breeze block walls, the broken floor tiles, the flickering overhead strip light that still hadn't been replaced. 'You really ought to have CCTV in here, you know,' she said – as if the omission was Cassie's fault.

'You think?' she shot back. 'We're always asking for a security system upgrade, but they keep knocking us back. Budget cuts, apparently.'

In the body store, the forensics officers had gone, leaving only the odd trace of black fingerprinting powder dusting the brushed steel surface of the fridge.

'This is where Mr Hardwick was stored.' Cassie indicated Harry's initials marked on the door to drawer sixteen.

'And do your records always match up with who's filed where?'

Trying to ignore that *'filed'*, Cassie said, 'Well, not *always*. But I like to think that we pick up any errors pretty fast.'

Flyte wasn't listening. She was frowning at the tall white fridge in the corner, which would have looked more at home in a domestic kitchen.

'That's the foetal fridge,' Cassie told her. 'Where we keep babies who haven't reached full term.'

She caught the quiver of distaste that crossed Flyte's face before she bent to stow her notebook in her bag, another sign of squeamishness that she wouldn't expect from a rookie cop, let alone a detective.

Flyte hoisted the strap of her bag onto her shoulder, ready to leave.

'So, what do you think happened to Mr Hardwick?' Cassie asked.

A penetrating glance. 'I think person or persons unknown gained access to the premises – probably over the weekend – and removed his body.'

Christ, the woman talked like a robot. But at least she didn't think it was an admin screw-up like the ignorant PC of earlier. Carl's theory – that Mr H had been taken by criminals trading in body parts – came back to her. But it still didn't make sense: with eleven people younger than him in the fridge, why choose the oldest?

Then something occurred to her. What if the critical word was '*choose*'?

Aware that she was sticking her neck out, she said, 'Mr Hardwick was too old for his body parts to be of much value. So maybe whoever took him wasn't looking for a random body.'

Flyte's gaze snapped back to her. 'Why do you say that?'

Going back to the doorway, Cassie said, 'This is the only way in, and the first door you come to opens onto drawers one to four.' She started to walk down the bank of fridge doors that lined the left-hand side of the room. 'But the thieves ignore this one . . . and the next . . . *and* the next . . .' Four or five metres from the doorway, she pointed out the initials on the final fridge door. 'They *choose* the drawer marked H.A.H.'

'Go on.' Flyte's eyes had followed her every move, her expression unreadable.

'Maybe they were looking for Harold Albert Hardwick specifically.'

'Really. And why do you think anyone would target a harmless old man?'

'I don't know.' Cassie shrugged. 'Maybe it was some kind of . . . revenge?'

'Revenge?' Flyte's impeccable eyebrows semaphored disbelief.

'Why not? Didn't some animal rights people dig up the body of an old lady as payback because her family bred guinea pigs for lab tests?'

Even as she said it, Cassie could hear how daft it sounded. An elderly and infirm widower who'd spent his life working for the engineering department of London Underground seemed an unlikely candidate for a murderous vendetta.

'I'll bear it in mind,' said Flyte, drily. 'But right now I'm not leaping to any conclusions re motive – guinea pig related or not.'

Flyte's affected pronunciation of 're', to rhyme with day, and her superior little smile made Cassie wonder how she'd even fleetingly considered her hot.

She crossed her arms. 'So you tell *me* why anyone would steal the body of an eighty-one-year-old diabetic with angina.'

Flyte's upper half twitched, reminding Cassie of Macavity when he was irritated. 'It's too early to say,' she snapped. 'But there are people who have an unhealthy fetish for death and dead bodies.' *People like you*, her lidded stare seemed to say, *with your piercings and your weird haircut.*

'Well, I'm glad to hear you're keeping an *open mind*.' Cassie's emphasis was unmissable.

Two pink spots had appeared high in Flyte's pale cheeks. She turned to go, but as they left the body store, Cassie caught the glance she threw over her shoulder. A glance that appeared to be assessing the distance between the doorway and drawer sixteen.

FLYTE

DS Phyllida Flyte decided to take the fast route back to the nick, along the canal.

From the intent frown she aimed at the towpath a passer-by might have gathered she was angry, but in truth she was simply trying to keep it together, to focus on the job in hand: the disappearance of Harold Hardwick's body. As loath as she'd been to admit it to that Goth girl morgue attendant, organ trading did seem an unlikely scenario given his advanced age, but she had no idea what the motive for the theft might be. The ritual use of body parts might perhaps be a more fruitful line of enquiry – it wasn't many years since the headless and limbless body of a child had been recovered from the Thames, a victim of African witchcraft practices.

But as hard as she tried to concentrate, her mind kept snapping back, the sights and smells of the mortuary crowding in, threatening to overwhelm her. It had been more than two years since she'd set foot in one, but when her new guv'nor, DI Bellwether, assigned her the Hardwick case, she'd said nothing. Camden was meant to be a fresh start and she had honestly thought that by now she could hold it together, trusting in her professionalism to get her through. But inevitably, it had resurrected the old feelings: the sensation that she was edging along the brink of an abyss, her feet threatening to slip. The temptation always to let go, to let herself fall into the bottomless blackness. For it to be over.

That's enough, she told herself.

The morgue girl had been keen to sell her theory that thieves had targeted Harry Hardwick in some colourful revenge plot – a little too keen, perhaps? Mortuary attendants were notorious for being misfits and weirdos – it went with the territory – and her entry card gave her round-the-clock access to the mortuary. If Cassie Raven wasn't involved, why then would she show such concern over the missing body of an elderly stranger?

Before climbing the stairs from towpath to street level, Flyte dug in her bag for a mirror and refreshed her makeup, carefully outlining her lips with liner before filling in with her favourite pale pink lipstick. She'd bought three in the same shade, having been caught out before by cosmetics manufacturers' enraging tendency to constantly renew their range. She hated this mania for novelty, for change, which infected every aspect of modern life.

The lipstick was perfect, apart from its moronic name: Giggle.

Her eye fell on the crude image of a scantily-clad Amy Winehouse glaring out from under her beehive, which some local 'artist' had daubed on the canal's brick siding, one of many tributes to the dead singer in the borough. Typical that Camden's chosen patron saint should be a victim of drug and alcohol abuse and that she should be commemorated in graffiti. It reminded her of Raven's look: the face studded with bolts and rings, the bizarre half-shaved haircut that showed her scalp, the edges of a tattoo visible at her neckline, lurid against her white skin. Why on earth would an otherwise attractive young woman do that to herself? It was a style calculated to flip the middle finger to nice, normal people – and one that on the streets of Camden appeared to be practically *de rigueur*.

It was two months, one week and three days since Flyte had moved to Camden to take up her CID post, and nothing had yet persuaded her to revise her initial loathing of the place. Camden had appeared to offer an escape route, a clean slate, far from Winchester, treacherous with remembered happiness. She missed its leafy tranquillity, its slower pace, and the simple good manners that people showed each other – but not the memories that crouched at every corner, ready to ambush her. Glimpsing a familiar park bench or table outside a pub had been enough to bring back an image of her and Matt, their heads close over a bottle of wine, planning their future. Those moments had ended abruptly after tragedy shouldered its way into their lives, brutal and uninvited.

After it happened, Hampshire Police had let her take a long sabbatical from her job in Major Crimes – a job she had loved – but when she'd finally gone back to work, she'd been forced to face facts. She simply couldn't do it anymore. The prospect of seeing the bodies of murder victims – and worse, interviewing their grieving families – was more than she could bear. Today's mortuary visit had left her reeling, and that was without even glimpsing a corpse.

Flyte took a shortcut through the market that sprawled north of the canal lock. Camden Market was a magnet for tourists, but all she could see was a scruffy bazaar piled high with tat: cheap imported jewellery, orange leather sandals, T-shirts splashed with the f-word and c-word, and all the water pipes, weighing scales and other paraphernalia the dedicated cannabis user could wish for. The place was in full swing: she could hear the frenetic beat of some hippie playing bongo drums, an appropriately brainless soundtrack to the scene. Pushing through the herd of sleepwalking tourists she almost trod on a dreadlocked beggar sitting cross-legged on the ground, a dog wearing a red bandana at his side, before passing a woman with a tattooed face and the tell-tale clockwork walk of a crackhead. Emerging onto the high street she had to duck around a pair of down-and-outs leaning on each other under a railway arch, clutching cans of super-strength lager.

Hideous. But also a reminder of the only thing in Camden's favour: it was nothing like Winchester.

Leaving the high street crowds for a side street, something caught her eye. Two men in the doorway of an abandoned book-shop, heads bent, standing too close together. The younger guy – IC3 – threw a too-casual glance over the shoulder of the older, balding IC1 man with his back to Flyte. Instantly recognising the approach of authority, he turned and legged it. By the time she'd reached the spot, the dealer was long gone, leaving his hapless customer standing there, trying his best to look unconcerned.

Flyte indicated his crotch. 'Hand it over, sir.'

For a moment it seemed as if he might not comply, but she held his gaze unblinkingly, and after a second or two he sighed, delving down the front of his jeans and putting a small plastic bag of marijuana, still warm, into her hand.

'I hope you're not going to make me late for work?' he said, adopting what she was starting to recognise as the aggrieved bluster of the London middle classes.

'If you'd like to call them I'd be happy to explain,' she deadpanned.

Five minutes later, she was presenting him to Dave, the officer on duty at the nick's reception desk.

After they'd been through the formalities, Dave asked one of the lads to put the guy in an interview room. She was about to follow them when he leaned both elbows on the desk and beckoned her over.

'That was your second possession bust in a week, am I right?' His voice friendly, confidential.

'Nine days. It was nine days ago, the last one.'

'OK, nine days. I'm not being funny, Phyllida, but the guy you just nicked? He's obviously just a personal user.' Holding up the plastic bag between finger and thumb, he raised an eyebrow. 'A tiny bit of weed like this? For a first offence, we usually just confiscate and caution.'

She felt her spine stiffen. 'Are you saying that if I see someone openly dealing drugs, I should just . . . ignore it?'

'Collar the dealer, by all means. But clogging up the nick with weekend spliff merchants like Jeremy there?' He gave a backward nod in the direction of the interview room. 'I'd have thought your time was better spent up on the third floor, solving serious crimes.'

She could feel a flush creeping up her face. 'I'm a police officer first and a detective second. If I see evidence of criminality, I shall continue to uphold the law.' She knew she sounded like a sixth-form prefect.

'Suit yourself,' he said with a friendly shrug, before straightening up again.

As she headed for the interview room, she was already regretting her response. If she were being honest, it was partly her instinctive reaction to Dave's look. Her old nick had enforced a strict grooming code and even after seeing him regularly over the last two months, she still couldn't get her head round a policeman with a beard.

Chapter Ten

Cassie got into work at 7 a.m. the next day – an hour earlier than her official shift start time. Owen Edwards had called the previous afternoon to arrange a viewing of his mother's body and she wanted to give herself plenty of time to make Mrs E presentable.

Doug hadn't been keen on her handling the viewing but she had managed to persuade him. When he got in an hour later, he reminded her of his one condition: 'Remember, not a word to him about his mum being your old teacher.'

She nodded. 'Is there any news from the cops? On Harry Hardwick?'

'Not a sausage.' Doug shook his head. 'I just spoke to DS Flyte at the station. They've viewed the council CCTV footage for Saturday night but apparently there's no camera close enough to pick up anyone coming into the mortuary.'

'There must be other cameras on the main road, surely?'

'I can't tell them how to run their investigation, Cassie.' He pulled a weary shrug. 'It's out of our hands now.'

After retrieving Mrs E's body from the fridge, Cassie saw that her eyes had drifted open during the night: a result of the *orbicularis oculi* muscles which controlled the eyelids relaxing as rigor mortis left the body.

'If I just close your eyes, they'll probably open again,' she murmured to her. 'Which wouldn't be very nice for Owen. But don't worry, we can fix that.'

Picking up a wisp of cotton wool with tweezers, she placed it on the surface of the eye, and gently lifted the upper eyelid over it, before repeating the exercise on the other eye: an old mortuary trick that created just enough friction to keep the eyes closed.

Mrs E's hair wouldn't be such a quick fix. It had got soaked when Cassie had washed her down after the PM, and now lay plastered flat against her skull. Using a hairdryer, Cassie dried the thick dark locks a handful at a time – styling it around Mrs E's face, before finishing it off with a few blasts of hairspray.

When the office called through to say that Owen Edwards was in reception, she experienced the sinking feeling that came with every family viewing. Eviscerating a dead body was a breeze compared to dealing with the flayed emotions of a bereaved relative, especially when the death was early and unexpected, like Mrs E's. The word condolence might sound stuffy and meaningless but Cassie was often reminded of its root in the beautiful Latin verb *condolore* – to suffer with another.

A big man, balding, overweight and perspiring in his cheap suit, Owen Edwards could surely only be in his early thirties, given Mrs E's age, but he looked a good decade older. He didn't appear to recognise her from her ill-judged visit to Mrs E's house: luckily, he'd only seen her from behind and the scrubs probably helped to disguise her.

In the viewing suite Cassie prepared him for how his mother would look, before asking, 'Have you ever seen a dead person before?'

'No.' He looked at her sharply – the first time he'd met her eyes – as if she'd accused him of something. She caught the acetone whiff of unmetabolised alcohol – he'd clearly over-done it the previous night, understandably, given that he'd just lost his mum. 'I mean, well, only on television, you know, war reports and so on.' He'd inherited his mother's aquiline nose, but none of her natural grace – and the Welsh accent that had sounded so eloquent and passionate on her lips sounded belligerent on his.

'Just be aware that it might take you a little while to recognise her.' People often struggled to connect the lifeless face with the living person they had known and loved.

He nodded, seeming impatient, like he had a far more impor-tant appointment elsewhere. But Cassie knew that grief could make people behave in unexpected ways.

Cassie opened the curtains, keeping a discreet eye on him in case he fainted – which wasn't unusual, even among men. *Especially* among men. In her experience, masculine bravado was often no match for the sight of a corpse.

Mrs E lay in profile, the deep red coverlet pulled up high enough to cover the train track of stitches with which Cassie had closed the midline incision. Owen didn't visibly react. A moment later the silence was broken by a musical sound, which threw her for a moment, until she realised that he was jingling the coins in his pocket.

'Is there anything you'd like to ask me?' – keeping her voice low and reassuring.

'Do you know how she died yet?'

Cassie explained that the death certificate would give the ultimate cause of his mother's death as drowning but that the underlying reason for her collapse couldn't be confirmed until a range of tests had been run on her blood, urine, and tissue.

'I hope you aren't suggesting my mother was on *drugs*?' He turned bulging eyes on her. 'Because I can tell you now, she never took so much as a para-cet-amol,' his accent dividing up the syllables.

From the crimson starburst that stained the white of Owen's right eye she guessed that he suffered from sky-high blood pressure.

'No, of course not. It's just when there's no obvious cause, we have to run routine toxicology tests to rule out any other factor. The pathologist thinks it's possible that your mum simply passed out in a hot bath.'

'She did mention suffering from dizzy spells, now and again,' he said slowly, looking up at the ceiling.

'Really? I don't recall any mention of dizzy spells in her GP records.'

'Well. She wasn't a great one for doctors.' That defensive note resurfacing in his voice. Cassie reached for the handle of the glass doors. 'Would you like to go inside, to spend some time with your mum?'

'No, no.' His eyes flickered toward the exit. 'I've seen the body – that's enough for me.' Another jingle from his pocket. 'Anyway, I've an appointment with the lawyers. I'm her executor, see.'

She let her hand fall. 'Of course. It's a difficult time – so much to do. Is there anything else, anything at all, I can help you with?'

'How soon can I book the cremation?

'As soon as the coroner approves the release of your mother's body, which will take a few days. After that, it's entirely up to you.'

Owen glanced at the door, as if checking his escape route.

'I meant to ask,' she said, as he made to go. 'Do you know if anyone else will be coming to see her?'

'Anyone else?' Owen stared at her.

Was it Cassie's imagination or did he seem shifty all of a sudden?

'Any other family, for instance, or close friends?'

His gaze slid away. 'No. There's only me.'

And without a backward glance at the woman who had given him life, Owen Edwards was off through the door like someone doing a late-night runner from a curry house.

Cassie checked the clock. In the four or five minutes the viewing had taken, the guy had barely glanced at his mother nor displayed any of the emotional responses she was used to seeing in the just-bereaved: sorrow, guilt, or even, sometimes, anger. And she couldn't recall anyone referring to their mother as 'the body' before: people always said, '*Mum*', or '*her*'.

'I don't know what to make of your Owen, Mrs E. Maybe he's just one of those people who gets freaked out around death and bodies.' She pulled out the sides of the body bag that had been tucked underneath Mrs E so she could zip it back up. 'I just wish I could have been able to tell him how you died.'

She had just closed the bag when she sensed it. A crackle in the air, like static before a thunderstorm. Pulling down the zip, she stared into Geraldine Edwards' lifeless face. The lips were motionless – a pale, set line. But the echo of the words she had clearly heard hung there still.

Cassandra. It's not my time yet.

Chapter Eleven

Having worked an early shift, Cassie was back home by mid-afternoon and took the opportunity to start work on the squirrel her grandmother had given her, which had been defrosting in the fridge. Her mind was still buzzing with what had happened that day and she was hoping that the simple physical task might bring some kind of clarity to her thoughts.

Laying the body belly-up on a chopping board, she made the incisions as instructed by the online tutorial before starting to carefully de-glove the skin. She'd bought the taxidermy course on a whim months ago when she and Rachel were still living together, but had put it on hold after Rachel had made a fuss over finding a dead mouse in the fridge next to the yoghurt. Now she was excited to see how the squirrel's internal anatomy compared with the human version.

Cassie's thoughts kept circling back to the moment when she'd heard Mrs E 'speak'. The experience had been as fleeting as ever – although this time it had arrived without warning, not preceded by the usual dreaminess – with Mrs E returning instantly to a state of unreachable, enigmatic silence.

Usually, she didn't examine these moments too closely, fearing that over-analysis might destroy her precious thread of connection with the dead. Now she tried to figure out where they came from. Rationally – scientifically – she knew that dead bodies couldn't speak. So were these 'messages' simply her own subconscious deductions, projected onto the dead?

It's not my time yet.

It was, after all, the sort of thing Cassie might expect a woman who died at fifty-one to say. But as hard as she tried, she couldn't entirely dismiss the notion that Mrs E's words contained a message – a declaration that her death had not been natural.

Owen's weirdly defensive manner came back to her, the way his eyes avoided hers, and his almost indecent haste to get away. The memory morphed queasily into an image of his meaty, perspiring face as he pushed his mother's head under the water.

She eased the squirrel's pelt over its head without having made a single unnecessary puncture. Now, with one hand holding the carcass steady, she used a scalpel to open it up from throat to groin, in imitation of the midline incision she performed a dozen times a week. Inside, she found the major organs laid out more or less like a human's but on doll's-house scale: the heart was no bigger than a kidney bean, the lungs like two baby almonds. The squirrel's brain was a different matter: pinker and smoother than a human brain, with none of its bulges and folds. She was racking her own brain for the Latin name for these undulations when the doorbell rang.

As she opened the front door, the answer pinged into her head: *gyri* and *sulci*. Miles away, it took her a few seconds to place the woman with the glacier eyes who stood on her doorstep.

'The mortuary said you were home. I tried to call but your mobile is going to voicemail.' DS Flyte's stare fell on

Cassie's gloved and bloody hands. 'I hope I'm not interrupting anything?'

She apparently expected Cassie to invite her and the uniformed cop at her shoulder inside.

'Has something happened at the mortuary?'

'No. We're simply continuing our investigation into the missing remains of Harold Hardwick. They said you'd left for the day. Can we come in?'

Cassie waved them towards the kitchen table before slipping off her bloodstained nitrile gloves. *So that's what being caught red-handed means*, she thought wryly.

She watched Flyte's eyes rake the room, taking in the full-length poster of a young, nude Iggy Pop, and the cluster of bleached animal skulls on the window ledge, and suddenly remembered the bit of weed she had at the back of the kitchen drawer.

Calm down, she told herself. *If the Stepford Cop had a warrant she'd have flashed it by now.*

Flyte's searchlight gaze fell on the eviscerated squirrel corpse stretched out on a chopping board on the worktop, alongside its tiny pile of organs. 'Is that a rabbit?' – her voice edged with disgust.

'It's a squirrel.' Feeling exposed, Cassie got up to stow the board in the fridge.

'You *eat* squirrel?'

Reminded of her squeamishness at the mortuary, Cassie decided Flyte was in the wrong career: she'd have made an excellent traffic warden.

'No, I'm a vegetarian,' she said, unable to keep a grin off her face, 'but I'm learning taxidermy.'

Flyte didn't return the smile. 'Don't you get enough of dead bodies in your day job?'

Cassie decided not to offer them tea. 'How is it I can help you exactly?'

'The line of enquiry we're pursuing in relation to Mr Hardwick's disappearance is that his remains were stolen by someone with . . . an unhealthy interest in dead bodies.' She met Cassie's gaze and this time there was no mistaking her implication: *someone like you.*

Ignoring the insinuation, Cassie said, 'If you mean a sexual interest, I'd say you were barking up the wrong tree. Every case of necrophilia I've ever heard of has involved the bodies of young people, usually women. No offence to Mr Hardwick, but old gents in their eighties don't tend to set the pulses racing.'

Flyte arranged her lips into a smile, her eyes never leaving Cassie's face. 'Whatever form the interest might have taken, I consider it to be the most promising line of enquiry. It need not necessarily be sexual . . .' she glanced at the little cairn of skulls on the windowsill. 'As I'm sure you're aware, body parts are used in witchcraft, Satanic rituals, that kind of thing.'

'So, how is it I can help? I'm as keen as you are to get poor Mr H back.'

Flyte pulled a document from her handbag, keeping her eyes stapled to Cassie's face. 'The security company has provided the records from the keypad entry points at the mortuary. As you know, all authorised personnel have their own unique code.'

'That's right.' Cassie noticed that Flyte's ice-blue irises were encircled by an unusually dark limbal ring – like the eyes of an Arctic wolf.

'The system records you entering the premises at 0650 last Friday,' she frowned down at the printout. 'And leaving at around 1500 hours. Could you confirm that you were the technician on call over that weekend?'

'Yes.'

Flyte's descent into full-on cop-speak was making Cassie's blood pressure spike.

'Are you often called into the mortuary out of hours?'

Cassie looked away. 'Occasionally. Sometimes the police need to bring someone in to identify a body. Or a family member might be desperate to see a loved one – we always try to make it work, whatever time it is.'

'But you told me that you weren't called back in after leaving on that Friday?'

'That's right.' *Where the hell was this going?*

DS Flyte handed her the document, which looked like a computer printout.

'This is the front entrance keypad record for the night in question.' Flyte placed a pink oval nail next to one of the lines of code. 'And as you see, it records you returning to the mortuary late on Saturday night.'

'*What?* That's not right.' But there it was: *Entry 23:58, passcode 4774.* Had she gone back to the mortuary that night? No, she reassured herself, the last time she'd been there 'unofficially' outside hours had been months ago. 'I don't care what it says. I didn't set foot in the mortuary last weekend.' She tried to recall where she'd been on Saturday night. 'I was at Kaos – it's a music bar in the Lock.'

'Can anyone vouch for your presence there around midnight?'

Cassie frowned: she had seen a few people she knew, but they'd all left to go to a club about eleven. 'The barman, Tito, knows me, he'll remember.' But when she pictured Tito that night – dancing behind the bar, eyes glazed – her certainty slipped. 'At least, he should do.'

Flyte made a note, before training her gaze back on Cassie. 'I'm told that you make a habit of talking to dead bodies.'

Sweet Jesus. So somebody knew her secret. Who'd been badmouthing her? Certainly not Carl or Doug, nor any of the pathologists – like they'd even notice.

She half-shrugged. 'I wasn't aware it was a crime.'

'What's all that about? Do many morticians chit chat with dead bodies?' – the mocking tone clearly designed to wind her up.

'Mortician is an American term,' said Cassie. 'In the UK we say mortuary technician – or anatomical pathology technician, if you prefer the proper terminology.'

'You haven't answered my question. What's the point of talking to a corpse? Isn't it a bit of a one-way conversation?'

The uniformed cop hadn't said a word so far but now he stifled a grin. Cassie could feel her fuse start to burn. 'I don't talk to the body. I talk to the person they once were.'

'Sorry? I'm still not getting it.'

'I'll try and look surprised.'

DS Flyte pressed her lips together – that pale pink lipstick she wore did nothing for her colourless complexion, thought Cassie.

'Are you aware that some of your colleagues consider you to be . . . somewhat *obsessed* with dead bodies?'

It had to be that prick of a chief porter, Darrell Fairweather, she decided. He'd made it clear from the off that he disliked her

72

simply because of the way she looked. Maybe one of his guys had overheard her while delivering a guest to the body store. She could just imagine him slagging her off to Flyte: *If I was you, I'd be questioning that Goth girl over at the mortuary – she's a right weirdo.*

'Porters love to gossip.' She looked straight at DS Flyte, who broke eye contact, confirming her hunch.

Should she try to explain her feelings towards the bodies in her care? That she sometimes imagined herself as a priestess or a modern-day Charon, ferrying them across the Styx to the underworld? Then she pictured Flyte's reaction.

'Is something funny?' Flyte demanded.

'Look, are we done here? I've got a squirrel to stuff.'

'No, we're not "done".' Colour flamed in Flyte's alabaster cheeks. 'I looked you up on the police database. You have a criminal record for possession of drugs.'

Stay cool.

'It was only a bit of weed and a line of sulphate – when I was *seventeen*. Anyway, what's that got to do with a missing body?'

'Selling bodies would be one way to fund a habit. Do you still take drugs?'

'Only the mainstream ones. Like vodka.' But beneath her cool exterior, the memory of her night with Tish-Tash was making Cassie's pulse race – and not in a good way. Never mind the weed in the kitchen drawer – she couldn't remember what she'd done with the empty wrap of coke at the club. Had she flushed it away or was it still in the pocket of the jeans she'd been wearing – now lying in the laundry basket – waiting to be sniffed out by a police dog?

'And did you declare this conviction when you applied for your job?'

'Yes. They viewed it as a juvenile misdemeanour. Which is precisely what it was' – sending her a defiant glare.

Flyte stared back for a long moment before closing her notebook, having apparently exhausted her weaponry.

Cassie took a careful breath. It looked like the use of her access code alone wasn't enough to justify arresting her. Still, if Flyte delved further back into the records and discovered the times she'd stayed overnight in the mortuary without any official reason to be there . . . it didn't bear thinking about.

The uniformed sidekick piped up. 'Is it all right if I use your loo?'

'Down the hall on the right.'

DS Flyte put her notebook back in her bag and snapped the catch shut. 'That's all for now, but we'll be wanting to question you again.'

She was at the front door when the uniform came back from the loo. 'Sarge,' he said. 'I think you'd better have a look at this.'

Cassie followed them into the bathroom where he pointed up at Ziggy, sitting in his usual place on top of the cabinet above the sink.

'Is that a human skull?' Flyte spoke casually, but Cassie heard the undertow of excitement in her voice.

Cassie half nodded, half shrugged.

'I assume you have the proper paperwork for it?'

The empty eye sockets above the grinning teeth seemed to look down at Cassie with a sardonic expression.

'Paperwork? But it's ancient . . .'

'Fine. I'll just need to see an antiquities licence certifying its age.' For the first time since they'd met, Flyte actually looked happy.

Cassie's heart had started thudding again. 'I haven't got a licence. I bought it at a boot fair in Hackney, for Christ's sake!'

'Then I'm afraid I must inform you that it's a criminal offence to be in possession of any human remains unless they're demonstrably at least a hundred years old.'

Flyte's voice remained unemotional but there was no mistaking the triumphant look plastered across her pale face.

Chapter Twelve

The next morning, Cassie went straight into Doug's office without taking her jacket off, to tell him about her access code being used and Flyte confiscating her skull, 'pending further investigations'.

'I bought it years ago, before I even worked here,' she told him. 'The guy at the boot fair said it was nineteenth century, from an old medical school. It never even occurred to me I needed a *licence*.'

'Are the police charging you?' Although outwardly calm, Doug hadn't stopped pacing his tiny office.

'Not yet; DS Flyte said it might take *weeks* to prove the skull's age.' She twisted her lip bolt. 'If they do charge me, I guess you'll have to inform the HTA?' A technician convicted of being in possession of undocumented human remains would surely be sacked in a heartbeat.

'Let's not get ahead of ourselves,' said Doug, running a hand over his balding head.

'The worst thing is, while that hard-arsed detective wastes time investigating me, she's not looking for the bastards who *did* steal poor Mr Hardwick.'

'What I don't understand is how on earth anyone could have got hold of your access code? Do you think someone could have seen you punching it in?'

She screwed up her eyes, replaying her daily arrival at work. 'They'd need to stand pretty close – I'm pretty sure I'd have noticed someone breathing down my neck.'

Doug pulled himself up to his full five foot eight. 'Look, I'm going to talk to DI Bellwether – tell him this sergeant of his is way off beam. I'm not prepared to have my staff harassed in this way.'

In the body store, Cassie checked that Mrs E and her other ladies and gents were all present and correct – since Mr Hardwick had gone missing she'd started doing all the stocktakes herself. Then a call came through from Penney & Sons, the undertakers.

'Morning, fruit bat,' came Luca's laidback drawl.

'Morning, fuckwit. Still breeding insects in that horrible beard of yours?'

Luca's big laugh always cheered her up. She'd had a fling with him a couple of years back, and now and again she found herself wishing it hadn't fizzled out – *just like all your relationships*, added a sly voice in her head. As someone who, like her, worked with the dead, Luca knew how emotionally draining it could be to deal with grieving relatives every day. Unlike Rachel, he had understood how sometimes you had to switch off the touchy-feely stuff when you left work.

'Listen, Cass. I've got an Owen Edwards on my case, asking when we can come over there and collect his mum?'

Cassie's gaze snapped towards Mrs E's drawer. 'Already? When did he call?'

'Umm. Yesterday, late morning? And again just ten minutes ago.'

Cassie did a quick calculation: Owen must have called the undertakers straight after leaving the mortuary yesterday.

'So . . . what should I tell him?' Luca asked.

'We haven't even got the coroner's release yet. What's his hurry?'

'He said something about going abroad for work. Needs to get the funeral out of the way before he can sort flights.'

Cassie turned to look at Mrs E's initials on the steel fridge door, hearing again what she had said, right after Owen had left.

It's not my time yet.

'Sorry?' said Luca.

'Nothing. Just talking to myself. Listen, Luca.'

'Ye-es?' When they were an item, he'd always been able to suss when she was working up to ask a favour.

'Could you . . . stall him for a bit? It's just . . . we're a bit behind on admin over here.'

'It's not like you to be slow with the paperwork. Are you slipping?'

'Yeah, well, it's been a crazy week.'

'No problem. I don't know what his rush is – people usually take ages to come up with a date the whole family can do.'

Luca agreed to tell Owen Edwards the crematorium was busy and that he would get back to him with the first available date.

It was a relief to have bought some time. Cassie's bad feeling about Mrs E's death and her shifty-seeming son hadn't gone away, and all her instincts told her to keep hold of the body for as long as possible. The police might still find something to make them reopen the case, something that would trigger a proper, forensic post-mortem, while there was still time.

Wishful thinking.

Cassie knew there was only one way to find out whether she was letting her imagination run riot or whether Mrs E's death really was suspicious – and that was to go looking for the evidence herself.

FLYTE

After her visit to Cassie Raven's flat, DS Flyte had spent the next morning trying – and failing – to get an audience with her boss, Detective Inspector Bellwether. So when she saw him in the lunch queue at the canteen, she had seized the opportunity to collar him.

As they slid their trays along the counter rails, she briefed him on her discovery that Raven's access code had been used to gain entry to the mortuary on the night Harry Hardwick's body had gone missing.

'Chips or mash with the pie?' asked the woman serving.

'Make it chips,' sighed Bellwether. 'It's turning into one of those days.'

Even in profile she could tell that Bellwether's expression – lugubrious at the best of times – had grown, if anything, progressively gloomier during her update.

'It's good news, isn't it, boss?'

'What, them having chips on today?'

'Um, no – I mean having a suspect for the theft of Harold Hardwick's body?'

His sideways glance told her – too late – that he'd been ribbing her. 'We're talking about the general mortuary next to the hospital, right?' He pushed his tray along towards the till. 'Barry White was still in the charts when that place was built. I'm guessing their entry system isn't exactly cutting edge.'

Flyte took her plate of ratatouille and salad, no dressing, from the woman behind the counter.

Bellwether went on. 'I'm just saying, I wouldn't rely too heavily on the entry records – you can bypass those old systems with a paperclip.'

'What about the human remains Raven keeps in her bathroom? I mean, what sort of person wants to have a skull watching her while she showers?'

Bellwether's look told her she might have spoken a bit too . . . vehemently. 'You said it yourself, Phyllida, these mortuary attendants can be a bit . . . off the wall, but she gets a five-star reference from her manager. If you're convinced she was involved you'll need to find something more concrete before you can charge her.'

Flyte reproached herself: making her criticism of Raven sound personal had been unprofessional. But there was something about the morgue girl that raised her hackles.

After taking his change from the cashier, he carried his tray over to the cutlery area, where she joined him a moment later. 'Boss, if I could have just a couple of uniforms, we could conduct proper door-to-door enquiries. Whoever stole the body would have had to drive a van into the mortuary car park, which is just off the main road. Even at midnight, somebody could have seen something.'

He stopped and looked at her properly for the first time. 'We've had four stabbings in ten days, Phyllida, and we're getting a lot of flak from upstairs and the press. That's where we need to put our resources – not investigating a crime against someone who's already dead.'

Looking over her shoulder towards the seating area, he gave an upward nod of acknowledgment to someone. 'Wrap it up sharpish,' he said, turning away. 'I need you back policing the living.'

Hell's bells. She stood there, people reaching past her for cutlery, realising what a fool she'd been. Bellwether had only sent her to the mortuary as a tick-box exercise to appease the coroner. He'd expected her to take a few statements, fill in the paperwork, and quietly shelve the case.

Part of her knew he was right: there were far worse crimes all over Camden crying out for their attention. But she just couldn't accept the idea of giving up on a helpless elderly man who'd met such an undignified end.

Harry Hardwick might not have any close relatives to fight his corner – but he still had Phyllida Flyte.

Chapter Thirteen

The colossal skeleton of the blue whale craned above Cassie's head, turning her into an overawed fourteen-year-old again. When she'd last visited the Natural History Museum, on a school trip, it had been Dippy the diplodocus that had enthralled her, although it hadn't been long before she had escaped with her mates to share an illicit cigarette in the grounds.

Cassie had taken a rare long lunch break to dash over to South Kensington in order to meet Eleni Petrides, an old friend from Mrs E's Biology evening class. They'd lost touch after Eleni went up north to study for a zoology degree but an online search revealed that she now worked in the museum research department.

Eleni had been a skinny little thing back then, peering at the world through the screen of an overlong fringe; now she'd acquired a smart pixie cut and a more confident air.

'Still rocking the Goth look, I see,' said Eleni admiringly. 'Have you still got that tattoo – the home-made one?'

Cassie pulled aside the neck of her top to flash her very first inking: a spider climbing a web on her shoulder done by a girl in her first squat – it wasn't bad for an amateur job.

'Remember how you were always trying to persuade me to get one?' Eleni widened her eyes.

'Changed your mind yet? Even nice girls have tasteful tats these days.' It was true: when she'd got her first tattoo done, they were still edgy. Now, they were about as transgressive as glamping at Glastonbury.

'My dad would go nuts!' Eleni laughed, covering her mouth with her hand in that way she had. It made Cassie smile, the way they'd fallen straight back into their old roles: she the older rebel, Len the half-scandalised, half-fascinated younger girl.

In the museum cafe, they caught up on the last five years. Eleni was still living at home, where her Cypriot-born mum was struggling with Eleni's recently adopted vegan diet – just like Cassie's grandmother had when she'd first stopped eating meat.

After they'd swapped stories of disastrous meals, Cassie's smile faded as she prepared to break the news about Mrs E. It had been three days since she'd unzipped the body bag to reveal that much-loved face, but the memory of that moment still made her catch her breath.

'Mrs E?!' Eleni's expression made her look like a crestfallen child. 'But . . . she wasn't old! I mean, not *old* old. Was it cancer?'

After hearing how Cassie had learned of Mrs E's death, Len's hands shot up to her face, as if in prayer. 'Oh my gosh, how terrible for you!'

Cassie had forgotten Len's endearing reluctance to swear, a legacy of her Greek Orthodox upbringing.

'I only saw her a few months ago,' Eleni added, shaking her head.

'Really?'

It turned out that Mrs E had brought a group of students to the museum during the summer and had emailed ahead to ask Eleni to act as their guide.

'But she'd retired from teaching by then,' said Cassie.

'I know! She said it was her "last hurrah".'

They exchanged a rueful smile.

'How is her fiancé taking it?' Eleni asked.

Cassie stared at her. 'Her what?'

'Didn't you know? Mrs E was engaged. We came here afterwards for coffee, and I noticed her engagement ring.'

Replaying her supermarket encounter with Mrs E, Cassie was surprised not to have spotted a ring on Mrs E's finger – it was the sort of thing she wouldn't usually miss.

'What did she say about this boyfriend?'

'Not much. Just that his name was . . . Christian? I'm pretty sure that was it.'

'No surname?'

A headshake. Eleni scrunched up her eyes. 'She said that they were thinking of living abroad. She clammed up again pretty fast, changed the subject – you know how cagey she could be.'

'Yeah, she always was a bit of a dark horse.' Even outside college, Mrs E had never shared much about her family or private life.

Eleni turned liquid brown eyes on Cassie. 'She seemed really . . . *happy*. Glowing, you know? It just doesn't seem possible that she's dead.'

Cassie fell silent. It was weird that her fiancé hadn't contacted the mortuary to arrange a viewing. In her experience, loved ones nearly always wanted to see the body, especially when death was sudden and unexpected. What was it Owen Edwards had said, when she'd asked if anyone else might want to view his mum? '*There's only me.*'

'Len, do you recall Mrs E ever mentioning a son, name of Owen?'

'A son? No. I always assumed she had no kids.'

Cassie nodded. In hindsight, it seemed odd that in all their hours of chat across the kitchen table at Patna Road, Mrs E's single reference to her only son had been one, almost accidental, mention.

'She was the only teacher we called "Mrs" E, rather than her first name, wasn't she?' said Len. 'I guess you know what it is . . . what it *was*, now?'

'Geraldine. Geraldine Olwyn Edwards.'

'Oh!' Eleni had remembered something. 'She did say she was on Facebook – surely the boyfriend must be tagged on her timeline?'

Cassie shook her head. 'She was only on it for a couple of months.'

'I can't imagine Mrs E on social media. Remember that old Nokia she had – the one with the prehistoric ring tone? And the way she used to talk – always *telephone* not phone and *television* instead of telly?'

'Yeah,' Cassie grinned. 'And she never said "goodbye" . . .'

'Always *Cheerio!*'

They laughed, but in a minor key.

'I still can't believe it,' said Eleni. 'And you were much closer to her than I was. How are you doing?' As Len reached out to touch the back of her hand Cassie felt herself stiffen.

'Me? I'm fine.'

Random physical contact always put her on edge: it had been another well-gnawed bone of contention between her and

Rachel, who'd often complained about what she called Cassie's 'emotional firewall'.

They walked slowly back towards the entrance hall, pausing beneath the massive skull of the blue whale.

Picking up a hint of unevenness in Eleni's gait, Cassie asked, 'Have you done something to your leg?'

'Oh, it's nothing,' Eleni grimaced. 'I've had a run of colds and it's left me a bit tired and achy.' Cassie remembered noticing how Eleni had put a hand on the cafe table to help herself up – the kind of thing a much older person might do.

'You do know, don't you, that you were her absolute favourite,' Eleni continued, her warm brown gaze seeking Cassie's.

'Really?'

'Gosh, yes! I think some of the others were jealous of how much attention she gave you.'

The buzz this gave Cassie was short-lived. 'Well, I didn't deserve it. I . . . lost touch with her a while back – all my fault. I kept meaning to give her a call. I guess I expected her to be there for ever – like Dippy.'

'You always were rubbish at keeping in touch,' said Eleni, softening the words with a smile. 'You never answered any of my messages after I went to uni.'

'*Mea maxima culpa.*' My most grievous fault. Cassie was uncomfortably aware of how hopeless she was at keeping up with old friends – truth be told, it sometimes seemed easier to her simply to make new ones.

'Well, now you've got my mobile number, there's no excuse.' Eleni gave her a mock-stern look.

A shaft of sunlight came through the glass canopy overhead, lighting up Eleni's face, and revealing deep shadows under her eyes.

Cassie closed her eyes against the light. *A series of colds that had left her friend 'tired and achy'. That hint of a limp.*

Muscle weakness, fatigue and a stuttering immune system . . . it came to Cassie what was ailing her old friend.

'Eleni, when did you go vegan?'

'About five or six months ago?'

'Do you take any vitamins or supplements?'

Eleni shook her head.

'I think you're suffering from vitamin D deficiency from coming off dairy,' Cassie told her. 'You need to sort that out or risk getting osteoporosis when you're older.'

Before Cassie left, she extracted a promise from Eleni: that she would take herself to the GP to get tested.

Chapter Fourteen

Back at the mortuary, Cassie had no time to dwell on the shock of Mrs E's marriage plans.

In the body store, she pulled out the drawer marked JMH. Nineteen-year-old Jordan Hewett had died in a head-on collision in the early hours while racing his mate on a suburban A road. Overtaking on a bend, his car hit a Volvo carrying an unlucky middle-aged couple coming the other way. The man driving was killed instantly, while his wife lay in the ICU facing life-changing injuries – at best.

'Hello, Jordan,' said Cassie gently, eyeing the carnival mask of dried blood that enveloped his eyes and forehead. 'I'm going to clean you up now, ready for the doctor. And we want you looking nice for your mum when she comes to see you.'

But she'd only just started sponging his face clean before she stopped, hand hovering over his forehead, pierced by an unexpected emotion. *Anger.* Unexpected, because treating everybody exactly the same was a matter of professional pride to her. She never passed judgement on those who'd harmed others – not even the man who'd rigged his car exhaust to gas himself and his two little girls in a brutal act of vengeance against his ex-wife.

Until now. In Jordan she was seeing the reckless teenage driver who'd taken her mum and dad from her when she was four years old, snatching away twenty-one years of parenting and denying her the love and nurturing that everyone else took for granted. For the first time in her life she was consumed by fury at the sheer injustice of it. But why now? Jordan was hardly the first killer-driver she'd had to look after. Forcing herself to calm down, she resumed her swabbing, although her heart was still beating unnaturally fast.

'We need to find out exactly what killed you, Jordan,' she murmured, making an effort to speak normally. 'It might seem to be obvious, but the coroner will want to know the specific cause of death.'

Beneath the dried blood, Jordan's face had suffered barely a scratch, and still wore the expression of dull surprise that must have come over it as he'd rounded the bend and seen death filling his windscreen. It was a different story below the neck: it looked like the steering column had crushed his chest with such force that it had dislocated both shoulders.

'You weren't wearing a seat belt, were you, Jordan?' She leaned closer but could hear nothing rising from his pale lips. The bodies of the young rarely 'spoke' to her. Maybe he was just one of the silent ones. Or perhaps her anger had chased away any chance of communication.

She started to turn him gently onto his front, hips and lower half first. But midway through turning his top half, she stopped, feeling the buzz that came with nailing the cause of death. 'You don't need to tell me anything, Jordan,' she murmured, patting him on the shoulder. 'Your body just spoke for you.'

Archie Cuff might only have one post-mortem list under his belt, but from the way he breezed in you'd think he was a veteran. 'Afternoon, guys. What have you got for me today?'

Cassie exchanged a look with Carl, who was prepping a customer at the other end of the autopsy suite. She'd been intending to make a fresh effort with Cuff, but his air of God-given superiority never failed to push her buttons.

'Our first customer is an RTA – a high-speed head-on collision at around three this morning,' she told him. 'Young male aged nineteen, in otherwise good health. Declared dead at the scene.'

'Boy racer?'

The look Cassie sent him said, *No shit, Sherlock.*

She waited to see if Cuff would mention the results of Kate Connery's lab tests which, according to a mate who worked in the tox lab, had been emailed to him the previous day. Apparently they showed sky-high levels of mast cell tryptase, a substance released by the immune system of someone suffering from anaphylactic shock. But all he said was, 'Right then, let's have a look at this body.' Would he at least ask her for her input this time?

No chance. After spending all of two or three minutes examining Jordan, Cuff said, 'With a gross chest trauma like that, my money's on a ruptured heart.'

As he strolled off, Cassie suppressed a grim smile. Well, if he wasn't interested in her opinion, she wasn't about to offer it.

Half an hour later, Cuff's air of certainty had deserted him. Standing at the dissecting bench, he frowned down at Jordan's dismembered heart. With a little shake of his head, he pulled the liver towards him again, muttering to himself. Carl caught Cassie's eye across the autopsy suite.

Picking up a mop, Cassie started to clean the blood off the floor around his bench. 'You going to be much longer, Dr Cuff? I'd like to get Jordan reconstituted soonish– his mum's coming in to see him.'

Giving no sign of hearing her, he wiped his forehead with the back of his gloved hand, leaving a smear of blood above one eyebrow.

'Is it not an open and shut case, after all, then?' she asked, all innocence.

Out of the corner of her eye she saw Carl turn his back, starting to crack up.

'The heart and lungs are intact,' said Cuff, talking more to himself than to her. 'And all the major vessels.'

Seeing his tense, pale face – like a twelve-year-old facing a nightmare exam paper – Cassie felt suddenly sorry for him.

'When Prof Arculus can't find an obvious cause in the organs, he usually takes another butcher's at the body,' she told him.

'Butcher's?' He stared at her, mystified.

'Butcher's hook – look,' she explained. *Where had that come from?* She'd never used rhyming slang in her life before. Out of the corner of her eye, she could see Carl's shoulders silently shaking.

'Right. Yes, of course.' He moved stiffly over to the eviscerated shell of Jason's body – but then just stood there, staring at it indecisively.

Cassie rolled her eyes. *For crying out loud.*

Going to stand behind Jordan, she put a hand on each shoulder and see-sawed them gently, which made his head flop from side to side like a broken puppet's, just like it had when she'd turned him over earlier. 'I'm no pathologist, but I'd say that was a C-spine fracture.'

Cuff's look of dawning comprehension was almost comic.

Jordan Hewlett's death certificate would give the direct cause of death as acute respiratory failure, emanating from a C1 vertebral fracture that had caused a complete traumatic spinal cord injury.

Put simply, the violent deceleration of the high-speed collision had snapped his neck. At least Cassie would be able to tell Jordan's mum that his death would have been instantaneous.

After Cuff had left, Cassie and Carl repaired the bodies and returned them to their chilly dormitory, before starting to clean up. Hearing Carl's soft chuckle, she looked up.

'*Butcher's hook*?' he said. 'Since when did you start talking cock-er-ney?'

'Oh, I'm fluent, me. Especially down the rub-a-dub-dub. After a few Britneys.'

'The look on his face . . .' Carl shook his head.

'Surely you mean his boat?'

'Did he even thank you, after you showed him the C-spine break?' asked Carl, leaning on his mop.

'What do you think?'

'Yeah, silly question.'

'He's not the first pathologist to miss a cervical fracture, but what gets me is when they're too arrogant to ask.'

As Cassie stowed Jordan's samples in the fridge, she felt an echo of her earlier fury. Maybe it was weird, but until that moment, she'd never really thought much about her parents' deaths, let alone the drunk driver who'd killed them. Losing them so young, before she'd laid down many memories, had always seemed to her a kind of blessing – sparing her the full trauma of bereavement.

Mrs E's death had shaken that comforting conviction, she realised. Maybe Rachel had been right after all: she really had been too young to process the bereavement properly, and beneath the unruffled surface of her life there lay an iceberg of hidden grief.

FLYTE

Saturday morning found Phyllida Flyte standing at the window of her first-floor flat. Sipping Darjeeling from a bone china mug, she watched traffic streaming around the one-way system and wondered again whether moving to Camden had been a mistake.

The stripped floorboards and marble fireplace of her flat had seemed characterful at first, but whenever a bus or lorry went past, the sash windows rattled. Worse, the rent on its two-and-a-bit rooms devoured almost 40 per cent of her monthly salary.

Having washed and dried her cup, she returned it to the cupboard, noticing with a pang the row of unused wine glasses, still carrying their Ikea price sticker, that she'd bought after moving in. At the time she'd pictured herself hosting soirees for the new, sophisticated circle of friends her move to London would bring. In reality, her CID colleagues were largely male, and their idea of night out was a marathon crawl around Camden's grotty pubs, competing with each other to tell increasingly disgusting jokes, and culminating in a greasy kebab in one of the local Greek tavernas. After enduring two of these outings, she'd ducked further invites as diplomatically as possible.

For all Camden's disappointments, Flyte knew she'd had no alternative. As much as she loved Winchester, it would always represent the past, echoing with how things might have turned out differently.

After fate – or a malign God – had laid waste to all their plans for the future, she and Matt had spent another fourteen months trying to make the marriage work, had even gone on a 'dream holiday' to Bali, but she suspected that by then they both knew it was over. Even after they separated, almost a year ago, she'd clung on in Winchester for a while before it finally dawned on her: if she didn't leave she would be stuck there forever, her grief paralysing her like amber embalming an insect.

At least in Camden – if she policed her thoughts properly– it was easier to keep the door to the past closed.

She checked the time: she was on duty from one and scheduled to attend Camden Town Tube station to assist in a stop-and-search operation targeting knives. They would confiscate and caution rather than arrest, the goal being to reduce the number of blades in circulation. Although the latest fatal stabbing had been a standoff between drug dealers, the majority of knifings were postcode related: kids who'd got knifed simply for straying into the 'wrong' area. Where the law was powerless, or irrelevant – as it was across swathes of inner London – it seemed to her that young men swiftly reverted to being territorial animals.

After consulting a map of the borough, she calculated that she'd have time to squeeze in some work on the Harry Hardwick case. Of course, when DI Bellwether had said, 'wrap it up sharpish', what he'd really meant was for her to quietly mothball the investigation. So what exactly was stopping her? she wondered.

It wasn't hard to work out: it was important to her to find Harry Hardwick's body and make sure that he, at least, got a proper funeral.

Flyte's first port of call was the petrol station on the busy Highfield Road, directly opposite the turning into the mortuary car park. The manager was an IC4 male, Pakistani at a guess, in his forties.

'DS Flyte, Camden CID.' She flashed her warrant card. 'I see you have a security camera covering the exit.'

'Too many drive-offs, lady. The police aren't interested, so I have to take the bastards to court myself.' Despite the profanity, there was no reproach in his tone.

'Do you still have the footage for last weekend?' She pinned him with a look that said he'd better not give her the run-around.

But the guy seemed keen to help, ushering her into the office, all the while relating his ongoing battle with people who drove off without paying for fuel. 'Cost me seven hundred pounds in lost payments last month, lady, and then I have to pay the bastard solicitors.'

He seemed cheerfully unaware of any offence his bad language might cause. Flyte wonder if she would ever become accustomed to Londoners' tendency to use swearwords as a kind of conversational condiment.

He powered up an ancient-looking PC, the cooling fan as noisy as a small jet engine.

'Last Saturday night you say, lady?' he said as he sifted through various .mov files.

That 'lady' was starting to irk her. But when he opened the file for Saturday night, her heart leapt: just as she'd hoped, the angle didn't just cover the petrol station exit but also the turn-off into the mortuary across the road.

'Could we take a look at the exit cam from about 23:30?' Cassie Raven's access code had been used two minutes before midnight.

As he fast-forwarded through the images, Flyte ignored the flow of cars exiting the garage, her eyes fixed instead on the mortuary turning opposite, half expecting to see Raven's slim figure and distinctive haircut stroll into view.

'Stop!' She had him rewind and replay one section frame by frame.

At 23:54, a battered-looking blue van slowed, before moving into the middle of the road to turn right into the mortuary. She'd already checked that the turning didn't lead anywhere else, so it had to be the body snatchers' van. It hung there for a few seconds, side-on to the camera, its passenger-side window a darkened rectangle, waiting for a gap in the oncoming traffic, before making the turn.

'OK. There.' Flyte leaned forward so her nose almost touched the screen, squinting at the rear view of the van. 'Back a few frames. Freeze.'

From the shape it was a Ford Transit, the white square of the number plate visible. But the reg number was a fuzzy blur.

'Fast forward, please,' she told the guy. There would be another chance when the van left.

'Lady . . .'

'And please, call me Sergeant Flyte.'

Shrugging, the guy hit fast forward. Within a few seconds the screen went black, with the van still inside the mortuary car park.

'What the . . . ?'

Pointing to the clock, which had stopped at one minute past twelve, he gave an apologetic wag of the head. 'Sorry, Lady Sergeant, garage closes at midnight.'

'Fishcakes!' she said, earning a mystified look from the man.

Halfway out of the door she stopped, feeling bad, not just for snapping at the guy but also for the way the police were routinely failing to protect him from what was straightforward theft. Should she go to DI Bellwether, suggest a borough-wide blitz to catch and prosecute drive-offs? Showing that the police took the crime seriously could deter others; she recalled that such an initiative had delivered results in Winchester.

But she could already hear Bellwether's stock response: 'This isn't Winchester, Phyllida.'

'Listen,' she told the manager. 'It's not ideal, I know, but I can probably get you one of those cardboard cut-out policemen? As a deterrent? Some forecourts swear by them.'

The guy's ever-present smile faded. 'We had one, Lady Sergeant.'

'Did it work?'

'On the second day, one of the youth set fire to him.'

Her next stop was the bar called Kaos, to check out Cassie Raven's supposed alibi for the previous Saturday night. The place was a dive: bare plaster walls decorated with the graffiti that passed for art in Camden, the sour reek of stale beer hanging in the air. Its only clientele was a pair of German tourists and a female punk with a blue Mohican nursing a beer at the bar, who greeted her with a scowl. The girl behind the bar, who sounded Eastern European, said that the barman whom Raven had named as her alibi had just arrived for his shift.

Tito's eyes widened when Flyte asked if he knew Cassie. 'Is she OK?'

The accent was Spanish. Of course. Having spent most of her adult life in overwhelmingly white and English Winchester, Camden's multicultural melee still had the power to make Flyte feel like she was the outsider. It reminded her of being a child again and having to start over at yet another new school, every time her dad took up a new posting. She'd dealt with the constant upheaval by insisting on keeping as much as she could unchanged: her mother didn't attempt to hide her exasperation at having to let out the only two dresses the ten-year-old Phyllida would wear, or at her daughter's insistence on the same lunchbox meal day in, day out: cheese and Branston on white bread, a chocolate marshmallow, and an apple, which had to be a Granny Smith. If a Golden Delicious were substituted it would travel home uneaten in her lunchbox after school.

'She's fine,' she said now. 'It's just a routine enquiry. She says she was in here, late last Saturday?'

He frowned for a moment, before dropping his gaze to the concrete bar top. 'Yes, she was in here.'

'When did she leave?'

Another pause. 'Around half eleven, twelve?'

'Are you sure?'

'Not a hundred per cent, but I think she went to a club?' Perhaps seeing something in Flyte's eyes, he added, 'I was a little drunk, so I couldn't swear to it, what time she left, I mean.'

Flyte smiled. The leeway was clearly designed to help Raven; but all he'd achieved was to expose her alibi as fatally flaky.

She asked to use the loo and when she emerged, Tito called her over. Indicating the blue Mohican girl, who was tapping at her phone, he said, 'Lexy has something you should see.'

Lexy handed Flyte her phone with a nasty smile. The screen showed a photo taken in the bar on that Saturday night, its graffiti-ed walls dimly lit. Sitting centre frame at a table, wearing a Ramones T-shirt, Cassie Raven toasted the camera with a margarita.

The timestamp said 00:06 – six minutes past midnight into Sunday morning.

Flyte eyeballed the punk girl: could she have hacked the metadata on her camera app to alter the time? It was possible, but she had to admit it wasn't plausible.

At the time somebody was stealing Harry Hardwick's body from the mortuary, Cassie Raven had been a mile away, getting drunk in one of Camden's innumerable lowlife bars.

Chapter Fifteen

As it was a Saturday and she had the day off, Cassie had a lie-in, but despite the soothing weight of a purring Macavity on her chest her thoughts were restless. The more she considered it, the more bizarre it seemed: in the five days since Mrs E had died, neither the mortuary office nor the funeral directors had heard a word from the mysterious Christian – her future husband.

Eleni had said that the couple planned to live abroad. Was he already based overseas? Maybe it was one of those long-distance relationships, which prompted a horrible thought: could he still be in the dark about Mrs E's death, increasingly worried that she wasn't answering her phone?

Relocating Macavity onto the duvet, which brought a mewl of reproach, she reached for her laptop and re-opened Geraldine Edwards' Facebook page, hoping to find some clue to the identity of the mysterious boyfriend. But half an hour later she was none the wiser. Mrs E's brief flirtation with social media hadn't survived the summer and no Christian was listed among her few dozen 'friends'.

Finding a fellow teacher at Mrs E's college called Maddy O'Hare on the list, Cassie fired off a message, saying she was a former student of Geraldine's and asking if they could meet up – keeping it deliberately vague, in case she hadn't heard about the death either.

Then, curious to see what Mrs E's house might fetch in Camden's ludicrous property market, she ran a search – and was shocked to find that the house on Patna Road had already been listed online. Under a picture of the exterior the blurb read '*Coming Soon! A unique opportunity to acquire a stunning four-bedroom early Victorian property on a Prime Street in the heart of Camden.*' Judging by similar houses, Mrs E's place could fetch as much as three million: enough to ensure that Owen Edwards could give up work tomorrow and buy an entire street of houses in Rhyl.

Owen's haste to cash in on his mother's death reminded Cassie of how uncaring he had seemed when viewing her body. Why, in all the years they'd been friends, had Mrs E been so reluctant to talk about her only child? Had there been bad blood between them? Bad enough for him to kill her?

Her eye fell on Mrs E's profile pic – a bottle of red wine and two glasses on an outdoor table – its golden light locating it way south of Camden, the second glass presumably belonging to the fiancé. In the background lay petrol-blue water – too calm to be the sea – and on the horizon a distant blocky smudge, oddly shaped, like a wedding cake.

Zooming into the photo, she peered at the label on the wine bottle in the foreground. *Bardolino.* Italian. The Italian Lakes? At the edge of frame was the partial head and shoulders of a male statue, slightly out of focus but clearly Roman in style, the hair exuberantly curly.

An image search for 'islands in the Italian Lakes' delivered a match. The distant island was Isola Bella on Lake Maggiore, an islet that some Renaissance-era oligarch had completely remodelled with layer upon layer of elaborate stone terracing.

After checking out a couple of dozen hotel websites, Cassie found three that seemed to have the right vantage point. Her eye snagged on the Hotel Bacchus Gardens and a grin crept across her face. *Bacchus.* She looked again at the Roman statue on the edge of the profile pic. That hair of his? Those weren't curls, they were bunches of grapes – the god of wine's traditional headdress.

Sending the gods a prayer of thanks for her classics A level, Cassie rewarded herself with another beer.

A few minutes later, she was spinning her story to Domenica, the girl on reception at the Hotel Bacchus Gardens.

'So I was on your lovely terrace when I overheard Geraldine talking about doing the trip to Isola Bella, and asked her if she knew the boat times.' Casting herself and her imaginary husband as a young couple on their first trip to Italy, Cassie claimed that they'd met 'Christian and Geraldine' on the hotel terrace one lunchtime. 'Such a lovely couple. You know how sometimes you just really hit it off with people? We ended up having dinner with them for the rest of our stay.'

No doubt bored silly in an out-of-season hotel, Domenica sounded like she welcomed the diversion.

'Anyway, we're here in London for a few days, and we're simply dying to catch up with them.' Cassie could hear her voice getting posher and posher – if she didn't tone it down she'd end up sounding like the Queen. 'Unfortunately, my husband has managed to *lose* Christian's phone number . . . and we only know Geraldine's surname. So, you see, you're our only hope!'

Domenica paused for a moment before saying, 'Yes, I remember them because Geraldine spoke some Italian. Such a charming lady. But . . . I'm afraid we are not permitted to give out the details from our guests.'

'Oh . . .' Cassie put a world of disappointment into the single syllable.

After a pause, Domenica dropped her voice. '*Aspetta* . . . But maybe I could pass your contact details on to the gentleman via email?'

Result! Cassie had just finished reading out her phone number when she heard the deep tones of a man's questioning voice down the line.

'Can I help you, madam? This is the manager speaking'– a voice as smooth and rich as tiramisu but underpinned by steel. Cassie rolled out a shorter version of her story, but it was clear that Signor Hotel Manager wasn't buying. Once he'd trotted out the dreaded phrase 'hotel policy' and said he could not sanction 'invading the privacy of our guests', she knew she was wasting her time.

After hanging up, she put her head back and hurled every curse she knew – including a few really filthy Polish ones – at the ceiling. From his vantage point on the arm of the sofa, Macavity opened one eye to assess the situation, before closing it again.

Then a message pinged up on her Facebook page: Maddy O'Hare had replied.

Chapter Sixteen

It was a ten-minute bus ride to Palmerston College, the adult education centre where Cassie had studied for her A levels. Maddy had said that she'd be there teaching on a weekend course for foreign students and would be happy to meet up to talk about 'poor Geraldine', which made it clear that she, at least, had already heard the news.

Cassie hadn't been back to Palmerston since sitting her final A level in classics. She'd taken up the subject after starting work at the mortuary, partly because human anatomy was a story told in Greek and Latin, but primarily because the mythology that the Ancient Greeks and Romans had spun around death fascinated her.

As she pushed open the oak front door of the redbrick Victorian pile, she was hit by its familiar smell – dust and dodgy electrics, overlaid with the same cocktail of mushroom soup and hot chocolate from the drinks machine. It triggered a cascade of memories: her quaking terror the first time she'd walked through that door, and the effort of will it had taken to drag herself here in the early days when she'd felt doomed to fail – feelings that had gradually given way to an anticipatory buzz.

Going to the reception window, she looked up to meet the quick brown eyes of Mrs Edwards.

Feeling herself start to sway, Cassie gripped the edge of the desk. 'I . . . '

'Are you all right, dear?'

Blinking rapidly, Cassie saw that the eyes belonged not to Mrs E, but to an Asian lady.

'Oh . . . I'm sorry. I'm here for . . .' but before she could complete the sentence, she heard a voice behind her.

Maddy O'Hare was in her late forties, hippyish-looking with her long grey-sprinkled hair and chunky ethnic-looking necklace. 'You must be Cassie,' she said, taking her hand and looking into her eyes. 'Geri was very proud of you, you know.'

Cassie just nodded, still a bit breathless after her . . . how to describe it? Daydream?

'It was such a shock,' Maddy said after taking her into an empty office. 'I hadn't seen her for a few weeks but since she retired she'd been looking so healthy – taking long walks in the park, swimming every day. To think that at her age she could just suddenly . . .' She put her hand to her mouth.

'I know. Listen, I was wondering about Mrs E's fiancé, Christian.'

Maddy smudged away tears with a wadded tissue. 'Yes, it must be just awful for him, to have their new life together just . . . torn away like that.'

'Do you think there's any chance that he might not know yet – about her death?'

'Oh, he must do, surely?' Maddy looked aghast. 'Unless he's away somewhere remote, on business?' She explained that he was an architect, based in Europe – somewhere in Germany, she thought – and his work involved a lot of travelling.

'Do you have any way of contacting him, just so we can make sure?'

That brought a wry little laugh. 'I don't even know his surname. Geri tended to keep her friends in separate silos, if you know what I mean.'

'What about her son Owen? Surely he would have got hold of Christian – to break the news to him?'

'Owen?' Maddy widened her eyes. 'I very much doubt it. Geri and he weren't in regular contact. The only time he ever called or visited was when he wanted something.'

Cassie noticed how Maddy crimped her lips after this, as if to stop herself from saying more. 'Do you know how she and Christian met?'

'On a dating site.'

'Wow, that must have been pretty out there for Mrs E.'

'It was! Especially as he was five or six years younger than her.'

Maddy told her that they'd joined up together back in the spring, not long before Geraldine took redundancy. Cassie remembered the photos of Mrs E celebrating her freedom: a woman embarking on a new chapter of her life and looking for romance. *Good on you, Mrs E* she thought.

'It was a bit of a whirlwind romance, from what I could gather,' said Maddy. 'His work made things tricky – but they did manage a holiday, somewhere in Italy. They were both mad about travel. She was thinking of selling the house and doing her bucket list.'

Cassie wondered if Owen had known about his mother's plans to spend his inheritance.

'That place must be worth a fortune now,' Maddy went on. 'But she said it was a total wreck when she bought it, back in the nineties.'

Cassie was trying to imagine a world in which a teacher could afford to buy a house – or even a one-bedroom flat – in Camden.

'How about you?' she asked Maddy. 'Did you have any luck with the online dating thing?'

'I only had one date. He gave me a day-by-day account of his golfing holiday in Marbella, for an hour straight.' They shared a wry look. 'That was enough for me.'

Cassie paused, trying to work out the best way to broach her doubts about Mrs E's son.

'So what did Owen make of his mum getting a new boyfriend?'

As Maddy frowned, staring off into the room, Cassie waited: years of working with bereaved families had taught her the power of a sympathetic silence.

Finally, the older woman spoke. 'You know, if Geri were still alive I wouldn't say anything – she was so sensitive about her privacy. But she did share some things with me. Owen is an alcoholic, which means he never holds a job down for long. And whenever he got fired – and from what I can gather he *always* got fired, eventually – he would turn up at Geri's looking for a handout.'

'And would she give him the money?'

Maddy nodded. 'Until recently. After she took redundancy she said, "that's it Maddy, if I don't say no to him now, he'll never sort himself out". She said she had to draw a line in the sand.'

'That must have been tough for her.'

'It was. Sure enough, a few months ago he came back, expecting another bailout. But once Geraldine makes her mind up about something, she won't be shifted.' Maddy shook her head, half-rueful, half-admiring. 'Apparently, he blamed Christian for "turning her against him" – got quite nasty about it.'

'Violent?'

'Not exactly, but she did say he got very aggressive with her. Luckily, Christian was there and he stepped in and threw him out.'

Despite Maddy's calm demeanour, Cassie noticed that since she'd started talking about Owen's hostility, she'd completely shredded the tissue she was holding. 'There's something else, isn't there,' she asked.

A nod. 'Two or three weeks ago, I was passing the end of her road, so I knocked on the off-chance of catching her in. She said she was just about to go out, so I didn't stay. But she wasn't herself.'

'How do you mean? Was she feeling poorly?'

'No, but she seemed . . . distracted. As I was leaving, I happened to glance back and saw her at an upstairs window.' Maddy lifted her hand as if holding back a curtain. 'She was peering at something down the street. Something didn't feel right, but I couldn't work out what was wrong.'

'But now you think you know.'

She stopped and looked at Cassie. 'I think she was . . . frightened.'

'Of Owen?'

'He's the first person I thought of.' Maddy bit her lower lip. 'But it's only a feeling. The awful thing is that was the last time I laid eyes on her.' Her voice fell to a whisper. 'I should have called her after that – maybe she *wasn't* feeling well. I could have persuaded her to go the doctor and she might still be alive today.'

Cassie said all the right reassuring things. But if the job had taught her one thing, it was this: there were no words that could assuage the regrets that the living felt towards the dead.

Chapter Seventeen

On Monday, Cassie found a workman at the mortuary front entrance installing a new swipe card entry system. It looked like the theft of Harry Hardwick had galvanised the authorities where years of badgering had failed.

Doug collared Cassie before she'd even had time to get out of her civvies.

Now she stood in his office, both hands pressed to her face. 'Poor Mr Hardwick!'

Early that morning, the police had retrieved a bundle wrapped in black bin liners from the canal, where a dog walker had spotted it floating against the lock gate. Inside was the body of an elderly man wearing a hospital wrist tag, smudged but still readable, bearing the name Harold Albert Hardwick.

Doug said that Mr Hardwick had been taken to the area mortuary at King's Cross where he'd been examined by the pathologist on call.

'He wasn't . . . mutilated or anything, was he?'

'No, thankfully the body was undamaged, except for the deterioration you'd expect after more than a week underwater. The police reckon the thieves dumped the body in the canal right after stealing him and didn't even bother to weigh him down properly, because the decomposition gases brought him to the surface.'

'Thank God he's been found.' She felt guilty that her preoccupation with Mrs E had pushed Harry Hardwick to the edge of her thoughts these past few days. The news of his recovery made her feel physically lighter – relieved that he hadn't been stolen for body parts, or fallen victim to the Satanists of DS Flyte's lurid imaginings.

'So do the cops have any more clue as to who took him – or why?'

'They're mystified. DI Bellwether reckons it might just have been youngsters mucking about. Some kind of dare – or a Halloween prank.'

'Halloween was more than a week before he went missing.' Cassie frowned. 'Anyway, how could kids have got hold of my access code?'

'The main thing is, he's been found.' Doug blew out a jet of breath with a sound like her gran's pressure cooker. Then he smiled for the first time she could remember since Harry Hardwick's disappearance. 'And I just got off the phone with the HTA. They've decided it wasn't our fault, given that we've repeatedly asked for a security upgrade. Now Mr Hardwick's been found, we're off the naughty step.'

'That's good.' Cassie fiddled with her lip bolt. 'But Doug, don't you still want to know who stole him, and why they then just . . . dumped him?'

'I know it's a bad business.' Doug looked away. 'The idea of someone getting in here and taking one of our customers – and believe me, I want to see them punished as much as you do. But DI Bellwether told me, off the record, that we'll probably never find out who did it.' His tone became confidential. 'If the whole thing just blows over at least it'll get that po-faced sergeant off your case.'

Cassie gave an unhappy shrug. He was right, of course.

Getting up from behind his desk, Doug put a fatherly hand on her shoulder 'I think we should try to draw a line under this and move on.'

She nodded.

'I tell you what. I'm going to raid the training budget and take everyone out for a team-building lunch.'

Later, at the local Greek taverna, with the cold retsina going down fast and the table crowded with plates of meze, there was raucous laughter and a tangible air of relief among Cassie's co-workers. Despite her efforts to join the celebratory mood, she couldn't shake the feeling that there was a ghost at the feast.

Doug tinked his wine glass with his knife. 'I want to thank everyone for being so professional during our recent drama. You've all been brilliant – just as I would expect.' He raised his glass. 'Here's to us – still the best mortuary in London.'

After a moment's hesitation Cassie lifted her glass too, before adding 'And to Harold Albert Hardwick.' Everyone went along with it, murmuring his name respectfully, but the awkward silence that followed made it clear that she'd killed the buzz.

Afterwards, the office workers headed back first, leaving Cassie and Carl at the table while Doug went to sort the bill. Carl, who'd already more than taken advantage of the free drink, was reaching for the retsina bottle when Cassie caught his eye. 'I hate to play killjoy, but I don't want you handling instruments half-cut.'

'You're probably right.' Pulling his slow smile, he poured himself some water.

She hesitated for a moment before saying, 'Doug seems really relieved the HTA are dropping their investigation.'

'Well, he could have lost his job, couldn't he, if they needed a fall guy.'

'True.' A disturbing thought had surfaced in Cassie's brain: if anyone could lay hands on the mortuary technicians' access codes it would surely be the mortuary manager.

Just then, Doug returned to the table. 'Are we ready, boys and girls?' Seeing his beaming, wine-flushed face, Cassie felt ashamed of herself for thinking that Doug could ever do anything so vile.

That evening, Cassie went to her grandmother's for dinner, but she didn't really enjoy her meal. And it wasn't the lunchtime meze that had killed her appetite.

Weronika cocked her head inquiringly. 'You're quiet tonight, *tygrysek*. What's going on?'

Cassie told her about the theft and dramatic reappearance of Mr Hardwick.

Weronika eyed her granddaughter's face, perceptive as ever. 'But there's something else troubling you, yes?'

Cassie frowned at the tangle of red pepper on her fork. 'You remember me talking about Mrs Edwards?'

'Of course I do, she was your science teacher at college. Scottish lady.'

'Welsh.'

Grandma dismissed this trivial distinction with a wave of her knife.

'She's dead.'

'No!' Putting down her cutlery, Weronika crossed herself. 'God rest her soul. But she was only young! What happened?'

Cassie pictured the email Prof. Arculus had sent over with the results of Mrs E's tests. No sign of underlying illness had been found and the tox report had come back clean, all bar a blood alcohol level more than twice the drink-drive limit – all of which seemed to confirm the Prof's initial assessment.

'It turns out it's not that hard to pass out and drown in a hot bath, especially if you've had a drink.'

'How terrible.' She reached out and touched Cassie's arm. 'I know how close the two of you were.'

'I know. I guess I thought she'd always be there.'

Cassie dropped her gaze. She hadn't mentioned her falling out with Mrs E – in fact, she rarely confided anything personal to her grandmother. She'd managed to keep the drugs and squatting off the old lady's radar and as for her complicated love life, she could hardly expect an elderly Catholic to understand. So she'd always recast her female lovers as 'friends', and Rachel as a 'flatmate'. If one of her relationships with a girlfriend ever went the distance, obviously she'd have to come clean, but it wasn't something she looked forward to.

She pushed her plate away. 'Babcia. There is something else. I've got my doubts about her death.'

'Doubts? What kind of doubts?'

'I just get . . . a bad feeling about her son. He seems to me like he has something to hide.'

'But it was a natural death, the body doctor said?'

'These things aren't always clear-cut.' People liked to think that the pathologist had all the answers, like they did on TV, but Cassie knew that the factors leading to someone's death were often elusive, whatever the certificate said.

'She was a widowed lady, yes? What a shame she didn't remarry.'

Cassie couldn't bring herself to say that Mrs E had recently got engaged.

Weronika patted the linen tablecloth, lost in a memory. 'I sometimes wish I'd remarried, after your grandfather died.'

Cassie didn't quite manage to hide her horror at this prospect. 'Did you ever consider it? Seriously?'

'Why not? I was only in my late fifties.' Her mouth curved into a wistful smile. 'I did have a romance, I suppose you might call it, with a widower at church.'

'But . . . it never went any further?'

Weronika smiled a private smile. 'We had sex, if that's what you mean.'

Yikes. Cassie took another gulp of water. 'So, what stopped you . . . marrying the guy?'

'I wasn't that much of a prospect.'

'Why ever not?' – embarrassment turning to outrage on her grandmother's behalf.

'Because at the time I had a bossy seven-year-old with a fixation on dead animals to look after.' She met her granddaughter's eyes. 'I think he found it difficult, knowing that she would always come first.'

Cassie was struck dumb: the sacrifices her grandmother must have made in taking her on hadn't really occurred to her before. Shamingly, she might even have viewed herself as a kind of consolation prize for a woman who'd lost her only child.

As she started clearing the table, Cassie glanced over at the framed photograph of her mother, a mantelpiece icon, frozen forever in her youth. As a child, she'd seen her parents as the prince and princess in a fairy tale, rather than real people. By her teenage years, this had curdled into an illogical resentment; she recalled the moment when her grandmother had said that her 'mama in heaven' would want her to behave better at school. Cassie had shot back, 'Well, she shouldn't have gone and died then!'

Cassie had been around the bereaved long enough to know that anger was grief's conjoined twin, but she'd always thought that losing her parents so young had allowed her to escape the ordeal. Now, she had to accept that Mrs E's death had unearthed feelings that had been lurking unseen all along, like the subcutaneous injuries that only a forensic post-mortem could detect.

Later, stacking the dishwasher, Cassie asked, 'Was Mum a good cook, Babcia? I can't remember.'

That brought a curious glance from her grandmother – Cassie rarely showed any interest in her parents. 'Oh, she was far more adventurous than me in the kitchen. She used to make Indian curry from scratch, with all the special spices. Not that you would eat it – you were a proper little fusspot!'

'Really? What about Dad – did he cook much?' This was riskier territory: Weronika had never hidden her dislike of her son-in-law Callum, preferring to act as if he'd never existed. As a result Cassie knew only that he was, in her grandmother's dismissive phrase, a 'Jack of all trades'. In between stints labouring on building sites or working as a market trader, he drove a minicab. Born in Ireland, but estranged from his family back home, he'd been good-looking, bequeathing to Cassie her near-black hair and dark blue eyes – information she had to take on trust since her grandmother claimed not to possess a single photo of him.

'Him? Cook? I doubt it,' Weronika said briskly. 'Now. Do you have time for a coffee?'

After Cassie left, she puzzled over what her dad might have done to provoke such lasting animosity from his mother-in-law. Had he been unfaithful? An alcoholic? Or just a bit of a waster? Maybe it was simply that a man who sold fruit and veg could never be good enough for Katherine, Weronika's adored only daughter.

Cassie turned off the lamplit street towards the canal. She wouldn't usually take the canal route home after dark, but tonight there was something she had to do. In the summer, the towpath would be crowded with people spilling over from the pubs and bars around Camden Lock, but now the only people she saw were a cyclist with no lights who whizzed past her and two girls having a drunken argument over which pub to go to.

She stopped at the canal's edge a few metres from the lock gate where Harry Hardwick had been found, and waited until the sound of the girls' voices faded, leaving only the background hum of the city and the lazy slap of water against brickwork. A band of fog, solid-looking, hung a hand's breadth above the canal surface. Dropping to a crouch she took the white carnations she'd bought out of their plastic sheath and stripped off the rubber band, before laying them in twos and threes on the black water.

'I'm so sorry we let you down, Harry,' she murmured. 'We're all so pleased to know that you're safe now.' Cassie had accepted that whoever had stolen Harry Hardwick's body would probably never be caught, but she liked to think that this small gesture would sanctify the place where he'd been found.

The flowers floated downstream, their white blooms punching through the gloom like lit candles, an unseen current bearing them towards the lock gate, just as it had carried poor old Harry.

They spun idly in an eddy, before the last one finally faded from sight, snuffed out by the darkness.

'*Recquiescet in pace*, Mr H. Rest in peace.'

Turning back along the towpath, she'd almost reached the canal bridge leading back to the high street, could hear house music booming out from the pub overlooking the lock, when she heard it. The swish of bike pedals turning at high speed coming up fast behind her. Just as she'd registered that the cyclist was going to pass too close, a blow landed on her left shoulder. Then the strap of her bag shot down her arm. There was a split second when she could have – should have – let it slip off over her wrist, but instinctively, she scissored her forearm upwards. The strap tightened with a sickening jerk, dragging her forward. She staggered, but by planting her Doc Martens wide managed to stay upright, and the bike came to a skidding stop, the rider forced to put one foot down on the towpath.

Cursing her, he jerked the bag down, pulling her to the ground, but she wouldn't give it up. She crunched herself into a ball as kicks thumped against her ribs, and lashed out wildly with her free arm. Her fist made contact with something soft, making her attacker yell. Then she heard shouts and glimpsed two guys running towards them from the direction of the bridge. Pulling his bike upright, the mugger got one foot on the pedal, still tugging at her bag. Cassie threw out her free hand and grabbed hold of the back spokes, throwing the bike off balance.

The shouting was closer now. Swearing, her attacker let go of the bag, but still she clung on to the spokes. Then she felt her jaw slam shut. He had back-kicked her under the chin. Her vision dimmed, and then . . . nothing.

Chapter Eighteen

'I'm very grateful to you for looking after me, but honestly, I'm OK now.'

Cassie wriggled to the edge of the hospital bed and reached for her leather jacket – noting with annoyance the gouges in the elbows where she'd been dragged along the towpath.

'When someone has lost consciousness like you did, we like to keep an eye on them for a while, in case they've suffered a concussion, or some other problem develops.' The nurse was the same earnest young man who'd assessed her, after one of her rescuers had brought her into A&E – disappearing before she'd had a chance to thank him properly.

She started to pull on her jacket, wincing as pain scythed through her right shoulder joint. 'I was only out for a minute max, they said. If I start feeling funny, I'll come straight back, I promise.'

'You really need to have someone stay with you tonight – in case you take a turn for the worse.'

'Sure.' She gave him her best winning smile, abandoning it as shards of pain drove deep into her jaw.

'That's going to be painful for a while,' he told her. 'You were very lucky it wasn't fractured.'

'Yeah, well I'm known for being thick-skinned – and bone-headed.' Moving her jaw cautiously from side to side she traced the pain to the right temporomandibular joint, where the mugger's back kick had smacked the lower mandible against the base of her skull. Lucky for her the guy had only been wearing trainers.

She'd almost made it out of the cubicle when she saw two uniformed cops, one male, one female, bearing down on her. *Great.*

Half an hour later, she'd given them her – *utterly pointless* – statement. All she could tell them about her attacker was that he had brown eyes, a complexion that might have been Asian, mixed race, or Mediterranean, and that he could ride a bike. The bottom half of his face had been hidden by a crimson scarf and like 90 per cent of Camden youth, he wore a black hoodie. No, she didn't think she'd be able to identify him if she saw him again.

The cops were sympathetic, but their body language said that, like her, they were just going through the motions: a crime had been reported, a statement taken, and Camden's street crime stats would click up one more digit.

'We'd have a better chance of catching him if he'd got your bag off you,' said the female cop, sounding faintly disappointed that Cassie had put up a fight. 'If he'd gone on a spending spree with your cards – we might have been alerted.'

Cassie must have looked sceptical because the male cop chipped in, 'We nicked a guy last week who used a stolen contactless to buy a chicken dinner in Nandos. The manager smelt a rat, and we turned up just as the guy was getting a refill of frozen yoghurt.'

The next morning, as she drifted up through layers of sleep, Cassie was gripped by the strange conviction that she'd been encased in cement from the waist up during the night. Opening her eyes, she tried to move. *No response.* Panic clamoured in her throat. Her limbs finally did respond, but her shoulder joints were so stiff she found she couldn't fully raise her arms.

Using the bedpost to lever herself to her feet, she padded slowly to the bathroom mirror. A streak of purple, like the lividity on a day-old corpse, stretched beneath the jawline almost up to her ear. As she applied a layer of slap and powder to cover it up, her overriding emotion was self-recrimination. What had she been thinking, hanging round the canal like that late at night? *What an idiot.* As for her attacker, the well of rage she felt towards him was too deep to even think about.

For a moment, she thought of phoning someone, before dismissing the idea. Who would she call? The closest thing she had to a proper friend, she realised, was probably Carl.

At least she was rostered off, which meant she could just lie around watching movies all day if she wanted. But after half an hour she felt the urge to get out of the flat.

There was barely anyone about on the towpath – it was too early for tourists, although the growing numbers of rough sleepers who bedded down around the canal were clearly already up and about, their empty sleeping bags lying around like the shed skins of insects emerging from their pupae.

Then she heard a voice. 'Cassie Raven? Is that you?' And saw a woolly hat above a pair of bleary eyes looking at her over the edge of a stained blue sleeping bag.

'Kieran? How're you doing?'

'I'm good!'

As he wriggled himself up into a sitting position the smell reached her: a potent cocktail of dirty clothes, cheap cider, and patchouli.

She and Kieran had once squatted together, sharing a disused office block and then a derelict pub along with an ever-changing assortment of artists, musicians, Goths, and New Agers. She was shocked to see that he'd aged a good ten years since she'd last seen him – his face grey, dirt-seamed, and pocked with sores – although he seemed as cheerful as ever. Even when he'd been wrestling with his twin demons, alcohol and ketamine, Kieran had always been one of those eternally sunny types who everyone loved to be around.

'What about you, Cass? Still cutting up stiffs?'

'Yep.' Feeling awkward talking down to him, she lowered herself carefully to a crouch, getting a stab of pain in the ribs where the mugger's kicks had landed.

Kieran winced in sympathy. 'You've hurt yourself.'

'Yeah. I got mugged last night, down by the bridge.'

'You're kidding me!' Kieran looked outraged. 'Where are the cops when you need them, eh?' He gestured at an empty nest of cardboard a few metres away. 'My mate got kicked around by some pissed-up twats the other night. It's not safe round here after dark.'

'Not like Hawley Road,' said Cassie.

The Hawley Road squat, a derelict, once-grand Georgian pub, had been legendary. After reaching a deal with the landlord to stay until planning permission to redevelop the site was granted, it had been their home for almost a year. They'd painted artwork on the inside walls and grown tomatoes and lettuces in the back yard. That baking hot summer was the happiest that Cassie had ever been.

'Yeah. Happy days.' A wistful look spread across Kieran's face. 'All the old squats over there have been demolished now, y'know.

They're building some flash new development. Camden's not the same anymore.'

Cassie didn't need to ask how Kieran came to be sleeping rough: the area's crazy property prices meant that commercial buildings rarely stayed empty for long enough to squat. And while homelessness was soaring, the number of hostel places was falling.

In any case, most hostels forbade drugs and alcohol, and from the look of him, Kieran was still using.

'Seen any of the old crew lately?' he asked.

'Not for ages,' she admitted, feeling a little rush of nostalgia, remembering the intense camaraderie that had come with belonging to a clan of outsiders.

Kieran nodded philosophically – they both knew that from the moment she'd stopped squatting and got a proper job she'd entered a parallel universe, a place in which people worked nine to five, went out to restaurants, held dinner parties . . . Cassie had a sudden urge to tell him that she still felt like an impostor in the straight world – like she didn't really belong there – and probably always would.

Kieran stood up, letting the sleeping bag fall along with the insulating layers of newspaper he'd cocooned himself in. 'I tell you what, I'll walk up as far as the high street with you, so we can have a natter.'

'OK.' Eyeing Kieran's facial sores and stained clothes, Cassie caught herself hoping that they wouldn't bump into anyone she knew, before pulling herself up. *Don't be such a dick, Cassie Raven: he was a good mate once.*

They walked along the towpath, chatting about the old days, Kieran periodically darting off to pick up any discarded dog ends that promised even a pinch of unsmoked tobacco, just as Cassie remembered doing in the old days.

Reaching the spot by the bridge where she'd been mugged, she slowed her step.

'Is this where it happened?' Kieran asked. He'd always been sharp, at least when he was sober.

She nodded.

'Why did you come back? Was you hoping they dropped something?'

'No.' She looked over the oily water for a moment. 'I came back because I won't be told where I can and can't walk.'

'Same old Cassie Raven.' Kieran grinned. 'Remember what we used to call you in the squat?'

'No . . .?'

'Teflon. Nothing left a scratch on you.'

Teflon. Was that what people had thought of her? That she was hard? Lacking in emotion? She wanted to say, *You should see me with dead people.*

After crossing the bridge, they came to a coffee shop. 'Why don't you join me?' Cassie tried not to look at the streaks of what might be dried ketchup – or blood – down the front of his denim jacket. 'Let me buy you a coffee, a sandwich, maybe?'

Kieran's laugh revealed an expanse of gum studded with a few ruined teeth. 'Nah, you're all right. I'd only freak out the customers.' He finished making his dog-end rollie one-handed, before running his tongue along the Rizla's gummed edge. 'I'd better be off. Gotta see a man about a dog.' He half closed one eye.

Off to buy gear, in other words – and who was she to judge?

'Here.' She shoved a twenty in the top pocket of his jacket. 'It's grand to see you, Kieran.'

'Bless you, Cassie Raven.' He pulled a wide grin. 'You take care of yourself.'

Cassie watched him go, his jaunty gait failing to disguise a dipping limp that made him look like Long John Silver navigating a sloping deck. Kieran could only be what – twenty-eight? Twenty-nine? – but he'd be lucky to make it to his fortieth birthday.

Waiting on her coffee, Cassie tried to recall the vagabond glamour that a life like Kieran's had held for her back when she was seventeen. Sure, she sometimes missed the camaraderie, but eight years on she was a totally different person – like the exasperated older sister of that naive girl.

Seeing Kieran had hammered something home to her. If Mrs E hadn't kept coming back to talk to the girl selling the *Big Issue*, hadn't encouraged her to return to education, hadn't gone the extra mile to steer her through night school, Cassie could easily be bedding down by the canal tonight, relying on booze and ketamine to keep the cold at bay.

Cassandra, it's not my time yet.

She owed Mrs E. And she had to do everything in her power to find out whether her death really had been just a terrible accident – or something more sinister.

Chapter Nineteen

Back at work the next day, Cassie decided to keep schtum about the mugging – the makeup was doing a good job of camouflage and she couldn't face having to tell her co-workers the story half a dozen times over, facing the mix of sympathy and prurient fascination generated by somebody else's trauma.

She was lowering a brain into a bucket of formalin, to firm up or 'fix' the soft tissue ready for dissection, when her phone rang. Seeing 'unknown caller' she almost ignored it but something made her strip off her glove and tap answer.

'Is this Ms Raven?' An unfamiliar male voice, well spoken.

'Who wants to know?'

'My name is Christian Maclaren.'

It took her a full second to process this information. 'Oh, hello,' she managed at last. 'How did you get my number?'

A gentle laugh came down the phone. 'A very helpful young woman from the Hotel Bacchus Gardens called me. She said you were anxious to "get back in touch"?'

Bravo, Domenica! She had clearly defied her boss and passed on Cassie's number. And going by Christian's drily amused tone, he'd played along with Cassie's cover story.

'I'm sorry about the cloak and dagger,' she said, with an embarrassed laugh. 'I couldn't think of any other way of getting your number. The thing is . . . I need to talk to you about Geraldine Edwards.' She waited, anxious to gauge his response.

'Geraldine? What about her?' Christian sounded no more than mildly perplexed – definitely not like a man whose fiancée had just died unexpectedly.

'I . . . can't talk about it over the phone,' she said. 'Are you in London at the moment?'

'I'm about to be – I'm flying into Heathrow early this evening.'

They agreed that Christian would text her later with a rendezvous.

Something didn't feel right, though. It had been over a week since Mrs E's body had been found. Surely if Christian hadn't heard from her in all that time he'd be saying, 'I'm really worried, I can't get hold of her'?

Maybe it was her constantly churning thoughts that made her go ballistic at Carl later that morning. Joseph Chivers, a pathologist they called Sloppy Joe, had left his usual tribute to Jackson Pollock executed in blood and organ fragments across every available surface of the autopsy suite and Cassie was helping Carl to clean up when she found a piece of what looked like kidney in an unlabelled sample jar at the back of the bench.

'For Christ's sake, Carl! What if I hadn't spotted that? It would have gone in the fridge and got mixed up with all the others.'

'I was just about to do it.'

The truculence in his voice lit her blue touch paper.

'Bullshit! You know we *never* leave a sample jar unlabelled, not even for two seconds. Imagine if that had gone off to histopathology with the rest. We wouldn't be able to confirm cause of death on Mr Lyttleton.'

'OK, OK. I'm sorry.' Carl raised his hands in surrender, his surliness gone.

Carl was usually so on the ball, but now Cassie was reminded of the stocktakes he'd missed that would have uncovered Harry Hardwick's disappearance earlier.

'Look, Carl,' – lowering her voice. 'After the Harry Hardwick business we're all under the spotlight, so we need to be watertight on procedure, OK? From now on, let's check and double-check.'

She scanned his face, picking up the red-rimmed eyes, and getting a whiff of alcohol leaking from his pores. 'Let me guess, you were out on the lash last night?'

An embarrassed shrug. 'Maybe I did overdo it a bit.'

'Are you up to working today? I don't want you anywhere near a scalpel if you're feeling shaky.' Cutting yourself while eviscerating the body of someone who might have had undiagnosed CJD or HIV could have devastating consequences.

'I'm totally fine. In fact, I was going to ask if I could get any extra shifts this week.'

'Maxed your credit card again?'

He pulled a sheepish grin.

Turning up hungover for an early shift wasn't really on, but Carl wasn't a repeat offender – besides, Cassie could hardly lecture him, after her night of drug-fuelled debauchery with Tish-Tash.

Pot. Kettle. A very British expression, but one of her grandmother's favourites.

That afternoon, the office passed on an ominously brief message from DS Flyte, asking Cassie to drop into the nick after her shift.

Was Flyte still trying to pin the theft of Mr Hardwick on her? Or was she about to be charged with illegal possession of Ziggy the skull? With Doug out of reach at a conference, Cassie could get no intel as to what the frozen-faced cop had in store for her. Either way, it could signal the end of her job.

Walking into reception at the police station took her straight back to her last visit here, after the ugly eviction when she'd been manhandled by the misogynist cop. So it knocked her back when the desk sergeant appeared, all smiles and sporting a full-on hipster beard.

After being shown into an interview room she found a familiar figure already sitting at the table.

'Professor Arculus! What the . . . ?'

He chuckled softly. 'A lady police detective called me to say she had confiscated a human skull from a keen student of anatomy. The coroner's office had informed her that I am the proud owner of an MSc in paleoanthropology – that's the study of old bones to you and me.'

DS Flyte came in carrying Ziggy in a plastic evidence bag, which she set on the table with a tight, unconvincing smile. 'This is an informal interview for informational purposes. Cassandra Raven is not under caution and therefore I won't be recording this interview.'

She fixed Cassie with a glacial look. 'As I explained, it is an offence to be in possession of human remains less than 100 years old. Professor Arculus has kindly agreed to give us the benefit of his specialist knowledge to advise on the age of the item.'

As Flyte pushed the bagged skull towards the Prof, Cassie noticed that although her nails were impeccably manicured and varnished, there was a strip of raw skin at the base of her right thumbnail where she'd picked at the cuticle. A tiny crack in the robotic exterior.

'May I?' Extracting the skull, Professor Arculus turned it this way and that, DS Flyte watching him intently. Superficially, she seemed as in control as ever, but Cassie noted the increased blink rate and her unnatural stillness. Flyte was stressed.

'Interesting,' he said after a moment.

Flyte held her pen poised over her notebook, the stillness of her chest revealing that she was holding her breath.

Christ, she must really hate me, Cassie thought with dismay.

'I'm afraid our friend here is definitely a good deal younger than 100 years old,' said Prof. Arculus.

Cassie's stomach plunged.

He turned the skull to face him. 'He's recent. Very recent.'

'Are you sure?' asked Flyte, her left hand clutching the pen so tightly her knucklebones gleamed through the tissue.

Cassie lost herself staring at Flyte's long slender fingers, recalling a mnemonic for the bones of the hand she'd come across online: *Senior Lecturers Take Prostitutes To The Carlton Hotel* . . . a ditty that had only confirmed her 'sexist wankers in rugger scarves' view of most medical students. Picturing the unique shape of each bone, she mentally ticked them off: *Scaphoid, Lunate, Triquetrum, Pisiform, Trapezium, Trapezoid, Capitate* . . . but what did the H in Hotel stand for . . . ?

The Prof had produced a penknife and chipped a fragment of bone off the base of the skullcap, before examining it through the bottom of his glasses.

Cassie could visualise the final hand bone, its hooked process sticking out. *Hamate! That was it*. From the Latin *hamulus*, or hook.

'Quite sure,' the Prof was saying. 'The technology to produce a skull this lifelike only came along in the nineteen-eighties.'

It took a moment for the words to sink in.

'Are you saying it's a . . . *fake*?' Flyte's voice rose on the last word in disbelief.

'That's right,' the Prof beamed. He set the skull back on the table and pocketed his penknife. 'Probably a Chinese import – but of very impressive quality. I wouldn't be surprised if it were originally manufactured for medical training.'

'Are you absolutely certain?'

Cassie saw that Flyte had grown even paler than usual, highlighting a fine spray of freckles across her nose.

The Prof looked at Flyte over the top of his glasses. 'Well . . . I do have a *little* experience of human anatomy, as a Home Office pathologist of thirty-five years.' His tone remained affable, but Cassie recognised a five-star slap down when she heard one.

When the Prof left the room, Cassie went to follow him, but was stopped at the door by Flyte – her gaze as warm and reassuring as an industrial blast chiller.

'Somebody has vouched for your presence at the music bar you mentioned last Saturday night.'

Cassie felt every muscle in her body relax.

'Of course, that doesn't change the fact that *somebody* used your access code to illegally enter the premises and steal Harold Hardwick's body.'

'I told you, I have no idea how they got hold of it.'

'The case is still under investigation.' Flyte pulled a tight smile. 'As is the possible motive for the theft.'

But Cassie sensed a hairline fissure in her usual glassy aura of certainty. 'I'm just glad you're still pursuing it,' she said, poking at the crack experimentally. 'I thought there might be pressure to drop it, after Mr Hardwick's body was found. Budget cuts and all that?'

The raw spasm that crossed Flyte's face told Cassie her guess was on target: the cops had more pressing concerns than the lost-and-found remains of an elderly gent with no close family. Catching sight of the wall clock, she realised with a pang that right about now Harry Hardwick was being laid to eternal rest in a plot in Chingford Cemetery.

Godspeed, Mr H.

The sight of her adversary retreating steel-spined down the corridor, stirred contradictory feelings in Cassie: Flyte was her enemy, but she felt a wave of respect for the uptight cop's reluctance to give up on a case that everyone else just wished would go away.

She found the Prof waiting for her in the street. 'All is well, I trust?' he asked. 'You're no longer facing the threat of incarceration at Her Majesty's Pleasure?'

'Looks like I'm a free woman, thanks to you.'

He dismissed the gratitude with a wave. 'But perhaps you might repay me by satisfying my curiosity about something. Your full name – Cassandra,' he rolled the syllables like a mouthful of port and walnuts. 'Were you perchance named after the soothsayer in *The Oresteia*?'

'I'm afraid not, Prof,' said Cassie. 'Rodney's girlfriend in *Only Fools and Horses*.'

'What a shame. I had rather hoped that snakes might whisper prophesies in your ear.' Hailing an approaching black cab, the Prof nodded towards the skull, which Cassie had forgotten she was still holding. 'As for our friend there – probably best to put him in your handbag. We don't want to frighten the horses.'

And with a valedictory wave he climbed into the cab, leaving her gazing down at the skull like a modern-day Hamlet in the graveyard.

FLYTE

'Let me get this straight,' DI Bellwether was saying. 'You're telling me you want to *broaden* the investigation into the old gent who was stolen from the mortuary?'

Flyte could see disbelief corrugating his forehead, but something made her press on. 'Yes, boss.'

'We already talked about this, Phyllida. The body was recovered two days ago, right?'

'Yes, but the case is still unsolved and we're all out of leads.'

'You said it! The only line of enquiry – your mortuary technician with the skull in her bathroom? Didn't that just blow up in your face?'

Flyte felt a flush creep up her throat. 'I know, boss, and I already apologised for being hasty about that. But together with the fact that her access code was used . . .'

'Her alibi stood up, right?'

Flyte pressed her nails into her palm. Focusing on Raven as the only suspect in the theft of Harry Hardwick's body had been a big mistake, leading Bellwether to call her entire judgement into question. With hindsight, she could see that she had been unduly swayed by the girl's weird look and her creepy flat strewn with skulls and disembowelled animals.

Ten weeks policing the streets of Camden should have made one thing clear to her: round here it was Phyllida Flyte and not Cassie Raven who was the odd one out.

'The whole thing sounds like some kind of tasteless joke to me,' Bellwether went on. 'I'm surprised no one's posted a selfie with the poor man on Instagram.' He glanced at his computer screen, clearly itching to get back to whatever he'd been doing before she'd knocked on his door.

'Listen, Phyllida. We've done everything possible to progress the case.' He started counting off on his fingers. 'Forensics drew a total blank. Nobody saw or heard anything. The CCTV of a random van entering the mortuary was too poor to deliver even a partial number plate . . . Have I missed anything?'

Flyte shook her head. 'But if I could just have a couple of uniforms to help me do some door-to-door, to see if anyone saw that van—'

Bellwether raised his hand to silence her, an incredulous smile on his face. 'You were at Friday's meeting, right? When I talked about priorities for this quarter?'

'Yes, boss. Challenging knife crime.'

'That's right. Since the *Crimewatch* coverage of Hanif Hassan's murder, I've got Area all over my case about the spike in knifings.'

Hanif Hassan had been the victim of an upsurge in knife crime, stabbed to death in a drug-dealing turf war a couple of weeks earlier. In itself, that wasn't especially noteworthy for Camden, but Hassan had been a star IT student and chess wizard who'd been filmed receiving an award from the mayor, so his death had got acres of coverage on primetime TV.

Flyte knew she should shut up, but something made her persist. 'But surely we shouldn't just ignore all the less serious crimes, should we, Guv?'

He glared at her. 'If I need a refresher course on positive policing, I'll know where to come.' His expression softened. 'Look, Phyllida, you're still settling in, and I know you're keen to make a good impression. But sometimes we just have to admit defeat on a case and move on. Until a fairy godmother comes along to wave a wand and double our budget, we need to pick our battles.'

Flyte stared at the floor, unable to tell him the truth: she might have accepted Cassie Raven's innocence but she still found it impossible to walk away from the Harry Hardwick case, even now that he'd been found and laid to rest. His funeral hadn't brought closure, as she had hoped: her need to see the culprits punished was undimmed. Trying to explain why to Bellwether was out of the question – he'd just send her straight to the occupational psychologist. A pointless waste of time.

'You're clearly a dedicated and diligent detective,' Bellwether continued. 'But – and don't take offence at this – I'm getting the impression that you can sometimes be a little bit . . . OCD?'

She bit her lip; it wasn't the first time she'd heard the accusation. And she knew that what mean people called her 'control-freakery' had only increased since she'd moved to London. It suddenly occurred to her why she'd taken such an extreme dislike to Cassie Raven: she stood for everything Flyte hated about Camden and her new life here. Perhaps even, by extension, everything that she had lost before coming here.

'Phyllida?' Bellwether's confiding half-smile invited her to agree with him.

'Maybe I am a bit, boss,' which is where she should have left it. 'But if you could assign me even one uniform . . .'

'The case is closed, Sergeant,' said Bellwether coldly, turning back to his computer screen. 'Shut the door on your way out.'

Outside in the corridor, Flyte uttered the strongest profanity she ever allowed herself.

'*Bugger.*'

Chapter Twenty

Christian's text had suggested that he and Cassie meet at the hotel in Fitzrovia where he was staying.

The facade of the Gainsborough Hotel resembled a cliff of stucco, its portal guarded by a uniformed doorman. Inside, Cassie found a lobby flanked by marble columns the height of a double-decker bus, topped with elaborately decorated capitals. The bar beyond was a sea of pale leather upholstery, black-clad waiters gliding to and fro to the tasteful tinkle of a jazz piano. She tugged straight her only grown-up jacket – the one she'd bought from Next for her job interview at the mortuary five years ago – glad that she'd made the effort to go home and change.

When she gave her name at the entrance desk she was led to a cream leather banquette where a trim, clean-cut man in his mid to late forties rose to greet her. Fair-haired and lightly tanned, Christian Maclaren wore a good suit and expensive-looking retro glasses.

'Flash place!' she said, glancing up at the statement chandelier overhead. 'Are you staying here?'

'Yes, it's delightfully OTT, isn't it?' he laughed. 'You don't get Doric columns at the Premier Inn.'

A waiter appeared at the table and Cassie asked for a tonic water with a slice of lemon. 'Two of those, please,' said Christian. 'And put it on my tab, would you?'

Since discovering that he and Mrs E had met on a dating site, it had occurred to Cassie that Christian might have a good reason for being hard to find. Everybody knew that dating apps were a hunting ground for 'catfish' – fraudsters who created fake dating profiles to target the unwary, with the aim of swindling them out of their cash.

But so far he appeared genuine enough. His air of quiet authority in these upmarket surroundings, the subtle fragrance of expensive male grooming products that rose off him, the discreet looping Cartier logo she spotted on one arm of his glasses – everything meshed with Maddy's report of him being a successful architect.

It was his easy smile and relaxed posture that confused her: he didn't come across as a man who'd heard nothing but deafening silence from his fiancée for the best part of a week.

'So how do you know Geraldine?' he asked.

'I used to be one of her students.'

'Oh, you're one of her little chicks!' His eyes crinkled. 'Now I think about it, she mentioned your name, several times.'

They fell silent as the waiter unloaded their drinks and a bowl of spiced nuts.

'So,' Christian's smile faded, giving way to a look of mild puzzlement. 'Does Geraldine know that you're here?'

So he had no idea.

'You haven't heard anything?' Cassie played for time, putting off the moment of truth.

He looked perplexed. 'You do know we're . . . no longer an item?'

'No I didn't. Can I ask how long ago you split up?'

'Six or seven weeks ago?'

News that made her job a bit easier.

'Christian, I'm afraid I have some sad news. Last week, Geraldine was found dead at home.'

She expected shock, grief – all perfectly natural responses to the sudden death of even an ex-lover. But the scale of his reaction was completely unexpected.

'*No!*' He stared at her, his face paling to the colour of old newspaper, before half rising out of his seat, agitated.

Cassie went into professional mode, jumping up to put a hand under one elbow. 'Come and sit down,' she murmured, gently propelling him back into his seat. 'You've had a terrible shock.' Seeing the waiter bustle over, she deflected him with a reassuring gesture.

Once he'd recovered a little, she fed him some tonic water. 'Small sips. Try to breathe.'

After a few minutes a little colour started to return to his face but he still looked five years older. 'I'm so sorry.' His voice was hoarse. 'It's just such a shock. You are absolutely sure?' His eyes met hers, searching for an alternative explanation.

'I'm afraid so.' Cassie explained how she'd seen Mrs E's body with her own eyes and how they thought she had died.

'She drowned in her own bath? It just doesn't seem possible,' he said. 'Geraldine was so . . . *full of life*. I don't recall her ever being even slightly under the weather.' He frowned, then looked at her. 'You don't think there's anything . . . fishy about it, do you?'

'Why do you say that?'

'Why else would you take all this trouble to find me?'

A reasonable question. Cassie pressed her fingers against her temples. 'Look, I'm probably just over-thinking things because she meant such a lot to me. The police aren't treating her death as suspicious . . .'

'But . . . ?'

'Can I ask, did you ever meet Geraldine's son?'

'Only once.' Christian's expression signalled his opinion of Owen. 'I had to physically eject him from her house when he turned up drunk.'

'What happened?'

He rotated his glass on its paper coaster. 'I threw him out. I didn't care for the way he was speaking to Geraldine.'

Cassie had to suppress a smile; he sounded like a character out of an old movie. She made a decision. 'Look, Christian, I have no reason at all to think Owen was involved in his mum's death, but . . . what you can tell me about their relationship?'

'He was always trying to get money out of her. That night he came round, I made myself scarce, so they could speak in private, but then I heard a chair falling over. I rushed into the kitchen and he had her backed right up in a corner, threatening her.'

'And that's when you threw him out?'

'After a bit of embarrassing middle-aged wrestling, yes.' She noticed him rotate his shoulder, the unconscious gesture of someone recalling an injury. 'Afterwards, Geraldine told me he was trying to talk her into some money-making scheme he'd dreamed up.'

'What type of thing?'

'It was something to do with the house. He was always trying to get her to downsize – no doubt so he could get another handout. But she was pretty shaken up and didn't want to talk about it.'

'She turned him down.'

'Point blank. I don't know if she stuck to her guns, because it wasn't long afterwards that we . . . split up.' From the sudden drop in volume on the last words it was obvious that the decision wasn't his.

'I'm sorry.'

'Perhaps it wasn't meant to be. Geraldine was far too good for me.'

He gazed at the floor, shoulders down, lost in his thoughts.

'I'm so sorry I had to tell you such terrible news. I'll leave you in peace now.' She touched his shoulder in parting. 'Feel free to call me, OK?'

In the foyer she paused beside one of the huge columns to look back. Christian still sat hunched in his chair, head bent, one hand cradling his brow. There was something so . . . *desolate* about his body language that it made her want to cry.

Outside in the London night, she was met by the bad-tempered growl of the traffic and the sting of rain. As she waited to cross the road, eyes screwed half-shut against the filthy weather, a double-decker bus trundled to a halt on the other side. Her gaze drifted over the blurred outlines of passengers behind its rain-smeared windows: a woman in a burka on her mobile; a workman, asleep against the window, his mouth hanging open; somebody with their head buried in what looked like the *Evening Standard*. As the bus started to move off, the *Standard* reader lowered the paper and looked out of the window – straight at Cassie.

It was Mrs Edwards, her lips a too-bright red against her white face, and she was frowning, but before Cassie's brain could even confirm what she was seeing, the bus's brakes sighed and it accelerated out of view.

Chapter Twenty-One

Cassie struggled to sleep that night, her thoughts constantly returning to the moment when she'd seen Mrs E on the bus.

The vision, or apparition – whatever you wanted to call it – had left her rattled. Despite her moments of communion with the dead, none of her charges had ever appeared outside the mortuary before. She didn't believe in ghosts, instead sharing the Ancient Greek view of death as a one-way journey across the River Styx into a darkness from which no one could return.

But what if Mrs E was still in limbo – had yet to complete her voyage to the Underworld?

Stuff and nonsense, as Mrs E would have said. She reminded herself that it wasn't uncommon for the recently bereaved to 'see' their dead loved ones. Like the just-widowed lady she'd recently dealt with who'd recognised the unmistakable outline of her husband paying for a food shop in Marks and Spencer. She'd been so convinced that she'd followed him out of the shop, along the street and down into a Tube station. She only caught up with him on the platform where he had turned to reveal – a stranger. For the first time, Cassie could grasp how powerfully real such a sighting could feel.

She finally went off to sleep, only for her pager to start bleeping in the early hours. The high-pitched tone might've freaked out any normal cat, but Macavity just gazed at her unblinkingly from the pillow beside her head. His sardonic look seemed to say, *That's some stupid job you've got* – a sentiment which, at that moment, Cassie couldn't argue with.

By the time her cab pulled up at the mortuary, the black van with *Penney & Sons, Funeral Directors* painted on the side was already there, its engine running to keep its occupants warm – the living ones, anyway. Bending to knock on the driver's window, she saw the bearded profile of her ex-boyfriend.

'Hey, Luca. Tell me you've got something nice and simple for me.'

He furrowed his brow in thought. 'What would you say to an old lady with end-stage cancer who passed away peacefully while saying her rosary?'

'Yeah, that would be perfect.'

Luca gave a sorrowful shake of the head. 'Sorry, I'm afraid you've failed the bonus question and lost out on the holiday to Vegas. The *right answer* is a junkie girl OD'd in a stairwell on the Fairfax.'

Cassie blew out a breath. 'Are her family coming, do you know?'

'No, she's a Jane Doe. But we just got a call from the nick – there's a cop dropping by shortly.'

Great. Cassie waved goodbye to any hope of a straightforward check-in and getting swiftly back to her bed.

After Luca had wheeled the new arrival into the body store, he said, 'By the way, I had Owen Edwards on the phone again, chewing my ear off. He was asking why we haven't picked up his mother's body yet.'

'When's the funeral?' she asked, praying it wasn't too soon.

143

'It's looking like next Wednesday.'

Six days away. 'So what's his rush?'

'He said he doesn't like the idea of his mum lying in the mortuary. He says he'd rather have her in the funeral home.'

'What's the difference between her lying in one of our fridges and one of yours?'

'That's more or less what I said to him, except I put it a bit more diplomatically than that.' Luca grinned. 'So, is she ready for collection?'

Should she just let Mrs E go? Owen might be a nasty piece of work – a sponging alcoholic waster who bullied his own mother – but without any solid evidence to persuade the cops that Mrs E's death was suspicious, there was no hope of getting her a proper forensic PM. The idea of dropping her half-arsed attempts at sleuthing and getting back to normal seemed suddenly tempting.

Her gaze drifted to the section of fridge where Mrs E lay and she remembered the vow she'd made to her. The body store's internal temperature never rose above four degrees Celsius, but once she'd been transferred to the crappy old fridge at Penney & Sons, her body would deteriorate faster, and any evidence of foul play could be lost.

'Luca . . .'

He gave her a long-suffering look.

'Could you tell him that we're all good to release the body at our end, but that you don't have any space at yours?'

'But I already told him we could pick her up as soon as we got the go-ahead from you.'

'Well . . .' Cassie bit her lip. 'You could say you've had a couple of rush jobs come in and you haven't got enough staff to do a pick-up.'

'A couple of rush jobs ...?' Luca bugged his eyes at her. 'We're funeral directors, not Yodel.'

Cassie had a brainwave. 'Why don't you tell him you've got a couple of Muslim funerals?' Islamic doctrine called for the dead to be buried the same day or, at worst, the following day before sunset – a schedule that was respected wherever possible, if no forensic post-mortem was required.

'But Muslims don't come to us – they have their own specialist undertakers.'

'He's not gonna know that, is he? He lives in Rhyl, for Christ's sake.'

Luca scratched his beard, before sending her a searching look. 'I don't know what you're up to, Cassie Raven, and I don't even want to know. But I'll put him off for now.'

'You're a pal,' she grinned. 'I owe you a roast dinner, with all the trimmings.'

'Roast beef and Yorkshires?'

'OK.' She could grit her teeth and cook a hunk of meat for a good cause.

He sent her a suggestive look. 'What about afters?'

'Now you're pushing your luck.' Reaching up to his shoulder she propelled him towards the door.

Returning to the OD'd Jane Doe, she unzipped the bag just enough to expose the face of a young girl – seventeen or eighteen years old. Olive-skinned, she'd been pretty, before death had turned her skin the colour of uncooked dough. There was a confused look in her hazel eyes, as if she'd fallen asleep on the Tube and had just woken up, way past her stop.

Turning the girl's left arm palm-upward she found the inner crook of her elbow stippled with recent track marks. Suddenly it seemed to Cassie that she was looking at herself at seventeen, and her own arm, the puncture marks pitching her back to the time she'd done heroin. Some guy at the squat whose name she couldn't remember had jacked her up, his belt black against the pale skin of her upper arm. A thread of blood blossoming in the clear liquid – unexpectedly beautiful – as he checked he was in the vein. Then the euphoria hitting her brain like a ten-ton truck made of candyfloss and the sensation of skydiving through the softest clouds, weightless, bathed in sunshine, all self-consciousness and anxiety steam-ironed away.

It had been the first and last time she'd touched heroin; she just hadn't trusted herself around anything that good. A few weeks later she'd met Mrs E and before long had left the squat and further temptation behind.

She gave the dead girl's shoulder a squeeze, detecting a trace of warmth beneath the chilling skin. 'You're safe now, sweet pea,' she told her. 'There's nothing to worry about anymore.'

The girl stared up at her quizzically and, as the air thickened and the overhead lights burned brighter, Cassie heard a single word.

Why?

The moment was shattered by the flicker of blue lights coming through the window, playing across the white plastic of the body bag. Looking into the girl's face, Cassie swore softly, knowing that the connection was lost.

Going to the front entrance she checked the entry cam and cursed more robustly at the all-too-familiar face on the screen.

'We can't go on meeting like this,' said DS Flyte with a dry look – the first time Cassie had heard her attempt any kind of joke.

'What's so urgent it can't wait till the morning?' Cassie demanded. But inside she was panicking – was Flyte still after her for Harry Hardwick? Had she been looking further back into the mortuary access records? If so, it could spell big trouble.

'I need to have a look at the dead girl found on the Fairfax estate,' said Flyte.

Thank Christ. Cassie followed the rapier-straight back down the corridor. 'You surely saw her already, at the scene?'

In the body store, Flyte turned to face Cassie, an uncharacteristic flicker of uncertainty crossing her face. 'Uniformed officers attended, and they didn't see fit to inform CID – I only found out about it half an hour ago.' A twitch ran through her upper body, signalling her disapproval.

'How come?'

'The girl looked like a rough sleeper and the sergeant found no evidence of foul play, so he called it as a straightforward OD.'

'And you think he got it wrong?'

She shrugged. 'Probably not. The girl still had a belt round her arm and there was a syringe lying right next to the body. But best practice dictates all unexplained deaths ought to be attended by a detective.'

Christ, the woman had a nerve. Five minutes ago she was accusing Cassie of bodysnatching, now she thought it was cool to turn up in the small hours asking for a favour.

Cassie folded her arms. 'So you're just here to tick a box.'

'Listen, they ought to have called me when the job came in.' She looked tired, her eyes darker today – the colour of a split flint. 'But . . . I think this particular sergeant has had a bellyful of OD'd smackheads.'

Or of tight-arsed female detectives, thought Cassie. She was about to tell her to come back in the morning when her gaze fell on the face of the dead girl. Whatever DS Flyte's faults, Cassie had a hunch that she would get the girl's profile onto the missing persons system faster than your average plod, which meant the family finding out sooner about their daughter's death.

'Could you give her a quick look over now?' asked Flyte. 'See if there's anything that might help us ID her?'

Unfolding her arms, Cassie unsheathed the body from its white plastic bag. The girl wore well-cut but grimy-looking jeans, a black T-shirt emblazoned with 'Trapstar' in a gothic font, and a thin bomber jacket. Her complexion was surprisingly clear, with none of the scabs and grazes from scratching the unremitting opiate itch that Cassie saw in long-term users.

Cassie started to examine her, lifting the T-shirt to check her torso. 'No bruising or other visible injuries.' She showed Flyte the track marks up her left arm. 'These are all pretty recent. Probably a new user who misjudged the dose. We see a lot of dead newbies, especially when there's some strong stuff doing the rounds.'

Cassie sensed Flyte's eyes on her – probably remembering her record for possession. 'This looks like the one that did for her,' she pointed out a fresh puncture mark in the main dorsal vein on the back of the girl's right hand.'

Moving down the body, she checked the girl's legs and feet. There were no track marks there, but she found something else on the right ankle. 'Look – this should help you track her down.'

It was a tattoo, two intertwined hearts wrapped in barbed wire, just above the bony swell where the tibia met the talus.

Cassie could make out a faint redness in the skin around the inked edges. 'I reckon it's only about a week old. I'll give you the names of the tattoo studios round here.'

Seeing the girl's bomber jacket slipping off the table, she reached out to catch it. Made of thin black satin, it was badly scuffed on the back but the bold black-and-white logo inside the collar caught her eye. 'Huh! Moschino.'

Flyte leaned in for a look. 'It's probably fake – or stolen.'

The girl's eyes had dulled, their last trace of expression drained away. Cassie drew a hand over the lids to close them.

'You know, we get a lot of dead junkies in here and most of them are rough sleepers, but not this girl.'

'What, because she's wearing Moschino?' Flyte pulled a sceptical face. 'She looks pretty grubby to me.'

'No, that's not it.' Cassie was picturing Kieran emerging from his newspaper cocoon down by the canal. 'If you're sleeping rough in November, you wear a lot of layers – if she'd been out all night dressed like this she'd die of hypothermia. Going by the pricy clobber and the fresh track marks, I'd say she's a middle-class girl slumming it. Her mum and dad are probably frantic.'

Shouldering her bag, Flyte looked as if she'd already mentally moved onto the next job.

All Cassie's dislike came rushing back. 'I am guessing you don't have children,' she snapped at her, taking in the immaculate black wool jacket, the buttons all done up, hair pulled into a chignon from which no hairs had escaped, the matte pink lipstick perfect. All this at three in the morning.

Catching a quiver around Flyte's mouth, Cassie regretted her words. Had Flyte tried – and failed – to have kids? It was a common enough story for a woman in her mid- to late-thirties.

'Anyway,' Cassie went on. 'If we're done here, I need to put this young lady to bed – and then I'm going back to mine.'

Easing the girl back into her body bag, she paused, noticing something. Felt around the collar of the girl's T-shirt, then touched her shoulder-length hair where it lay against the plastic.

'What are you doing?' asked Flyte, already halfway to the door.

'Her T-shirt, here, and round the back, it's damp. And so's her hair, underneath.'

'Are you sure?'

'She was found under cover, you say?' Cassie was trying to picture the girl's last moments. 'I don't think she OD'd outside. It happened indoors, and somebody tried to revive her.'

'Splashed water in her face, you mean?'

Cassie nodded, her face darkening as she pictured the scenario. 'When they couldn't rouse her, they dragged her out to the stairwell and left her there.'

'Jesus!' Flyte's face twisted with disgust.

Cassie felt sick. There had been an unbreakable code back when she'd been squatting: if somebody OD'd, you always called an ambulance, even if it meant risking a visit from the cops.

Flyte lingered, looking at the girl. 'I'll bear it in mind,' she said finally. 'If we ever find out who she is.'

At the main entrance, Flyte paused in the half open door, and Cassie noticed her picking away at her cuticle, the skin there even redder than before. 'Thanks for letting me see her. I want her family to be informed as soon as possible.'

Dropping her gaze, she busied herself pulling on a pair of black suede gloves that accentuated her long fingers. 'Look, regarding the Harold Hardwick case. We've pursued all possible leads, but strictly off the record, it's fair to say that it is no longer under active investigation.'

'Does that mean I'm off the hook?'

'I would say that's a reasonable assumption.'

Flyte raised her eyes, and Cassie was taken aback to detect an apology of sorts there – presumably for suspecting her in the first place.

Her surge of relief was followed by a backwash of guilt. So that was that: the cops weren't going to commit any more resources to solving the disappearance of an old gent – especially one without any family to demand answers on his behalf.

There was something else in Flyte's expression beside contrition, Cassie realised – regret on her part too, that the people who stole Harry Hardwick's body would never now face retribution.

Chapter Twenty-Two

By the time an Uber had dropped Cassie back home, sunlight was climbing her block, painting its windows fool's gold.

Getting any proper sleep after these late-night callouts was a nightmare. She dozed fitfully, twitching through lurid dreams. In one, the junkie girl had come to life and was banging on the inside of the mortuary fridge, a hellish cacophony that finally woke her.

Blinking in the dim light, she saw the outline of a woman. Slender-backed in a silk slip, she was applying lipstick in the dressing table mirror. The woman turned, her lips a startling vermilion against bone-white skin. *Mrs E.* A tramline of black stitches ran down from the suprasternal notch, disappearing beneath the slip.

'There's no time to waste, Cassandra,' she said.

Cassie awoke with a jolt, properly this time, the sheet wound too-tight around her like a damp shroud. The room stood empty, except for Macavity sitting on the end of the bed, cleaning himself. Cold daylight and traffic noise filtered through the thin curtain, the boiler clattering into life in the kitchen. She had the day off, and would usually try to get some more sleep. But with Mrs E's funeral looming, the dream's message was spot on: time really was running out.

She fed the cat and took a shower. By the time she'd towelled herself dry, Cassie knew what she had to do.

Giving herself no time to consider the risk she'd be taking, she pulled on the Next jacket and trousers she'd worn to meet Christian, removed all her piercings and styled her hair to cover her undercut. After applying enough makeup to cover the last traces of her bruise, she checked herself out in the mirror and gave a satisfied nod. She'd pass.

Beside the canal, the morning mist wrapped a clammy hand around her face. She felt bad nudging awake rough sleepers: the first few, who looked like they hailed from the Balkans or the Middle East, didn't speak much English, and none of them seemed to know Kieran. Finally, she found a Camden local who suggested a couple of places where he might have kipped down.

Ten minutes later, she came across a familiar-looking blue sleeping bag curled in the doorway of an office block.

'Kieran?' she murmured, dropping to a crouch.

There was an awful moment when she thought he might be dead – she saw far too many rough sleepers on her mortuary table. Then a bobble hat emerged from the bag, followed by bleary eyes. 'Cassie Raven?' – his voice clogged with sleep. 'What's this then? Room service?' Struggling up to a sitting position he took the grease-stained paper bag from her, while she opened the thermos to pour him some coffee.

'Bacon and HP sauce,' he said through a mouthful. 'Good memory!'

'It's probably a bit cold by now – I looked for you by the canal first.'

'Nah, I've moved on. Some Romanian bloke took my favourite spot. Not that I'm complaining, he was a lot worse off than me, poor bastard. Anyway, it's getting proper chilly by the canal.' He took in her trouser suit. 'You scrub up nice Cassie Raven. Funeral or court appearance?'

'Very funny. Listen, Kieran, I'm after a favour.'

'Fire away,' he said, taking a slug of coffee. 'Ooh, brandy! Are you trying to get me drunk?' He waggled his eyebrows suggestively.

'You used to have some gizmos for picking locks, when we were squatting? You taught me how to use them once.'

Setting his bacon sandwich aside, he delved into the sleeping bag and ferreted around, producing a slim plastic wallet. 'There you go. I haven't used 'em in a couple of years. Nowhere left to squat round here.'

Pulling out a padlock, he gave her a refresher course in lock picking. She was a bit rusty to start with, but after a few minutes probing and wiggling with the tension tool and trying the different size lock picks, she started to get a feel for it again. Finally, the padlock snapped open.

'There you go! You're a natural-born housebreaker,' said Kieran, with a wink.

'So can I borrow them, just for today?'

'Course. Just don't get caught, and if the rozzers do pick you up, say you bought them on Amazon as a hobby.'

'Are they illegal then?'

'Yeah. Just carrying them around is "going equipped to burgle".' He laughed, flashing his sparse collection of teeth. 'You're an outlaw again, Cassie Raven.'

At the end of the street she turned to give Kieran a wave. He responded with a thumbs-up, and it struck her that he hadn't even asked how she was going to use them. That felt good, as if she'd been temporarily readmitted to the brotherhood of the street. For all its hardships, the period she'd spent in the squatting life still felt like the only time she'd really belonged somewhere.

Entering the cobbled backstreet that led to the garden entrance of Mrs E's property, she experienced her first twinge of doubt. The last time she'd been here the overhanging trees had been in full leaf, giving cover to the garden door. Now their winter-bare limbs left it cruelly exposed. After checking the street was empty, she inserted the tension tool into the vintage Yale lock to widen the aperture, before using her other hand to introduce the lock pick. If anyone challenged her, she was going to say she was from Jarvis Jones, the estate agents selling the house, and pretend she'd brought the wrong key.

The lock was stiff with age, but after a couple of minutes she heard the gratifying *tock*! of the final lever surrendering – and imagined a grinning Kieran saying *Bingo*!

Inside, she followed the rough track through the trees. When the Victorian builders had constructed Patna Road the peculiarities of the terrace's layout had left an extra parcel of land at the end of the garden at number 12 – almost as big as the garden itself – which Mrs E had left as natural woodland. Cassie remembered her saying that she often came here first thing in the morning to listen to the birdsong.

She was safe enough here, hidden by the rustling branches of beech and silver birch, but as the drifts of darkening gold leaves underfoot gave way to a brick-paved garden path she became agonisingly aware of her vulnerability: if a neighbour caught sight of her from an upstairs window, they might call the police.

Reaching the rear of the house she was relieved to see the old, defunct alarm box still on the back wall: she'd been worried that Mrs E might have decided to upgrade to one that worked. At the back door to the kitchen, where she was safely out of sight, she got to work with the lock picks again. The first one was easy, but the more recent Chubb had five levers that each needed to be separately slipped. By the time she reached the last one, her fingers were sweaty, making the job even harder, but finally, there came a relieving click.

Pushing the door open, she stood half in, half out of the kitchen, listening. The only sound was the soft ticking of an electric clock over the kitchen table – the same old scrubbed wooden table where she and Mrs E had sat drinking coffee and chatting so many times.

The familiar smell of the place made her stomach dip, but she had no time for sentimentality: she had a job to do . . . although Christ only knew what it was. Did she really expect to find some damning evidence against Owen just lying around?

Pushing her doubts aside she did a quick sweep of the ground floor – nothing of obvious interest – before setting off up the stairs. Framed photographs lined the wall: ancient black and white studio portraits of stern-faced ancestors, and a wedding – presumably Mrs E's parents, judging by the starch-skirted fifties get-ups the women wore. The first colour photograph depicted a young boy, standing on the doorstep of a whitewashed cottage, sulky-faced in a stiff blazer: recognisable as an eleven- or twelve-year-old Owen, followed by more recent ones of other kids, presumably the children of friends.

At the top of the stairs, the last photo showed Cassie brandishing her A level results, a mixture of disbelief and triumph splitting her face. Mrs E had taken pics of the whole class using a brick-like old-school camera, but only Cassie's photo had made it onto her wall. Discovering that it still there in spite of their bust-up made her feel both guilty and happy.

The master bedroom stood on the first floor, its floor-to-ceiling windows overlooking the garden. It was as if Mrs E had stepped out of the room barely a minute ago: a pair of shoes lay beside the bed, as if just kicked off, there was an open book lying face-down on the bedside table, and, on the dressing table a makeup brush haloed by an arc of powder.

When Cassie's gaze fell on a cream-coloured silk slip slung over the back of a white-painted rattan chair, she sat heavily on the edge of the bed. *What the fuck did she think she was playing at? What would Mrs E say if she could see her here?*

There was a faint creak and Cassie sensed something in her peripheral vision. Electricity crackled over her scalp as she was gripped by a powerful conviction: if she just turned her head forty-five degrees, she would see Mrs E sitting on the rattan chair an arm's length away.

She held her breath, torn between wanting to turn and scared of what she might see.

Then came the faintest waft of air, like an exhaled breath, and with it a tantalisingly familiar fragrance – sweet and woody. Cassie whipped around, her pulse hammering in her throat. The chair was empty, but the discarded slip that had been hanging there now lay coiled on the floor. Scooping it up, she pressed it to her face. There was that scent again – *Calèche* by Hermès,

Mrs E's favourite – and a fugitive warmth, as if the slip had only been taken off a moment ago.

Cassie smiled at herself: it was hardly surprising to smell Mrs E's perfume in her own bedroom. As for the slip's residual warmth, hadn't it been lying in a shaft of sunlight when she first came in?

All the same, the moment left her feeling as if her presence here had her old friend's blessing.

The cabinets either side of the king-size bed produced nothing of interest: one held tights, hairbands, the usual female paraphernalia, and a book Cassie hadn't heard of – *The Magus* by John Fowles. The one on the other side was empty, which was to be expected, given that Mrs E and Christian had broken up.

Hanging on the wall beside the bed was a framed picture: a tiny faded Polaroid, it showed an absurdly young and gawky Mrs E sitting up in a hospital bed, a newborn baby wearing a pink crochet hat – presumably Owen – in her arms. Although she was smiling dutifully for the camera, her eyes looked uncharacteristically anxious.

Finding nothing of interest in the dressing-table drawers, Cassie moved on to the massive carved wardrobe – perhaps handed down from Mrs E's Welsh ancestors. It held some surprisingly upmarket gear: an Agnes B navy linen duster coat, an asymmetrical dress by Whistles, a clutch of other chic but unflashy labels. A long red military-style coat that triggered a stab of recognition – it had been Mrs E's winter favourite.

The glossy and beribboned bags all this stuff had arrived in lay neatly folded at the bottom of the wardrobe which made Cassie smile, remembering Mrs E's thrifty dislike of waste. Noticing a stack of shoeboxes on a shelf above the clothes-rail and finding it too high to reach, she fetched the rattan armchair to climb onto. Pulling out a shoebox covered in chartreuse-green figured velvet, a beautiful object in its own right, she discovered that it wasn't empty.

She emptied the contents onto the bed. A pressed dried flower – bougainvillea from the look of it – a silk scarf of a startling kingfisher blue, a champagne cork, a postcard of a medieval mosaic at some place called Ravenna and, paper-clipped to the back of it, a photo of Mrs E and Christian.

They'd been snapped at a sunny restaurant table, presumably during their holiday to Italy, their smiles holding an edge of 'hurry up and get it over with' embarrassment. Mrs E looked radiant, the vivid blue scarf in the shoebox looped round her throat was the perfect foil for her dark hair and olive complexion. Cassie felt a sudden burning behind her eyes – not over Mrs E's death, exactly, but the poignancy of her finding love in later life, only for it to not work out. But then her own brief excursion into the jungle of online dating had demonstrated how digital hookups had a tendency to accelerate too fast before a spectacular crash and burn.

The room next door looked like Mrs E's study. High-ceilinged and lined with books, mostly on science and history topics, it was bare except for a sturdy-looking desk and chair. The desk drawers held a stapler, paper clips and the like but no documents or correspondence. Sitting in the battered swivel chair, Cassie noticed that while the top four or five shelves were tightly filled with books, the lowest shelf nearest the desk held fewer, leaving some of them leaning on each other like pub drunks. Examining the shelf more closely she traced out a faint squared-off outline in the dust that extended to the shelf edge. She guessed that it had once been home to box files full of documents, before someone – Owen, presumably – had removed them, shuffling the books along to fill the hole.

No sign of a laptop – although when she untangled the cables at the back of the old fashioned printer beside the desk she found a lead with a USB connector. So Owen had removed his mother's computer, too. But so what? As next of kin he was no doubt within his rights.

Cassie walked over to the bay window – grateful that muslin curtains and the trees lining the street shielded her from any nosy neighbours. This had probably been where Maddy had seen Mrs E peering out, looking frightened.

Her eyes fell on the old-school printer again and something made her turn it on. It bleeped and churned for an age before flashing a red light. The words 'Paper Jam' flashed up on the display. Pulling out the paper tray Cassie peered into the guts of the machine – but could see nothing. It took her a while to find the release lever, but when she finally cranked open the back of the machine she found a neatly concertinaed piece of A4 caught in the workings.

Smoothing it out on the desk she saw it was a printout from a genealogy website – the kind that people used to trace their family tree. It recorded the marriage, two years earlier, of Julia Geraldine Torrance and Barry Dennis Renwick. The marriage district was given as Chester, up north. If her geography was right, that wasn't far from North Wales, where Mrs E had grown up.

Cassie stared at the printout till her vision blurred. *Geraldine.* Mrs E's given name and the bride's middle name. A family connection? If not, why had she tried to print it out?

Pocketing the document, she went back into the bedroom, and sitting on the bed, took another look at the framed photo of Mrs E and the newborn Owen. It would have been the last thing she'd seen at night and the first thing she opened her eyes to in the morning. Wasn't that odd, given how he had treated her?

And that pink baby hat. An unusual colour choice for a boy, especially back then. Mrs E also did look absurdly young – practically a teenager. A thought occurred to Cassie. What if the baby she was holding wasn't Owen at all, but a previous child?

Might the mysterious Julia Geraldine Torrance have been Mrs E's love child, born before her marriage and adopted – the baby's middle name the only surviving link to her birth mother? Back in the early eighties it wouldn't have been unusual for young unmarried mothers to be pressured into giving up their babies for adoption – especially in rural Wales.

Maybe Mrs E had come across the marriage record while searching for her lost child, now a grown woman. Did Owen know? He might view a half sister as a potential rival for his mother's affections – and more importantly, her money.

After taking a snap of the photo, Cassie was shocked to see the time: she'd already been in Mrs E's house for fifty minutes,

But she had one last job still to do.

Outside the bathroom door she hesitated before grasping the doorknob. A steep-sided Victorian style bathtub with claw feet dominated the space – the place where Mrs E's life had ended ten days ago.

It was chilly in here – the top window had been left open to air the place. Tracing a musty smell to the bathmat she dropped to a crouch and lifted the corner – getting a whiff reminiscent of mushrooms past their sell-by date. The mat's underside still felt slightly damp. Had it got soaked when the paramedics lifted the body out of the bath? Or during a struggle, when Mrs E tried to fight off somebody trying to drown her?

Feeling an urge to immerse herself in Mrs E's last moments, Cassie turned on the hot tap full pelt. As steam started billowing upwards she put her hand under the stream, before snatching it away again: the water temperature must be set to scalding. And if Mrs E had felt suddenly faint in the over-hot water, she could see that scaling the cliff of white enamel would have been a challenge – even without anyone pushing her under.

Turning off the taps, she pulled out the plug. As she watched the water swirling down the drain, she said out loud, 'What happened, Mrs E?'

Her gaze drifted around the room before coming to a stop. The warm water vapour condensing in the cold air had misted over the bathroom mirror, revealing something written there in the steam.

Cassie stood up. Made out two words in shaky capitals:

'BEING FOLLOWED'

Chapter Twenty-Three

Cassie was still staring at the mirror, trying to work out why Mrs E would write the words, when she heard something. The unmistakable sound of a key turning in the front door.

She stood there paralysed. Until the distant burble of voices – unmistakably male – followed by the thud of the front door closing, jolted her out of her frozen state. Softly closing the door she flattened herself against the wall on the hinge side, so she'd be hidden if someone only glanced in.

The volume of the conversation dropped as the men – two of them – went towards the back of the house and she heard the kitchen door opening. But almost immediately they came back into the hall.

Who the fuck were they? Probably the estate agent with a house hunter – which meant she'd need a better hiding place before they came upstairs. But as the voices got louder, she realised they were already on their way up.

Too late. Now what? Pretend to be the cleaner? Not in this get-up, she thought, looking down at her suit.

The squeak of a stair tread right outside, followed by something that stopped the breath in her throat.

'You'll get a pretty good view from up here.' The rise and fall of a Welsh accent, just a couple of metres away. *Owen Edwards.*

Cassie held her breath. Heard the voices pass the bathroom door and move into Mrs E's bedroom.

'As you can see it'll make a good-sized plot, once the trees are felled.' Owen's voice, with that familiar aggrieved and aggressive tone.

'And what exactly did planning tell you?' The other man's voice deeper and business-like.

They moved further out of earshot, and Cassie could only make out fragments of their conversation: 'no objection in principle' . . . 'housing plan' . . . 'six units'.

Then the penny dropped. This must be the money-making scheme Owen had been trying to bully his mother into, the time when Christian had thrown him out. He'd been planning to sell off her beloved patch of woodland to a property developer to build flats, and now she was dead he was free to pursue his plan. *Bastard.*

If Owen had simply brought the guy up here for a better view of the plot, rather than the full tour, she just had to sit tight till they'd gone. Suddenly remembering her mobile, she delved into her pocket to switch it to silent.

Nada.

She tried the other pocket. Remembered getting it out in the bedroom to take a picture of the photograph by the bed.

Jesus Christ. She must have left it in there. If Owen spotted it, he would surely search the place once he'd got rid of the developer – and she didn't like to think what would happen when he found her.

After what felt like an age, she heard them emerge onto the landing. Another few seconds and they'd be past the bathroom door and heading downstairs. If Owen hadn't noticed her phone, she could still escape undiscovered.

But the footsteps seemed to stop right outside, the two men so close now that she could smell the musky aftershave one of them was wearing.

'Do you mind if I use your loo?' asked the property developer guy. Cassie felt her whole body go rigid.

'Be my guest,' said Owen. Seeing the door handle turn, Cassie felt a rush of acid burn the back of her throat.

Then Owen's voice again. 'On second thoughts, better use the one downstairs – this one's a bit temperamental.'

A few minutes later she heard the downstairs loo flush, followed by the slam of the front door. She cocked her head for a long moment, straining to hear whether Owen had stayed behind to investigate the mystery phone in his mother's bedroom.

Silence had never sounded so sweet. She allowed herself to slide down the wall, all the way to the floor.

She noticed that the mist on the bathroom mirror had cleared, leaving no trace of the words she'd glimpsed there.

No time to hang around. She had to find her phone and get out of this place.

Back in the master bedroom she found it lying on the bed and sent up a prayer of thanks to Fortuna, Roman goddess of luck, that Owen hadn't spotted it.

Chapter Twenty-Four

Even after she'd reached the safety of her flat, Cassie was still riding the wave of adrenalin caused by her escapade – the buzz reminding her of a cocaine high.

Changing out of her estate agent disguise, she started to calm down, to assess what her reckless act had actually achieved. Did the name 'Geraldine' in that mysterious marriage record signify anything? Or was her theory about Mrs E's love child simply her imagination running wild? As for Owen's plan to allow some developer to concrete over his mother's woodland – heartless it might be, but probably entirely above board.

'BEING FOLLOWED'

Mrs E must have scrawled the words while running her bath – but why write them on the bathroom mirror instead of calling the police? Maybe she suspected that she would be brushed off – a woman living alone, probably prone to paranoia. Yet *something* had driven her to record her fears – however impermanently – just before she died.

A knock at the door broke her train of thought. On the doorstep she found her grandmother, bundled up in her old Persian lamb coat, a red beret on her head. A young Asian guy Cassie had never seen before stood beside her, carrying a large floral-patterned holdall and wearing a sheepish expression.

'Babcia?! What are you doing here?'

Not wanting to worry her grandmother, Cassie had planned to stay away until the bruises from the mugging had gone completely. She had phoned her to say that she was suffering from a bad cold and might not be over for a bit. Throwing a swift glance in the hall mirror it was a relief to see that her makeup was still doing its camouflage job.

'Give this nice young man a pound, would you, Cassandra?' Weronika asked, seeming not to notice her granddaughter's guilty confusion.

At the old lady's instruction, the guy set the bulging bag on the kitchen table. Then, refusing the couple of quid Cassie tried to give him with a gracious gesture, he hightailed it out of the front door.

'Was he a cab driver?' asked Cassie.

'Cab driver? As if I've got money to throw away on cabs!' Weronika scoffed, starting to unpack the holdall: a cabbage, followed by a bag of apples. 'I got here on the number twenty-nine just fine. But the lift was broken so I asked that nice young man to help me up the stairs.'

Picking up one of the plastic freezer boxes her grandmother had piled on the table, Cassie said, 'There's enough food here for a month. Did I miss the nuclear siren?'

'You said you were poorly, and I didn't want you eating junk food. So I made you some vegetarian meals to put in the freezer.' She gave her granddaughter an assessing look. 'Your colour's good – are you starting to feel better?'

Cassie gave a guilty nod. 'Just a bit tired still.'

Weronika brandished a jar of gherkins. 'The brined ones – your favourites. Full of vitamin C.'

'This is really kind of you, Babcia, but I should be doing *your* shopping, not the other way round.' Cassie was feeling worse and worse about her white lie. 'You sit down. I'm going make us some dinner, then we can watch a bit of telly, and then I'll get you an Uber home – which *I'm paying for*. No arguments.'

Leaning down, she kissed her grandmother's sweet-smelling papery cheek.

'It's a good job I brought the cabbage,' Weronika said.

'What, so now I don't eat enough vegetables?!'

The old lady gave her a searing look. 'No, but you need a cabbage leaf poultice on that bruise of yours.'

Cassie's hand shot to her jaw, cursing those sharp eyes.

After hearing about the mugging, Weronika went quiet for a long moment. 'So, the *skurwysyn* who did this, do you think you would recognise him if you saw him again?'

Despite having barely any Polish, Cassie knew that *skurwysyn* was one of the very worst swear words, and one she'd never heard her gran use before.

'Unlikely. He had a sort of scarf over the bottom half of his face.'

'Bandana. They call it a bandana. Some of the gangs use them to identify themselves. What colour was it?'

'Red,' said Cassie.

'Hmm. Could be Castlehaven Boyz. But I think Barclay Road Crew wear red, too.'

Cassie was taken aback. 'How the hell do you know this stuff?'

Her grandmother pulled a hankie from her sleeve to blow her nose, but Cassie could tell she was playing for time.

'Well?'

'You remember that youngster I caught selling filth to young people in my block?'

168

Weronika revealed that, a couple of days after giving the drug dealer a talking-to, she'd received a visit.

'A different young man turned up at my front door and told me if I didn't keep my nose out of other people's business I would get cut.'

'Oh my God. What did you do?' asked Cassie, wide-eyed with alarm.

'I asked him in and gave him some kremowka.'

'You asked a gangsta in for cream cake?!'

'Why not? He was so thin.' The old lady shrugged. 'He was there for an hour. He talked to me about his babcia who died last year and cried a little. We parted friends.'

'You parted . . . For Christ's sake, Babcia!'

'Please don't curse, Cassandra. It sounds ugly from a woman.'

'Why didn't you tell me this before? You're going to get yourself in serious trouble one of these days.'

'Nonsense,' said the old lady, lifting her chin. 'I didn't survive six months in a communist prison cell just to live like a slave in a free country.'

Having heard this argument in varying forms all her life, Cassie didn't bother trying to press the issue.

A complacent little smile crept across her grandmother's lips. 'After that day I never saw one dealer selling drugs in my block. Not one.'

Cassie shook her head, speechless.

'I still see him around the estate sometimes,' she went on. 'If you like, I could ask about the bandana . . .?'

'No! Don't even think about it.'

The old lady shrugged her acquiescence.

'Now,' said Cassie. 'I'm going to cook us some mushroom pierogi, and then we can watch *Strictly*, like normal people.'

After her grandmother left, Cassie sat at her kitchen table and went over what she knew about Owen Edwards. It was clear that when his mother turned down his property development idea, he had threatened her. A couple of months later she died out of the blue. And now, before even waiting for her cremation, he was resurrecting his plan to flog her woodland to a property developer.

In six days' time, Mrs E's body would be going up in smoke and with it, any evidence to prove that she'd been murdered. And there wasn't a thing Cassie could do to stop it.

Not on her own, anyway.

She paced up and down the flat, trying to think of some alternative to what she was about to do.

There wasn't one. Pullling a card out of her purse she dialled the number.

'Detective Sergeant Flyte.' Hearing DS Flyte's words ping down the line like cold gravel, Cassie almost hung up. Asking a cop for help made her feel faintly sick.

'It's Cassie Raven'– anxiety ratcheting her voice up half an octave. 'I was wondering if we could meet.'

Chapter Twenty-Five

After Cassie flat-out refused to discuss anything over the phone, Flyte had finally agreed to meet her the following morning. Cassie named a coffee shop almost a mile from the mortuary: if someone from work saw her talking to the cops it would throw up a lot of awkward questions. A pathologist might speak directly to the cops; a technician, never.

'So what's this all about?' Flyte fixed Cassie with those pale eyes.

Having allowed Flyte to view the OD'd junkie girl out of hours, Cassie had hoped she could call in the favour, but now they were face to face she felt her confidence waning.

'Can we talk off the record? My boss doesn't know I'm meeting you.'

Flyte took a sip of her tea – Earl Grey, black, with a slice of lemon. 'So long as you're not about to confess to some heinous crime.' She pulled her dry almost-smile.

'It's about the body of a woman who came in just over a week ago. You lot – I mean, the police – aren't treating it as suspicious, but . . .'

'But you're not sure.'

Cassie laid out the circumstances of Geraldine Edwards' sudden death without mentioning their connection, figuring that if she kept it professional, Flyte might take her doubts more seriously.

By the time she'd finished, a tiny frownline had appeared between Flyte's perfect brows. 'But the pathologist thinks she passed out and drowned – having found nothing to suggest foul play at the post-mortem? Are you saying he missed something?'

'No, no. You've met Prof. Arculus, he's one of the best in the business, but you know what a routine post-mortem is like. It takes forty-five minutes tops – it's nowhere near as comprehensive as a forensic PM.'

Flyte's sideways nod appeared to take that on board. 'I assume there was nothing unusual in her bloodstream or we'd already have been informed.'

Cassie shook her head. 'Only alcohol. But again, unless it's a forensic PM, the stuff they test for is relatively limited. There are literally hundreds more drugs and poisons that would only show up if you ran specific assays for them.'

'Understood. But you can hardly expect us to splash four thousand pounds of taxpayers' money on a forensic PM without having a line of enquiry.' Flyte took a leisurely sip of tea. 'What exactly is it that makes you think there's something suspicious about her death?'

Cassie had to be careful: Flyte wouldn't take kindly to her freelance sleuthing, let alone her foray into house-breaking. 'It started when her son Owen came to view the body. I got a really bad feeling about him.'

'A really bad feeling?' Flyte's eyebrow twitched upward.

'Look, I've seen hundreds of grieving family members. But him? I got the strong impression that he was glad to see the back of her.'

'Maybe he was. Plenty of kids hate their parents.'

Cassie could practically see Flyte's scepticism descending between them like a Perspex screen. 'Yes, and I've met tons of them, but they don't act like he did,' she insisted. Transfixed by the perfect pink lip-print Flyte had left on the rim of her white china cup, she struggled to find the right words. 'There's always some kind of emotion. Anger, guilt, self-pity . . . *something*.'

'And that's it? You think the son's a murderer because he didn't emote over Mummy's dead body?' – a mocking edge to her tone.

'It's not just that,' said Cassie. 'She owned a massive Victorian house which he put on the market straightaway . . . '

' . . . which he's perfectly entitled to do if he's the executor so long as contracts aren't exchanged until he gets probate.'

Cassie was tempted to reveal Owen's plan to sell Mrs E's woodland to a property developer but couldn't think of a credible way she might have heard about it. The same went for that '*being followed*', which Mrs E had written in the bathroom steam.

'Listen, I've never met anyone in such a hurry to get a body released and cremated.' By now Cassie was craning across the table, as if by closing the distance between them she could change Flyte's mind. 'I'm telling you, there's something off about the whole thing.' She brought the palm of her hand down on the table between them with a force that rattled the crockery.

During the silence that followed, Flyte fished the lemon slice out of her empty cup, and tore the flesh from the rind with her teeth – a startlingly primitive gesture from someone so self-controlled. After discarding the peel on her saucer, she wiped her fingertips on a paper napkin.

'This Geraldine Edwards. How did you know her?'

Cassie sat back abruptly. So Flyte had known all along that she was hiding something, had been goading her into an emotional reaction. *Just like a cop.*

'She was my science teacher.'

She expected her revelation to end the conversation, but instead Flyte put her elbows on the table and steepled long fingers under her chin.

'She must have meant a great deal to you, for you to call me.'

There was something in Flyte's voice that Cassie hadn't heard before – a genuine-sounding empathy.

'Yes, she did. She was . . . like family to me.'

'OK.' Flyte gave a sympathetic nod. 'So now we've got that straight, why don't you tell me the whole story?'

Cassie shared what she'd discovered: that Owen was an alcoholic who repeatedly asked his mother for bailouts, Maddy's report of the row with Mrs E not long before her death – and her feeling that she'd been scared of someone, probably her son, at the end.

'You say your Mrs E was widowed a long time ago. What about a boyfriend?'

Cassie shook her head; she had decided not to mention Christian. The news of Mrs E's death had clearly come as a terrible shock to him. She'd seen people fake grief for public consumption in the viewing suite, and had no doubt that she could distinguish it from the genuine kind. Knowing the cops would routinely treat the lover, or ex-lover, as suspect number one in any murder case, she didn't want Flyte wasting valuable time that should be spent focusing on the real suspect.

'I know it sounds a bit vague, the bad vibes I get off Owen,' she said. 'But it is my job to pick up on things. And people say I'm good at it.'

'Really. Perhaps you could give me an example.' A sceptical half-smile hovered around Flyte's lips.

'All right . . . You use your right hand to write with – and a bit awkwardly, like you were taught to overcome your natural preference. But you're instinctively left-handed.' Flyte set down the cup she was holding in her left hand. 'Together with your . . . preoccupation with grammar, I would bet that means you weren't state schooled. So a private school – and an old-fashioned one, somewhere out in the sticks maybe?'

Flyte squirmed in her seat.

'But your accent doesn't strike me as born-posh and I get a mix of regions in there, including maybe the north-east? So, I don't know, maybe your parents moved around a lot for work and you went to a bunch of different schools?'

After staring at her for a moment, Flyte said quietly, 'My father was in the army, which meant I went to four different primary schools before I was ten. When he was posted to Cyprus they sent me to boarding school in Northumbria.'

'I'd also say that you're quite recently divorced . . .'

'Separated,' Flyte snapped. 'Why do you assume that?'

'You went on holiday somewhere hot just before the split.' Cassie indicated her left hand. 'There's still a faint tan line on your ring finger.'

She stopped herself, suddenly aware that this might be painful territory – especially if her earlier guess had been right and Flyte and her husband had tried and failed to have a baby.

'OK, so you notice things,' said Flyte, dropping her hand out of view. 'Just assuming for a moment that this Owen Edwards did murder his mother, how might he have done it, in your professional opinion?'

175

'I don't know.' Cassie pictured herself picking the ancient lock to Mrs E's back door. 'He might still have had a key to her house. He could have crept in while she was in the bath and pushed her under. He's a pretty big guy.'

'But if she fought for her life, surely you would have found defensive injuries – bruises, for instance?'

'Not necessarily. Recent contusions can be invisible on the surface, which is why we remove parts of the skin in a forensic PM.'

Flyte put the tip of her tongue between her teeth. Her incisors were unusually pointed, Cassie noticed, adding to the wolfish effect of her eyes. 'It was a category two death so a detective will have attended,' she murmured, half to herself. 'All right. I'll have a look at the report from the scene.'

'That's great . . .'

'. . . but if everything seems to be in order – which I suspect it will – that's it. Understood?'

The look Flyte sent her told Cassie that something between them had changed: the cop–suspect vibe was gone, and in its place was something more like a cautious respect.

Cassie hesitated, but not for long. It was the best she could hope for. 'OK. But you need to know there isn't much time. He's got the cremation booked in for next Wednesday.'

Flyte put her notebook back in her bag and ran an exploratory hand over her flawless chignon, which seemed to pass the test.

Cassie found herself picturing what she'd look like first thing in the morning, sleep-blurred, her hair loose.

'By the way,' said Flyte. 'You were right about the overdosed girl found on the Fairfax estate.'

'How do you mean?'

'She wasn't a rough sleeper. Her name was Rosie Harrison. Seventeen years old, from a nice family. She was a straight-A student, but she'd had a row with her mum after coming home with that tattoo on her ankle. She stormed out, went to stay with her boyfriend – who, it turns out, is a heroin addict living on the Fairfax, one floor up from where her body was found.'

They shared a look – remembering Cassie's hunch that after the girl had overdosed somebody had dumped her in the stairwell to die.

'And of course he knows nothing about her OD-ing, I suppose?' asked Cassie.

'He claims he saw her inject herself with the heroin but says she was fine when he went out shortly afterwards. When she wasn't at the flat later he assumed she'd gone home to her mum. We think he might even have injected her himself, but we can't prove it.'

Cassie pictured the scuff marks on the back of the girl's Moschino jacket 'And instead of dialling 999 he dragged her down a flight of stairs to die, alone and in the freezing cold. To save his own skin.'

'So it seems. I'd love to charge him with manslaughter, but there's no CCTV so it'll be hard to prove.'

What kind of person would do that? Remembering the girl's single word '*Why*?' Cassie's lips set in a line. Rosie had loved this guy.

Her eyes closed and she was back under the mortuary lights, seeing again the quizzical look in the girl's hazel eyes, the line of trackmarks on her left arm – and the fresh puncture wound on the back of her hand. Her *right* hand.

She heard Flyte say, 'What's the matter?'

177

Surfacing, Cassie opened her eyes to meet Flyte's curious look. 'Only ten per cent of the population are left-handed like you.'

'I don't follow . . .'

'Rosie had track marks in her left arm, but the most recent puncture mark – her last ever hit – was in the back of her *right* hand. That's not unusual – users rotate injection sites to prevent their veins scarring up. But if she was right-handed then it would be almost impossible for her to inject herself there, especially for a novice.'

'Really?'

'Yeah, really. I've seen plenty of people shoot up and it's not easy even using your dominant hand.'

Flyte narrowed her eyes. 'Show me.'

Cassie mimed pulling a ligature tight around the top half of her right arm and holding it tight against her ribs, before making a fist with her right hand. With her left hand she brought an imaginary syringe to the vein in the back of the right hand.

'You need to get the point of the needle into the vein but without going through it. Then you have to pull back the plunger one-handed to draw blood and check you're in the vein,' demonstrating the precision that the manoeuvre required. 'And then carefully depress the plunger to inject the gear: move the needle-tip more than a few mil you're out of the vein and into muscle.'

'A waste of a hit?' asked Flyte.

Cassie nodded. 'If Rosie was right-handed and injected herself, then why didn't she use the vein in her left hand?'

Flyte stared at her for a moment. Then a smile bloomed on her face, giving it a sudden, startling prettiness. 'I'll check with her mum. If you're right then we can argue that the boyfriend did inject her – and lied about it under caution.'

Chapter Twenty-Six

'What are you so cheery about?' Carl asked Cassie, hearing her whistling as she worked that morning. Alerted by the grumpiness in his voice she looked up, taking in his unwashed hair and reddened eyes. Another night on the lager from the look of him. But she was feeling too upbeat to take him to task.

Going to retrieve a customer from the body store she reached down to Mrs E's drawer and touched her initials, 'GOE', black against the steel surface. 'There's a detective on the case, Mrs E,' she murmured.

Would Flyte discover something in time? A line of inquiry, in the cop jargon, that would get Mrs E a proper forensic post-mortem? Cassie had to believe that she would.

There was an urgent rapping from the window between admin and the autopsy suite. It was Doug. Unsmiling, he nodded at her, before jabbing a finger at Carl.

Translation: *Both of you, in my office, now.*

A few minutes later they both stood in front of his desk, with Carl getting Doug's disappointed look on full beam. 'I've just had Roger from the crematorium on the phone chewing my ear off. Any idea why that might be, Carl?'

'No, boss,' said Carl. He sounded as laidback as ever, but Cassie had clocked the heel of his right boot beating out a rapid tattoo on the office carpet.

'Well, let me enlighten you. It was you who did the evisceration on Pauline Palmer last Wednesday, wasn't it?'

'Um, the name rings a bell . . . '

'Mrs Palmer was cremated this morning. Do you remember anything special about her body?'

Cassie had a sudden, awful intuition as to where this was going.

Carl's foot stopped drumming. 'She . . . she had a pacemaker.'

'And what happens to a pacemaker when it's subjected to one thousand degrees Celsius?'

'The lithium batteries explode, boss.'

Cassie closed her eyes: the thought of a body entrusted to their care exploding in the crematorium furnace made her feel physically ill.

'Christ, Doug,' she said. 'It didn't go off when the family was still there, did it?'

'Luckily for us, they'd already left by the time it happened. But Roger is foaming at the mouth. By some miracle it didn't damage the cremator – otherwise it would have cost thousands to fix.' Shifting his gaze back to Carl, Doug said, 'How the hell could you forget to remove a pacemaker? It's not complicated, Carl, it's post-mortem procedure for dummies.'

Carl muttered an apology. Glancing at him, Cassie could see he was genuinely gutted.

'That's all very well,' Doug shook his head. 'But sorry just doesn't cut it for something this serious. I'm afraid I'm going to have to consider disciplinary action.'

After dismissing Carl, Doug pressed his fist into his upper abdomen: it looked like the news had brought on another of his bouts of stomach acid.

'Can I get you an alka seltzer?' asked Cassie.

But Doug went on as if he hadn't heard her. 'I must say I thought better of Carl – he's usually so on the ball.'

Cassie felt heavy with guilt. Carl had been drinking a lot recently, and the string of hangovers had probably contributed to his screw-up, but as senior technician, she should have picked it up. She usually made a point of ensuring that all pacemakers and defibrillators had been removed from the bodies awaiting collection, but she couldn't recall double-checking Mrs Palmer. Since Mrs E's death she'd been letting things slide at work, she realised.

'He is only twenty-two, Doug. Could you cut him some slack, just this once?'

Puffing out his cheeks, Doug blew out a long stream of air. 'Maybe. But you need to keep a close eye on him, Cassie. First the Harry Hardwick fiasco, now this. We'll be getting a reputation.'

Back in the autopsy suite, she found Carl scrubbing the work surface with punishing vigour. Seeing her, he stopped, and she was taken aback by how stricken he looked. 'Cassie, I'm really sorry. I'm such a twat. I even remember thinking *I've got to get that pacemaker out before they pick Mrs P up at two o'clock.*' He turned the scrubbing brush over and over in his hands. 'And then . . . it just went clean out of my head.'

Cassie was torn between anger at his lapse, guilt at her own failure to spot such a terrible blunder, and the desire to console him. 'Look, Carl, there's no point beating yourself up about it. I've haven't exactly been Ms Efficiency myself lately.' He sent her an appreciative look, his lips thinned with emotion.

She wondered if Carl's recent alcohol intake was more than just the binge drinking almost everyone went through at his age.

She put a hand on his shoulder 'Carl, you've not been your usual cheerful self recently. Is there anything you want to talk about? As a mate?'

With a headshake he broke her gaze but not before she caught a shocking sight: the glint of tears in his eyes.

FLYTE

'DS Sloman.'

'Hi Steve. It's Phyllida Flyte. How are you?' – making an effort to inject what she hoped would pass for warmth into her voice.

'Fine, thanks.' His tone was neutral – or was it outright unfriendly? Without seeing his expression Flyte found it hard to tell, but she'd decided that her white lie would be easier to sell over the phone than in person.

'I wanted to pick your brains about a recent death you attended, in Patna Road?'

'Oh yes? Why's that then?' Wariness bristled down the line.

It was almost certainly a waste of time, agreeing to look into the death of Cassie Raven's former science teacher. It was obvious that the girl was emotionally involved, and in Flyte's experience, emotion was the enemy of clear thinking – the enemy of a lot of things, come to that. And asking questions about the case was bound to imply she was calling into doubt the actions of a fellow detective – hence Sloman's prickly tone. Still, a promise was a promise, she told herself.

'I'm giving a talk to some probies about attending a category two death, and I heard about the woman who died in the bath? I thought it would make an interesting case study for them – you know, correct procedure, what kind of questions a detective might ask, et cetera.' She tried out a chuckle. 'Funnily enough, it's the only kind of scene I've never attended.'

A creak as Sloman leaned back in his chair. 'So you're what, wanting to walk them through the investigative process?'

'Yes, exactly.' His tone had defrosted a few degrees, his vanity clearly piqued at the prospect of his pearls of wisdom being passed onto a bunch of probationers fresh out of Hendon.

He paused. 'Are you going to throw in the correct procedure if they come across a skull in someone's bathroom?' A sly grin in his voice.

Flyte dredged up a laugh at the lame witticism. Christ, would the sniggering never stop? Only yesterday some comedian had left a plastic skull on a leather thong draped over her computer screen. Although she'd pasted on a smile, the incident had left her feeling more of an outsider than ever.

'All right, no probs,' he said. 'Have you got a pen?'

Sloman took her through his actions at the scene on the morning Geraldine Edwards' body was discovered, while she interjected bland-sounding questions and the odd flattering comment.

'Right,' she said, after he finished. 'And just so I can explain the reasoning, how did you rule out it being a suspicious death?'

'There was no sign of a struggle or forced entry, the doors were all double locked from the inside, and the neighbours didn't see or hear anything out of the ordinary. There was a whisky bottle and glass next to the bath – and the tox report confirmed a sky-high blood alcohol level.' His voice dropped confidentially. 'Pretty straightforward verdict – middle-aged spinster has a funny turn in the bath after a few too many whiskies. Game over.'

'Right.' She managed to stop herself pointing out that Geraldine Edwards had been a widow, not a 'spinster' – as if her marital status were even relevant. 'And the next of kin?'

'A son up in wild and woolly North Wales, so a uniform called the local nick and they did the death knock.'

'I assume you established his whereabouts around the time of the death – just for the record, of course?'

A pause, before he said, 'This is all just for your probie talk, right?' A note of suspicion had entered his voice.

'Absolutely. But you know me, I like to be thorough!'

'That's one word for it.' His laugh had a snarky edge. 'From memory he was at a conference that night. Bristol, I think.'

After Flyte hung up, she wondered if her little deception would come back to bite her. What was she playing at, sticking her neck out for Cassie Raven? OK, it was true that she owed her one. That morning the mother of heroin overdose girl Rosie Harrison had confirmed that her daughter had been right-handed, giving Flyte grounds to bring the druggie boyfriend in for a second interview.

But she had to admit that wasn't the only reason. For all Cassie Raven's bolshy attitude, tattoos and piercings – the gentleness with which she'd handled Rosie's dead body had left a profound impression on Flyte. It was the way anybody would want to see their child dealt with.

She gave her head a shake to derail that train of thought.

She'd also been impressed by how conscientious Raven had been in examining Rosie – picking up details that could easily have been overlooked. Flyte respected people who were meticulous in the execution of their duties. In her experience, it was a regrettably short list – and one that didn't include DS Steve Sloman, judging by his report on the scene at Geraldine Edwards' house.

Checking back through her notes, she made a list of Sloman's failings. His description of the scene was vague and lacking crucial detail, and his interview with Geraldine Edwards' cleaner, who had found the body, had been perfunctory to say the least. He'd only spoken to the next-door neighbours to one side of the Edwards house: the ones on the other side had been out, but he hadn't bothered sending a uniform to try again later.

Her conclusion: that Sloman had decided almost immediately that the death was an accident, pure and simple, and the rest of his investigation, if you could even call it that, had just been going through the motions.

Part of her was itching to dive into this case, not least because Sloman's slapdash policing offended her professional principles.

But realistically, what could she do? DI Bellwether had already labelled her as 'OCD' for not wanting to give up on the Harry Hardwick case. Whatever her misgivings, she couldn't risk his wrath by asking to reopen a routine case just because somebody had filed a sloppy scene report.

Chapter Twenty-Seven

Cassie stayed late that day, catching up on the admin she'd allowed to mount up and devising a system to prevent any repeat of the terrible indignity inflicted on poor Mrs Palmer in the crematorium furnace.

But she felt jumpy, distracted, and on the walk home she gave in to the impulse to call DS Flyte: it couldn't hurt to ask if she'd made any progress.

'So, I spoke to the detective who attended your old teacher's house after she was found. I've also had a good look through the report from the scene.'

Flyte's uncharacteristically breezy tone felt wrong to Cassie – like it was a facade for something.

'And?' Cassie could feel her heart start to thump.

'I'm afraid he found nothing whatsoever to suggest foul play.'

'That's it? I could have told you that.'

'I'm not sure what more you expect me to do. I said that I would double-check the report, to ensure that nothing obvious had been overlooked – and that's precisely what I did.'

She sounded irritable but Cassie sensed defensiveness. 'So, you think he did a thorough job?'

A micro-pause. 'That's hardly for me to say.'

'That's a no, then' – clutching the phone hard.

'I didn't say that,' Flyte retorted. 'It's just . . . not my place to comment on a fellow detective's actions.'

'But you would have done things differently.'

An impatient sigh. 'That's not what—'

'You know what I think?' Cassie gave in to a surge of rage. 'You think he missed something. But you're not prepared to rock the boat.'

She hung up without giving Flyte a chance to respond.

Persuading Flyte to investigate the death had been her last throw of the dice – the final chance to get Mrs E a forensic post-mortem. And she had failed her. Picturing her body lying in a metal drawer Cassie felt a hot prickling at the back of her eyes.

Turning right around she headed back into Camden, bound for the Vibe bar. She deserved a serious drink and, who knows, she might even run into Tish-Tash. *Fuck it*, a line or two wouldn't hurt either . . .

Then her steps slowed as a powerful sensation took hold of her. She wasn't alone. There was nobody in sight but she felt sure that Mrs E was walking quietly beside her – a reassuring, invisible presence.

A memory came back to her. The chemistry lesson where Mrs E had demonstrated what happened when potassium encountered water. The lump of soft silvery metal had fizzed in the beaker for a moment before erupting in a shower of sparks and flame that brought shrieks and laughter from the class.

You set fire to my mind, Cassie murmured.

Fifteen minutes later, instead of getting pissed in the Vibe bar, she was lying face down in the chair at InkStains, her back exposed. Holding out her phone she showed an image to Kobe, who'd been her go-to tattooer for years.

'It's an equation that describes a chemical reaction,' she explained.

'OK, so . . . H_2O is water, but what does the K stand for?'

'Potassium. When you add it to water it ignites the hydrogen. It's pretty spectacular.'

'Cool. And you want it down your spine, right?'

'Yeah. And the initials G.O.E. in gothic font underneath.'

It was a two-hour job and since Kobe – thankfully – didn't like to chat while he worked, she had bags of time to think.

With the vertebrae so close to the surface, the pain of the tattoo gun working its way down her spine was pretty intense, but Cassie didn't care. It was worth it to have her body carry an indelible memento of the woman who had set fire to her mind. But as her pain-killing hormones kicked in, and the gun's deep buzzing lulled her into a reverie, a troubling thought surfaced. Why had it never occurred to her to commemorate her parents this way? Or in any way, come to that?

Sure, she visited her mother's grave in Finchley Cemetery twice a year with her grandmother to mark the anniversaries of her birth and death, but it was a ritual she went along with more out of duty than any personal need. As for her dad, he went completely unremembered – Babcia said that he was buried in a family plot somewhere in Ireland, she didn't even know where, and in the face of her unyielding animosity towards him, Cassie had never pressed the point.

Now she found herself wanting to find out more – about both her parents.

'Sorry to turn up so late.' Following her grandmother into the toasty-warm flat, Cassie shucked off her jacket, grateful to relieve the pressure on the sunburn feeling of the fresh tattoo down her spine.

'Late? It's not even ten o'clock! I was watching a film.'

They went into the living room, where Cassie could see a freeze frame of John Wayne under a cowboy hat on the TV – it looked like Babcia had been re-watching *The Searchers* for about the hundredth time.

Scanning her granddaughter's expression, Weronika asked, 'Shall I make you a cocoa with cream – and a little *conac*, perhaps?'

The first time Babcia had made her cocoa topped with whipped cream had been when the ten-year-old Cassie had come home prizeless and tearful from a school sports day. Weronika hadn't been able to get time off from her job at Safeway, leaving Cassie as the only child there with no mum or dad to cheer her on. But intermingled with the disappointment of the day had been the guilty feeling of relief that her gran hadn't come.

As Cassie got older, the school-gate embarrassment of seeing her grandmother's permed grey hair and old-fashioned tweed coat alongside the ripped jeans and wedge heels of her friends' mums had become almost unbearable. By secondary school, the mean girls were openly taking the piss – mocking her grandmother's heavy accent and pretending to throw up at the pierogi and golombki in Cassie's lunchbox.

Things came to a head when she caught one girl in the corridor, socks rolled down, doing an impression of Babcia's bustling old-lady walk. Pushing her up against the wall Cassie gave her a thumping that only ended when a passing

teacher pulled her off. She would never reveal what had pro-
voked the attack – which earned her a month-long suspen-
sion – but it was the last time anyone took the piss out of her
grandmother.

As she carried their hot drinks into the living room, she said,
'Babcia . . . could we look at your photos of Mum?'

Her grandmother's look of delighted surprise jabbed at
Cassie's conscience – how many times had she ducked what
she'd always thought of as the photo album ordeal?

Setting a large battered cardboard box on the floor, Gran pulled
out an album and opened it across their laps. 'Ah! Here's your
mama dressed up for her first party – it was her fifth birthday.' A
little girl wearing an old-fashioned party dress of pale blue silk,
with a skirt that stuck stiffly out from the waist; her face was wide-
eyed, tense with excitement.

'Posh frock!'

'Posh? Bless you!' Grandma laughed. 'I made it from an
off-cut of curtain material I got at the market.' She patted the
album. 'She's the mirror image of you at the same age.'

'Really?' This strange little girl with her plaits and knee-high
white socks looked so retro, so *other*, that she might have been
beamed down from another planet.

But one of the later pictures of her mum did jump out at
her, effortlessly vaulting the decades. It captured the young
Katherine walking through Camden Market on a summer's
day. She looked about nineteen or twenty, which would make
it the early nineties. The shadows were sharp-edged, the sunny
areas bleached of detail – even the air looked hot. Her denim
cutoffs exposed long slender legs, and the sunshine picked out
glints of auburn in the wavy hair falling to her shoulders. Her

expression – happy yet laughingly self-conscious at having her picture taken – was the kind of look you'd only give a lover.

'Dad must have taken this,' said Cassie.

Seeing her grandmother purse her lips, Cassie felt again the everlasting taboo against any mention of her father.

'Gran, I know you think he wasn't good enough for Mum,' she tried. 'Maybe you're right and he was a bit of waster and everything, but he was still my father.'

The old lady's lips had thinned to a streak, but something made Cassie persist. 'Do you blame him for the crash, is that it?' Perhaps what she'd always been told – the reckless boy racer in a stolen car – wasn't the whole story. 'Was the crash Dad's fault really? Had he been drinking?'

With a tiny shake of her head, the old lady closed the album.

But Cassie couldn't stop herself. 'I don't even have a photo of him, for God's sake. You must have some idea how to get hold of his family? I ought at least to visit his grave.'

'I have no idea about his family – or where he's buried.' Babcia's gaze slid away.

Returning the album to its box, she gave the cover a stroke before putting the lid back on. 'Cassandra, *tygrysek* . . . It is natural for you to be curious about your father, I understand this.' Looking into Cassie's eyes she gripped her hand so tight it made the knuckles grate. 'But you have to trust me on this one subject: you were fortunate not to know him.'

Her expression was so fierce that Cassie could see there was no point in persisting.

What on earth had her dad done to earn such hostility? Or was it just the misplaced aggression of a woman who believed her beloved only child would still be alive if only she'd never met her future husband, had never climbed into the car with him that night? It was a way of thinking that Cassie saw constantly in the bereaved: a self-torturing litany of 'what ifs' and 'if onlys'– an endlessly branching roadmap of alternative events or choices that might have averted the death of their loved one.

The memory of her dad making a spoonful of food swoop like an airplane came back to her – but this time with a new detail: his curly head bent over the dish with a look of concentration, fishing something out with the spoon.

After Weronika returned from putting the album away, there was a charged silence, which she was the first to break. 'I can tell something is bothering you lately, *tygrysek*.' Her voice gentle now. 'Is it something to do with that lady teacher, your friend who died?'

'Sometimes I feel as if the dead speak to me.'

Cassie was taken aback by her own words: having kept her moments of communion with the dead secret for five years, she'd told Tish-Tash – a random stranger – and now her grandmother, in the space of a few days.

'It happened with Mrs Edwards,' she went on. 'Except this time, I keep seeing her as well – outside the mortuary.'

If Weronika was shocked, she did a good job of hiding it. After a long moment she said, 'When somebody you love dies, they are still with you.' She hit her chest softly with her fist. 'I mean *really* with you. Three days after your mama died, I came in and saw her sitting right where you are now, braiding her beautiful hair.'

Looking down at the sofa cushion, Cassie shivered. For the first time in years she pictured her mother's smile, which brought a feeling of loss so violent that it hollowed out her stomach.

Had Mrs E's death torn the lid off her grief, bringing the memory of her parents' deaths flooding back? Was that why she was having these visions?

'It's like she's trying to tell me something's wrong – that she shouldn't have died,' she said. 'Does that sound completely crazy?'

'No, not crazy. Not if you love someone.' Her grandmother's eyes cut away to the photograph of her daughter on the mantelpiece. 'You know, it is twenty years since I lost my Katherine, but she still speaks to me sometimes. And when it happens, it's a wonderful gift.'

Cassie thought, yet didn't say, *Does she ever talk about me?*

Chapter Twenty-Eight

The following day was a Saturday and Cassie wasn't even on call but she'd agreed to go into the mortuary at the end of the day to prep for a forensic post-mortem scheduled for the crack of dawn Monday morning. Since a forensic PM's findings could mean the difference between a killer going to jail or getting away with it, every step of the procedure had to be 100 per cent watertight.

At around five she sat down with Deborah in admin, who'd come in especially, to go through the paperwork.

'The deceased is Hanif Hassan, date of birth April seventh 2001,' Deborah read off the screen, before clucking her tongue against the roof of her mouth. 'Same age as my youngest. He's that stabbing they showed on the telly, isn't he?'

Cassie nodded. She'd been the APT on call the night that the cops had brought in Hanif's body a couple of weeks back. His killer had pursued him for nearly a mile, all the way from the northern end of the borough back to the tower block where he lived with his mum. Security cameras had captured much of the chase including the moment Hanif's pursuer had followed him into his block. The knife attack, which took place off camera and without witnesses, had left Hanif with the single stab wound to the thigh which had killed him.

The CCTV footage had led to the arrest of Regis Kane, a local gang leader who ran the drug trade in the network of streets around the notorious Castlehaven Estate. Kane was now in a cell in Wormwood Scrubs awaiting trial for Hanif's murder.

'Drugs, I suppose?' Deborah sighed.

'Yeah. It's kind of a sad story, actually.' Cassie relayed what the cops had told her. Apparently, Hanif Hassan had been tipped for a big future in computer programming, having recently won the IT Student of the Year award, presented to him by the mayor. Unfortunately, Hanif was helping to fund his studies by dealing a bit of weed on the side. He only sold to people he knew, but on the day in question somebody spotted him on turf controlled by Kane, who apparently ran the drug trade around the Castlehaven Estate.

Recalling her night with Tish-Tash, when she'd scored off one of the Somali kids outside the Vibe bar, Cassie felt a flush warming her neck. She'd only paid twenty quid for her wrap of coke, but she knew that all those twenties bankrolled a blood-soaked trade.

Busy hunting for an email, Deborah didn't notice her discomfort. 'Here we go. Right, so the defence pathologist will be a Mr Anton Ferriman.'

Professor Arculus had conducted the official forensic post-mortem on Hanif and confirmed the stab wound to the upper thigh, which had nicked the femoral artery, as the fatal injury. Kane had been charged with murder, but now his defence counsel was exercising his right to have an independent pathologist conduct a second post-mortem on Hanif's body.

Deborah pulled a sceptical face. 'Why are they even bothering? Murder's murder, isn't it?'

'You might think so,' said Cassie. 'But all the defence PM needs to do is inject a smidgen of doubt.' She remembered one case where the pathologist hired by the defence argued that the victim of a beating had been suffering from a pre-existing cardiac condition which had been the underlying cause of death, leading to the acquittal of the accused.

'It's bonkers, isn't it,' sighed Deborah.

Leaving Deborah closing down her computer, Cassie got an unexpected phone call from Carl.

'I was wondering if you fancied a jar, once you're done there?' he asked.

'I'd love to, but I've still got to get the forensic suite prepped.'

'You're not pulling a late one though, are you?'

She checked the time on her phone. 'No. I should be out of here by eight at the latest but after that I think I'm going to get an early night.' Carl sounded a bit jumpy – and it occurred to Cassie that he'd probably been wanting to chat about his looming disciplinary. 'Has Doug talked to you yet about the pacemaker debacle?' she asked.

'I've got a meeting with him first thing Monday.' His voice dropped to a murmur. 'Any idea what he's got planned for me?'

Cassie hesitated: she couldn't let on that she had negotiated Doug down from a written to a verbal warning. 'Not exactly, but don't go losing any sleep over it, OK?'

'OK. Thanks, Cass.'

'And don't come in smelling like a Wetherspoon's.'

Distracted by Carl's troubles, Cassie found herself standing in the main autopsy suite when it was the forensic suite, out back, that she needed to prep.

Unlocking the door she stepped inside, the stink of formalin raking the back of her nose and bringing tears to her eyes. She opened the fridge – smaller than the main body store, with just six drawers – and checked the name and date of birth on Hanif's label against her paperwork.

'Not long now, Hanif,' she told him, through the body bag. 'We'll get you back to your mum just as soon as we can.'

Cassie didn't expect Hanif to reply; she'd never heard any of her forensic charges 'speak' – perhaps because she didn't perform the evisceration in these cases. The pathologist would be the only person permitted to touch Hanif's body on Monday, to eliminate any risk of contaminating the evidence. Her job would simply be to stand there handing him instruments and sample pots.

Still, she always looked forward to a forensic PM. If the pathologist deemed it necessary, the skin would be flayed from the body, leaving the machinery of muscles, tendons, and blood vessels exposed, like an anatomical model. Trying to explain the strange thrill she felt at the sight to her grandmother once, Cassie had struggled to find the words. Weronika had thought for a moment before saying, '*It must be like glimpsing the mind of God*', which had come close.

Her first task was to clear the dissection bench, which was crowded with lidded white pails containing brains soaking in formalin – a process that firmed up the soft tissue prior to dissection. The pails weighed a ton, making it a two-handed job, and by the time she'd moved them all to the far end of the suite her shoulder joints ached. Before she could even start on giving the place a proper clean, her phone rang. It was Deborah. Just as she was leaving an old gent whose wife had died in the hospital earlier that day had called to ask if he could view her body.

'Should I tell him to come in on Monday?' she offered.

Cassie pictured an elderly man, no doubt just emerging from the initial numbing shock of losing his life partner, gripped by the urgent need to see her.

'No, don't do that.' She checked the time. Half an hour to prep the wife's body, another hour, say, for the viewing. She could sort the forensic suite afterwards. It was going to be a late one, after all. 'Tell him to come over at eight o'clock, that should give me plenty of time to get her ready.'

Maurice, a well-spoken gent in his eighties, arrived half an hour late. He had the vacant gaze of someone befuddled by loss, but had clearly taken care over his appearance for the visit. Cassie noted his freshly pressed shirt and tie, the smell of fresh polish coming up from what were probably his best shoes, the tiny smear of blood from a razor cut under his jaw.

She sat with him by his dead wife Naomi's side as he reminisced about their fifty-three years of life together. Rushing him was out of the question, and it was a good two hours before he agreed with her gentle suggestion that perhaps he should get a good night's sleep and come back to see Naomi in the morning.

His visit put Cassie so far behind schedule that by the time the forensic suite was cleaned and ready for action, it was gone midnight. She was just running a final check of all the sterilised instruments and sample jars, when she heard it.

The rumble of a diesel engine drawing up outside.

Chapter Twenty-Nine

Cassie's first thought was that she must have missed a message from the undertakers about a late-night delivery. But when she reached into her pocket for her mobile to check she realised she'd left it in the viewing room.

Since the forensic suite was windowless, she decided to head to the office, which overlooked the parking area. But as she stepped into the corridor, she felt a finger of cold air stroke her face.

Somebody had opened the front door. But who? The undertakers didn't have swipe cards.

Hearing the soft thud of the front door closing, her scalp contracted, beads of sweat breaking out on her upper lip – her amygdala telling her what her frontal cortex was slower to admit: the mortuary had an intruder. Straining her ears, she heard an insistent whisper from the entrance hallway.

Make that intruders, plural.

Her hearing on hyper-alert, she picked up the mouse-squeak of trainers on the lino floor of the corridor. Slipping back inside the forensic suite, she engaged the lock as softly as she could behind her.

The lack of any other exit caused a brief flutter of panic but she told herself she had a good solid door between her and them, whoever they were. Junkies, most likely, looking for drugs or petty cash – and there were plenty of unlocked doors off the corridor for them to try.

This comforting thought was shattered by the sound of low, urgent voices right outside. Two men, one sounding younger than the other. She heard snippets of their conversation: ' . . . Need to get it right' – from the deeper, older voice. 'Place gives me the fucking creeps' – the whiny voice of the younger guy. Then the older one again: 'Give it to me, bruv . . .'

A thud, followed by a splintering sound, made Cassie jump.

Jesus fucking Christ. They were trying to jemmy the door open at the hinges. The wood groaned. It was standing firm, but for how long?

She decided to announce her presence.

'The cops are coming,' she said through the door, keeping her voice calm, the pitch low and authoritative. 'If I was you, I'd get out now.'

The assault on the door stopped and there was silence, followed by a whispered argument – the young one, sounding panicked, clearly wanting to leave; the other, deeper voice overruling him. She heard the older man chuckle. ' . . . bitch is lyin', bruv.' Then he spoke through the door. 'Listen up, we coming in anyway – you let us in, and we won't fuck you up, a'right?'

Cassie didn't let herself dwell on the cold promise in that deep, unconcerned voice. Backing into the suite, she looked around for a weapon. A moment later, another sickening impact and a metallic squeal as the door came under renewed assault. She scanned the armoury of scalpels, saws, and rib shears lined up on the dissecting bench. They might look dangerous, but right now she'd trade them all for a baseball bat.

A crack like gunfire echoed through the suite as the bottom door hinge gave way, bringing whoops from the men outside.

Cassie eyes went to the lock-release mechanism. If she gave in and opened the door, maybe they wouldn't hurt her? *Yeah, right.*

Seconds later, the door finally gave way, crashing to the floor.

From the corridor the two men peered into the darkness within.

'Where the fuck she gone?' muttered the younger one.

The older one took a step towards the threshold of the darkened room, his wrecking bar raised to shoulder height.

He saw a flash of something white coming towards him and a scary face studded with metal. The face split in a scream as it heaved the white thing in his direction. A great tongue of liquid looped out of the bucket and hung in the air for a split second like a freeze frame. Then it broke over him – and something heavy hit him in the chest.

Dropping his weapon he pulled up his sweatshirt, desperately trying to scrub the stinging liquid off his face. 'Acid! The bitch burned me!' Then his eye fell on the thing that had struck him, which now lay nestled between his trainers.

He blinked twice, before he saw what it was. *A human brain.*

Cassie appeared in the doorway, brandishing another loaded bucket, but the men had already turned to run, skidding on the wet lino.

Chapter Thirty

Her 999 call brought three squad cars, sirens screaming, to the mortuary. The cops found the front door open and Cassie on her knees in the corridor, coaxing a human brain back into a white plastic bucket. As they would tell their colleagues back at the nick, she was murmuring to it, the way you'd talk to an injured pet.

Now, she was sitting in the office being force-fed sweetened tea by Doug, while the cops cordoned off all the areas where the intruders had set foot.

'Stop worrying about the brain, Cassie, you did the right thing.'

She rocked back and forth, her arms locked around her knees. 'But what if the lab can't get a decent section off it?'

'It'll be fine – brains are tougher than you think. Strictly between you and me, I dropped one down a flight of stairs once.'

She looked doubtful. 'And they still got a usable sample?'

'Yes. Now drink up your tea. Could you manage a biscuit?'

She shook her head.

'You still look awfully pale. I've half a mind to send you home in a cab and tell them they'll have to question you in the morning. It's nearly one o'clock, you know.'

'It's OK. I'd rather be here.' The idea of going home, leaving Mrs E and all her other charges alone and defenceless after the violation of the break-in was unthinkable.

Through her mental fog, Cassie heard the unmistakable tones of DS Flyte outside the office, coldly berating one of the uniformed officers for some oversight.

She came in glowering, but on seeing Cassie curled up in an armchair cradling her cup of tea, her scowl dissolved. She pulled up a chair beside her.

'How are you doing?'

'OK.'

'Sounds like you gave them a bloody good scare. Good for you.' Flyte's usual cold spikiness had melted away – *like frost on a winter rose,* thought Cassie, suddenly – and her eyes held only compassion. 'Cassie, are you up to talking about it while it's still fresh in your mind?'

Cassie nodded. While Doug disappeared to make more tea, she tried to dredge up everything she could about the break-in. *Tried,* because although it had all happened less than an hour ago, her memory had splintered the episode into a series of random images, making a straightforward timeline hard to nail.

'What about the men. Could you pull them out of a video lineup, do you think?' asked Flyte.

Cassie lifted a shoulder. 'I'm really not sure. I only saw them for a split second. It's all a bit of a blur, to be honest.'

She gave the best description of the two men she could manage: the older one maybe late twenties and mixed race; his sidekick barely eighteen, with the doe eyes and delicate features of a Somalian or Eritrean.

'Don't worry,' said Flyte. 'You're still in shock. This chemical you chucked over them? Will they be needing treatment for burns?'

'Formalin – dilute formaldehyde. No, not really, so long as they wash it off quickly.'

Disappointment briefly creased Flyte's face. 'Did you get any idea of what they might be after?'

She shook her head. 'The forensic suite is the only interior door with a security lock. Maybe they thought they'd find drugs inside?'

There was a knock at the door and one of the uniformed cops put his head round. 'Forensics are here, Sarge.'

Flyte gave him barely a nod before turning back to Cassie. 'You might find yourself remembering a bit more after you've had some sleep. I'll get one of the guys to run you home.'

Cassie shook her head. 'I . . . I don't like the idea of leaving after . . . what happened.'

'I understand,' said Flyte, eyeing her face. 'I tell you what. How about I stay here until the security firm comes to reset the system. Even if that's not till the morning.'

Cassie nodded, before getting to her feet, a bit wobbly still. At the door she turned. 'Thank you, Sergeant Flyte.'

'You're welcome.' A flush coloured her pale cheeks. 'And call me Phyllida.'

Chapter Thirty-One

Cassie woke with a jolt, blinking in the sullen glare of a low winter sun – she'd fallen into bed fully clothed, forgetting to draw the blinds. A moment of confusion, before the previous night's events came tumbling back.

The pitiful scratching at the bedroom door was probably what had woken her: Macavity's breakfast was long overdue.

Even after getting up she still felt dazed, unable to remember the break-in properly. All she could recall were fragments – like the agonised squeal of the door hinge giving way.

After a cup of syrupy-strong stove-top coffee, the fog in her brain parted for a moment, and she realised something.

Two mortuary break-ins in a fortnight was no coincidence.

Last night's intruders had to be the same people who had stolen Harry Hardwick's body. Which ruled out at a stroke two possible motives for the theft: it hadn't been some one-off prank, and neither had they been targeting Mr Hardwick. So what *had* they been up to?

Maybe Carl had been on the right track from the start: that they were body snatchers out to harvest reusable body parts from the recently dead. Whoever commissioned the theft would have ordered a younger, more valuable body, but maybe the thieves had screwed up. That would explain why they'd dumped poor old Harry in the canal – and had come back last night for another go.

A snippet of their conversation came back to her: something about 'getting it right' – meaning that they needed to get it right *this time*. . .?

But . . . there was something wrong with this scenario that Cassie couldn't quite nail – her befuddled brain trying and failing to join the dots. After getting changed, her gaze fell on the set of lock picks she'd borrowed from Kieran, still sitting on the worktop. With Flyte likely to turn up here to interview her, it would be a good idea to return them to their owner.

Down by the canal the air was cold and crisp, helping to clear her thoughts. Last night's mortuary invasion had scared her witless – of course it had – but she took some comfort from knowing that the intruders clearly weren't expecting to encounter anyone with a pulse; she'd simply been in the wrong place at the wrong time.

She spotted a familiar splash of bright blue beside the towpath up ahead. It was Kieran, sitting up in his sleeping bag, his shaggy head bent over the task of rolling up.

'I was hoping I'd see you, Cassie Raven,' he said, giving her his ruined grin.

'Sorry,' she dug the lock picks out of her pocket. 'I meant to bring them back before.'

'Ah, no worries, it wasn't that.' He threw a look up and down the towpath before beckoning her closer.

She dropped to a crouch and Kieran shuffled towards her, releasing a meaty gust from his sleeping bag. 'I heard something interesting on the grapevine a few days back.' His face was alive with intrigue. 'Some gangbangers had a stiff they wanted to get shot of.'

'Yeah?' said Cassie, aiming for no more than casual interest.

'The word is, they nicked it from the morgue.'

'Really?'

'You haven't lost anyone then?' He grinned at her questioningly.

She managed a chuckle. 'We had a full house last time I looked!' Which was true.

'Yeah, I thought it was probably bollocks. Why would anyone nick a stiff?' He drew his tongue along the edge of the Rizla.

'Who were these supposed bodysnatchers, anyway?' asked Cassie, raising a sceptical eyebrow.

'Castlehaven Boyz. Nasty little fuckers from up Kentish Town way.'

Castlehaven Boyz . . .

'Never heard of them. So what happened to this so-called stolen body?'

'I never heard, to be honest.'

'Someone's been pulling your leg, I reckon,' she said, feeling a rush of relief that the early morning recovery of Mr H had kept the story out of the press.

'Yeah, well we have to make our own entertainment round here,' admitted Kieran cheerfully, before lighting his rollie with a flourish.

The conversation set Cassie's brain whirring. Had Castlehaven Boyz been commissioned to break into the mortuary by someone in the body parts trade? But then her earlier, niggling doubt about this theory clicked into place. If you were coming back to steal a younger body, then why wouldn't you return to the main body store, where there were a dozen bodies to choose from?

And why would you take on the locked door of the forensic suite?

Reaching the lock gate where Harry's body had been found, she stopped in her tracks.

There was only one body in the forensic body store – and it belonged to Hanif Hassan, who had been murdered by gang leader Regis Kane. And since Kane ran the drug trade around the Castlehaven Estate, Castlehaven Boyz had to be his gang.

Pulling out her phone, she called Deborah's mobile.

After fielding her shocked enquiries about the previous night's events, saying that yes, she was fine, etc. etc., Cassie finally got a question in edgeways.

'Listen, Deborah, I'm sorry to bother you on a Sunday, but it's been bugging me all morning. You know our young guest Hanif, who's due to have the forensic PM . . . When we filled in the forms, we did put his full name in the box, didn't we?'

'Ah bless you,' said Deborah. 'You shouldn't be worrying about things like that after what you've been through! Doug has postponed the PM till next week.'

Cassie rolled her eyes. 'I know it's silly, but like I say, I can't get it out of my head. I know you've got remote access to the system so I was wondering, could you bear to take a quick look, just to humour me?'

On any other day, Deborah might have come over all jobsworth about it, but today she was Ms Co-operation. Moments later, she came back on the phone. 'I've got his form up in front of me and it's all filled in, so no need to worry.'

'Oh, good ... Deborah, just remind me what his middle name was, would you?'

'Umm ... It's Aziz.'

Cassie experienced the same thrill she'd had as a child, when her final twist had rendered every side of the Rubik's Cube a single unbroken colour.

Chapter Thirty-Two

By the time DS Flyte arrived at the mortuary an hour later Cassie had her gameplan worked out.

'Have you remembered something about the break-in?' asked Flyte as she crossed the threshold. Cassie was amused to see that her only concession to weekend wear was a slightly less formal jacket than usual and a crew-necked top instead of a proper shirt.

'Not exactly,' she said, reflecting that she still couldn't think of her as Phyllida. 'But I know what it was about – and who did it.' With just the two of them there, she was able to speak freely.

'What do you mean?'

Cassie was startled by the vulpine intensity of her stare: apparently the touchy-feely Flyte she'd glimpsed in the early hours of that morning was firmly back in her box.

She stuck out her chin. 'I'll share my . . . thinking with you, on one condition. That you reopen the investigation into Geraldine Edwards' death – and I mean properly this time.'

Flyte's pink lips parted in astonishment. 'Are you trying to do a deal with me?'

Cassie folded her arms, feeling the swift but steady thump of her heart against her sternum. 'I'd rather call it . . . an understanding.' The revelation that had come to her on the towpath was the only leverage she had, and she was determined to use it to get justice for Mrs E.

Flyte narrowed her eyes, probably deciding whether to pull the old 'obstructing the police' routine. Instead she said, 'It's not that easy, you know. I can't just . . . wade into somebody else's case.'

Cassie just shrugged, offering nothing.

'You don't understand,' Flyte insisted. 'I would need specific permission from my boss.'

'So ask him for it.' Their eyes locked. It wasn't the first time they'd clashed but this time it felt to Cassie as if the standoff was tinged with mutual respect.

Flyte opened one hand – a sign that she was wavering. 'Look, he'll probably just tell me to get lost . . . '

'But . . . ?'

'But if you really can give me something that might solve the Harry Hardwick case, and last night's break-in, something substantive, I mean, I'll ask. On the strict understanding that if he says no, there's nothing I can do.'

Any other cop would have told her to sod off – not least because the theft of an old man's body wasn't worth the grief – but Cassie's antennae had picked something up: for some unknown reason, Phyllida Flyte was invested in the Harry Hardwick case.

Cassie started off down the corridor, indicating that Flyte should follow.

'The men from last night? They have to be the same mob who broke in and took Harry Hardwick's body two weeks ago.'

'Go on.' Going by Flyte's expression, she'd already worked that out.

Cassie reached the door marked *Body Store*. 'So, imagine you come in the front door, and you're looking for a body – this is the first place you'd check out, right?'

Pushing it open, she went over to the giant refrigerator with the initials inscribed in black marker pen on its polished steel doors. 'You remember the system? When a new body gets checked in, we mark up the berth where they'll be staying.'

Flyte nodded, impatient.

Indicating the initials 'PJF' on one door, Cassie opened it and pulled the drawer out on its rollers to reveal the shrouded head and shoulders of the occupant inside. Locating a small label on the side of the body bag, she beckoned Flyte.

Bending down Flyte read out: '*Peter James Fenner.*'

'Right. But imagine you're a midnight intruder in a hell of a hurry. The name label isn't easy to find, is it?' Closing the door with a thunk, she tapped on the big black initials. 'I think that when you see this you assume that the body inside will be the one you're after.'

Flyte was listening intently. 'What was Harry Hardwick's full name?'

'Harold Albert Hardwick.'

'So the first break-in, you reckon they were looking for someone with the initials H.A.H.'

Cassie nodded.

'But not Harry Hardwick?'

She shook her head.

Flyte huffed, her impatience returning. 'Are you going to tell me who they were after or not?'

'Remember that Asian kid, the small-time drug dealer who got knifed a couple of weeks ago?' Cassie pulled the post-mortem paperwork from the pocket of her scrubs. 'He's been in the forensic fridge out the back ever since. He's down to have a second post-mortem tomorrow, ordered by his killer's defence team.'

Practically snatching the form out of her hands, Flyte scanned it. Then her head jerked up, her pale pink lips forming a perfect 'O'.

'That's right,' said Cassie. 'They were after Hanif Aziz Hassan all along.'

FLYTE

Flyte was enjoying a rare experience – the undivided attention of her boss DI Bellwether, whom she'd called on his mobile. Sounding irritated at first to be disturbed on a Sunday, his tone had changed as he'd listened to her story.

'So, according to your theory, Regis Kane sent a couple of his crew to steal the body of Hanif Hassan in order to prevent the second post-mortem that his own defence was about to conduct?'

'Yes, boss. Kane has spent the last few weeks stuck in the Scrubs brooding on the prospect of getting life – with a seriously long tariff. I think he came up with a plan. If Hanif's body should suddenly disappear, he would be denied his legal right to have it re-examined by an independent pathologist.'

Kane would know that the CCTV footage of him chasing Hanif Hassan put him squarely in the frame for the murder, but the lack of any eyewitnesses to the killing itself meant he could get creative with the facts.

'If I were Kane I would claim that it was Hanif who pulled the knife,' Flyte went on, 'and say that in the desperate struggle to defend himself, Hanif accidentally got stabbed with his own blade.'

'So he would argue that the injury was inflicted in self-defence, with no intent to kill?'

'Exactly – the knife had both men's prints on it remember. And the defence could argue that without a second post-mortem on

Hanif's body Kane's version of events couldn't be tested against the position and angle of the stab wound.'

'I'd hate to think that any jury would be stupid enough to fall for it.' Bellwether leaned back in his chair. 'But I can imagine the song and dance Kane's brief would have made about Hanif's body being the most important exhibit. And some people might hesitate to sentence a young man to life in those circumstances.'

'Exactly. At the very least, it would have muddied the waters. In any event, faced with a life sentence, Kane probably thought he had nothing to lose.'

Bellwether nodded thoughtfully. 'Let's say you're right, and Kane is behind both mortuary break-ins. But if he sent his boys to steal a seventeen-year-old Asian kid, how do they end up with an eighty-one-year-old white guy?'

Flyte walked him through Cassie Raven's theory – how, after going into the wrong body store, Kane's men saw the initials H.A.H. inked on the door, and grabbed the body-bagged occupant inside, assuming it was Hanif Aziz Hassan. 'Picture the scene, boss. They're a couple of young gang members in a mortuary at midnight with only a phone for a torch. They're not exactly keen to hang around.'

'Fair point. So they stick the body in the back of a van, only to find out later that they've collected the wrong takeaway order.'

'Then Kane sends them back for another crack last night, just before the second post-mortem.'

Bellwether went quiet for a moment before saying, 'OK. Let's put a car on twenty-four-hour surveillance at the mortuary, at least until Hanif's PM, in case Kane's boys are thinking third time lucky.'

It bothered Flyte, still having no idea how the intruders had gained entry. Especially as this time the security firm claimed there was no record of a swipe card being used to gain entry anywhere near the time of the break-in.

'Given the connection with Hanif Hassan's murder, you'll need to brief the boys and girls in Major Crimes,' Bellwether went on. 'And since they'll have all the latest intel on Kane and his Castlehaven Boyz, they should take over both mortuary break-ins as well.'

He paused, perhaps expecting her to put up a fight, but when she said nothing, he went on, 'Well done, Phyllida. Good work.' His tone made it clear he considered the conversation over. But when she didn't end the call he asked warily, 'Was there something else?'

Flyte would have preferred to pursue the men who'd desecrated Harry Hardwick's body herself, but knowing that the investigation into the theft was back on was enough for her. Now she had to deliver her side of the bargain she'd struck with Cassie Raven.

'Yes, boss. I'd like to take another look at a sudden death Steve Sloman attended eleven days ago. A fifty-one-year-old female found in the bath. It's gone down as a category two but there are a couple of things I'd like to double-check.'

'Have you talked to Steve about it?'

'I have, but I'm afraid I had to be a bit economical with the truth. The fact is I got a confidential tip-off.'

He eyed her 'What did the post-mortem say?'

'Death by drowning. The pathologist thinks she might have blacked out, but according to her medical records she was in excellent health up to that point.'

'And this informant of yours – they're saying there's more to it than meets the eye?'

'Yes. It might come to nothing, but I'd like to re-interview the dead woman's cleaner, who found the body, just in case.' As Flyte anxiously awaited Bellwether's response, she realised that something had crept up on her unawares. For some reason she was unable to fathom, it was important to her not to let Cassie Raven down.

She heard Bellwether sigh on the other end of the line. 'Well, fair enough, Phyllida. I guess you've earned it. Lucky for you, Steve has just gone on paternity leave, so you can proceed without putting his nose out of joint. Keep it to yourself though. And if you do find anything off about the death, you report back directly to me.'

Chapter Thirty-Three

Cassie was on her way home from her meeting with Flyte when she heard her phone ding. A text from Carl – at last. Since he must surely have heard about the mortuary invasion by now, she'd been feeling a bit hurt that he hadn't called to check on her. Even now, his message was mysteriously curt: *'I'm in the Hawley. I need to talk to you'.*

The pub was five minutes away. From the moment she saw him, hunched over a pint on the roof terrace, she knew something was very wrong.

'What's up, Carl?'

She was confused to see his eyes skitter away from hers.

'Y'know, it's always impressed me, how committed you are to the job,' he said. 'I mean, you really care about it, don't you?'

He didn't seem to be taking the piss, so Cassie gave a half-nod, half-shrug. *Where was this going?*

'Even the way you talk to the bodies. I used to think that was a bit . . . weird? But then I got it. You still see them as people, not just corpses.'

Cassie's shock lasted only a moment: after sharing a workspace for over a year, it was inevitable that Carl had overheard her chatting to her charges – but it was clear he had something bigger to get off his chest.

'The thing is, Cassie, I'm not like you. I don't have your . . . dedication. To me, it's just a job.'

'Carl, if you're worrying about that pacemaker you missed . . .'

He put away a big slug of beer. 'Do you know how much money I put in the fruit machine downstairs before I texted you?'– his voice freighted with disgust. 'Sixty quid.' He pulled the chain of an invisible toilet. 'Gone.'

Cassie remembered him hinting at money worries lately – but if he was trying to solve them by throwing cash into fruit machines, he must be more desperate than she thought. 'Carl, look, if you've got cashflow issues, maybe I can help? You could come and kip on my sofa for a bit, save the rent . . .'

'Don't do that!' he burst out, startling her. 'Sorry, Cassie. But I can't handle you being nice to me, not after what I did.'

After what he did?

And then everything fell into place with a sickening, world-shifting lurch.

'How much did they pay you, Carl?' She felt . . . precarious, like she was stepping out onto a frozen lake.

Staring down at the tabletop, Carl told her everything in a rapid hoarse whisper: how the odd flutter on a football match or a tenner on the lottery had morphed into something more serious – an addiction to fixed-odds betting terminals, which let punters gamble up to a hundred quid per spin.

'If I lost, I'd gamble more to make it back, and if I won, I'd gamble more, sure I was on a winning streak. One day, I lost seven hundred quid in twenty minutes. *Seven hundred quid.*' A spasm of self-loathing contorted his face. 'That same day, a guy starts chatting to me at the coffee machine. Asks me if I want to make a bit of cash.'

'He'd been watching you, seeing you dig yourself into a big fat hole.'

He glanced up at her. 'I guess so. I owed nearly twelve grand by then. We go for a jar and it turns out he knows I work at the mortuary – Christ knows how. He says he might have a job for me that would pay serious money, without me having to lift a finger. He even gives me a grand in cash upfront – a golden hello, he called it.'

Cassie's mind was racing ahead. *Of course!* She saw her index finger punching her access code into the mortuary entry pad, Carl at her shoulder, motorcycle helmet under his arm – a scene repeated on countless mornings. When she had told Flyte that nobody could get close enough to steal her access code she hadn't even considered Carl.

'They wanted you to get them into the mortuary at night,' she said, surprised at how calm she sounded.

Carl put both hands over his eyes, reminding Cassie of a blindfolded man facing execution. 'I meant to pull out of it, pay them back. But after I lost the grand they gave me on the machines, they had me over a barrel. By then, my credit cards were maxed and I was two months behind with the rent.'

'So, what's the going rate for a mortuary access code?' – anger tightening her voice.

'Fifteen grand.' A shamed whisper.

Petty cash to a gangsta like Regis Kane.

'Then, after they fucked up the first time, going to the wrong body store and taking Mr Hardwick, they put the screws on, said they wanted their money back. Like it was my fault!'

Cassie remembered Carl in the pub after Harry Hardwick went missing – his anxious fingers fraying the beer mat. And the rash of benders he'd been going on. *No wonder.*

'This guy turned up at my flat . . .' Carl, usually so unruffled, suddenly looked like a kid who'd seen the bogeyman climb out of his wardrobe. 'He was the real deal, Cassie.'

'So you helped them break in a second time.'

Until then, he'd been avoiding her eyes, but now he sent her a pleading look. 'You weren't supposed to be there. Nobody was. I checked . . .'

'That was why you asked if I was staying late that night.' She stared at him. 'Because you knew they were coming back. But we had the new swipe cards by then, so how . . . ?'

'I found a way to leave the door on the latch.'

Cassie thought about it: the door had a soft-close mechanism, which meant she probably wouldn't have clocked it, if she'd left on time that night. 'What if I had noticed, and locked the door properly on my way out?'

'They had my swipe card as a last resort.' He leaned across the table. 'Look, Cassie, I know it doesn't count for much, but when I heard what happened to you last night, I called my contact and said enough's enough – I'm out.'

'What did he say?'

'He said no problem – and gave me till the end of the week to pay back the fifteen grand.'

His sardonic smile made him look like the old Carl for a moment, as if none of this was really happening.

'I need a drink,' she said, getting to her feet.

Waiting for her order at the bar, she replayed the way that Regis Kane and his Castlehaven Boyz had targeted Carl, like jackals circling an injured herd member. She felt sorry for him, but mostly angry that he had been prepared to sacrifice a body in their care – and by giving up *her* access code.

'Are you all right there?' The barmaid was frowning at her, looking worried.

Cassie waved away her concern and ordered a large vodka. She had just joined the dots. Her grandmother had mentioned that Castlehaven Boyz wore red as their gang colours . . . and her towpath mugger had worn a scarlet bandana over his face. A mugging that had happened the day she got her swipe card.

Carl must have told his contact when the new cards were being issued – never thinking that someone would follow her to steal her bag and swipe card, no doubt as back-up in case Carl changed his mind. She wondered whether to tell him, before deciding he was already feeling bad enough.

She hadn't even sat back down before he said, 'What those bastards did to you, the thought that they might have hurt you . . . Cassie, I'm so sorry. It was all my fault. I feel terrible.' He blinked. 'It made me realise I've got to sort myself out. This morning I called one of those helplines for problem gamblers.'

'That's a good start.' Cassie sank half her vodka, felt its hot bite start to distance her from the hurt of Carl's confession.

He sought her eyes. 'Do you think you can ever . . . forgive me?'

'For what happened to me? Yes.' She gave a little shake of her head. 'But not for what happened to Harry Hardwick. We were supposed to be looking after him.'

Carl gave a miserable nod.

'What are you going to do?' she asked.

'I'm not sticking around. I've got a mate in . . . well, probably best I don't tell you where, but a long way out of town. He reconditions vintage bikes. He's got more work than he can handle so he's asked me to help him out.'

Carl had been a motorbike mechanic before re-training as an APT. Cassie was about to point out that if he did a runner the police would put two and two together before stopping herself. If he stayed in Camden, the cops would be the least of his problems.

FLYTE

'I have worked for her eleven years now – such a lovely lady,' Imelda told DS Flyte.

It was Monday morning and the two of them were standing in Geraldine Edwards' kitchen, Flyte towering over the cleaner – a small and sturdy Portuguese lady in her sixties.

'When I first came here I couldn't speak English, so Geraldine gave me lessons twice a week – for nothing. But if I didn't do my homework she would say to me' – she assumed a stern look – '"Imelda, there is no gain without pain!"' Her smile didn't erase the sadness in her eyes.

'Did you ever meet her son, Owen?'

'I don't call *him* a son.' Imelda's mouth turned down. 'All the years I work here, he never even sent a birthday card, a Christmas card. She didn't like to talk about him – I could tell he had broken her heart.'

'Did Geraldine ever mention him visiting? Especially just before her death?'

'No.' Imelda frowned to herself. 'But a few weeks before she passed away, she did say that I should never let *anyone* in the house when she wasn't here,' her eyes widening on the 'anyone'.

'You think she meant Owen.'

A nod.

A card for a local locksmith propped on the kitchen work-top told Flyte that Geraldine might have been anxious about security, but since the locks on back and front doors were decades old she clearly hadn't got round to having new ones fitted before she died. And Imelda didn't know whether Owen had a spare set.

On the first floor, Imelda stopped at the bathroom door and shook her head. 'I'm sorry. I haven't been inside since it happened.'

'I do understand how difficult it must be, I really do.' Flyte held the older woman's gaze. 'But you might remember something that you missed that first time, when you were upset at finding Geraldine. Something important.'

Bracing her shoulders, Imelda pushed open the door.

The steep-sided Victorian-style bath was perfectly designed to drown in, if Geraldine Edwards really had just blacked out. 'When you found her, Imelda, was she completely submerged?'

Imelda nodded wordlessly, lips pursed against tears, one fist pressed to her chest.

'And the report said there was a bottle of whisky and an empty glass . . . here?' Flyte indicated a table within easy reach of the bath.

Imelda looked away, probably embarrassed by her employer drinking spirits while taking a bath, then nodded. 'I remember the detective picking them up to smell inside.' She mimed his actions.

'And what happened to them?'

'I washed up the glass and put the bottle in the recycling.'

Flyte tried not to show her irritation: both items should have been preserved as evidence in case the death became suspicious;

now there was no chance to fingerprint them or test their contents. 'Is everything else as you found it that night?' She looked around the bathroom, inviting Imelda to share her survey.

'Yes, I think so. Apart from the sandwich.'

'Sandwich?'

'Yes, it was right here, next to the glass – a cheese sandwich. I cleared it up after they took her away – I didn't want rats running round in poor Geraldine's house.'

'Don't worry, it's fine, you did the right thing.' Flyte managed a smile but inside she was raging at Sloman: first a disappearing glass and bottle, and now a missing sandwich.

Crouching to examine the bathmat – which smelled of damp – she asked, 'Did you happen to notice whether the bathmat was wet when you found her?'

Imelda's eyes narrowed as she tried to remember. 'When I came in, I rushed over and kneeled down, to try to lift her poor head above the water . . .' Her face quivered for a moment before she was able to go on. She shook her head. 'I think I would have noticed if the mat was wet.'

Which suggested it had got soaked during the removal of the body rather than during a life-and-death struggle. 'You told my colleague that Geraldine telephoned you at about ten the night before you found her. What did she call about?'

'Nothing important. Only to ask me to bring some bleach in the morning.'

'Could you try to remember exactly what was said?'

Imelda scrunched her eyes half-shut. 'She said she was sorry to call so late. She had forgotten to buy bleach at the supermarket and asked would I be kind enough to pick some up on the way – she was always a very polite lady. Then she said she thought she might be coming down with a cold. She had the shivers and was going to run a nice hot bath to get warm before going to bed.'

Flyte detected a return of the uneasiness Imelda had shown over the whisky. 'How did she sound to you?'

'I thought she sounded ... tired.' Imelda turned away, ostensibly to pick up a towel from the rail.

'Imelda. Did she really just sound "tired" ... or something else?'

'Well ... she liked to have a nightcap.' Imelda lifted her chin defensively. 'But I don't want you thinking she was ... a drinker.'

Imelda's protectiveness towards her dead employer touched and exasperated Flyte. It sounded as though Geraldine Edwards was halfway to hammered by the time she climbed in the bath, which made the pathologist's verdict of death by accidental drowning all the more plausible.

Flyte opened the bathroom cabinet and peered inside. Female toiletries crowded the bottom shelf, but the upper shelf stood empty.

'Is this how it always looked? The upper shelf left empty like this?'

Imelda gaze slid away 'I'm not sure ...' but the colour blooming in her cheeks said otherwise.

'You've remembered something,' said Flyte, regarding her steadily.

'Mrs Edwards, she was a very private lady ... ' Imelda's hand went to the crucifix hanging round her neck.

'Imelda, privacy doesn't matter to the dead. I need to make sure that we haven't missed anything suspicious about Geraldine's death. You obviously cared about her, so I know you would want that, too.'

A pause. 'I did see some . . . man's things in there once. A razor, some shaving foam . . . But last time I looked, a couple of months ago, they were gone.'

'OK, so Geraldine had a boyfriend. Do you know how they met? Did she ever mention him?'

'No! This is not the sort of thing we would ever talk about.' Imelda's eyes had widened; she evidently found the idea of a middle-aged woman having a sex life deeply uncomfortable.

'I understand. Did you get the impression he stayed over often? Did he keep any clothes here, for instance?'

'No. I did find a man's handkerchief once.'

'Imelda, did you tell the other detective about this boyfriend, or ex-boyfriend?'

Imelda didn't need to answer. Her expression said it all: she had kept the scandalous business of Geraldine Edwards' paramour a secret.

Did Cassie Raven know about him, too? *Probably.* A realisation that upset Flyte more than she would have expected.

'One last thing. I assume Geraldine owned a computer but I haven't seen one.'

She shrugged. 'Perhaps her son took it away?'

'Maybe. Has anything else disappeared?'

Imelda shook her head. 'Nothing. Except for a photograph.'

'What photograph?'

'Geraldine when she was very young, with her baby. It was on the wall by the bed. But today – pouff! – it has disappeared.'

Chapter Thirty-Four

'Owen says he's only expecting half a dozen guests,' said Luca. 'He said a small family funeral was "what she would have wanted".'

'The bastard!' Cassie burst out. 'She was a teacher, for Christ's sake! She taught hundreds of people, and I know she'd have wanted them there.'

Just after Cassie got in to the mortuary, Luca had called to tell her the final details of Mrs E's funeral, which was scheduled for four o'clock on Wednesday – just two days away – at Golders Green crematorium.

She tried to focus on work, but couldn't stop looking at the clock, seeing the relentless sweep of the second hand, knowing that in forty-eight hours' time Mrs E's body would have been reduced to a few handfuls of ash and bone.

Was Phyllida Flyte sticking to her promise? Or had she been wrong to trust her?

For the first time ever, Cassie was finding work a chore rather than a privilege – she had barely exchanged a word with the poor locum who'd turned up to cover for Carl after he'd called in sick. She kept picturing him on his motorbike, racing down a motorway on his way to exile somewhere in the sticks. Every step of the mortuary routine was a bitter reminder of all the laughs the two of them had shared, their moans about the bureaucracy, their daft in-jokes . . . memories that his betrayal had contaminated forever.

Deborah's voice came through on the speakerphone from the office to say that DS Flyte was on the phone.

'Did you know Geraldine Edwards had a boyfriend?' she snapped, without preamble.

'*Ex*-boyfriend. Ex-fiancé, actually.'

'And might I ask why you didn't share this information?' – her words clipped and icy.

'Uh . . . because they split up ages ago?'

'That's irrelevant. He should have been questioned.'

'Why?'

Flyte made an exasperated sound. 'In any unexplained death, it's standard practice to question the spouse or lover.'

'It's *Owen* you should be questioning,' Cassie protested. 'Christian went to bits when he heard about Mrs E's death.'

There was a frigid pause. 'Are you telling me you've *met* this man?'

Oops.

'Yes. And after five years dealing with people who've lost a loved one, I know when someone is genuinely hurting.'

'Really. And how many murderers have you interrogated?' Flyte's words came down the line like bullets.

'Look, I'm telling you, *he didn't know* Mrs E was dead.' Cassie got a flash-frame image of the blood draining from Christian's face. 'He practically passed out when I told him. I'm telling you, there's no way he was faking it.'

'Your faith in your powers of intuition is highly reassuring.'

Flyte's sarcasm tipped Cassie over the edge. 'Why aren't you chasing Owen? He's the one who stands to make millions out of his mother's death. And the funeral's the day after tomorrow!'

'I'm afraid you'll have to leave the conduct of the investigation to me,' said Flyte. 'But right now, I want the contact details for this Christian guy and everything you know about their relationship.'

The silence lasted so long it grew scar tissue.

'Look, Cassie.' Making what sounded like a monumental effort, Flyte softened her tone. 'If you want me to review this case properly, then you have to help me.'

Cassie knew she had no alternative: if she didn't tell Flyte what she wanted to know, she would simply drop the case.

Ten minutes later she hung up, with an unwelcome sight looming in the glass of the door: the floppy fringe of that smugtard Archie Cuff, above – what else? – a navy blue Barbour jacket. She thought with a pang of the look she and Carl would be exchanging right now.

'Good morning, Cassie.'

'Hi,' she muttered, before turning her back on him. A moment later she glanced back and found him still standing there like an idiot.

'I wanted to apologise,' he said, clearing his throat. 'The other day, when I couldn't find a cause of death on that RTA. The young guy with the C-spine fracture?'

She nodded, remembering Cuff's failure to identify the broken neck that killed Jordan the boy racer, until she'd put him out of his misery.

'I just wanted to say that it was . . . arrogant of me not to ask you. Our profs always tell us how important it is to ask the technician's opinion. I'm totally aware that you people know your stuff . . .'

You people . . . ? She wished Carl was here for this.

' . . . I mean, you've seen hundreds – if not thousands – more bodies than me, and assisted at countless PMs. You were right about that anaphylactic shock case, after all. And Professor Arculus speaks very highly of you. In fact, he told me you're *primus inter pares*. Which means—'

'First among equals.'

The expression on Cuff's face reminded her of a Polish saying her grandmother was fond of: *'like a dog who's been shown a card trick'*.

'I picked up a bit of Latin doing classics A level,' she explained, before folding her arms. 'OK, so why didn't you? Ask me my opinion?'

He gaped at her – this probably wasn't in the 'apology script' he'd been taught at Harrow.

He ran a hand through his ginger mop, grimacing at the ceiling. 'I suppose because this is my first time working in a mortuary. And if I'm being honest . . . I'm probably feeling a bit out of my depth?'

Wow. Quite an admission from a master of the universe.

'Apology accepted,' she said, turning to get back to work.

'Hang on.' Rummaging in his bag, he produced a bottle of Chopin, her favourite – wildly expensive – Polish vodka. 'Peace offering. I asked Douglas what your poison was.'

As she took the bottle, he beamed at her – and she couldn't help but return the smile. Maybe she'd got it wrong about Archie Cuff.

233

For the next couple of hours they worked amicably together through the PM list, even exchanging the odd joke.

After Cuff left, Cassie replayed her conversation with Flyte. Had she been wrong to keep schtum about Christian? She suddenly felt unsure of her instincts. After all, hadn't she been hasty in dismissing Cuff as just another arrogant hooray, while being prepared to trust Carl with her life?

She decided to call Christian. He was, after all, entitled to know the details of his former fiancée's funeral.

He picked up on the second ring. 'I'm so glad you called. Is there any chance we could meet up for a drink, or a coffee this evening? Hearing about Geraldine was a terrible shock, but being able to talk to someone who was close to her – well, it was a great help.'

Cassie agreed. Seeing Mrs E's ex again face to face would help her to decide whether her instincts about him had been seriously awry.

As she left later that day, she passed the squad car that was posted outside the mortuary 24/7 now, and caught herself exchanging smiles with the two cops inside. It was the first time she could recall the sight of a police uniform making her feel reassured rather than nervous.

As she headed for home, that feeling of security drained away, replaced by a neck-pricking sensation that someone was watching her. Remembering the words '*BEING FOLLOWED*' on Mrs E's bathroom mirror, she threw a casual look over her shoulder to scan the street behind, but could only see a well-dressed woman wearing sunglasses who was focused on her phone, and a middle-aged guy walking his dog. Ducking into a housing estate that had a labyrinthine layout she knew backwards, she threw a couple of sharp turns, finally emerging on a back street that would take her towards her flat.

She knew it was probably just an attack of paranoia after the break-in, but after dousing a couple of gangstas in formalin it was best not to take any chances.

FLYTE

Flyte knew that finding anything that might properly be called a lead – and ideally before the body was cremated in two days' time – was an impossibly tall order.

Cassie Raven hadn't made things any easier: deciding Geraldine's ex wasn't a suspect, on a personal whim! But then, if she weren't so pig-headed, Flyte wouldn't be revisiting a death that might well have been written off as accidental too swiftly.

She remembered a few days ago, overhearing one of the DCs describe her in mocking tones as the department's 'queen of lost causes' for her reluctance to let the Harry Hardwick case drop. She was upset, at first, to hear what her new colleagues thought of her, but that soon gave way to a perverse feeling of pride in her own single-mindedness. Maybe she and Cassie Raven did have something in common after all.

Investigating Geraldine Edwards' death had made her realise something else: she missed working murder cases. Her CID work tended to fall into two categories: the pointless – witness the wasted hours she'd spent at hospital bedsides trying to persuade teenage gang members to name who'd stabbed them; and the tedious – in ten weeks she must have taken two dozen statements from victims of credit card fraud.

After leaving a voicemail on Christian Maclaren's mobile asking him to call her, she ran an online search. His website featured photos of his architectural commissions – mostly featureless high-rise office blocks in eastern Europe – and he also had a LinkedIn profile, which meshed with Cassie's description of him. But Flyte wanted more background before interviewing him.

After checking out the Facebook profile of Geraldine's best friend and fellow teacher Maddy O'Hare, she called the number Cassie had given her, saying that she had a few questions before closing the case file on the death. Maddy confirmed 'Geri's' troubled relationship with Owen and without much coaxing, repeated what Cassie had mentioned: that her friend had appeared to be scared of something – or someone – not long before she died.

'What can you tell me about this dating site you both signed up to, where Geraldine first met Christian?'

'Ocean? Well, I can tell you they weren't cheap!' said Maddy. 'Geri called them "reassuringly expensive". But they seemed very professional.'

'What was their security like? Did they run any identity checks?'

'Yes. I was surprised how thoroughly they checked us out. It was all a bit of a pain actually . . .'

Ocean didn't sound like the kind of flaky, low-rent site that would be vulnerable to dating fraud, but you never knew.

'One last thing,' Flyte asked. 'Geraldine didn't own a smartphone, and I couldn't find a computer at the house, so how did she go online?'

'Geraldine definitely had a laptop because I gave her my old one. It was practically steam-powered, but it did the job."

At Ocean, she was put through to the managing director's PA, who sounded keen to help – until Flyte asked for Maclaren's membership history and profile details. The girl refused point blank to release anything without the authority of the managing director, Lucy Halliwell, who was 'in a meeting'.

Forseeing days of phone and email ping-pong – time she didn't have – Flyte decided to turn up and doorstep this Halliwell woman: the sight of a police warrant card could be a powerful persuader.

Ocean occupied the ground floor of a sixties office block just off the north end of Tottenham Court Road. Within minutes of arriving, Flyte was installed in a conference room with a coffee. She didn't have to wait long before Lucy Halliwell came in, finishing up a call on her mobile. An attractive woman in her forties, she wore immaculate wide-legged black trousers and a short-sleeved teal jumper with a pricy-looking, complicated chunk of metal round her neck: the kind of dressed-down look that cost a fortune to pull off.

'I'm so sorry about that,' she said, after hanging up. 'I hope you've been looked after?' Well-spoken, she radiated an air of untroubled command.

'I'm investigating the sudden death of one of your members.'

'I'm very sorry to hear that.' Her eyebrows tried, and failed, to arch regretfully – Botox, probably.

'She met a man through your dating site, so I am keen to discover what security procedures your applicants go through.'

'We prefer to call ourselves a premium relationship service,' Halliwell corrected her gently. 'In-depth vetting is the core element of what we offer. Everyone who applies must provide a bank account reference and agree to undergo identity checks, including their occupation.'

'Surely a really determined fraudster could find a way round the checks?'

Halliwell gave a little smiling shake of her head. 'Our systems are designed to guarantee that our members know precisely to whom they are talking.'

'Is it fair to say that your target market is middle-aged professional people?'

Halliwell gave an affirmative tip of her glossy head.

'That must make them an attractive target for online scammers,' Flyte suggested. 'Young people don't usually have anything to steal.'

'I think you'll find the reason people choose us is precisely because they're aware of that risk and wish to mitigate it.'

Flyte had noticed that the veneer of the boardroom table was splitting at the edges, the room's once fashionable wallpaper lifting here and there at the seams. In-depth security didn't come cheap, and companies were always looking for ways to shave outgoings. Were Halliwell's claims just corporate waffle?

'Out of interest, how many applicants do you reject?' she asked.

A flicker of annoyance ruffled Halliwell's unnaturally smooth forehead. 'Not a huge number, but that's precisely because our security protocols deter fraudsters.'

Breaking through Halliwell's smug corporate schtick was like trying to crack toughened glass with a plastic spoon. Flyte flipped open her notebook. 'I need details of your former member Christian Maclaren. And his online communications with anyone on the site.'

'You're aware, I'm sure, that all such information is covered by data protection legislation,' said Halliwell, with a sorrowful smile. 'We would require an official application for access.'

Flyte held her gaze. 'And I'm sure you're aware that we would have no trouble securing the necessary order, should we be forced to go down that route.'

Halliwell tapped a glossy nail on the tabletop, her eyes never leaving Flyte's. 'You're saying that this Maclaren is a suspect in your investigation?'

Flyte hesitated. 'It's one line of enquiry.'

Halliwell's fractionally raised eyebrow said she didn't buy it.

Flyte cursed inwardly: with Geraldine Edwards' funeral looming, she didn't want to waste time making an application under the Regulation of Investigatory Powers Act. Leaning forward, she adopted a confidential tone. 'Dating frauds attract a lot of media interest. If we were to discover that a fraudster had found a loophole in your systems . . . well, it would be good to be able to say that we had your full cooperation from the outset.' Flyte felt her pulse quicken: veiled threats weren't usually her style.

The tip of Halliwell's tongue made a brief appearance between nude-coloured lips. 'I have complete confidence in the integrity of our security protocols,' she said. 'But . . . as a company, we have a duty to treat any request by law enforcement agencies with the utmost seriousness.'

Flyte had to clench her jaw to keep from smiling.

Lucy Halliwell led Flyte down a shabby flight of stairs and into a low-ceilinged basement office lit by fluorescent strip lights.

Prints of old movie posters lined the walls in an attempt to hide the spots where damp had bubbled the paintwork.

'This is where we hide the IT department,' Halliwell murmured, a hint of apology in her voice. Old drives and screens lay piled on the floor alongside overflowing cardboard boxes, and cacaphonous rock music blasted out of a portable speaker.

'Dan's our information analyst,' said Lucy, heading towards a young bearded man, intently focused on his computer. As he moved his mouse with practised nonchalance to shut something down, Flyte wondered what he'd been viewing – Facebook? Or Pornhub? 'Dan, where's Beth?'

'Oh hi, Lucy,' he said, with an insincere smile. 'She's in the cubbyhole,' indicating a nearby doorway.

Inside the tiny office, a woman in her late thirties, at a guess, sat at a computer workstation. On the wall above was tacked another film poster: Audrey Hepburn and Gregory Peck perched on a Vespa. *Roman Holiday.*

'Beth is in charge of membership services,' said Halliwell. 'Could you help DS Flyte with some information? Within the parameters we discussed on the phone.' The meaningful look she sent her underling didn't escape Flyte.

'Of course, Lucy. I'd be happy to' – Beth's cautious expression suggesting that Halliwell was the kind of boss who would need constant appeasing.

After Lucy had gone, Flyte drew up a chair. 'Have you worked here long?'

'Um . . . about eight months?' Beth looked bemused to find a cop sitting in her workspace.

'The office is a bit of dump, isn't it?' murmured Flyte, trying to put her at ease.

241

A smile crept across Beth's face. 'A makeover would be nice, but apparently we're not a "customer facing" part of the business.'

'And how is business?' Keeping her tone light.

'It's OK, I guess.' Beth used both hands to push her dark shoulder-length hair behind her ears, one pierced on the outer curve. 'Considering there's a new dating site coming online practically every week.' Her style was what Camden types called grunge, and Flyte called unkempt.

She saw a corkboard pinned with wedding photos – a dozen or more couples, all in various stages of middle age, beamed from the steps of churches and register offices. 'It must be a nice feeling, when it works out.'

Beth nodded, smiling. 'It's the best thing about the job. Seeing people who belong together find each other.'

'I'd already guessed that you're a confirmed romantic,' Flyte nodded up at the film poster of Hepburn and Peck.

'I adore that movie.' Beth pressed a hand to her heart like a lovesick teenager. 'Those two were made to be together, but the world wouldn't allow it.'

Slightly taken aback to see Beth's eyes glistening, Flyte refrained from pointing out that the characters' love affair was founded on a deception – Hepburn the innocent princess posing as a tourist, Peck the unscrupulous journalist playing along in search of a scoop. You might even call it an early case of catfishing, she reflected, if Peck's character hadn't gone on to redeem himself in the final scene.

'OK, so here's the personal profile of the guy you're interested in,' said Beth, angling the screen towards Flyte. 'This is what other members would have seen while he was with us.'

Maclaren's profile described him as a forty-five-year-old architect with his own practice, never married, no kids, and gave his hobbies as art, travel, film and theatre, and outdoor pursuits. His photos were unremarkable – except for one, which showed Maclaren at the tiller of a sailing boat, looking handsome and purposeful. He wore a cable knit jumper and what looked like a grand's worth of watch on his wrist: a glamorous shot guaranteed to get plenty of favourites on a dating site.

Beth agreed to mail over his profile and accompanying pics, but when Flyte tried her luck by asking to see his bank reference, the shutters came down.

'I'm really sorry, but Lucy said . . .' Beth's swivel chair squeaked as she shifted position, clearly embarrassed.

'I know, no confidential member information,' Flyte smiled to show she didn't hold it against her. 'Anything else you can tell me?'

Beth brought up another page. 'It looks like he joined in March, and cancelled his membership in June, if that's any help?'

'Did he have contact with anyone other than Geraldine Edwards?' chancing her arm again.

Beth's gaze flickered towards the open door. Following her look, Flyte saw her colleague Dan sitting in Beth's line of sight. At first glance, he seemed focused on his computer, but Flyte could see that although he was wearing headphones, the side facing them wasn't quite covering his ear.

Flyte gave a pantomime shiver. 'Do you mind if I . . . ?' before standing to close the door. 'I hate draughts. We were discussing Maclaren's other contacts?'

Beth dropped her voice. 'He only made that single contact, with Geraldine Edwards.'

Fishcakes. It was hardly the MO of a dating fraudster.

'Is any of this helping at all?' Beth asked.

'To be honest? Not really.'

Beth glanced at the door and spoke in a murmur. 'This Maclaren guy, he hasn't . . . done anything terrible has he?'

Flyte met her gaze. 'I don't know yet, Beth. It's possible.' Maclaren hadn't returned her call yet, but perhaps he was travelling.

Beth fiddled with a lock of her hair. 'Because if I thought a woman had been hurt because of anything we did, or failed to do . . .'

The phone on the desk rang, and with an apologetic smile she picked up.

During the brief exchange that followed, Flyte noted the extension number on the handset. After hanging up, Beth grimaced an apology. 'That was Lucy, saying we should be done by now?'

Flyte smiled to conceal a wince at Beth's upward intonation.

'No problem. I appreciate all your help.' Getting to her feet she put her card on Beth's keyboard. 'In case you should ever want to contact me, in confidence.'

She left her looking down at the card, playing with her hair.

Chapter Thirty-Five

That evening, presenting herself at the luxe reception of the trendy Shoreditch club where Christian had suggested they meet, Cassie felt out of place: not, for once, because of her piercings, but because she'd had to come straight from work in jeans and a T-shirt.

After being directed up a glass staircase to the mezzanine level, Cassie's feelings of discomfort intensified as she passed a woman coming down. Wearing shades and stylishly dressed from her velvet beanie down to her plum patent leather Doc Martens, the woman's brief sideways glance made Cassie feel as if she'd been judged and found sartorially wanting.

'You're early!' said Christian, getting up to greet her.

'Sorry, I managed to get away quicker than I thought.'

'Don't apologise – it's lovely to see you.'

He was still smartly turned out, but she was shocked to see how haggard he looked compared with the last time they'd met. A half-full highball glass stood in front of him, and in the place opposite, another, empty but for a slice of lemon. 'I hope I haven't interrupted anything?' asked Cassie.

'No, no. Just a tedious business meeting, all over now.'

'This is a great place,' she said after the waiter had taken her order, taking in the cavernous brick interior, low-lit by a thousand tiny bulbs hanging in clusters from above. 'It's an old church, right?'

'Yes. We used to come here, Geraldine and I.' A smile haunted his lips. 'She called it her "sod the inheritance" indulgence.'

The perfect opening to explore her theory that Mrs E might have had a love child before she was married. 'Did Geraldine intend to leave all her money to Owen, do you know?'

'I always assumed so. Not that we ever discussed dying.' He blew out a breath. 'Why would we? She should have had another thirty years, or more.' He turned his glass on its paper coaster. 'Why do you ask?'

'I just wondered if she ever said anything about another child – a girl? Born before Owen came along?'

He looked blank. 'She never mentioned it to me.' He wasn't wearing glasses today, which made him look more . . . vulnerable. His expression reminded her of Maurice, the elderly gent who'd come to view his dead wife the night of the break-in – befuddled, not quite there.

'I'm so sorry to probe. It must have been tough for you, finding out about Geraldine's death the way you did.'

He nodded slowly. 'You've probably worked out that I hadn't really got over her. If I'm honest, I suppose I still thought . . . hoped . . . that we might get back together.' He pinched his lower lip so hard Cassie saw it whiten. 'The hardest thing is the thought that if we'd stayed together, she might still be alive. That . . . that I might have been able to prevent her death.'

He said it as if he really believed he could have saved her. It was a kind of magical thinking that Cassie often saw in the newly bereaved.

'"Life's but a walking shadow",' he said to himself.

'Shakespeare?'

'Yes, *Macbeth*.' Christian's way of speaking might have suggested private schooling and yet Cassie detected the hint of something overly careful about the way he enunciated certain words that suggested his current accent might not be the one he'd been raised with.

'Where did you grow up?' Seeing his startled look, she added, 'I'm sorry, I shouldn't be so nosy.'

'No, no, that's fine.' Smiling, he raised a hand. 'I was born the wrong side of the river, in Brixton. Long before the hipsters moved in.'

'Do your parents still live there?'

He sipped his drink. 'I never knew my father, and my mother died when I was thirteen – she was an alcoholic.'

'I'm so sorry. Do you have any brothers or sisters?'

'A sister.' He frowned into his drink.

'You're not close?'

'We used to be . . . very close.' A fond look crept over his face. 'We were both taken into care, as it's laughingly called, when I was nine. They kept placing us in separate foster homes, but we always ran away to find each other, so in the end they let us stay in the children's home. I loved having a little sister.'

'But not any more?'

'We . . . fell out.' His expression signalled a mix of emotions – his obvious affection battling with exasperation, or even anger.

'Family is forever though, isn't it?' Cassie hated to think of him enduring his grief alone. 'I'm an only child and I'd give anything to have a sister, or a brother.'

Taking a cocktail stick, Christian started to pass it between his index and middle fingers, twirling it in a fluid movement, apparently unconsciously. It was a trick Cassie had spent hours trying to learn off a mate in the back of her year eight maths class – without success.

'I haven't been able to stop thinking about Geraldine's death since you told me – especially your doubts about it,' he said eventually. 'I couldn't bear . . . it would be far worse if it were more than just a terrible accident.' His voice fell to a horrified whisper. 'The idea that somebody might have *killed* her.'

She touched his arm, feeling guilt at his tortured expression.

'Look, Christian. There's not a speck of evidence to suggest that.'

'But you clearly have your suspicions. Do you think the police investigated it properly?'

So Flyte hadn't been in touch yet. Should she forewarn him? Cassie was torn: although they barely knew each other, the bond of grief that they shared over Mrs E had made her feel close to him. And siding with a cop didn't come easily. But having pushed Flyte into investigating Mrs E's death, it just didn't feel right to interfere in her process.

'What about her blood tests? Did they find anything . . . untoward?' he went on.

'No, nothing.'

He dropped his gaze but Cassie wondered whether she'd caught something in his eyes – a flicker of relief?

'Geraldine never . . . did drugs, did she, as far as you know?

'Good God no!' His amusement seemed genuine. 'Not unless you count a good Scotch and the occasional sneaky cigarette.'

'Listen, Christian, there are dozens of accidental deaths every day. I'm probably just over-thinking it, looking for a reason . . .'

She stopped, trying to find the words. 'Because I can't face the fact I'll never see her again.'

Cassie saw competing emotions fighting it out on Christian's face: fear that someone had murdered the woman he'd loved versus the hope that the death really had been a freak accident. For the moment, hope seemed to have won.

Back on the Northern line, heading home, Cassie went over the meeting in her head, trying to analyse it the way Professor Arculus would a body. But she found nothing to shake her conviction that Christian was a man struggling with genuine grief – and shock – over the death of his ex-fiancée. The only mildly puzzling moment had been his question about her toxicology results.

Maybe Christian was fretting that Mrs E had taken an overdose, worried that after they split up, and with teaching no longer in her life, she might have fallen into a depressive spiral?

The idea that Mrs E might have committed suicide was almost worse than the fear she'd been murdered. To think of her suffering alone after Cassie had lost touch with her would be unbearable. But thinking it through rationally, she felt reassured: the standard toxicology screen tested for more than three hundred substances, which covered every drug a normal person could realistically have laid hands on.

Chapter Thirty-Six

The next morning Cassie was on her way into work, head down against the chill slanting drizzle and lost in thoughts of Mrs E's funeral when she almost walked straight into him. A big balding man who loomed out of the shadow of a railway bridge; a man whose outline she recognised immediately.

'It was you, wasn't it, who splashed my mother's funeral all over Facebook?' Owen swayed a little on the balls of his feet.

In fact it was Maddy who'd posted the details of the funeral due to be held the following afternoon. But Cassie realised she'd probably been tagged – allowing Owen to identify her as the girl from the mortuary.

'I knew there was something fun-ny about you from day one.' Owen pushed his face into hers, bringing with it a sickly gust of alcohol – he must have enjoyed a liquid breakfast. 'Then the undertakers say they're not picking up the body till today. And now I've got the police calling me with a load of questions.' He stabbed a finger in her face, stopping just short of touching her. 'I'm not an id-i-ot. I know you've been stirring up trouble, see?'

The air of suppressed violence he gave off made Cassie's skin prickle. 'Aren't you pleased that so many people want to come and pay their last respects to your mother?' she asked, sounding calmer than she felt.

'What's it got to do with you? You were just one of her bloody *students*.' She felt a fleck of spittle land on her eyelid. 'She never had any time for her only son – oh, no, but she loved her *students*.'

'And we loved her – with good reason,' she snapped. 'She deserved to be loved.'

'Oh, she was *loved* all right,' his face gargoyling. 'Dis-gusting. A woman her age.'

Cassie experienced a spurt of pure rage. 'If you mean Christian, then I'm glad she found somebody. Why couldn't you have been happy for her?'

He loomed towards her and she braced herself for a blow but instead he subsided, angry jowls drooping. 'Why didn't she love me?' he asked plaintively – as if Cassie might know the answer. 'She never did. I was never good enough, never clever enough.'

Cassie scanned his drunken, self-pitying expression. It was true that Mrs E hadn't suffered fools gladly. Might she have been a less than sympathetic mother when her son failed to meet her high standards?

She sought his eyes. 'When you've just lost someone, feelings can be very raw. It's easy for things to become exaggerated. I'm sure she did love you.'

He looked down at her, as if he'd forgotten she was there.

'You listen to me,' he said, in a voice soft with menace. 'You're sticking your nose into things you don't understa—' He stopped, eyes narrowed, and looked her up and down assessingly. 'I saw you sniffing around my mother's house the day I got down here!' A nasty smile spread over his face as if something else had just dawned on him. 'And that was you who was inside her house the other day, wasn't it?' he crowed. 'I thought I'd seen a strange mobile phone but when I went back to look for it it had vanished.'

251

Cassie shook her head. 'I don't know what you're talking about' – but she could feel her face going bright red as she pictured herself retrieving the phone from the bed.

Owen seemed to relax, his body language radiating triumph. 'That's why the back door was open – the cleaner swore she'd left it locked.' He jabbed a fat finger inches from her face. 'You look here now. You keep your sticky beak out of my business from now on, see? Or I'll tell the police you broke in and get them to fingerprint the place.'

'I think you've got me confused with somebody else,' said Cassie, starting to back away.

Turning, she walked off as fast as she could without breaking into a jog.

He didn't move to follow her, but called out, 'If you dare turn up at the funeral tomorrow, I'll have you physically ejected!'

She scurried down the lane to the mortuary, her heart pummelling her sternum. Once inside, she pulled up Flyte's number on her phone, still breathing hard.

Her thumb hovered over the call button. Flyte needed to know what just happened with Owen, what kind of a man he was. But she realised he'd been careful not to lay a finger on her, nor threaten violence. And anyway, he held all the cards now: if he did report a break-in at Patna Road, the cops would find her fresh fingerprints all over Mrs E's bedroom. Fingerprints that were already on the database from her arrest for possession when she was seventeen. A breaking and entering charge wouldn't just mean the end of her career; it could derail Flyte's investigation of Mrs E's death, destroying the last chance to save her body from cremation.

FLYTE

Flyte had about as much time for 'gut feelings' as she had for horoscopes: instinct was no substitute for evidence, a motive – and a suspect. She hadn't given up on the Geraldine Edwards case, even if the body – the only piece of potential evidence – was about to go up in flames tomorrow. The cremation itself wouldn't end the investigation, but if she didn't get somewhere fast she'd soon have DI Bellwether breathing down her neck.

She pushed open the door to interview room four.

Getting to his feet, Owen Edwards put out his hand, leaving her no choice but to take it. 'It's a pleasure to meet you, Detective Sergeant.'

Fighting the urge to wipe her palm on her trousers, she sat down opposite him.

'Is this going to take long?' he asked, an ingratiating smile fattening his thread-veined cheeks. 'I've got a mountain of things to attend to for tomorrow's funeral, as you can imagine.'

Did she detect anxiety in his expression as he said this – worrying, perhaps, that the funeral might be halted? She'd never been that good at picking up people's 'tells'; her successes had all been down to the logic and shoe leather approach to policing.

'Not too long, I hope, Mr Edwards. Just trying to tie everything up for the final report.'

253

'But we know there's nothing funny about her death?' His Welsh accent breaking the word in the middle: fun-ny.

'Nothing that we're aware of.'

'Because the coroner's office gave the go-ahead for the funeral after receiving the pathologist's report.'

'That's right.' She sent him a cool look. 'But since your mother's death was unexpected, we wouldn't want to leave any stone unturned, would we?' She leafed through her notes. 'The cleaning lady, Imelda, tells me that your mother had a personal computer, which has gone missing from the house.'

'I thought it was safer to take anything valuable out of there' – his smile starting to sag. 'You get druggies and all sorts moving into empty houses in London, don't you?'

The whiff of stale booze reached Flyte from across the table. 'And her mobile phone?'

'I . . . I threw it out. It was ancient.'

'I see. And where is the computer now?'

'Why do you ask?' With every question, Owen's expression had become less and less sycophantic.

'It might give us important information, such as who she was in contact with in the days preceding her death.' Or, indeed, whether the bad feeling between mother and son had got to the point where she had good reason to be frightened of him.

Owen's eyes darted around the room. 'I wiped the hard drive and took it to the dump.'

'So you changed your mind fairly swiftly about the value of these items.' She introduced a note of cold gravity to her tone. 'I must warn you that it is an offence to destroy anything that might give the coroner information of relevance to your mother's death before the inquest.'

Flyte knew that it was an empty threat: the inquest was largely a formality, only taking place because the post-mortem had found no definitive cause of death. Still, it didn't hurt to keep Owen on edge.

'I assume your mother left a will?'

'It's filed at the solicitors, all in order.'

'The estate agent says you're selling the house with a separate parcel of land.' She raised an eyebrow. 'That should fetch a significant price. Are you the sole beneficiary?'

'I am.' He jutted his chin out. 'Who else would she leave it to?'

There was a knock at the door and a uniformed officer put his head in. 'Sorry to disturb, Sarge. There's a message from someone you've been trying to get hold of.'

He handed her a slip of paper that said: *'Christian Maclaren called. He'd be pleased to meet you first thing tomorrow morning. He's left you a voicemail.'*

The message reminded Flyte of the gnomic text Cassie Raven had sent her just before the interview: *'Ask Owen Edwards how he felt about his mother having a sex life.'* Exasperatingly, she'd offered no explanation as to why this might be a fruitful line of questioning, but then Flyte had underestimated the girl's deductive powers before.

'Moving onto your mother's private life, Mr Edwards. How did you get on with her fiancé, Christian Maclaren?

'Ex-fiancé,' Owen snapped. His complexion, florid to begin with, took on a darker hue.

'Is it fair to say that you didn't like each other?'

'I hardly met the man!'

A politician's answer – as in, no answer at all. 'I hear that he had to escort you out of the house once, after you and your mother had a row?'

Owen's eyes slitted and for a split second she thought he might explode. 'That was just a . . . silly misunderstanding,' he blustered.

'What did you make of your mother having a lover?'

His face quivered with the effort of self-control. 'Middle-aged madness, I call it. Must have been her hormones having a final fling.'

His hands were so tightly bunched on the tabletop that the knuckles looked like ivory chess pieces. He certainly acted like a man with something to hide – but placing him at the scene, let alone finding enough evidence to build a murder case? That was a different matter.

'Just remind me for the record where you were on the night your mother died?'

'I was in Bristol for a conference, as I already told your boss.'

'Detective Sergeant Sloman is my colleague, actually,' she said, with a tight smile. 'Which hotel did you stay in?'

'Like I told him, I grabbed a few hours' sleep in the car. I thought it would save a few bob.'

An uncheckable alibi – how very convenient.

Their eyes locked. Flyte wondered how far she could push it, when he wasn't under caution and she had not an iota of evidence against him.

'Are we done here?' he asked.

'Yes, we're done,' she said, closing her notebook.

He got to his feet, unable to suppress a complacent smile.

She smiled back. 'For the time being.'

Chapter Thirty-Seven

Cassie did her job on automatic all morning, her eyes constantly cutting to the clock, its heartless hands eating through the hours. The undertakers would be coming by that evening to collect Mrs E's body in readiness for tomorrow's funeral.

By lunchtime she must have checked her phone thirty or forty times for a message from Flyte, but nothing. Finally, a text. With her usual charmless brevity it said simply, '*We need to meet*'.

At the coffee shop, she found Flyte installed at a corner table, her back to the room. Her blonde chignon was impeccable as ever, with not a single stray hair on the nape of her long, and undeniably lovely neck. Cassie suppressed a smile: maybe she literally never let her hair down.

Flyte nodded a cool greeting. 'I got you an espresso.'

'Oh brilliant. Thanks.' After their last encounter, when Flyte had bitten her head off for failing to mention Christian Maclaren's existence, Cassie was determined to be on her best behaviour.

But she'd barely sat down when Flyte silently pushed something across the table. A computer printout that Cassie instantly recognised as a record of the mortuary's old entry system, like the one that had made her a suspect in the theft of Harry Hardwick's body.

'I'd almost forgotten that I asked the security company for the mortuary entry records going back twelve months when this arrived,' she said coolly. 'Would you care to explain what you were doing there in the middle of the night at various times over the last seven months?'

Cassie felt her stomach swoop at the suspicious look she saw back in Flyte's eyes, but she managed a shrug. 'I already told you, I'm often on call and sometimes I have to go in during the night.'

'For *the whole night*?' Flyte pointed out lines that she had highlighted on the printout. 'There are three occasions when you started your shift during the daytime – and never went home.'

Cassie folded her arms. 'Everyone knows the old entry system was unreliable – that's why we got a new one.'

'Look, I'm sticking my neck out for you, looking into Geraldine Edwards' death!' Anger pinked Flyte's cheeks. 'I need to know that you're not involved in anything illegal!'

Their eyes met, and Cassie realised something: if she was going to keep Flyte on board she had to take a massive leap of faith.

She took a breath and blew it out. 'OK. You remember that crazy hot day we had back in April? A nine-year-old boy called Oliver was mucking around with his mates by the canal and jumped in for a dare. Anyway, he got into trouble and drowned. His body had to be recovered by divers. I was on duty when his mum Natalie came in to view him.' She felt her face clench at the memory. 'Single mum, no dad around – Oliver was her only child.'

'Go on,' said Flyte her voice just above a whisper.

'She sat with him the whole afternoon and well into the evening. Later on, her best friend came to join her. By ten o'clock, we were both trying to persuade her to go home and get some sleep, come back in the morning. But she just couldn't bring herself to leave.'

She shot a look at Flyte, who was staring into her coffee cup.

'Anyway, eventually it all came out. Oliver had always been scared of the dark and she couldn't bear the thought of him lying alone inside the drawer of the body store.'

Flyte gave an involuntary gasp.

'Yeah, it was pretty upsetting,' said Cassie, eyeing her stricken expression – surprised again by how thin-skinned she was for a cop. Then she suddenly recognised the look: Phyllida Flyte had experienced devastating grief – and had barely begun to deal with it. *Frozen at the denial stage.*

'So. You . . . you offered to stay with him.'

'I told Natalie I'd kip down on the floor of the viewing suite to look after him until the undertakers came in the morning.' Cassie shrugged. 'After that, whenever we had a child in the mortuary overnight, it became sort of a routine to spend the night there with them.' Rather than share the truth about these nights with Rachel she'd always spun her the line that she'd got drunk with Carl and fallen asleep on his couch.

'So it was like a vigil.'

Cassie nodded, unable to read Flyte's expression as she picked up the printout and put it back in her bag.

'So . . . you're not going to tell my boss?' asked Cassie.

'Of course not. It's hardly a police matter.' Flyte gave her the kind of reassuring look you might give a friend.

Cassie realised that something in the atmosphere between them had changed.

Flyte tore open a packet of sweetener, the candy pink matching the colour of her perfectly oval, lacquered nails, and poured it into her coffee. 'Did you get the photographs I sent you earlier?'

'Uh, no? Sorry, I'm rubbish at checking my email.' Cassie scrabbled in her bag for her phone.

'Here.' Flyte tapped at her own phone screen before passing it over. 'Just for the record, is this the Christian Maclaren you met?'

Cassie swiped through the gallery of photos and shrugged. 'Yes, that's him. But what about Owen – have you interviewed him? What did you make of him?'

'There's no evidence to suggest that Owen had any role in his mother's death' – a tetchy edge back in her voice.

But Cassie detected frustration at her own lack of progress.

'Evidence or not, you don't trust him, do you?'

Flyte huffed a bit, before admitting, 'I don't *like* him, but thinking someone's a creep doesn't carry a great deal of weight with the Crown Prosecution Service.'

'There's something else you should know.' Deciding to take another risk, Cassie reported an edited version of how Owen had ambushed her that morning.

Flyte sat up straight. 'Did he touch you or threaten you in any way?'

'No. But he did say something weird. That I was "sticking my nose in things I didn't understand".'

'Any idea what he might mean by that?'

Cassie shook her head.

'Could he simply have been referring to the difficult relationship with his mother?' Flyte pressed.

'I don't know.'

Seeing the look of resignation return to Flyte's face, Cassie was gripped by the fear that she was about to jack it all in. 'There must be *something* we can do.'

'I tried, Cassie, really I did.' Flyte folded her paper napkin. 'I'm sorry. But I've got a pile of other stuff in my in-tray.'

Cassie recalled her break-in at Patna Road – and what she'd found stuck in Mrs E's printer – the record of a marriage, a couple of years back, between the mysterious Barry Dennis Renwick and Julia Geraldine Torrance.

'Listen. What if Mrs E had given birth to another child before she was married and had been forced to give her up for adoption?' she said. 'If she'd started looking for her lost child, trying to make contact, Owen might have freaked out? Maybe he would be worried that she was about to change her will and he'd lose out.'

Flyte looked mildly amused. 'And you have evidence, I presume, for this plan to disinherit Owen in favour of an unacknowledged love child, do you? You can't just decide on your perpetrator and then dream up some fantasy motive that fits the bill.'

'*Circulus in probando*,' Cassie murmured to herself.

'Sorry?'

'A circular argument.' Cassie tried to twirl a teaspoon between her fingers, attempting to mimic Christian's trick without success.

'You said "give *her* up for adoption".' Flyte's eyes narrowed. 'Where did this theory come from?'

What the hell, thought Cassie. 'It was something I found at Mrs E's house in Patna Road. I went there with an estate agent, pretending I was looking to buy.' She hoped it sounded halfway plausible.

Flyte's expression told her it didn't.

'He let me look round on my own for a bit while he made some calls. And I found something – the record of a marriage printed off a genealogy website – and the bride's middle name was Geraldine.'

Their eyes met and in the long silence that followed, an unspoken agreement was reached – Flyte knew that Cassie's story about how she'd got into Geraldine Edwards' house was a steaming pile of crap, but she wasn't going to call her out on it.

'Give me the names,' she snapped, pulling out her notebook.

'Thank you . . . Phyllida,' the name feeling awkward in her mouth.

'I'll check it out, but don't get your hopes up.' Flyte picked up her bag. 'You do know the most likely explanation of Geraldine's death is still that it was just a tragic accident? Her cleaner told me that she mentioned feeling poorly the night she died.'

'Really? There was no mention of it in the police report – they usually make a note of things like that.'

'Yes, well.' Flyte's look said it all. 'Geraldine said that she was coming down with a cold and complained of having the shivers. Hence the hot bath and the whisky. She even took her supper into the bath.'

Casting her mind back to the post-mortem, Cassie frowned. 'There was no food in her stomach.'

'There was a cheese sandwich next to the bath but she hadn't got round to eating it.'

Cassie frowned. Taking a sandwich into the bath? That didn't sound like Mrs E, with her love of cooking and her sense of *order*. Even if she was only having a biscuit she'd put it on a plate and sit at the table to eat it. But she knew that such vague qualms would cut no ice with Flyte.

Parting company out on the pavement, they avoided each other's eyes and Cassie realised something: since she'd confessed to her overnight vigil with Oliver there had been a subtle but fundamental shift in their relationship. If it hadn't been for that moment of fellow feeling, she wouldn't have dreamed of more or less admitting her illegal break-in to a cop.

Cassie was reminded of Julius Caesar's words as he took his momentous decision to cross the Rubicon.

Alea iacta est.

The die is cast.

Chapter Thirty-Eight

Luca had agreed to pick up Mrs E's body after five that evening, outside usual collection hours. Cassie wanted to ensure that everyone else had gone home, so she could be alone with Mrs E and say her goodbyes properly, without fear of being overheard.

As the clock hands crept close to five, the feeling of dread that had lain in Cassie's stomach all day was joined by the jangling jumpiness she used to get before her exams.

The rattle of Mrs E's fridge drawer opening split the silence and Cassie imagined the other ladies and gents behind the walls of steel stirring from their slumber to bid farewell to their departing companion. After transferring the white-shrouded figure onto a wheeled stretcher, Cassie unzipped Mrs E's body bag.

Her face had lost some of its volume, making it look more solemn than she ever had in life, but she was still the same old Mrs E. Cassie half expected those hooded eyes to snap open at any moment and ask her to state the special theory of relativity.

'I wish you could tell me what's going on, Mrs E,' she told her. 'Anything that might help to get your funeral postponed. Were you trying to find your daughter and Owen found out? Was it him you thought was following you, just before you died? Or someone else?'

She stared into the waxen face for more than a minute, straining for some further illumination of those words '*It's not my time yet*' – and why she had been seeing her old friend and teacher over the last two weeks. But there was nothing, only the hum of the giant fridge and the ticking of the faulty light overhead.

A familiar rumble outside announced the arrival of Luca's van. Reaching into her pocket, Cassie took something out of her scrubs. Tucking her physics A level certificate beneath Mrs E's body, she rested a hand on her shoulder for a moment before slowly closing the body bag.

As she wheeled the trolley out of the body store and down the corridor, memories crowded in on her: Mrs E dissolving into helpless laughter after some classroom experiment went wrong; her whoop of triumph at Cassie's A level results; the look of quiet pride in her dark eyes as Cassie related some mortuary anecdote over coffee.

Abruptly, Cassie stopped wheeling, feeling breathless and panicky. By this time tomorrow her old friend and teacher would be gone, reduced to a few pounds of cinder and ash. But then another memory surfaced: Mrs E writing something on the white board in her looping hand: *The First Law of Thermodynamics,* and her voice saying, '*Matter cannot be destroyed.*' A reminder that even after flames consumed her body, it would survive in the form of indivisible and indestructible chemical elements.

Mrs E was telling Cassie she was still with her – and always would be.

At the front door, Luca took in her expression and offered only a nod of greeting. Taking the trolley from her hands, he wheeled it towards the waiting van, piloting it with unusual vigilance around the potholes in the tarmac.

Once Mrs E was safely on board, he closed the rear doors and paused, casting a look back at Cassie, as if asking her permission to leave.

She gave a nod, and a moment later, the van moved off. As it paused at the exit to the street, Cassie raised her hand in farewell.

'Cheerio, Mrs E,' she murmured, as it disappeared round the corner.

Chapter Thirty-Nine

As Cassie headed for home, feeling exhausted, her phone rang and Christian's name appeared on the display.

'I'm meeting a police detective first thing tomorrow,' he told her. 'She wants to talk to me about Geraldine.'

'I'm sorry about that. I should really have called to warn you that I'd given her your number.' Cassie felt torn – she and Christian had become close through their shared love of Mrs E, and yet she was aware of the debt she owed Phyllida Flyte for sticking her neck out over the case.

'Please don't apologise. Does this means they've decided that Geraldine's death *was* suspicious?'

'Not yet – but they are . . . taking another look at it.'

He didn't sound worried at the prospect of getting quizzed by the cops but he did sound different somehow. Cassie ducked into a shop doorway so she could hear him better. 'You might find DS Flyte a bit . . . hard-core, but I think she's really good at her job.'

'I'll do whatever I can to help her find out what happened. If somebody did hurt Geri then they must face justice. It's the least I can do.'

She realised what was different about him. From their previous encounters she would have described Christian as easy-going –

the kind of man who would choose the path of least resistance. But now his tone was more decisive.

'Did you get the funeral details I sent you?' she asked.

'Yes. And I really hope I'll be there. But . . . Cassie, I want you to know that I loved Geraldine.'

'I know . . .'

'I mean I *really* loved her – she . . . changed my life.'

'Mine too. She was that kind of person.'

'Could I ask you a favour, Cassie?'

She pressed the phone to her ear.

'If I don't make it to the funeral – would you please say goodbye to her for me?'

The hairs crackled upright on her forearms. *What the fuck was going on?*

But before she could question him further, he'd hung up.

Chapter Forty

The conversation left Cassie in a spin. Christian had been talking like a man who had made a decision of some kind. Whatever it was he had decided must surely be connected with Mrs E. But what was it?

Cassie's stomach had started to churn: did Christian Maclaren know more about her death than he'd been letting on after all?

A double-decker bus grumbled past her through the dusk, slowing to pull in at a bus stop. The sight took Cassie back to the very first time she'd 'seen' Mrs E after her death – glimpsed through a bus window, right after she'd left the Gainsborough Hotel and that first meeting with Christian. She could still see Mrs E's white face, and the way she'd frowned. Like she used to do in class when there was some kind of flaw in somebody's argument.

Something stirred at the back of Cassie's mind: a distant, discordant note sounding deep in her memory – or a desperately annoying itch she couldn't quite reach. It was something to do with the Gainsborough Hotel. But she couldn't say what.

The bus was taking on its last few passengers. Seeing it was a number 88, which would go to Oxford Street, she gave in to an impulse and ran to catch it.

Twenty minutes later, Cassie was climbing the steps to the Gainsborough's grand entrance, hoping that the visit might jog her memory.

Last time, the place had impressed her, but now she examined it more critically the glamour seemed only skin-deep. There was a polyester sheen to the doorman's jacket and stains on the carpet underfoot. Something made her go over to one of the massive classical columns that flanked the lobby, and set her palm against it. Instead of the cool kiss of marble, she felt plasterwork.

Fake.

Hadn't Christian made some joky comment about these columns? Her gaze travelled idly upwards, ending at the elaborately decorated capital where it met the lobby ceiling.

Pulling her hand from the plasterwork as if it was red hot, she rushed outside, ignoring the doorman's startled look as she shot out of the revolving door.

It seemed like an age before Flyte answered her phone.

'Christian Maclaren isn't an architect!' Cassie said, the words bursting out of her.

'What are you talking about?'

She took a moment to breathe. 'There's a pair of classical columns in the Gainsborough Hotel lobby. The capitals – that's the decorative bit around the top – are Corinthian, the most detailed and elaborate of all the ancient classical designs.'

'I don't—'

'Hear me out. When I met Christian there – it was one of the first things he said to me – about why he liked the place. He said something like, "You won't see Doric columns at the Premier Inn".'

'You've lost me.'

'The capitals of Doric columns are the earliest and *simplest* design, with hardly any decoration. They're impossible to confuse with the Corinthian.'

'Couldn't he just have made a mistake?' Flyte sounded sceptical.

Cassie grimaced with exasperation. 'No way! It's Classical Architecture 101. I learned it at *A level*, for Christ's sake, and architects study for, like, seven years! Trust me, it's not something a genuine architect would get wrong.'

'I'll bear it in mind when I interview him.' But Cassie could tell she wasn't convinced.

'If he lied about being an architect what else might he be lying about?'

'Look, I hear you, OK?'

Knowing from experience that trying to browbeat Flyte was counter-productive, Cassie literally bit her lip. She moved on to the strange phone call she'd received from Christian – and her impression that he'd made up his mind to 'do something'.

'What kind of thing?'

Cassie heard again the steeliness in his voice. 'I have no idea,' she admitted.

FLYTE

It was the morning of Geraldine Edwards' funeral and on her way into the nick, Flyte trod in the half-eaten remains of some southern fried chicken – one of hundreds of discarded takeaway meals that littered Camden's early morning streets, along with innumerable cans, bottles, and the occasional homeless person asleep in a shop doorway. She stopped to scrape off the breaded nugget impaled on her heel onto the kerb.

She was already in a bad mood after a late night spent investigating the mysterious marriage record Cassie Raven had found at Geraldine Edwards' house. Cassie's hunch that Geraldine was about to disinherit her son Owen in favour of the illegitimate child she'd given up for adoption had sounded like the overheated storyline of some daytime soap – and turned out to be just as credible. When Flyte had finally managed to track down Julia Torrance's birth certificate, it recorded her birth date as May 1969, which made her a mere two years younger than Geraldine Edwards, her supposed birth mother.

The late-night overdose of blue light from her laptop screen had kept her awake till the early hours, but lack of sleep wasn't the only thing making her feel out of sorts. Cassie's account of how she gained access to the Edwards' house was so obviously a fabrication that Flyte couldn't stop asking herself why she'd let it pass. For the first time in fourteen years as a serving police officer she was uncomfortably aware of having crossed some kind of line.

It all stemmed from Cassie's unexpected admission of her overnight vigils with dead children at the mortuary, a revelation that had transformed Flyte's view of her, to the extent that she struggled now to recall why she'd taken such a dislike to her in the first place. It seemed obvious now that all those tattoos and piercings camouflaged a genuine empathy for others.

She arrived at work just before nine, giving herself enough time ahead of Christian Maclaren's interview to check out Cassie's other theory – that he wasn't a genuine architect. Even if someone like Cassie really did know her way around classical architecture, Flyte wasn't convinced that confusing his Corinthian and Doric columns made Maclaren a fake.

A call to the Royal Institute of British Architects turned up no record of him, but they explained that RIBA membership was optional and advised her to check with the Architect Registration Board.

'You could just search our register online, you know,' sighed the woman she spoke to in the ARB records department.

Flyte spoke through gritted teeth. 'This is a police investigation. Forgive me if I'd rather trust a human being than an online search box.'

After spelling out Maclaren's name she was left listening to modern jazz but, mercifully, not for long.

'There is nobody of that name on the register.' The jobsworth was back.

'Are you saying that he's definitely not an architect?'

'We are the regulatory body for the profession in the UK.' The woman spoke as if addressing a small, dim child. 'If he's not registered with us and is practising as an architect, he's breaking the law.'

Phyllida Flyte felt her spine stiffen. So Cassie had been right: Maclaren was an impostor. That meant his dating profile at Ocean, his website, the images of buildings he'd supposedly designed, were all fake. The only possible reason for constructing such an elaborate fiction: to present yourself as a well-paid, eligible professional to women like Geraldine Edwards.

She realised that it was gone 9.45, which meant Maclaren was fifteen minutes late for his interview. After getting no response from his mobile she waited another fifteen.

Then she called DI Bellwether.

She had to strain to hear him above the high-pitched noise of two small children squabbling in the background. 'Sorry to bother you, boss. Have I called you on a day off?'

'No, no. I'll be in a bit later.' He lowered his voice. 'Between you and me, I'm looking forward to it.'

She told him that Geraldine Edwards' former fiancé was a fake with a fraudulent dating profile.

'Interesting. So – have you got anything solid to link him to the Edwards' death?'

'Not yet, but he was meant to be coming in for interview over half an hour ago and he hasn't shown up.'

The voice of a little girl speaking in a stage whisper came down the line 'Daddy. Come and see the bunny I drew!'

Flyte felt her throat contract. Bellwether had covered the mic, but she could still make out his muffled voice. 'Daddy's on a work call, sweetheart. I'll come and see it in a minute.'

A high-pitched 'Daddy! Pleeease!!!' pealed down the line.

Flyte was hijacked by a vision as beautiful as it was terrible: her and Matt on a beach somewhere, playing with a little girl in the surf, the parents they might have become, the life they should all have had together, if only Flyte had gone to the GP earlier, if only the hospital had reacted faster, if only she had been born alive.

The unbearable litany that had ruled her life for so long and that would never be laid to rest.

She pressed a hand against her eyes. As the image faded to black she felt the yawning darkness below, reaching up to claim her.

'Phyllida? I've really got to go.'

With an enormous effort she mastered herself and managed to say, 'Could we put in a RIPA application to Maclaren's mobile provider, boss? I suspect he's actually UK-based so once we get an address we could doorstep him. The Edwards funeral is this afternoon.'

A sigh whistled down the line. 'You don't have enough to justify it, Phyllida. And upstairs are telling us to be more judicious with our use of RIPAs. He might still turn up, after all.'

'But . . .'

'Keep trying his number and let's catch up when I get in.'

Chapter Forty-One

The alarm woke Cassie from an uneasy doze that morning at 7 a.m. She'd booked the day off work to attend Mrs E's funeral at four but her overriding thought was how to prove to Flyte that Christian Maclaren was a fraud and stop the body being cremated.

Since her lightning-bolt revelation over Maclaren's architectural slip-up, she'd spent a restless night re-examining their every encounter through a new lens. What might she have missed, or misguidedly dismissed, first time round, blindsided by how grief-stricken he had seemed?

The designer glasses he'd worn the first time they met, but not the second: had they been just for show, useful props for his role as a successful architect? Like his beautiful speaking voice, with its occasional lapse into a London accent, which now seemed a deliberate part of his act – part of the persona he put on.

Most of all she kept returning to his flicker of anxiety when he had quizzed her about Mrs E's toxicology results. Had Christian slipped her some toxic substance? Something that the standard screening hadn't picked up? Knowing her liking for a nightcap, he might have gained entry to her house and put something in the whisky bottle.

In the shower, she mentally revisited the images Flyte had sent her from Christian's dating profile. Mainly they showed him in his suit and posed in various locations – on his laptop at an outdoor cafe, working at his 'desk', outside Tate Modern – all easy enough to fake.

But one image stuck out.

Wearing only her bathrobe, she plonked herself down beside Macavity on the sofa, earning herself a hard stare, and opened the image of Christian steering the sailing boat. Going by his hairline, it pre-dated the other shots by five years or more. It would have been easy enough to hire the boat for the photo, of course, and now she looked it afresh, his pose – one tanned forearm planted in foreground, the resolute way he was gazing into the distance – all had the air of being staged.

And there was something else about the image that jarred.

'What's wrong with this picture, Macavity?' He opened one eye, before closing it again, a single twitch of his tail indicating irritation.

Zooming in, it dawned on her what didn't quite gel. The sky behind Christian was filled with a glorious orange sunset, but the warm light on his face suggested he was *facing* the sun. Either the shot had been professionally lit, or skilfully composed from more than one image. But why go to such unnecessary lengths – hiring a boat, crafting the shot so professionally – when his other images were perfectly acceptable for an online dating profile?

Cassie remembered it was possible to run a reverse image search: using a picture file's digital signature to find other locations where it had been posted online. If any of Maclaren's profile pics turned up somewhere else, maybe they'd provide a clue to his real identity.

Finding the website, she dragged all the shots into the search box and sat staring at the progress bar while the software searched the web. Results for the most recent shots came up first.

No match. No match. Match.

A little jolt of excitement, which evaporated when she realised the location was only his fictitious LinkedIn profile. Another positive match took her to his company website.

No match. No match.

The shot of him steering the sailboat took the longest.

'Come on,' she muttered, watching the progress bar chomp its way through millions of websites.

Match.

After clicking on the link, she blinked at the page that came up on her screen, uncomprehending.

FLYTE

'Is that detective sergeant Flyte?' Phyllida Flyte took a moment to identify the vaguely familiar female voice as belonging to Beth Montagu, the woman who looked after membership records at Ocean.

'I'm calling in confidence, like you said?' – sounding nervous. From the traffic noise in the background, she'd stepped out of the office to make the call.

'Of course. What's on your mind, Beth?'

'The guy you were asking about – Christian Maclaren? I haven't been able to stop thinking about him. The idea that someone might have used our site to hurt somebody . . . it's been giving me sleepless nights.'

Flyte made an encouraging noise.

'So . . . I had a look back at his details. You remember he stated in his profile that he's based in Hamburg?'

'Yes?'

'After your visit I double-checked – and his subscriptions were paid out of his London bank account. It's probably nothing, but I just thought, I don't know, that it might help?'

Flyte allowed herself a smile.

'It might well do, Beth. Do you have a billing address for the account?'

There was a long pause before Beth said, 'I suppose there are a hundred ways you could have got his address, right?'

The address she read down the line was in SW2, which meant nothing to Flyte, but seeing one of the DCs pass her desk she collared him. Josh was the one she'd overheard mocking her as 'queen of lost causes' – but she knew he lived south of the river.

'That's gonna be Brixton, Sarge.'

'Where they had the riots?'

'Yeah,' He eyed her, evidently suppressing a smile. 'Before I was born. Nowadays a flat there would set you back half a million.'

She gaped at him – in Winchester, £500,000 would buy a three-bedroom house.

'What are you working on?' Josh looked curious. 'Anything I can help with?'

'I don't know yet.' She looked him in the eye. 'It'll probably just turn out to be another one of my "lost causes".'

He at least had the grace to blush.

Flyte was wondering whether Bellwether would let her go to doorstep someone outside the borough when she got an internal call. There was a Cassandra Raven in reception.

Raven's excitement was palpable, her words spilling out before they even reached the interview room.

'I got an Uber here – I knew you wouldn't believe me if I tried telling you over the phone. I had to show you this.' She pushed her phone in Flyte's face.

As the image came into focus, the skin on Flyte's neck tingled. It was an ad for a posh brand of watch, the kind you saw in glossy magazines – and the image of a handsome man steering a sailing boat was instantly recognisable.

'This was on Maclaren's dating profile,' she turned to stare at Cassie.

As soon as you knew it was an ad, it was impossible to see it any other way: the glossy production values, the man's phony thousand-yard stare, the wristwatch he wore helpfully large in the foreground.

'There's more,' said Cassie. Tapping on her screen she brought up the same image on another site, this time minus the logo and sales pitch. 'This is an archived web page from six years ago,' she said, before zooming up the blurb next to the shot. '"Six foot two, with blond hair and china-blue eyes, Alex Barclay is available for dramas, commercials, and voiceovers . . ."'

'This is from a casting agency,' said Flyte. Sometimes you had to say something out loud to make it real.

Cassie met her gaze and nodded.

'That's right. Christian Maclaren is an actor.'

Chapter Forty-Two

Having proved to Flyte that 'Christian Maclaren' was a small-time former actor calling himself Alex Barclay, all Cassie could do was leave her to it. After the first super-charged rush of her discovery, she was hitting the comedown. She knew that stopping a funeral scheduled for that afternoon was a near impossible task – especially now that 'Maclaren' had done a disappearing act.

His acting training helped to explain how he had pulled the wool over her eyes so completely. His visceral shock and grief at the news of Mrs E's death had been so convincing that even now she found it hard to see it for what it was: a performance.

She made her way to Camden Market to pick out flowers for the funeral: a florist's wreath had seemed too sombre and impersonal, and remembering Mrs E's glorious, semi-wild garden, she was determined to choose something less formal. She wondered if Owen might cause trouble when he saw her at the crematorium: he could still grass her up to the cops for breaking into his mother's house.

Fuck it. Nothing was going to stop her attending Mrs E's funeral, not even the threat of a criminal conviction.

At the market, the range of flowers was limited by the season, and she agonised over what to choose. Lilies struck her as morbidly funereal, the smiley-faces of sunflowers a bit too cheerful, gerberas too tropical: Mrs E had once said that she didn't entirely approve of plants that looked too exotic for the English climate. Smiling at the memory, Cassie chose an armful of blowsy, deep pink peonies – classic cottage-garden flowers, even if in November they must have clocked up a shedload of air miles.

By the time they'd been wrapped and paid for, a watery sunshine had pierced the ceiling of winter grey, and the market was nearing full throttle. Navigating the clogged aisles was like playing human pinball: office workers out to score a swift lunch colliding with ambling, zombie-like tourists. Forced to sidestep a girl with green dreads zipping past on a kick scooter, Cassie pressed the precious peonies closer to her chest, her anxiety levels rising.

Then something caught her eye up ahead, a still figure amid the roiling throng. A dark glossy head above a red coat.

She turned and looked directly at Cassie, before turning to move swiftly away from her. *Mrs E.* Her message was clear. *Follow me.*

Cassie put her head down and carved a path through the press of bodies, one arm cradling the bouquet of flowers against her chest. She was so determined to keep the tall figure in sight that she barely dared blink. '*Excuse me . . . sorry . . . sorry . . .*' – her ruthless progress bringing a volley of glares and tuts. Mrs E was moving faster now, threading through the crush like a darning needle through wool, forcing Cassie to speed up.

Just as she felt sure she was getting closer, the sheaf of peonies started to slip from her grasp. Cursing, she slowed for a moment to zip them inside her leather jacket, and . . . *Boof*! Somebody barged into her from behind so hard it threw her off balance. Arms flailing, Cassie teetered on her left foot for a split second. She hit the tarmac hard, hearing a *hufff* as the air shot out of her lungs.

Muffled noise. A tangle of hands reaching down. A melee of voices, suddenly loud. 'Did you see that?' . . . 'What a rude woman!' . . . 'Is she OK?' . . . 'What happened?' . . . 'Give her some air.'

Out of the chaos loomed a giant pickled walnut, like the ones Gran loved, before resolving itself into the face of an old man. 'Are you all right, love?'

' . . .' Where she meant there to be words, Cassie heard only a wheezing sound. Panic rose in her throat.

'She's winded, the poor thing.' A woman's voice now – American. 'Can we get a chair over here?'

Finally, Cassie drew a ragged breath. Someone handed her a bottle of water and she drank, spilling it down her front.

'Hurt anywhere, does it, love?' The old geezer again – clearly one of the stallholders. She wanted to tell him that her father used to sell fruit and veg here once but couldn't form the words.

'Uhhn.' She took a swift inventory. 'I'm . . . OK.'

The American lady guided her into a chair – eyes crinkled with concern. 'You should really go get checked out in the hospital.'

'Thank you.' Cassie shook her head. 'But I can't go to hospital. Not today.'

She looked down at her jeans, the knee ripped out of one leg, and flexed her wrist. Pain scythed through it and a voice in her head diagnosed a possible sprain to the scapholunate ligament. And going by her sore backside she'd have a big fat bruise later. *Nothing serious.*

Then she noticed the heads of the peonies lolling against the black leather of her jacket, their poor necks broken, and started to cry.

FLYTE

Bellwether sat back in his chair. 'Well, well, so Christian Maclaren's entire persona is a fabrication.'

'That's right, boss. Up until six years ago he was working as a model and bit-part actor under the name Alex Barclay. Although according to the casting agency, the watch ad was the only major job he ever got.'

She had laid it all out for him: Maclaren's fictitious website, the fake bank account he must have set up in order to join Ocean, the Hamburg number that diverted callers to a professional messaging service. 'This was a sophisticated and complex fraud. But when it came to choosing pics for his dating profile, he couldn't resist using the best photo he'd ever had taken.'

'Caught out by vanity,' Bellwether nodded. 'So, throughout his relationship with Geraldine Edwards, he was impersonating a successful architect with a glamorous lifestyle, obviously intending to defraud her.'

'Exactly. According to her best friend, Geraldine was thinking of selling the house after they got married to go travelling. His next step would have been to clear out the joint bank account and disappear. Instead, Geraldine breaks off the engagement, perhaps smelling a rat, and just a few weeks later, she's found dead in the bath.'

Bellwether thumbed the button on his pen top, click-click, click-click. 'You think that he murdered her to prevent her exposing him.'

'I think it's a reasonable working hypothesis. I've got an address for him now – he lives in Brixton.'

Flyte glanced at the time – less than five hours till the funeral. 'Boss . . . do you think we can persuade the coroner to stop the cremation until I can interview Maclaren?'

Despite all her efforts to prepare him, Bellwether looked startled. 'When's it happening?'

'Four o'clock.'

He pulled a face. 'That's a big ask, Phyllida. He'll probably say the investigation into Maclaren can continue without the body. You might have established motive but we'd need a lot more before we can charge him with murder.'

'Will you give it a try though, boss?'

As Bellwether carried on clicking his pen, Flyte fought down an urge to reach across the desk and snap it in half.

Finally, he spoke. 'I'll give him a call, but don't hold your breath.'

Malcolm Bellwether was rewarded with a 100-watt smile – and was startled to realise that Phyllida Flyte was a rather beautiful woman. 'Ask Brixton nick to send a local uniform to keep an eye on this guy's address until you get down there.'

'Actually, boss . . . I already called Brixton. They're sending a squad car.' She was finding his expression hard to read. 'Sorry. Is that what you call me being a bit OCD?'

A grin spread across his face. 'No, Phyllida. That's what I call thinking ahead.'

She could feel her cheeks flushing.

'Phyllida?' he said as she turned to go. 'I'm just curious. What put you onto Maclaren being a fake in the first place?'

She hesitated, picturing Cassie Raven, the multiply-pierced mortuary attendant with an unexpected knowledge of classical architecture.

'If I told you, boss, you wouldn't believe me.'

Chapter Forty-Three

Cassie apologised for the umpteenth time to the American lady who'd looked after her. She had no idea why she had lost it so completely over some broken flowers – couldn't remember the last time she'd cried like that, not even when Rachel had moved out. Her Good Samaritan, a widow called Rosemary from Vermont, brushed off the apologies and insisted on accompanying Cassie back to the flower stall to buy more peonies.

'How are you feeling now, dear?' she asked, while Cassie selected her second bunch of the day.

'Much better.' In truth, she was still feeling a bit wobbly, but then shock could do that – it had been a nasty fall. She rubbed the tender place on her buttock.

'You look way too pale to me,' said Rosemary. 'And you should get that wrist checked out.'

'It's just a slight sprain,' she said, flexing it.

Still looking doubtful, Rosemary patted Cassie's shoulder in an affectionate parting gesture. 'I hope the funeral goes all right, dear. I'm so sorry for your loss.'

As Cassie watched the kind lady disappear into the crowd, she had to hold her breath to quell the sob gathering in her throat. It occurred to her that Mrs E's funeral would be the first she'd ever attended. When her mum and dad died, her grandmother had decided that at four she was too young to be exposed to such an upsetting experience. Cassie had never before questioned the decision, but now she felt a spurt of hot rage. What had Babcia been thinking – denying her the chance to say goodbye to her parents?

The stallholder gave her the wrapped bouquet and she handed over a twenty. But as she reached out to take the change, the coins seemed to come alive, slithering between her clammy fingers. Sideswiped by a wave of dizziness, she gripped the edge of the stall, but when she opened her mouth to thank the stallholder for retrieving her dropped coins, the words came out all mushy.

This time, the ground looming up to embrace her felt like an old friend.

FLYTE

With siren wailing and a blue light clapped to the roof of the pool car, Flyte drove like a demon to 18B Highlever Court, Christian Maclaren/Alex Barclay's Brixton address. A squad car was already in position outside the flat, under strict instructions to apprehend the suspect only if he tried to leave: if he were forewarned, he could simply disappear.

Using the hands-free, she put in a call to Josh. When Bellwether had offered her a DC to help investigate Maclaren, he'd been her first choice. He might be a cheeky little swine but he was the brightest of the bunch in CID.

'Did you look into Maclaren's Brixton address?' she demanded.

'Yes, Sarge. The bills are all in the name of Christian Maclaren.'

Flyte dropped into second to negotiate a line of traffic queueing at a roundabout, cars pulling left and right at the sound of the siren.

'But I called Land Registry and that's not the name they have on record as the owner of the flat.'

'Hang on two secs.' Finding a truck blocking her way onto the roundabout, apparently deaf to the siren, she leaned on the horn. Passing the truck she caught a glimpse of the driver's startled face, mobile pressed to his ear. Shame she had no time to pull him over.

'Go on, Josh.'

She could hear him tapping at his keyboard. 'Yeah, the name on the title deeds is B.D. Renwick.'

'Fuck.' Feeling the car drift, Flyte had to give the steering wheel a corrective tug.

'Sarge?' Josh sounded shocked; he'd never heard the Ice Maiden swear before.

Barry Dennis Renwick. The name of the bridegroom on the marriage record Cassie Raven had found at Patna Road.

So Barry Renwick, aka Christian Maclaren, had married Julia Torrance two years before starting his affair with Geraldine Edwards. Clearly, Geraldine had become suspicious and unearthed evidence of her fiancé's former marriage – and his false identity. Presumably she had confronted him and threatened him with the police.

It seemed likely that Julia Torrance was another of Barry Renwick's victims. Had she, like Geraldine, met him through a dating site?

'Josh, I need you to track someone down for me.' After giving him his instructions, she swung the car into an empty bus lane and floored the accelerator.

'How does he choose his victims?' she mused out loud.

She remembered Beth at Ocean saying that Geraldine Edwards was the only woman Maclaren had made contact with. But how did he know that the women he targeted owned assets or wealth that made them worth pursuing? Could he have found a way to hack into the databases of dating sites to identify property-rich victims?

After she had located the two reassuringly burly male uniforms from Brixton nick waiting in an unmarked car, they all made their way to Maclaren's block. Flyte and the uniform called Dave went inside, while the second guy, Miles, went to cover any rear escape routes.

Outside Renwick's flat there was an estate agent's board advertising it as 'SOLD'. Maybe he was trying to do a runner before the police caught up with him. *Too late, matey,* she thought with grim satisfaction as she leaned on the bell. Her heart was beating hard but steadily as she wondered how Renwick – aka Maclaren – would react to finding the law on his doorstep.

But from the flat's interior there came only silence, even after she'd shouted through the letterbox.

She answered Dave's questioning look with a nod. Motioning her to move aside he hefted the tomato-red Enforcer, swinging it in a backward arc, taking aim at the door lock. A mighty cra-ack! was followed by a tinkling sound as both glass panels shattered from the impact. One more blow, and the door's lock gave way.

'Police!' Dave barrelled down the hall, eyeballing each room in turn, Flyte following behind. A quick check of living room, bedroom, and bathroom revealed no sign of anyone. The kitchen diner was empty, too.

I've missed him, she thought.

Her eye fell on a brown paper bag on the kitchen worktop. Inside, unopened takeaway cartons gave off the unmistakable aroma of curry, and nearby, a naan bread lay neatly quartered on a chopping board. She tapped it with a fingernail – rock hard.

'Sarge, take a look at this.' At the kitchen table, laid for two, a bottle of Chablis, open but unpoured, sat in a puddle of water. Next to it, a glossy magazine, its cover bisected by a neat line of white powder.

A rust-coloured smear on the skirting board caught her eye. On the wall she found its cousin: a constellation of fine red-brown dots at seated head height. They exchanged a look.

In the only bedroom, which was barely wide enough for a standard double bed, she pulled open the wardrobe – empty but for a series of expensive-looking suits and a rack of silk ties – before dropping to a crouch by the side of the bed. She ducked her head to check underneath – and met the china-blue gaze of the man in the watch ad.

Barry Renwick, aka Christian Maclaren, lay with his head on one side, pillowed in a pool of congealed blood. This time, his brooding thousand-yard stare would last for all eternity.

Chapter Forty-Four

She could hear her mother calling her down for breakfast.

'Cassie, wake up!'

But how could that be, when she had no memory of what her mother's voice sounded like?

Then a deeper voice, more insistent – Mrs E. 'Cassie! Can you hear me?'

A shard of blinding white light.

'Pupils are responsive,' said Mrs E.

But I was your best pupil, she wanted to say.

Something pinched the back of her hand. She tried to cry out but somebody had sewn her lips together. Tried again. 'Nnnng . . .'

A shadow moved over her face. 'She's coming round.'

She opened her eyes a crack. Above her lab coat, Mrs E wore a mask depicting a cute Asian guy. 'Why the mask?' asked Cassie, her voice a mumble.

'There you are! Hi, Cassie. I'm Dr Sanjay. Do you know where you are?'

No clue, she realised.

'You're in hospital. Have you taken any drugs today?'

Closing her eyes, she shook her head crossly – why couldn't they shut up so she could sleep?

'Can you remember what happened?'

She tried, but her memory was fogged, like a car windscreen in a rainstorm. 'I broke the peonies.' Something hot tracked down the side of her face. *Tears,* she realised.

A muttered exchange over her chest. 'Peonies?'

'Yes, the paramedics said she collapsed half an hour ago while buying flowers.'

A tiny gap appeared in the fog and she slipped through it. 'Am I . . . sick?'

'Yes, but we're looking after you. How are you feeling at the moment?'

'Cold.' An urgent twisting in her gut. 'Hungry.'

'Do you suffer from problems with your thyroid or liver? Have you ever been diagnosed with low blood sugar? Are you fasting?'

The barrage of questions enraged her.

'Fuck *off.*'

'Irritability,' said the voice above her.

For some reason an image of Harry Hardwick's untamed eyebrows popped into her mind, followed by fragments of the conversation with the sister on his ward. Something about him shouting at the nurses. Saying that they were starving him, that was it.

Another pang of hunger clutched at her stomach. Then another image. Mrs E, in her lab coat, cutting something up at the dissection bench. A pig pancreas. Pointing her scalpel at something, she spoke sternly. '*Cassandra. Remember what this is called.*'

Cassie opened her eyes a crack. 'The Islets of Langerhans,' she said, her words coming out surprisingly clear.

A cloudburst of chatter broke over her. But Cassie let her eyes close and submitted to the great pillowy darkness.

FLYTE

Releasing a crackle from her protective suit, Flyte dropped to a crouch for another look at Barry Renwick's body. They had pulled the bed aside so the pathologist could view him properly. Renwick no longer bore any resemblance to his glamorous alter ego, international architect Christian Maclaren; dead, he could be any bloke you might see propping up the bar in a Brixton pub.

Back in the kitchen, she quizzed the pathologist – a tall, taciturn man who was peeling off nitrile gloves – for his initial opinion on the cause of death. 'A single stab wound to the neck,' he said. 'Time of death probably between about eight and ten last night.'

Her eye fell on the chopping board with its four neat segments of naan bread, but no sign of the knife used to slice it. 'A kitchen knife, maybe?'

'Very possibly. Straight-bladed, I'd say, and about six or seven inches long. The assailant must have approached from the rear' – he went over to where the bloodstains indicated Renwick had been sitting, and raised his left hand before arcing it down with surprising gusto – 'striking downwards, into the base of the neck.'

'If he bled to death, why isn't there more blood?'

'The injury appears to have missed the major vessels, but it partially severed the trachea. I suspect he choked on his own blood.'

Renwick's body had been lying on a black bin bag, which the murderer had clearly used to make it easier to drag him into the bedroom.

The table laid for two, the unopened takeaway – all suggested that Renwick had known – and trusted – his killer.

She stared at the line of white powder on the magazine cover.

Had Renwick been murdered by his dealer? It might seem the obvious conclusion, but the fact that the killer had struck just hours before Renwick had been due to talk to her about Geraldine Edwards' death was a red flag. Was the murder really just coincidence – or had somebody wanted to silence him?

Although Renwick's mobile phone was nowhere to be found, robbery was an unlikely motive in light of what Flyte had found in the living room: a pile of gadgets, some still in their Amazon boxes, including a Panasonic 4k stills and movie camera, editing software, and a MacBook Pro, still virginal in its white sleeve. A treasure trove worth five or six thousand pounds. Barry clearly fancied himself as the next Martin Scorsese.

The flat contained no personal items – no photographs, mementoes, or any other clue to the man or his history. Almost as if they had been deliberately erased.

Going back to the kitchen, Flyte turned her attention to the kitchen bin, lifting out the liner with gloved hands, hoping to find the takeaway receipt. Teabags, discarded junk mail, but no receipt. Then, at the very bottom, something interesting.

A stain-blotched newspaper cutting, yellow with age. A photo showed a company of actors – which the caption identified as an amateur dramatic group called the Stockwell Players – taking their post-performance bow. Standing centre stage, a handsome young man: Barry Renwick – probably in his late twenties going by the clean jawline and unthinned hair. He held aloft the hand of a much younger girl, slender and wearing a floor-length medieval-style dress, who'd been caught in profile, gazing up at him admiringly. The caption gushed about the 'touching performance of *Romeo and Juliet*'. In small print at the page edge, the words 'South London Press'.

The heart-shaped magnet she found among the debris suggested that until very recently the clipping had enjoyed pride of place on the fridge. Slipping the cutting into an evidence bag, Flyte wondered what had prompted Renwick to bin this souvenir of his acting career.

She went to the front door, where Dave the uniform was stringing tape across the doorway.

'Drug-related was it, Sarge?' he asked. 'They usually are, round here.'

'It's one line of enquiry. Did you speak to the neighbours?'

'Yep.' Pulling another length of tape from the reel he stuck one end to the top of the doorframe.

'So did anyone hear or see any visitors, late last night?'

'No. Nothing. The old dear on that side,' a jerk of the head, 'did say there was a bloke knocking at the door, but that was yesterday lunchtime. She said he was banging for so long that she stuck her head out.'

'And?'

'It was just a delivery for Renwick. The bloke said he'd take it back to the depot.'

'Any description?' Flyte gave up trying to hide her exasperation.

'A middle-aged bloke, she said, well built like me.' He nodded down at his considerable frame. 'Definitely not the drug-dealing type.'

Flyte decided life was too short to challenge Dave's preconceptions. 'That's it?'

'Yep.' He unspooled some more tape. 'Except that he was a boyo.'

'A what?'

He looked at her as if she were a moron. 'He had a Welsh accent.'

Chapter Forty-Five

Colours churned behind Cassie's eyes like oil in a lava lamp. Wine-dark red brightened to orange, then to peach; the soundtrack a not unpleasant, murmuring hubbub. She smiled, enjoying the show, until she was spewed forth into viciously bright light, the murmur giving way to clatter and strident voices.

This must be what birth felt like.

'Hello, Cassie.' A man's face, Asian, loomed before her. 'How are you feeling?'

She tried to move her right arm but was stopped by a tugging pain in the back of her hand.

'Umm, better, I think.'

'You're on a dextrose drip.'

'What?'

'You're very lucky we found out what was wrong with you in time – although I have to admit you gave us a big hint.'

A doctor, she realised, although she had no clue what he was on about.

'The Islets of Langerhans?' he prompted.

A memory came rushing back: Mrs E pointing her scalpel at a dissected pig pancreas. *'The Islets of Langerhans,'* she was saying. *'It sounds like the name of some windswept island group in the Baltic, doesn't it? A romantic name for patches of endocrine tissue within the pancreas, with the unromantic but essential job of making some of the body's most important enzymes and hormones. Can anyone remember what these cells produce?'*

All the disparate fragments that had been floating around in her brain like so much space junk started to click together.

Mild-mannered Harry Hardwick had shouted at the nurses for starving him, after suffering a hypoglycaemic episode caused by his diabetes. Hunger and irritability were known side effects of an insulin surge.

So was feeling cold.

Mrs E had taken a hot bath because she felt chilly, and her late-night sandwich suggested hunger pangs.

Before Cassie had passed out, she too had felt bone-cold, hungry, and remembered swearing at the doctor.

Neither she nor Mrs E suffered from diabetes, but their symptoms all pointed in one direction.

Can anyone remember what these cells produce?'

'Insulin,' said Cassie.

Dr Sanjay was speaking. 'That's right. Your bloods show that you've suffered an insulin overdose.'

'I know.'

'Are you studying medicine? Is that how you got hold of the insulin?' He gave her a sympathetic look. 'I've asked the psychiatric registrar to drop by for a chat.'

She struggled up onto her elbows. 'No, listen. I didn't *take* insulin; I was injected with it.'

The collision in the market had been no accident, and she would bet her sore backside was the injection site. Seeing Dr Sanjay's expression, she said, 'Look, I'm not mentally ill. I'm an anatomical pathology technician. I work in the mortuary.'

Cassie felt suddenly tearful. Harry Hardwick and Mrs E had saved her life.

And now she knew what had killed Mrs E.

But how to prove it?

'Doctor, I need you to make a call for me.'

Chapter Forty-Six

Cassie opened her eyes to meet the worried gaze of Phyllida Flyte.

'I got here as fast as I could. They wouldn't tell me anything on the phone.' She sounded breathless, her eyes soft with concern. 'What happened?'

Propping herself upright on the pillows, Cassie explained about her blood-test results and what had happened to her in the market.

'You're saying somebody injected you with a hypodermic full of insulin – and you didn't notice?' The sympathetic tone acquiring a tinge of scepticism.

Cassie gritted her teeth. 'They're insulin pens these days, with superfine four-millimetre needles. And I didn't feel anything because whoever did it body-barged me so hard it knocked me over.'

'Could you identify this person?'

'No, he must have crept up behind me.' Cassie remembered 'seeing' Mrs E and having to race to keep up with her. Had she been trying to draw her away from danger? Or had Cassie herself subconsciously clocked the threat?

'He? You saw him then?'

'Well . . . no, but I guess I was assuming it must have been Christian?'

'He has a cast-iron alibi,' said Flyte crisply, her expression hard to decipher.

A passing nurse paused to give Cassie a meaningful look, followed by a nod towards a paper cup on the bedside table. Grimacing, she swigged some of the Lucozade they were feeding her to restore her blood-sugar levels.

'Don't you see, that must be how Mrs E was murdered,' she went on once the nurse was gone. 'Someone bashes into her in a crowded place and jabs her. Half an hour later the insulin spike starts to send her hypoglycaemic – her blood sugar dives, and her temperature plummets. She makes a sandwich, and gets into a hot bath to warm up, but goes into an insulin coma and drowns.'

Flyte seemed to be listening intently but her expression gave nothing away.

'Now, if she had just gone to bed, like the killer expected, she'd have been dead by the morning – and her liver would have metabolised the insulin, leaving no trace of it in her body. Understand?' Flyte nodded. 'But here's the thing. The killer *didn't* expect her to get into a bath and drown. And because she died *before* the insulin killed her, there should be unnaturally high levels of it left in her body.'

'So why didn't it show up in the tox report?'

'Because detecting insulin post-mortem is highly specialised. It's not something the lab would routinely test for.' Cassie was making a big effort not to show her impatience. 'You said she told her cleaner she was feeling unwell that night. And that she was slurring her words. That's another symptom of hypoglycaemia.'

'Or of having one too many whiskies,' Flyte shrugged.

Cassie slapped her palm down on the bed cover. 'So I get injected with insulin, I get the same symptoms as Mrs E just before she died – and it's all just a coincidence?' Aware of a sudden hush, she glanced over at the bed opposite. A visiting family – a mum and dad and their teenage daughter – clustered around the bed of an old lady had fallen silent and were clearly earwigging on the conversation.

She brought her voice down a notch. 'We have to stop the funeral and get her body back to the mortuary.'

'Cassie, the funeral's less than an hour away.' Flyte shook her head. 'My boss said he'd try the coroner's office, but I wouldn't hold your breath. Anyway, even if the body is cremated, isn't the lab required to keep all the post-mortem samples until the inquest? Why don't we simply ask them to re-test Geraldine's blood for insulin?'

'Insulin is unstable in blood – it won't be traceable by now.' Cassie felt like banging her head on the bedside cabinet. 'Our only hope is to find the injection site and test the surrounding tissue. And for that we need the body!'

The last bit came out louder than she intended. The family opposite were gawping openly now, the mum whispering to her daughter as if discussing the latest twist in a TV drama.

Flyte waited a moment before saying, 'It's understandable that you're upset. You've been under a lot of pressure recently, with Mrs E dying like that.'

At first, Cassie couldn't quite identify her subtle change of tone. Then she got it: for the first time in ages, Flyte was back talking to her like a cop would address a suspect.

Flyte glanced at her watch before turning a look on Cassie that radiated professional sympathy. 'Cassie, I have to ask. You didn't . . . harm *yourself*, did you? To stop the funeral and get a forensic PM for Mrs E?'

Cassie stared at her. So that was it. Flyte had just been pretending to believe her, all the while thinking what the doctors still clearly suspected – that she had injected the insulin herself.

'I would like you to leave now,' she said, turning her face into the pillow.

'Cassie . . .'

'Just go.'

Cassie's disappointment was seasoned with a certain bitter satisfaction: it proved that she should never have trusted a cop.

FLYTE

'*We have come here today to remember before God our sister Geraldine Olwyn Edwards, to give thanks for her life, and to commend her to God, our Merciful Redeemer . . .*'

The words sounded newly minted in the rolling Welsh cadences of the minister, a small, hump-backed yet animated old man who spoke as if he'd known the dead woman all her life. Perhaps Geraldine had stipulated in her will that he conduct the service; Flyte couldn't imagine her son making the effort.

Her eye fell on Owen Edwards' broad back squeezed into a dark shiny jacket in the front pew. He had no idea that she'd slipped in and was watching from the shadows at the rear of the church, nor that he'd be coming back to the nick after the service for questioning about the murder of Barry Renwick.

The elderly neighbour had identified Owen as the 'delivery man' who had knocked at Renwick's door on the day of his murder from his Facebook profile pic. Cassie Raven had been right to suspect that he'd been hiding something about his mother's death, and now Flyte was entertaining the idea that he and Renwick were possible accomplices, who had conspired in a plan to murder Geraldine Edwards and split the proceeds of her estate. Maybe they subsequently fell out – or Owen had killed Renwick simply to avoid having to share the booty. The only thing that didn't quite fit was their reported tussle the night Owen had turned up drunk at his mother's house. Had that simply been a piece of theatre laid on for Geraldine's benefit?

Flyte checked her phone again for any last-minute message from Bellwether, despite knowing it was surely too late now to halt the funeral. The chapel was full – the pews packed with a hundred mourners or more, including a woman who Flyte recognised from Facebook as Geraldine's friend Maddy O'Hare, along with dozens of younger people – no doubt the dead woman's former students.

The minister turned to face the flower-decked coffin on its conveyor belt. 'We now commit the body of our sister, Geraldine Edwards, to God's mercy . . . earth to earth, ashes to ashes, dust to dust.'

Flyte thought she had forearmed herself in readiness for the funeral, but hearing those ancient words – so terrible in their bleak finality – caught her unawares. Suddenly she was back in the delivery suite, two years and two months ago.

Nobody had said any words over her baby daughter. She had wanted a proper funeral, but Matt had resisted – a twenty-eight-week stillborn 'wasn't the same' as a child who had lived to draw breath, he'd argued, and anyway what was the point of upsetting themselves even more? Using reason, when the only possible response was an unreasoning howl of anger and pain.

But she didn't blame Matt; she blamed herself for not putting up a fight. Addled by grief and the trauma of the birth, after just two precious hours with her little girl she had let them take her away to the mortuary, to be stowed on a shelf in what Cassie Raven had called the foetal fridge.

Now the organ struck up a soft refrain, and the coffin started its journey towards the curtains.

Closing her eyes, Flyte pictured the perfect little face, eyelashes soot-dark against creamy cheeks.

Darling Poppy, she murmured under her breath – the first time that she'd uttered the name since that day. She braced herself for some collapse or cataclysm – but none came.

Dust to dust ... terrible words, yes, but at the same time strangely consoling, with their promise of continuity, of returning to where we came from.

A woman nearby had started to cry, the soft sound of her weeping an underscore to the organ's lament. Opening her eyes, Flyte saw it was Geraldine's friend Maddy. Several of the other mourners were smudging away tears, too, but Owen Edwards appeared unmoved, his watchful gaze fixed on his mother's coffin – did he fear a last-minute intervention that might yet save it from the flames?

Flyte glanced at the door, half-expecting to see Cassie Raven, still in her hospital gown, burst in to stop the ceremony. She remembered the expression of betrayal on Cassie's face when she'd pressed her on whether the insulin overdose might have been self-inflicted.

Having thought it over, Flyte had ruled out the idea. She really couldn't see Cassie going to such extreme lengths – she was just too smart. But it had been bruising to hear the old defiance back in the girl's voice. Maybe she'd been kidding herself, thinking they were on the way to becoming friends.

So who had attacked Cassie? Not Barry Renwick, who'd been twelve hours dead by then, and she couldn't picture the well-upholstered Owen Edwards chasing Cassie for any distance, let alone getting close enough to jab her without somebody noticing. She had told Josh to go down the market tomorrow at the time of the attack to look for witnesses.

The music faded away as the curtains closed behind the coffin, and the priest said a few final words. Then the organ started up again and the mourners stood to file out of the pews – Flyte's cue to move towards the central aisle. She waited while Owen went to shake the hand of the priest, bending to say something in his ear, a complacent smirk on his face.

Then he turned and saw her, and the smile slid from his face like ice cream thrown at a wall.

Chapter Forty-Seven

Cassie checked her phone again. Four thirty-five. The funeral service would be over by now. Flyte had promised to call if she had news from the coroner, which meant any hope of an eleventh-hour halt to the cremation was dead.

She visualised the chapel, heard the hum of the conveyor belt carrying Mrs E's coffin through the curtains towards the cremator. It wouldn't go straight into the flames – that was a Hollywood myth – but into the receiving room for final paperwork checks. Nonetheless, Mrs E's body, and with it any surviving evidence that she'd been poisoned by insulin, was just minutes away from destruction.

As Cassie's last hope drained away, a wave of weariness came over her. Until now, she'd been running on adrenalin, but the doctor had warned that her blood sugar rollercoaster ride would catch up with her.

'I'm so sorry, Mrs E,' she murmured. 'I did everything I could.'

She felt her muscles slackening, her eyelids drooping, but despite her weariness, there was a noise needling her, stopping her from falling asleep – the insistent beeping of a heart monitor from one of the nearby beds.

Her eyes snapped open.

Christ. Why didn't I think of that before?

FLYTE

'Where were you yesterday evening?' Flyte asked Owen Edwards, glancing at the recorder to ensure the red light was on.

'At the Central Inn in Holborn.'

'You didn't go out the whole evening?'

He fidgeted. 'Well, only to get a bit of dinner. I was in bed by around nine thirty.'

'Where exactly did you eat?'

She could see the sweat sheening his jowls. He'd spent the journey to the nick fulminating at being hauled in for questioning on the day of his mother's funeral, but now he was in the hot seat facing Flyte and Josh, he appeared to have mislaid his outrage.

'I couldn't tell you, in all honesty. It was just an ordinary cafe . . .'

'So when we check the hotel's security cameras, it will show you coming back and turning in at around nine thirty?' Her tone was matter of fact but her flat gaze told him she didn't believe him.

'There or thereabouts.'

From Holborn he could have reached Renwick's flat by Tube in forty minutes, much faster by taxi, but if the pathologist's estimate was right, Renwick had died no earlier than ten. If Edwards was the killer then he had to be lying about the time he'd gone to bed.

Edwards set both hands palms-down on the table, clearly trying to regain control of the situation. 'Now, look here, officer. You haven't even told me what all this is about.'

She looked up from her notebook. 'Are you familiar with the name Barry Renwick?'

Shaking his head, Edwards touched his chin, before hastily dropping his hand – perhaps realising the gesture was straight out of the barefaced liars' playbook.

'That's not entirely true though, is it, Owen? You did know Barry Renwick, or, as he was known to your mother, Christian Maclaren.'

Edwards' gaze pinballed around the room. Finding nowhere to hide, it came back to rest on her. 'It was that bastard who killed her,' he said, raising his chin. 'Why aren't you interrogating him instead of me?'

Well, well. 'Killed whom?'

'My mother.' His eyes narrowed to slits. 'The dirty thieving scumbag was after her money from the start. I kept telling her, he only wants to marry you to get his hands on the house.'

'Why were you so suspicious of him?'

'As if some high-flying architect would be interested in a woman of her age,' he scoffed, looking at her, then Josh, as if inviting them to agree with him, but finding only stony expressions. He folded his arms. 'Well, it turned out I was right all along.'

'Please explain.'

'After my mother died, I found an email on her laptop she'd sent to her so-called fiancé accusing him of being an impostor. She'd found out, see, that he wasn't even called Maclaren – he'd married some other woman under the name Renwick. He made a business out of defrauding lonely women.'

Julia Torrance.

'Did your mother say how she'd found him out?'

A headshake. 'No, but I'll say one thing for my mother: she was a clever woman. Despite her moment of menopausal madness.'

Flyte had to look down at her notebook to hide her expression. 'Did he reply?'

He shrugged. 'Oh yes, he sent her half a dozen emails. He admitted it all and gave her a load of crocodile tears about how sorry he was for everything he'd done.'

'But you wiped the drive and dumped the laptop.'

He nodded.

'Knowingly destroying evidence of significance to a police investigation into your mother's death. That's a very serious offence.'

'I was just trying to protect her good name, like any son would.'

'I think you wanted to collect your inheritance without the complications of a possible murder trial.'

Edwards shot her an angry look out of red-veined eyes.

Flyte stared right back at him. 'You asked me why we were interviewing you and not Barry Renwick.'

'Bloody right I did.'

'I'm hoping you can help us with that. Because Mr Renwick was found dead at his home this morning, with a stab wound to the throat.'

'What . . .?' Rising from his seat, he lunged across the table. 'You're not saying I did it?' Josh jumped up, shooting out an arm to protect her.

Flyte hadn't moved a centimetre. 'Sit down, Mr Edwards.' She waited for him to retake his seat. 'Did you and Renwick do a deal to get rid of your mother? You knew she considered you to be a drunk and a waster – were you worried that she might cut you out of her will?'

'You're off your bloody head! A lot of bull-shit, that is!'

'Did you and Renwick fall out over the money? Did the row get out of hand, was that it?'

'Utt-er rubb-ish.' Folding his arms, he turned his face to the wall.

'So what were you doing at Barry Renwick's flat in Brixton yesterday?'

His head snapped back to face her, and his gaze crawled over her face, clearly calculating whether she could prove that he'd been there.

'I . . . I went to tell him not to show his face at the funeral.'

'And the second time, when you went back later that night?'

'I bloody never!'

'Because we have a forensic team checking the flat for prints and DNA right this minute.'

Breathing heavily, Owen Edwards leaned forward. 'I came here in good faith,' he hissed, 'but I'm not saying another word without a solicitor.'

Chapter Forty-Eight

Batting away Dr Sanjay's gentle remonstrations, Cassie discharged herself from the hospital and walked the two hundred metres through the darkening car park to the mortuary, where she grabbed a clean set of scrubs. A glance in the changing room mirror revealed a face the colour of skimmed milk, but the only other after-effect of her insulin overdose was a deep exhaustion, like she'd just stepped off a long-haul flight.

Hearing the buzzer she went to the front entrance where she found the tall bearded figure of Luca silhouetted against the deepening twilight.

He handed her the delivery chit. 'So, somebody forgot to remove a pacemaker from a body, did they?' He widened his eyes in mock surprise. 'Twice in a week too! What are the odds?'

'Better safe than sorry, Luca,' she smiled. 'Nobody wants a lithium battery exploding in a cremator.'

Luca shook his head at her – part exasperated, part admiring.

The line she'd spun Roger the crematorium manager on the phone about another overlooked pacemaker had been a high-risk manoeuvre – and one that could get her the sack. But right at that moment her only feeling was huge relief at having saved Mrs E's body from destruction.

'The funny thing is,' Luca went on, still wearing a quizzical smile, 'just as we were putting her in the van, Roger came out. Told me the pacemaker mistake was actually a stroke of luck.'

That pulled Cassie up short. 'What did he mean?'

'He'd just got a call from the coroner telling him *not* to cremate Geraldine Edwards after all, because her body needed sending back to the mortuary for a full forensic PM.'

'*Really*?' So Flyte had done the business, after all.

'Yeah. If it wasn't for the pacemaker issue, she'd already have gone into the furnace by the time the coroner called.'

After she'd wheeled Mrs E into the autopsy suite, Cassie unzipped the body bag. 'Sorry about all the to-ing and fro-ing,' she told her, 'but you know why I had to do it.'

Cassie blinked. When she'd last seen Mrs E, her face had settled into a sombre expression that wasn't at all like her. But unless she was imagining it, there was now the ghost of a smile curving those lifeless lips: the kind of smile she used to give Cassie in class, when she raised her hand to answer a question.

Using an illuminated magnifying glass, she started to go over Mrs E's body centimetre by centimetre, searching for anything resembling a puncture wound. The chief toxicologist over at the lab in Hammersmith had told her that insulin might still be detectable, but only in tissue taken directly from an injection site. Drawing a blank, she gently turned Mrs E's body onto its front. The skin on her back was discoloured where the blood had settled, making the job more difficult. She worked systematically from the shoulders downwards, moving from side to side.

On the upper slope of Mrs E's left buttock she found something. A smudge of purple, no bigger than a grain of rice.

How could she have missed it at the PM? Then she remembered something Prof. Arculus had once told her: bruises could continue to develop after death.

Hearing the door open behind her, she turned to see Archie Cuff wearing his blue Barbour and a ridiculous hat with fur-lined earflaps.

'Hello there,' he grinned. 'What's all this about then? I was down my rugby club, limbering up for a heroic bender, when you called.'

Prof. Arculus had been Cassie's first choice, of course, but he was out of the country visiting First World War battlefields in the Somme – one of his passions.

'Come and have a look at this, will you.'

Bending down he looked through the magnifier.

'Do you see that? There?' she asked. Right in the bull's-eye of the bruise was a tiny dot. 'Could it be an injection site?'

'Hmm. It's possible,' said Archie, before nodding towards the closure stitches at the base of Mrs E's scalp. 'But hasn't this cadav— I mean, this lady, already had her PM?'

'Yep. But now the police think it might have been murder so they want a forensic.' She'd been planning to blag her way through this bit, but now her story had the added advantage of being true. 'They suspect she might have died from insulin poisoning.'

'How exotic!' Cuff's eyebrows shot up. 'So what do you need me for? Won't it have to wait till the Prof gets back?'

'We need to get a tissue sample over to the lab asap.' The chances of detecting insulin – already small – were dwindling with every passing day. 'I really appreciate you coming back,' she went on, swallowing her pride. 'I know you finished your list hours ago. Prof Arculus has approved it – he'll sign off on the paperwork when he gets back tomorrow.'

He gave her a look she couldn't work out. 'OK, I'll do it. On one condition.'

'Which is?'

'That you'll join me for a Ruby one evening.'

'A what?'

'Tsk tsk. A Ruby Murray.' His eyes were twinkling. 'And I thought you were fluent in rhyming slang.'

'Funny guy,' she said.

Maybe Archie Cuff could do banter after all.

FLYTE

It was the day after she'd interviewed Owen Edwards, and Flyte was feeling cautiously optimistic that the evidence to charge him with Barry Renwick's murder was almost within her grasp.

She had just got off the phone with the pathologist at Brixton Mortuary when Josh called her over. 'Sarge, there's something you need to see.' He nodded at his screen.

Judging by the look on his face, it wasn't a good something.

As he played her the clip from a CCTV camera, she felt her mouth drying to the texture of a rich tea biscuit. Dated two days earlier, the night Barry Renwick had died, it started with a long shot of a big man barrelling in through the revolving door of a hotel foyer. The image was fuzzy and it wasn't until he turned unsteadily towards the lift, narrowly avoiding a collision with a coffee table, that his face became visible. But she already knew who it was: Owen Edwards, returning from what must have been an extremely well-lubricated 'dinner' – and the time stamp in the corner of the screen read 21:26 – twenty-six minutes past nine.

'Bollocks,' she muttered, getting a sideways look from Josh, who had now heard her swear twice in twenty-four hours.

The forensic PM on Barry Renwick had confirmed the pathologist's initial finding that he had choked on his own blood, and had put his time of death at between 10 p.m. and 11 p.m. By which time, according to the CCTV footage, Owen Edwards was five miles away, sleeping off his binge.

'He doesn't go out again?' she asked.

Josh shook his head. 'Nope. There's a security cam on his corridor and he doesn't appear again till the morning.'

The whole picture had shifted again. If Owen Edwards hadn't murdered Barry Renwick, then who had? And was the same unknown assassin responsible for murdering Geraldine – and if Cassie Raven was right – trying to kill her, too?

'There goes our prime suspect – and our motive,' she said.

'What about the coke found at Renwick's place?' asked Josh.

Flyte pictured again the neat line of white powder, which had tested positive as cocaine. But the more she thought about it, the more calculated it seemed – like a theatrical prop labelled 'CLUE' left deliberately for the police to find.

She shook her head. 'I just don't buy the "drug deal gone wrong" scenario. Renwick's murder has to be connected to his plan to defraud Geraldine Edwards. Did you dig up any more about his previous?'

The national database had revealed that fifteen years earlier Renwick had been sentenced to six months in jail for two counts of obtaining money by deception.

'The case notes say that he used to film weddings,' said Josh. 'He did a few, but then started taking deposits and not turning up. He had a female accomplice, apparently, who dealt with the clients.'

'Girlfriend?'

He shrugged. 'When the police busted him, Renwick refused to name her. His refusal to cooperate is probably what got him a custodial sentence.'

'Very gallant of him.'

Josh had also located Renwick's ex-wife, Julia Torrance – although she no longer lived at the address given on the marriage register. Three months after marrying Renwick she had sold her house for £1.4 million and then, a year to the day after the wedding – at the earliest juncture permitted by law – she'd filed for divorce. Tellingly, her solicitor had to use a special procedure for divorce cases in which there was no known address for the respondent. Barry Renwick had apparently disappeared, no doubt to spend the proceeds of his hapless wife's property. But at least Julia Torrance had escaped with her life.

'I've asked Chester nick to send a uniform to her house to give her a knock, Sarge.' He looked up from the screen. 'Do you think she's a possible suspect?'

'For killing Renwick?' Flyte had considered the idea. 'It's not impossible.' She took her coat off the back off the chair. 'Call me if you get anything useful.'

'Where are you off to, Sarge?'

'The hospital, to see if Cassie Raven has remembered anything about yesterday.'

Josh's smile faded. 'I thought you knew.'

'Knew what?'

'She discharged herself yesterday evening.'

A chilly dread descended on Flyte. In hospital, Cassie had been relatively safe. Out on the street, there was a distinct possibility that whoever had tried to kill her might try their luck again.

Chapter Forty-Nine

Cassie had told her grandmother a white lie to explain why she'd needed to stay over the previous night, claiming that her boiler had broken down. In truth, after her traumatic day, she'd felt in need of some TLC and Polish comfort food.

The calls from Flyte had started around nine that morning. Cassie had ignored them, still furious that she hadn't believed her story, but seeing her name came up on the display for the fifth or sixth time, curiosity got the better of her.

'What were you thinking of, discharging yourself like that?' Flyte barked down the phone. 'The doctor said it's a serious matter, an insulin overdose.'

'Self-inflicted, according to you,' Cassie shot back.

An exasperated sigh. 'I'm a police officer – it's my job to ask the awkward questions.' Then her tone softened. 'But look, Cassie, I . . . I do believe you.'

Cassie wasn't ready to accept the olive branch. 'Whatever. I'm fine now.' In fact she still felt a bit shaky and hadn't argued when Doug ordered her to take the day off.

'Listen to me. Somebody tried to kill you and right now we have no idea who. Keeping you safe is my . . . is our responsibility. What if they come after you again? Where are you right now?'

Hearing the concern in Flyte's voice, Cassie relented. 'I'm at my gran's – I stayed here last night.' Obviously, the fact that her insulin-wielding attacker was still on the loose had crossed her mind. She'd even accepted Archie Cuff's offer to walk her home the previous evening. They'd had good banter on the way and Cassie had got the vibe that romance might be on the cards if she was interested – and to her surprise, she realised that she might be.

What's up with me? she thought. Having already got far closer than was sensible to a cop, now she was thinking of shagging a hooray?

'I'm glad to hear it. Why don't you stay put? I've got an officer attending the market this morning to look for witnesses, and I need to take a statement from you.'

Cassie sighed. In the light of day she was feeling more relaxed about going home – confident she'd be able to shake off anyone trying to follow her.

Flyte said, 'The quicker we can work out who attacked you, the better our chances of catching Geraldine's killer.'

As a ploy it was transparent – but hard to dispute. 'OK, I'll wait. But don't be long.'

DS Flyte gave up trying to make out what the guard was saying over the underground train's antediluvian public address system, but since they'd been sitting in a tunnel for ten minutes, she didn't really need telling that there was a problem. She cursed her decision to take the Tube to Cassie's grandmother's flat, located on Camden's southern fringe. She'd been trying to save time: choosing a two-stop journey from Chalk Farm to Mornington Crescent over a twenty-minute walk on pavements viscous with tourists.

Strictly speaking, she ought to have sent Josh to interview Cassie. Instead she found herself once again sticking her neck out for the impossible creature – and still no more able to explain why.

At the housing estate where Weronika Janek lived she found an out-of-order notice taped to the lift. Six flights of stairs later, she was out of breath and sweating under her coat.

A tiny old lady with intelligent eyes, answered the door promptly but with an apologetic look. 'I'm very sorry, officer, but you've just missed her.'

Checking her phone, Flyte saw a text from Cassie saying she'd had to go home to feed her cat, *for crying out loud*, leaving her no option but to turn around and head back the way she came.

When Cassie reached her own block, she eyed the stairs before deciding against the climb. Despite sleeping ten hours straight the previous night, the walk home had taken it out of her. By the time the lift came, two other people had joined her: an attractive woman carrying a clipboard and wearing cool boots, and a young guy with a flashy ring on his pinkie, expensive tracksuit bottoms, and the obligatory hoodie. After hitting the button for the ninth floor, she asked which floor they wanted, but hoodie guy ignored her, leaning across to punch it himself, deliberately invading her space.

Using her peripheral vision, she checked him out. From his fresh features he couldn't be more than sixteen or seventeen, but he'd already mastered the dead-eyed stare and fuck-you body language of the entry-level gangsta. Guys like him were hardly unusual in her block – and with half of them it was no more than a defence mechanism – but just in case, she opted to get off at the floor below hers and take the stairs the rest of the way. At her front door she checked that the landing was clear behind her before going inside and double-locking the door.

Staring up at her from the doormat was a picture postcard showing some random sand dunes, somewhere on the UK coast. The scrawled message on the back read simply: 'You wouldn't Adam and Eve how nice it is here'. The postmark read Exeter and she didn't need a signature to know it was from Carl – letting her know he was OK, that he'd reached his place of exile in one piece.

With Phyllida Flyte on the way over, she decided it might be wise to burn it. She'd just finished wafting the smoke out the window and was sluicing the ashes down the sink when the doorbell rang. She peered through the spyhole, and saw it wasn't Flyte, but the clipboard woman from the lift.

Flyte wasn't going to risk the Tube again: hailing the first black cab she saw, she gave the driver Cassie's address.

As the cab lurched forward, her mobile rang. It was Josh – and from the tiresome tattoo of bongo drums in the background he must be calling from the market.

'Any progress?'

'I couldn't find anyone who actually saw her go down,' he said. 'But one of the stallholders said he saw the scrum right after it happened. He went to see what was up and heard somebody say something about a "rude woman".'

'Meaning?'

'He took it to mean that whoever knocked Cassie over was a female.'

A female. Flyte had always pictured Cassie's attacker as a man. But this new information made perfect sense: it would have been easier for a woman to get close to another woman in a public place without attracting unwelcome attention.

It would also explain how the killer had got close enough to jab Geraldine Edwards. She remembered her cleaner Imelda saying that the night Geraldine died, she had just returned from the supermarket.

An innocent-seeming collision in a crowded place before she went on her way, unaware of the toxin surging through her bloodstream.

But who the hell was the mysterious female assassin?

'I'm sorry, I'm a bit busy . . .' said Cassie.

'It'll only take five minutes, I promise.'

Clipboard lady was from a market research company and persistent in a charming way, but Cassie wasn't tempted – not even by the prospect of a generous twenty quid, just for answering a few questions about hair and beauty products.

'I'm really sorry,' she said again, sugaring the rejection with a smile and going to close the door.

The woman pressed the clipboard to her chest, and dropped her eyes, but not before Cassie caught the quiver that crossed her face. 'I'm the one who should be sorry,' the woman murmured, dropping the sales patter. 'I was being pushy.'

'Are you OK?'

The woman drew a shaky breath. 'I'm fine. I probably came back to work too early.' She started to tear up. 'You see I . . . I lost someone recently.'

'I'm so sorry to hear that,' said Cassie, suddenly feeling mean. 'Can I get you a drink of water?'

'No, please, I wouldn't hear of it.' She flapped a hand at her eyes as if the tears were a cloud of insects she could fan away. 'God, this is so unprofessional.'

Cassie opened the door a little wider. 'Come in for a cuppa,' she said, relenting. 'And once you're feeling a bit better, we'll do this survey of yours.'

It only took a couple of minutes for Flyte's cab to reach Camden High Street, but by the time it reached the railway bridge, the traffic had started to congeal.

She stared out at the passers-by crowding the pavement. *Go back to the fundamentals.* If, as seemed likely, Renwick had met Julia Torrance through an online dating site, how had he identified property-rich women like her and Geraldine upfront? Given the elaborate nature of the scam, she couldn't see him taking a scattergun approach – grooming multiple women online and having to meet them individually in order to find out who owned valuable properties. And Beth Montagu at Ocean had revealed that Geraldine was Renwick's only contact on the site. So there had to be some flaw in their supposedly cast-iron security systems that allowed him to pinpoint his victims upfront.

She called Geraldine's friend Maddy, getting hold of her just as she was about to go into class. 'Did Geraldine say how quickly she and Christian made contact after she joined Ocean?'

'He messaged her the first day. Which was a bit galling since I'd already been on there for two weeks without so much as a sniff,' said Maddy with a chuckle.

'You said they were very security conscious when you joined up. What sort of information did they ask for?'

'Um, I had to fill in a long form, and send in a payslip.'

'On this form, did they ask whether you were a homeowner?'

A pause. 'Yes. I remember thinking that they might reject me because I rent my place.'

Whereas Geraldine would have ticked the owner-occupier box which, together with her address, would have marked her out as someone who owned a house in one of Camden's grandest streets.

But how might Renwick have got hold of such highly sensitive information? Could he really have hacked into Ocean's database and stolen members' details?

Only that week Flyte had received a spam call offering her a 'once-in-a-lifetime investment opportunity' – suspiciously soon after she'd entered her details online to get information on a stocks and shares ISA. Had Ocean been selling on its valuable membership database, together with members' confidential and personal information? A serious breach of data privacy laws, but hardly uncommon among unscrupulous firms. Lucy Halliwell, Ocean's MD, might appear polished and respectable but she wouldn't be the first company director to use dubious means to keep her business afloat.

Flyte coughed into her handkerchief – the sooty taste of diesel was irritating the back of her throat – and realised that the cab had been stationary for some time, its windscreen filled with the rear ends of cars and trucks snaking into the distance.

She tapped on the glass partition.

'They're replacing a gas main up ahead,' the driver threw over his shoulder.

'Can't you take another route?'

He shook his head. 'Sorry, sweetheart. There is no other route to where you're going: the canal's in the way.'

Slumping back in her seat, she pulled up the number for Ocean on her phone. By providing Barry Renwick's address, Beth Montagu had already proven she wasn't unthinkingly loyal to the company, and as membership manager she might even be aware if Lucy Halliwell really was selling off members' data.

Reaching Ocean's recorded message, Flyte tapped in extension 131, the number she'd memorised from the handset in Beth's cubbyhole.

It rang a few times, then clicked onto another line before being picked up.

'Lucy Halliwell.'

Interesting. What was Halliwell doing, taking her underling's calls?

'It's DS Flyte. I was actually calling Beth Montagu, to clarify something about Maclaren's profile.'

There was a meaningful pause. 'I'm sure you're aware, officer, that any such requests to my staff should be directed through me.' Her voice as smooth and glassy as those nails of hers.

'I'm afraid we don't always have time to observe corporate protocol in a murder investigation. But since we're chatting, perhaps you can help me with something else that's come up?'

'I'll try, of course.'

'Would it surprise you to discover that some of your members' confidential information had ended up in the wrong hands?'

There was a longer pause. 'I . . . that is, Ocean has a *very* robust policy on personal data. The confidentiality of our members' personal information is absolutely sacrosanct.'

Same old corporate hot air – but until Flyte received the go-ahead to trawl Ocean's systems, she had little to gain by pushing the point.

She was about to hang up when curiosity got the better of her. 'By the way, can I ask why you're fielding Beth's calls?'

'Beth isn't in today.'

Something in Halliwell's tone – an uptick of anxiety – caught Flyte's attention.

'Is she off sick?'

'We're not sure actually. She didn't turn up for work – and we haven't been able to reach her. I was thinking of calling the hospital, actually.'

'The hospital? Isn't that a bit over-dramatic?'

'Well . . . ' She hesitated. 'Beth has . . . a serious medical condition.'

Flyte felt her scalp contract. Then her brain caught up.

A woman could get close to another woman. A woman was more likely to be trusted.

Once she started going through her script, market researcher lady quickly regained her cool. But Cassie knew how grief could blow up in sudden and violent squalls, and recede just as swiftly.

'On a scale of one to ten, with one meaning "strongly disagree" and ten meaning "strongly agree", how would you rate the following statement: "*Regular pedicures are an essential part of a woman's beauty routine.*"'

Cassie bugged her eyes. 'Is there a "who cares" answer?' Her mobile lit up with an incoming call but on seeing *Phyllida Flyte* appear on the display, she dismissed it with a jab of her thumb.

'I'll make that a one then, shall I?' the lady smiled, before ticking the box. She was filling in the survey old-school style, with pencil and paper – maybe carrying a tablet around Camden estates was considered too risky.

Stifling a sigh, Cassie reached for another chocolate biscuit. 'Are you sure you can't help me out here, before I eat them all?' Dr Sanjay had said it was important that she ate regularly, even if she didn't feel hungry.

The woman pulled a rueful grimace, 'I'd love to. But I'm on a no-sugar diet.' Using both hands she swept her dark hair behind her ears: the one facing Cassie had been pierced on the outer edge, but held no earring.

'Let me top you up at least.'

As Cassie poured the tea, her eye fell again on the woman's boots – plum-coloured patent leather Doc Martens – enviably stylish footwear for a door-to-door pollster. She felt sure she'd seen them somewhere else recently: had it been online? Or had somebody down the Vibe bar been wearing a pair?

The woman frowned down at the questionnaire, spinning her pencil round the first and second finger of her right hand. 'That's it! We're all done.' Delving into her little leather money belt, the woman handed Cassie a twenty-pound note. 'Sorry about earlier.' She bit her lip. 'I don't know what came over me.'

'Hey, it's no problem,' said Cassie, suddenly on the verge of tears herself. 'I know what it's like to lose somebody.'

The woman didn't seem to notice. 'Do you mind if I use your loo?'

After directing her to the bathroom, Cassie collected their mugs and took them to the sink. As she washed up, she tried to recall where she'd seen those distinctive DMs before. She frowned at her reflection in the kitchen window, cursing the insulin overdose for slowing her brain to a crawl.

Then it hit her. The club in Shoreditch where she'd last met 'Christian'. The woman who'd passed her on the stairs had been wearing the exact same boots. Which made her realise something else. Although that woman had shades on and her hair tucked under a beanie, the way she had carried herself was a lot like pollster lady. Another image flew into Cassie's mind. The empty glass sitting opposite Christian that day – a business meeting, he'd said.

Cassie suddenly knew that the person 'Christian' had been meeting that day was the woman currently using her bathroom.

Whatever she was doing here, it couldn't be good.

Cassie caught a shift in the reflection in the window over the sink. Saw the woman's outline silhouetted in the kitchen doorway behind her. Something about the way she was moving made Cassie's stomach swoop.

Stealthy. That was the word.

Cassie shifted and turned in one movement, hurling the mug at her head. It missed, smashing on the tiled floor, and the woman flew towards her, right arm scissoring down. There was a banshee screech as steel met the steel of the sink where Cassie had been standing. As she raised the knife again, Cassie twisted out of the way and threw up her right arm, taking a glancing blow to the underside of her forearm. *Classic defensive injury*, part of her brain noted, as her other hand shot out to grab for the knife. She got a half-hold on the handle and they wrestled over it face to face for a horrible moment. The woman made no sound, but her eyes blazed with hatred.

Who the hell was she?

Feeling herself losing the tug of war, Cassie suddenly stopped pulling, transferring all her force into a giant shove. The woman staggered backwards, off balance but still holding the knife, fury contorting her face.

Running for the door, Cassie flung herself through, before slamming it behind her. The same with the front door. Outside, she took the stairs down one level, then another, and ran along the landing, banging at random doors. Bang bang bang . . . *No answer* . . . Ring ring . . . *no answer* . . . Where the hell was everyone? Out at work? . . . Or too scared to open up? Her heart jumped when she saw a curtain move in one front window, but it was a frail old man who peeked out, mouth agape with fear. Hand to ear, Cassie mimicked a phone call, shouted 'Call the cops!' Racing back to the stairwell she heard the clatter of footsteps on the stairs overhead.

Reaching the bottom she hesitated by the bins area, breathing heavily from the exertion. *What to do*? But the sound of those boots coming down the stairs behind her – fast – spurred her into a sprint across the turf, focused on putting the maximum possible distance between her and her pursuer. The estate was deserted this time of day: she needed to get somewhere busy. *The market.* As she took the stairs leading down to the canal, she risked a look back over her shoulder. The woman was only a hundred metres behind, gaze fixed on her target, running, her long stride efficient-looking. She had to be at least ten years older than Cassie, and on any other day Cassie would have felt confident of winning the race, but the insulin overdose had left her muscles feeling shaky and weak.

Reaching the canal, she scanned the towpath ahead – but there was not a soul to be seen. Hardly anyone strayed up here – the 'wrong' end of the canal – a good mile from the market. She set off at a run again, her lungs already complaining. As her right arm swung, she saw it inscribe a fine spatter of blood on the towpath, dripping off her little finger from the slash wound on her arm.

Then, a sight that galvanised her. Two figures fifty metres away, just going under one of the bridges that crossed the canal. Dropping her head she put on a sprint. They had paused in the shadows of the bridge. As she got closer, she threw another look over her shoulder. The woman was on the towpath now: even over that short distance she'd gained on Cassie.

She drew level with the two men. 'Hey . . .' panting desperately. 'That woman . . .' but she didn't even bother finishing the sentence. They both shot the breathless girl a single, incurious look, before returning to their business, a package changing hands for a fold of notes.

Run. Just keep . . . running. Lungs burning. Thigh muscles on fire – but worse, starting to quiver already.

Another backward glance. The woman was now barely forty strides away – so close that Cassie could see her expression. She looked almost relaxed, as if there was no question how this would end.

After Flyte had finished questioning Halliwell, she hung up and rapped the cab's glass partition again, thrusting her warrant card under the driver's nose. 'I'm a detective sergeant with Camden CID and this is an emergency. Put your hazards on and let's go.'

He waved at the solid traffic up ahead 'You could be the Queen of the May, darling – there's no way through this lot. You'd be quicker jumping out and walking up the canal.'

To reach the towpath, Flyte had to fight her way through the market, teeming with lunchtime crowds. She caught the

burning-compost reek of skunk punching through the barbe-
cued chicken smell, but it didn't even occur to her to look for
who was smoking it. She re-checked her phone: still nothing
from Cassie. No way of knowing whether she'd seen Flyte's text
warning her of the danger she was in.

Now she was crossing the first bridge, shouldering her way
through the drifting shoals of sightseers taking pictures of what
passed for a view round here – a dank and scuzzy canal, walls
defaced with graffiti.

A couple of minutes on and the crowds started to thin,
allowing her to speed up to a jog. Again, she went over the
clues she'd missed at Renwick's flat. The neatly quartered naan
bread, the bottle of Chablis – a woman's touch. The bin bag
under Renwick's corpse to make it easier for the slightly built
Beth to drag him into the bedroom. And that newspaper clipping of *Romeo and Juliet* in the bin – the teenage Juliet had to
be a younger version of Beth Montagu – she had even assumed
Romeo's surname when applying for the job at Ocean.

All of it easy to see now. Beth Montagu and Barry Renwick
had been accomplices, presumably lovers, but it had been Beth
who had injected Cassie with the insulin she used to control her
diabetes.

Flyte had to fight down a rising sense of panic. Even in life-
threatening situations she'd been able to rely on her training to
remain calm. So why did her fears for Cassie feel so overwhelm-
ing? Out of her churning thoughts, a voice broke the surface.

Because Cassie Raven has got under your skin.

Ahead of Cassie there was still no sign of life on the towpath.
She focused on running, just running, the only sound aside

from the ragged in-out of her breath the whirr of wings from the occasional panicked moorhen as she raced past.

A stiletto of pain skewered her left thigh, an attack of cramp that slowed her to a limping jog. Then an ominous sound – the steady beat of the woman's footsteps behind her. A metronome counting down the seconds.

Up ahead she saw the canal curve to the left, and pictured the bridge that lay just beyond, its stairs going up to the road. Reaching the point in the bend where she would become invisible to her pursuer, she put on a final, wobbling sprint. Out from under the bridge, then a sharp about-turn up the first flight of steps. On the half-landing, her breath coming hard and shallow, muscles screaming, she got one knee up onto the brick balustrade, heaving the rest of her body after it. Trying to quiet her breathing, she crouched there, blinking down at the towpath a few metres below.

The dark head of the woman emerged from beneath the bridge, her pace slowing in confusion. Cassie's stomach flipped to see the blade already clutched in her hand. *Wait till she's underneath*, she told herself. Seeing the woman's face started to tilt upwards, Cassie half-jumped, half-fell on her.

A shockingly long moment – before they landed in a tangle on the canal's edge, Cassie's ankle sending up a shriek of pain as she hit the deck. The woman's body partly broke her fall, but the impact was still enough to expel her last breath. Gasping for air, the oily water of the canal horribly close to her face, Cassie wrestled to get a grip on the thrashing figure half beneath her. She could feel the woman's hand – her knife hand – flailing around. Cassie desperately tried to capture it, but time and time again, it slipped from her sticky grasp. Drop by drop she felt the fight drain out of her.

Catching sight of her own chest, Cassie was struck by a distant sense of dismay. Her T-shirt, once a light blue, was now stained a deep and vivid red.

A buzzing in her ears was pierced by a shout. A female voice, braced with authority.

Phyllida Flyte's face looms above her, those pretty pink lips moving but no sound coming out, like she's been muted. The face disappears: it's just another of her apparitions. Then the shock of cold air on Cassie's midriff as her T-shirt is tugged upward. She wants to joke – 'I thought you'd never ask' – but can't find enough breath to form the words.

Then Phyllida's face was back and this time the volume had been restored. 'Cassie! Listen to me. You're OK. It's her blood – not yours.'

As Phyllida manoeuvred her away from the canal's edge, Cassie got a glimpse of her attacker. She had stopped moving. A scarf of scarlet was looped around her neck, pooling in the notches above her clavicles and tumbling onto the concrete below.

An image came back to Cassie then – the woman spinning her pen through her fingers, just like she'd seen Christian do with a cocktail stick – the kind of trick that kids teach each other. *Of course.*

She tried to catch the eye of Flyte, who was pressing something against the woman's neck.

'What is it, Cassie?'

'Her … she's … '…' she managed to lift a hand in her attacker's direction. 'Sh … she's Barry Renwick's sister.'

FLYTE

The following day, DS Flyte and Josh made their way to the hospital's private wing, where the woman calling herself Beth Montagu was being treated.

A uniformed cop stood on watch outside her room. 'Hi Ben,' said Flyte. 'Is the doctor still in with her?'

'Yeah. He's been in there a while. The paramedics said you saved the psycho from bleeding to death.' He sent her a sly look. 'How does that make you feel?'

'Wishing I hadn't been such a swot on the advanced first-aid course.'

He gave an appreciative snort.

A week ago, Flyte would probably have reminded him it was their job to preserve life, even the life of a suspected murderer – might even have quoted the 'duty of care' wording from the Met safety manual at him. But the attack on Cassie had shifted something fundamental in her outlook. For the first time in fourteen years as a police officer, she had allowed herself to become personally involved – and what was more, she didn't care.

A youngish male doctor emerged from the room.

Flyte showed her warrant card before asking, 'How's she doing?'

'We had to give her three units of blood, but she's out of immediate danger.' He lowered his voice. 'You were right about her being diabetic: her blood sugar levels were dangerously high. If you hadn't told us when she came in, she'd be in a coma by now – or worse.'

Flyte heard Ben pointedly clearing his throat behind her.

'Can we talk to her?'

'Yes. She's been asking to speak to the police ever since she regained consciousness.'

Beth Montagu was tethered to a bag of blood that drip-fed life into the back of her hand, her face candlewax-pale above the throat bandage covering the near-fatal wound made by the knife she'd been holding when Cassie had jumped her. But questioning her about that would have to wait until they found witnesses to back Cassie's claim that Beth Montagu had been pursuing her.

Flyte hadn't even opened her mouth before Beth said, 'I asked to see you because I wanted to tell you everything I know.' She sounded heartfelt.

She kept her eyes lowered while Flyte read the caution, occasionally smudging away tears – had there been a script, the stage direction would have read 'bravely'.

'So, Beth – or, as we should call you, Elizabeth Renwick. When did you and your brother Barry decide to target wealthy women on the Ocean database?'

Flyte enjoyed the way that Elizabeth's eyes had narrowed on being addressed by her real name.

Cassie Raven's hunch about the pair's relationship had proved to be correct – Josh had confirmed the connection when he'd followed up the newspaper report on their performance of *Romeo and Juliet*. The Stockwell Players were still going strong and he'd been able to retrieve an old programme from their archive. His digging also revealed that Elizabeth and Barry Renwick had been born to the same chaotic, alcoholic mother by two different, unnamed fathers. Barry had been put on the 'at risk' register as a toddler and later, not long after his baby sister was born, they were both removed to spend the rest of their childhood in care.

Despite the exposure of her true identity, Elizabeth made a swift recovery, turning her tear-stained gaze up to Flyte. 'If I'd ever had even the slightest idea that he was planning to defraud anyone, I never would have helped him.'

'Really. So what did you think he was up to exactly when he asked for details of women with valuable properties like Geraldine Edwards?'

'That's not how it happened. I helped him because . . . I didn't want him to get hurt.' Seeming not to notice Flyte's expression, she steepled her eyebrows. 'I simply passed on the profiles of women who seemed . . . genuine. Women who I could imagine becoming my future sister-in-law.'

God, she was good though. The diffident Beth Montagu in the cubbyhole at Ocean had all but disappeared, to be replaced by Elizabeth Renwick's latest, and most tragic role – the loyal, loving sister, riven by regret.

'And you really expect a jury to buy that, do you?' Flyte sent her a flat stare – but even as she said it, she felt a ripple of unease.

'I love my brother,' she plucked mournfully at the bedclothes – a gesture straight out of some forties movie. 'I just . . . I just want him to be happy.'

Flyte put the photocopy of an application form on the coverlet in front of her. 'If it was all so innocent, then why did you use a false identity and NI number to apply for the job at Ocean?'

Elizabeth didn't miss a beat. 'I can explain that. At a previous job my boss found out I had type-1 diabetes and that was the end of my promotion chances. I know there's supposed to be a law against disability discrimination, but you try proving it.' She gave a sad little shake of her head. 'Knowing that my old employer had my private medical information on file, I decided it was safer to reinvent myself. After joining Ocean I did have a hypoglycaemic attack at work one day, and Lucy was very understanding. But by then . . .' – a regretful little intake of breath – 'it was too late to admit my real name.'

Pulling out a polythene evidence bag, Flyte showed her the newspaper cutting showing her and her brother playing Romeo and Juliet. 'I think you and Barry have been partners in crime for a long time. Did it all start with the amateur dramatics? You discovered you were good at pretending to be other people, didn't you? And realised it was a way to make money.'

A squiggle appeared between Elizabeth's brows – wondering, no doubt, where the clipping had come from after she had cleared every trace of anything that might connect them from Barry's flat. 'It was just a hobby, nothing sinister. The children's home where we were brought up had a drama club and we both got the bug. Life in the home could be . . . difficult, so the chance to escape into a role was rather wonderful.'

Picturing Elizabeth Renwick in the dock, Flyte imagined how this touching history would play with the more credulous members of the jury. She looked down at her notebook. 'What role did you play in your brother's scheme to defraud people who wanted their weddings filmed?'

'I don't know anything about that.'

The reply was too fast to be truthful. 'I think you do, Elizabeth. I checked the witness statements and you fit the description of his female accomplice to a tee. But Barry took the rap for the whole thing, didn't he? Protecting his little sister.'

'That's not true!' Elizabeth widened her eyes. 'It's always been me trying to keep him on the straight and narrow. When his behaviour started to change recently, I knew he must be taking cocaine again.'

The claim was predictable. It had to have been Elizabeth herself who'd planted the line of coke at his flat, a piece of conspicuous stagecraft to support the storyline of a drug deal gone wrong.

'And then when you turned up, investigating the death of that poor woman,' she pressed a hand to her chest, 'I got really worried. Why do you think I called you? I knew he needed to be stopped.'

You stopped him all right, thought Flyte.

Major Crimes didn't want Elizabeth Renwick questioned about her brother's murder before they had any evidence to place her in his flat that night. But Geraldine Edwards was another matter.

'Do you deny suggesting Geraldine Edwards to your brother as a target? A lady whom, as you know, died unexpectedly two weeks ago.'

Elizabeth dropped her eyes to the coverlet. 'I suppose . . . it makes no difference now . . .' Her voice was hoarse with counterfeit emotion.

Flyte stared at her, fascinated despite herself.

'Barry stayed over at my place a couple of weeks back. We fell out because he was taking drugs again, which made me feel just awful about passing Geraldine's name on to him. He admitted he was only on the site to "bag himself a rich woman".' A sad little headshake. 'Then, a couple of days later, I noticed something was missing.' She paused – a nice bit of dramatic timing – before meeting Flyte's gaze. 'He'd stolen a box of my insulin pens.'

It was only then that it dawned on Flyte. Elizabeth Renwick didn't really care whether she bought the story or not: this was all just a dress rehearsal for her biggest role yet: the loving sister who would need to persuade a jury of her innocence. Picturing her in the dock, Flyte had an uneasy presentiment of how it would end: Elizabeth Renwick would be given the benefit of the doubt, while her dead brother shouldered the blame for the murder of Geraldine Edwards.

That was the trouble with the dead: they weren't around to defend themselves.

Chapter Fifty

'Remember the last time you were here? When you confiscated my skull?' Limping across the kitchen to hand Phyllida Flyte her tea, Cassie sent her an exploratory grin.

All she got back was a tight smile, followed by the polite enquiry, 'How's the leg?' – nodding down at the fracture boot that encased the lower half of Cassie's right leg. It'd been four days since Elizabeth Renwick had chased her along the canal tow-path leaving her with five stitches in her arm and a broken ankle.

'Sore. Itchy. But I'll take a stable fracture over a knife in the guts any day.' She took a slug of tea. No point sharing the other legacy of the attack: the times she'd come bolt awake in the dark, shivering and sweaty in her sheets, trying to blot out the horrible look on Elizabeth Renwick's face as she'd lunged at her. 'It *is* gonna put the mockers on my line-dancing career though' – her admittedly lame joke getting zero response from Flyte.

In fact, she seemed stiffer if anything, the uptight cop persona firmly back in the driving seat, reluctant even to make eye contact.

They drank their tea in silence before Cassie spoke again. 'I haven't really thanked you properly for what you did.'

'I didn't do anything.' Flyte lifted a shoulder. 'By the time I got there you'd taken care of it yourself.'

'But you didn't have to come after me like that . . . ' Cassie tailed off, remembering the moment on the towpath when Flyte's face had appeared above her – the sudden conviction that everything would be all right. 'So, seriously, thank you for, you know, going the extra mile.'

'You're welcome.' Still Flyte barely glanced at her.

'Isn't it brilliant about the tox report?' Cassie tried. That morning the toxicology unit had reported that they'd identified the chemical signature of pharmaceutical insulin in Geraldine Edwards' tissue sample.

Flyte made a regretful face. 'Look, it's helpful, obviously . . .'

'Helpful? This Renwick woman is a diabetic and she uses the same brand of synthetic insulin that Mrs E and I OD'd on. And she chased me for a mile with a blade. She's so obviously guilty!'

'We haven't found any witnesses to her chasing you yet – she's claiming that it was you who committed assault, when you ambushed her. And as you know, both of you left prints on the knife.'

'You've got to be kidding! She sat *right there* asking me about freaking *pedicures* – before she tried to eviscerate me. How are you ever supposed to put anyone away?' Cassie stopped. Finding herself siding with the cops was a disorientating experience, like looking through her grandmother's glasses.

Cassie still couldn't get over what a total muppet she'd been, letting Elizabeth Renwick into her flat. But then Elizabeth had known exactly which buttons to press – turning on the tears, saying she'd lost someone – obviously having learned from her bastard of a brother that Cassie worked with the bereaved.

'It might help if we knew how she found out where you live,' said Flyte. 'Did you ever share your address with her brother, for instance?'

Cassie shook her head. She'd only ever shared her email with 'Christian', when she'd sent him the details of Mrs E's funeral. Then she remembered. That day when she'd got the feeling that someone was following her, on her way home from the mortuary – the well-dressed woman in sunglasses behind her, apparently focused on her mobile. Maybe she'd shaken her off on that occasion, but Elizabeth would have had plenty of opportunities to follow her home another time.

Flyte listened in silence before taking a careful sip of tea – the way she was avoiding Cassie's gaze suggesting more bad news to come. 'Cassie ... there's something else I need to tell you. Elizabeth Renwick is going to claim that it was her brother who murdered Geraldine. She says that he stole the insulin from her.'

'What? She's lying, right?'

Flyte nodded 'Barry was in the conspiracy up to his neck, but everything points to Elizabeth doing the actual deed. Unfortunately, we're still a long way from proving that it was Elizabeth who killed Geraldine – and her own brother.'

Cassie was still digesting the news that Christian Maclaren – aka sleazy fraudster Barry Renwick – now lay in a mortuary drawer, murdered by his little sister.

'Have you remembered anything that "Christian" might have let slip that could help us to charge her?'

Cassie heard him saying – *I loved having a little sister* – and pictured the sadness in his eyes. 'Like I said, I just got the impression they'd been very close, before having some sort of bust-up. But to murder your own brother . . .? Why do you think she did it?'

'I suspect she was gambling that eliminating him would effectively end any further investigation of Geraldine's death, and with it, any risk of her being implicated. And she was careful to cover her tracks – there's no trace of her visit to the flat that night, no witnesses, no CCTV sightings. Even the takeaway was ordered via an unregistered mobile.' Flyte dug out her notebook. 'There is some good news though. Something that arose out of my . . . fortuitous discovery of Renwick's marriage to Julia Torrance.'

Their eyes locked – and Cassie suddenly understood the dilemma that Flyte must have wrestled with. Unable to reveal that it was Cassie who had found the marriage record after breaking into Mrs E's house, Flyte had been forced to lie, presumably saying that she'd found it herself during her own, legitimate visit to Patna Road.

Cassie drank some tea to hide an admiring smile: for a rulebook junkie like Flyte it must have been a big deal to do something less than 100 per cent kosher – and to trust Cassie to keep the white lie under wraps.

Flyte brought her up to date on Julia Torrance's brief marriage to Renwick, whom she'd met through a dating site based in Manchester. Julia had sold her house so that the couple could buy a place in the Algarve but instead, right after completion, Renwick transferred half the proceeds out of their joint account and disappeared. Julia hired a financial investigator, but the money – £700,000 – had already conga-ed its way through a string of overseas accounts, and eventually she'd had to accept that there was no hope of getting it back.

'She didn't tell the police?' asked Cassie.

'She felt too humiliated to report it at the time. But now she knows that Renwick had other victims, she's keen to help.'

Unable to speak, Cassie bit her lip so hard she tasted blood – a deliberate act of penance for her stupidity in falling for Renwick's act – and for all the other things she'd got wrong. Like her crazy theory that Mrs E had a previous love child, solely on the basis of a pink baby hat and Julia Torrance having the middle name Geraldine. It was obvious now that the baby the young Mrs E had been cradling in the framed Polaroid by her bed was Owen after all – a treasured memory perhaps, of a simpler time, before their relationship soured.

'They met through a dating site called Rapport, based in Manchester.' Flyte put a printout in front of her. 'See anyone you recognise?'

Under the heading 'Meet the Rapport Team' lay a grid of photographs. Cassie ran her eye down the smiling faces, before returning to a woman with short, flame-red hair. She certainly had an uncanny ability to change up her look, but those eyes sent a trickle of ice-water down Cassie's neck.

'That's her.'

Elizabeth Renwick had used a different false identity to secure the post of Rapport's membership manager – a job that enabled her to select the recently widowed Julia Torrance as a promising victim.

'It isn't enough to charge her with Geraldine's murder,' warned Flyte. 'But it does prove that she was an active partner in the conspiracy to defraud both women, which will almost certainly mean a custodial sentence.'

'Big deal,' muttered Cassie. Reaching for the knitting needle her grandmother had lent her she bent to scratch her leg inside the fracture boot. 'I can see why she had to kill Mrs E – and her brother. But why was she so keen to get rid of me?'

'Barry was clearly reporting your suspicions about Geraldine's death back to her. When you told him the police were investigating, she must have panicked – maybe worried that he had unwittingly incriminated her during one of your meetings. With him gone and Geraldine about to be cremated – you were the last loose end.'

Cassie said nothing. That might have been how Elizabeth had rationalised it to herself, but what she had seen in her eyes four days ago wasn't the look of someone simply tidying up loose ends.

She had no idea why, but Elizabeth Renwick hated her.

Chapter Fifty-One

After Flyte left, Cassie found herself puzzling over their encounter. Apart from their moment of silent collaboration over the Patna Rd break-in, she had picked up some new awkwardness in Flyte that she couldn't explain.

Mulling it over, she went to the kitchen sink for a glass of water. As the tap ran, her eye fell on a jagged groove gouged into the draining board, a bright zigzag against the duller surrounding metal. The breath stopped in her throat as she saw again the flash of the blade coming towards her, the tortured squeal of steel on steel.

It dawned on her that it wasn't just the aftermath of the attack she was struggling with. The experience had brought a brutal fact home to her: *one day, she would die.* There was a date marked in the calendar when Cassie Raven would cease to exist. Rationally, she already knew it, of course – her day job made the inevitability of death hard to ignore – but having to face the fact of her own mortality at the age of twenty-five, that was totally different.

Hard on the heels of that thought had come others. Would anyone come to her funeral? Would she ever find someone to share her life with? Let alone have kids?

She found herself dialling Rachel's number.

'Listen, Rach I'm sorry to bother you. I just wanted to tell you something.'

'I'm listening.' She sounded cautious, but not discouraging.

'You know those times I said I slept over at Carl's? Well, you were right, I wasn't being honest.'

She heard a little in-breath.

'But look, I wasn't sleeping with anyone else either. The fact is . . . I was at the mortuary.'

'You . . . slept at the mortuary? What for?'

After Cassie told her about staying with the body of nine-year-old Oliver, and her other overnight stays with dead children, Rachel made a noise that mixed affection and exasperation. 'That's a lovely thing to do. But why didn't you tell me?'

The truthful answer: because the admission would have skated too close to her sacred bond with the dead, which she wasn't about to confess to – then or now.

Instead she said, 'I suppose I wasn't sure how you'd take it. You might have noticed, when we were together . . . I'm not that great at sharing?'

Rachel left a diplomatic pause before saying, 'Well, thank you. I appreciate you telling me.'

After hanging up, Cassie was surprised to find herself feeling more philosophical about their failed relationship. Maybe telling Rachel the truth had somehow helped to close that chapter.

After rolling a single-skin joint, she logged into her email for the first time in days – and stared uncomprehendingly at the name that jumped out at her from the list of unopened messages.

She'd never got an email from beyond the grave before.

It had been sent from Christian Maclaren's email address the night before Mrs E's funeral – and only a couple of hours before he'd been murdered.

'Dear Cassie,' it began. 'My real name is Barry Renwick, and this is the hardest letter I've ever had to write.'

He started with a confession, how when he'd first contacted Geraldine, his sole aim had been to steal from her – going on to admit that it wouldn't have been his first offence of this kind. But then he made a startling declaration: he had shelved the whole plan after finding himself genuinely falling in love with 'darling Geri'.

Cassie made a noise of furious disbelief: conspiring to murder someone was a funny way of showing love.

According to Renwick, when Geraldine found him out, he had confessed everything. Accepting that there could be no future for them, he asked if there was anything he could do to try to make amends. 'She said something I'll never forget. She challenged me to "become a better man".' A challenge he was taking up, he claimed, by reviving his previous business filming weddings and other events, in order to earn 'an honest living'.

Cassie skim-read the next paragraph, which laid out Renwick's enduring feelings of shame and guilt, before she was pulled up short by a sentence that was partly underlined.

Renwick wrote: 'I admit I was a fraudster. But you must believe me when I say <u>I had nothing to do with Geri's death</u>.'

Cassie pinched out her barely smoked joint – she needed to think straight.

Was this all simply a last-ditch bid by Renwick to exonerate himself as the police closed in? If so, what had he been hoping to achieve? His protestations of innocence were hardly likely to persuade the cops.

If he really *was* telling the truth, it would explain a lot: above all, his devastated reaction when Cassie had first told him Mrs E was dead. His shock and grief had struck her as 100 per cent genuine – so much so that it had scrambled Cassie's usually acute radar for reading people and situations.

She read on. 'The times you and I met,' he wrote. 'I kept trying to escape the truth. But eventually I could no longer deny what was staring me in the face. That my sister Elizabeth murdered Geri.' He said he was meeting her that evening, with the aim of persuading her to hand herself in. 'If she refuses, I am going to tell DS Flyte the whole story. I love my sister, but she has to face the consequences of what she did.' Cassie remembered Renwick's flicker of unease over Mrs E's toxicology results. Knowing that her death was unexplained and that his sister was a lifelong diabetic who self-injected insulin, he had evidently started putting two and two together.

Renwick's confession brought only a crushing sense of frustration. What had he achieved by confronting his sister, other than to sign his own death warrant?

But Barry Renwick had kept his biggest bombshell till last.

FLYTE

DS Flyte – accompanied by Josh – opened the door to interview room one, where Elizabeth Renwick sat alongside her defence solicitor, who was murmuring something in her ear.

It was six days since Elizabeth had tried to knife Cassie and Flyte was amused to see that she had discarded her usual grunge-chic in favour of pearl earrings and a demure high-necked white blouse: a look evidently calculated to broadcast the message 'innocent victim', and one which Flyte expected to see a lot more of in court.

After Josh started the recording, Flyte read out the caution, at which point the brief – a wiry guy with dark floppy hair and intelligent eyes – interjected. 'Before we begin, I would like it put on the record that I made a request for prior sight of this "new evidence" you say you have against my client – and that my request was denied.'

'Duly noted,' said Flyte. She and DI Bellwether had already had a telephone conference with the CPS who had decided that it was defensible to give Renwick no prior warning of the evidence she was about to see.

Opening her laptop, Flyte angled it to ensure that Renwick and her solicitor could see the screen clearly. The brief looked uneasy, but Elizabeth's expression held only complacency tinged with curiosity – apparently confident that she'd left no trace of her crimes.

Flyte said, 'I am about to play Elizabeth Renwick an audio-visual file sixteen minutes in length. We'll be viewing a copy – the original has been sealed as evidence.'

The footage started just before 10 p.m. with Barry Renwick's face looming into fish-eyed close-up as he adjusted the camera and checked the audio levels. Flyte had found it unnerving, on her first viewing, to look into the eyes of someone with no idea he had less than an hour to live.

This time she was entirely focused on Elizabeth Renwick's reaction to the footage. She had become very still, but otherwise was maintaining an outward calm.

At 22:13, the motion-sensitive camera sprang back to life, triggered by Elizabeth's arrival with the takeaway. Its wide angle took in the whole kitchen, capturing her unpacking the boxes of curry onto the kitchen worktop, while Barry uncorked the wine behind her at the kitchen table.

Elizabeth seemed in good spirits, singing along to what sounded like Oasis in the background. It had worried Flyte at first, when she'd started playing music on her phone, but the audio of the conversation between brother and sister still cut through nice and clear.

When Barry told his sister he was meeting the police detective investigating 'Geri's death' the following day, Elizabeth didn't reply, or even look up, although her lips did stop moving to the lyrics.

He came over to her and put his hands on her shoulders. 'Look, Lizzie, I know you've always denied it, but we both know it was you who . . . who killed Geraldine.'

'Stop the film.' The solicitor, who had been shifting around in his seat with growing agitation, fixed a look on Flyte. 'I suggest we halt the interview so that I can confer with my client,' he said, glancing at Elizabeth for agreement. Her gaze was fixed on the screen, which showed Barry frozen, his hands on his sister's shoulders, an encouraging half smile on his face. If Flyte had to describe Elizabeth's expression, she would call it wistful.

'Elizabeth?' prompted the solicitor.

'I want to see it.' Her tone brooked no argument.

'I would have to advise—'

She made a savage gesture with one hand and the solicitor subsided with a resigned shrug.

Flyte nodded to Josh to restart the film. Barry had ended his email to Cassie by sharing the final part of his plan: to confront his sister over Geraldine Edwards' murder and secretly film the conversation in the hope she might confess. If he failed to persuade her to turn herself in to the police, he planned to hand the footage over to Flyte at their meeting the following day.

Officers dispatched back to Renwick's flat had swiftly located the pinhole camera hidden in a smoke detector. When they couldn't locate the receiver Flyte had been left on tenterhooks, before finally getting the news that they'd found it, tucked inside the casing of the boiler. On the film, Elizabeth made no response to Barry's accusation; instead, picking up a kitchen knife from the worktop, she started to quarter the naan bread with energetic strokes.

'I've seen the way it's been eating you up,' Barry went on, hands still on her shoulders, his voice affectionate. 'Lizzie, Lizbet, you won't find any peace until you admit to what you did. Come with me tomorrow to see the detective and we'll tell her everything, together.'

Elizabeth wheeled around to face him, Flyte's eyes going to the knife she still held in her hand.

'I had to do it!' she burst out. 'When you said she knew everything, I just . . . freaked.' She made a pleading face. 'What if she had gone to the police?'

Flyte thought she detected Barry's shoulders slumping a fraction at his little sister's admission: perhaps until that moment he'd still been hoping against hope that he'd got it wrong.

'I told you, if that happened I would take the blame myself, keep you out of it,' he said.

Elizabeth gave a vehement shake of her head. 'I couldn't let you do that. I had to get her out of the way, to protect both of us.'

In the interview room, Elizabeth's solicitor tried to catch her eye, but she ignored him.

On the film she was telling Barry: 'She could have ruined everything – surely you can see that?' – sounding for all the world like a teenager trying to wheedle her way out of trouble after exceeding her phone allowance.

'Look, Lizzie, I have tried to understand what you might have been thinking when you . . . did it. But it's not . . . normal.' Renwick's voice grew ragged. 'Remember that time in the home? When you went for that girl with the scissors?'

'Penny Harrison.' The name was spat out.

He looked down at her. 'She was lucky there was a first aider on hand. And you were lucky not to get sent to a secure unit.'

'Only because you stood up for me! Told them what a cow she could be. You always looked after me – how could you betray me now and let them put me in prison?'

'Lizzie, they'll send you to a hospital, not prison. You need help.' He tidied the hair off her face – a parental gesture. 'You know that I'll stand by you. I'll be doing time as well, remember.'

'No! It would be like going back into care. Why do we have to?' She smiled up at him. 'Why don't we go away, just you and me. Remember our Rome idea? Taking an apartment near the Trevi Fountain and riding around on a Vespa?'

In the interview room, Elizabeth had leaned forward a little, her eyes glued on the scene unfolding on the laptop as if she were the only person in the room. At the mention of Rome, Flyte was confused to see a hopeful smile tug at the corners of Elizabeth's mouth, before realising that she was right back there in her brother's kitchen, convinced that somehow, this time, she might persuade him.

Barry patted his sister's upper arm, the one that still held the knife. 'Maybe when we get out.'

Her head drooped against his shoulder and there was a long silence. Finally she spoke. 'You're going to do it anyway, aren't you? You're going to betray me.'

Barry took her by the shoulders and bent to look into her eyes. 'It's not a betrayal, Lizzie. I'm doing it because I love you.'

She gave a little girl nod, appearing to concede. 'I love you, too.'

'Let's sit down and have a drink, talk it over properly' – and with a final squeeze of her shoulder, he returned to the kitchen table and sat down, his back to his sister.

Knowing what was coming, Flyte's hands balled reflexively into fists under the table.

Elizabeth Renwick crossed the tiny kitchen in two or three strides. A blur of upraised arm, a wink of steel on the downstroke and Barry tipped sideways, both hands at his neck, making a choking noise. As he crashed to the floor, Elizabeth took a quick step backwards.

Flyte was watching her reaction to the footage. Up until this moment, Elizabeth had remained almost preternaturally still, but just before the attack, she had craned forward, like a moviegoer gripped by the denouement.

Flyte pressed pause. 'As you know, Elizabeth, the film goes on to record you watching as your brother drowned in his own blood. Two and a half minutes during which you could have helped him, possibly even saved his life.'

Elizabeth turned eyes narrowed with hate on Flyte, who stared straight back at her.

'It's a funny way to show you love someone, isn't it, Elizabeth? Cold-blooded murder.'

Without warning, Elizabeth slumped sideways in her chair, eyes half closed, lips goldfishing for air. Her solicitor didn't miss a beat, 'Since my client has been taken ill, I am terminating this interview. Please call a doctor immediately.'

Within a minute or so, Elizabeth had staged a semi-recovery and her brief was helping her to her feet. Before leaving the room, he turned to murmur to Flyte, 'I imagine my client will be enjoying your hospitality until charges are brought?' His look admitting what they both knew: the gig was well and truly up.

Once they had left, Flyte and Josh exchanged a grin.

'I just want to check something,' said Flyte, pressing rewind.

As Elizabeth stood over the dying Barry, it looked like her lips were moving, but her words were no longer audible.

When the volume was increased to maximum, it became clear. Elizabeth Renwick hadn't been saying anything; as she watched her brother choke to death, she'd been singing along to 'Wonderwall'.

Pointing to the timecode, Josh shook his head in disbelief 'Less than seventeen minutes for a nice night in with a curry to turn into a snuff movie.'

Flyte rewound, back to the moment when Barry sat down at the table, right after telling his sister he was going to hand her over the police. 'Look at Barry's body language, when she comes at him.'

She clicked through it frame by frame. In the final seconds before Elizabeth struck, Barry's hands were flat on the table, his head slightly bowed, his body oddly still – as if bracing himself.

'He *knows* what she's about to do,' said Josh, shaking his head slowly. 'So why on earth does he just sit there?'

Flyte was asking herself the same question. Barry Renwick must have known how his volatile sister might react – yet he had made no effort to protect himself. An outlandish idea came to her: had Renwick sacrificed himself in order to ensure justice for Geraldine Edwards by recording his own murder?

Flyte and Josh took the lift back down to the office. After a moment's silence he said, 'Sarge, I wanted to let you know, one of the guys has been saying that you nicked the Edwards case off Steve Sloman while he's away on paternity leave?'

She gave him a disbelieving look.

'I know,' he said. 'So I told him that if you hadn't taken another look at it and kept plugging away, well, that nutcase female in there would have got away with murder. Anyway, just so you know, everybody else agreed with me.'

She smiled, feeling her cheeks colour up.

As they left the lift, his expression grew shy. 'It's my birthday today,' he said. 'Come for a bevvy with the gang?'

Her lips were already forming a polite excuse when she heard herself say 'I'd love to. I owe you a few pints for all your hard work.'

The pub was pretty scuzzy, like most of Camden's cop drinking haunts, but after a couple of Sauvignons it dawned on Flyte that she was enjoying herself. Every time she tried to get a round, one of her colleagues would wave her money away and insist on buying, to congratulate her on the Edwards case. After an hour of this, Flyte realised she was feeling something she hadn't felt since leaving Winchester nick, that she was part of a team again.

Nonetheless, she excused herself before the Greek taverna stage of the evening – impatient to get home, to do what she'd been thinking about all day.

Back at the flat, she took the bag containing the photo frame she'd bought into the bedroom. When she'd seen the pale blue mother of pearl frame on an antique stall in the market on her way to work, it had crystallised something that had been on her mind since Geraldine Edwards' funeral – something she'd not been able to do in all the time since it had happened.

Opening the bottom drawer of her wardrobe she retrieved the carved walnut box, the one she'd once kept her childhood treasures in. Unwrapping the photograph from its nest of soft pink fabric, she slid it carefully into the frame.

Then she lay back on the bed, holding the tiny babygro against her chest, and for the first time in twenty-six months allowed herself to look into the beautiful, serene face of her baby girl.

Chapter Fifty-Two

Phyllida Flyte had suggested they meet at their usual coffee shop the following morning and Cassie was about to go in when she spotted Kieran – although it took her a moment to recognise her old squatting buddy.

'Wow, Kieran, that's some jacket.'

What stood out wasn't so much the ski jacket's lurid lime-green hue, nor the fact that it was two sizes too big for him, but its leopard skin pattern.

'It's the dogs', isn't it?' As he performed a wobbly twirl, she caught the whiff of extra-strong lager. 'The nice old girl at the Age Concern shop gave it to me for nothing. Can you believe the posh wanker who donated it never even wore it?'

Cassie could totally believe it, so instead of replying she asked how he was, trying not to let her eyes linger on the fresh bruise at the side of his temple, hopefully the result of nothing more sinister than a tumble when he was off his head.

'I'm good, Cassie Raven, never better.' His gappy but joyous grin made her marvel again that, in spite of a life that appeared so irredeemably shit, Kieran managed to stay so upbeat. The Special Brew probably helped.

Recognising the tall slim figure with the ramrod walk approaching from the direction of the high street, she lifted her hand in a wave. Kieran followed her gaze for a moment before shooting Cassie a sly look 'Who's the hottie? New girlfriend?'

Cassie shook her head, laughing 'She's a *cop*, Kieran.'

'You're shitting me!' He checked her out again. 'The feds get better looking every day.' Following his gaze, Cassie had to admit he was right: despite the uptight vibe she gave off even at a distance Phyllida Flyte had the kind of beauty that turned heads.

When Flyte reached them there was an awkward exchange of hellos, before she leaned in to examine Kieran's bruised face. 'That looks like a nasty knock you took there. Do you want to report an assault?' The empathy in her voice took Cassie back to the night of the mortuary invasion, and the unexpected kindness Flyte had shown her.

'Nah, bless you. I walked into a door,' said Kieran.

Cassie persuaded him to wait while she bought him a sandwich. But inside the coffee shop, when she tried to pay for Kieran's bacon baguette Flyte shook her head. 'After everything you've done, I reckon the Met can stand your pal breakfast.'

Outside Kieran said, 'You're a mate, Cassie Raven.'

'Don't thank me, thank the feds.'

His eyebrows went up. 'Fuck a duck!' Peeling the lid from his caramel latte he took a thoughtful slurp. 'She seems really nice – for a cop.' He winked at her. 'You two make a good-looking couple, y'know.'

Cassie laughed 'There's nothing like that . . .'

'Never say never, Cassie Raven. You could do a lot worse.' He zipped up his ski jacket with the purposeful air of a man anticipating a busy day at the office. 'I'd better be off.'

After getting a table, she and Flyte sipped their drinks in silence for a long moment, making Cassie wonder whether the awkward vibe of their last meeting was the new normal. Maybe Flyte's friendliness had been an act all along, adopted purely to keep her onside during the investigation – a thought she was surprised to find upsetting.

'So...you wanted to see me?' Cassie asked.

'Rosie Harrison's boyfriend has admitted to administering the heroin overdose that killed her.'

Cassie pictured the puzzled look in young Rosie's eyes and the injection site that didn't fit with her being right-handed. 'Oh, that's great news.'

'He folded as soon as I confronted him with the facts.' Flyte gave one of her tight little smiles. 'He admitted that when she OD'd he panicked and dragged her outside "to wake her up".'

'Right. And left her there without even calling 999. Bastard.'

'He says he meant to but zonked out when he got back inside.' Flyte raised her cup in a toast, meeting Cassie's eyes properly for the first time. 'We've charged him with manslaughter.'

Cassie returned the gesture.

'Any news on Renwick's sister? Will his recording get her put away for killing Geraldine?'

Flyte nodded. 'We think she'll plead guilty to manslaughter by reason of diminished responsibility, citing a mental disorder. They're probably hoping she'll serve her sentence in a special hospital rather than prison.'

'Does that mean she could get out sooner?'

Flyte shook her head. 'Unlikely, given the seriousness of her crimes – and her history of violence.' A glance down at her notebook. 'There was a road rage incident a few years ago. She chased down a female driver who'd overtaken her and tried to throttle her. The victim declined to press charges. And when she was only thirteen she attacked another girl at the residential home with a pair of scissors, left her needing five stitches in her face.'

Seeing a flash frame of Elizabeth Renwick, silvery blade in her upraised hand, Cassie had to bear down on a shudder. 'Do you know why?'

'The care home report says the victim had a crush on Barry. The two girls were making costumes for some play when she told Elizabeth he'd asked her out. Her response was to reach for the nearest weapon.'

'She was jealous?'

'Apparently, Elizabeth worshipped him. It sounds as though the two of them were inseparable in the home. Elizabeth was notorious for being volatile, prone to lashing out, while Barry played protector and tried to keep her out of trouble.'

'So in her eyes they really *were* Romeo and Juliet,' said Cassie. 'Another good reason to hate Mrs E, after Barry went off script and fell in love with her.'

Flyte nodded. 'I think that's the real reason she killed Geraldine – for daring to come between her and her precious brother. It might explain why she tried to kill you, too.'

'Me?'

'She was probably jealous of his friendship with a good-looking young woman.'

Their eyes collided. Cassie felt herself blush – and was puzzled to see colour creeping up Flyte's cheeks as well. They each busied themselves with their drinks.

'Do you believe Barry really *was* determined to change,' asked Cassie, 'like he said in his email?'

Flyte gave a half shrug, half nod. 'He recently exchanged contracts on his flat and had given his solicitors instructions to transfer the proceeds to Julia Torrance's bank account. He told them it was to "settle an old debt".'

So Renwick had taken up Mrs E's challenge. Cassie was shocked to feel tears building behind her eyes.

Maybe Flyte noticed because she asked, 'How are you bearing up? You've been through a hell of a lot in the last couple of weeks.'

'I just feel such an idiot for *trusting* Christian – I mean Barry. Why wasn't I more sceptical?'

'If you *had* been more sceptical, you never would have shared your doubts over Geraldine's death with him,' said Flyte, 'and he might never have suspected his sister of murder.' When Cassie just shrugged, she leaned towards her across the table. 'Listen, Cassie. You helped Renwick rediscover his conscience. If that hadn't happened we wouldn't be where we are now – getting justice for Geraldine.' Cassie met Phyllida Flyte's gaze, the glacier-blue irises with their darker limbic ring, which had once reminded her of an Arctic wolf.

'That was nothing to do with me – it was all down to Mrs E.'

Flyte frowned, uncomprehending.

'What you said about his conscience, getting his sister to confess and dying in the process,' said Cassie. 'It was his love for Geraldine that made him do that. She made him want to be a better man.'

Cassie was suddenly hyper-aware that their hands lay a finger-length apart on the table. 'Why did you want to meet up?' the question came out unplanned, startling her.

'What do you mean?'

'It's just . . .' she met Flyte's clear, serious gaze. 'You could have told me all this on the phone, couldn't you?'

Flyte's pink lips opened and closed again, and she looked off into the room as if searching for the answer. When her eyes returned to Cassie's they held the look of someone forced into a painful admission.

'Honestly? I suppose I just wanted to see you again.'

Chapter Fifty-Three

Taking the lift up to her grandmother's where she was having lunch, Cassie realised that it was twenty days since she had first heard Mrs E 'speak'.

She no longer asked herself whether those words, and the apparitions that had followed, were real – or just projections bubbling up from her subconscious.

The important thing was that they had initiated a chain of events that would end with Elizabeth Renwick facing retribution for her crimes. And Cassie liked to think that, after a life spent in pursuit of objective facts, Mrs E would take satisfaction from knowing that the truth had been uncovered.

Her relationship with Phyllida Flyte, on the other hand, was a puzzle with no easy answer. Did she want friendship, or something more? Either way, it had plunged Cassie into confusion. Was she attracted to her? *Yes.* But the idea of becoming friends, let alone lovers, with a cop was way out of her comfort zone.

At the flat, Cassie found her grandmother glued to the TV news. Cassie's broken ankle had left her no choice but to share an edited version of recent events with her, and the old lady had reacted calmly enough. After crossing herself, she'd reached up to take Cassie's face in both hands, fixing her with those beady eyes. 'Thank God you're a survivor, *tygrysek*, like me.'

Cassie had reached a big decision. It was high time she and her grandmother had a proper talk about the mystery she sensed swirling around her parents' death – what exactly had happened the night of the crash, why Cassie hadn't been allowed to attend their funeral, and above all, why Babcia was so relentlessly hostile towards her father.

Now, her grandmother was saying, 'Cassandra, do you remember that rapist who attacked all those women walking home from train stations? They've let him out of prison after *four years* and now he's raped someone else.'

Something in her gran's voice made Cassie look over. She was perched on the very edge of the sofa, her body tense. The news had given way to a football report, but she still sat as if frozen, staring at the TV.

'Babcia? Are you OK?'

Appearing to surface, she looked over, and Cassie saw that the colour had drained from her face. '*Dobrze,*' she murmured, lapsing into Polish.

Seeing her about to stand, Cassie leapt up. 'You sit and drink your tea. Let me look after the soup.'

A few minutes later, Cassie was stirring the panful of barszcz on the stove, when she heard the *crack-tinkle* of breaking crockery. She found Babcia slumped sideways on the sofa, her eyes closed, the porcelain cup broken into half a dozen pieces on the glass-topped coffee table.

Some forty hellish minutes later Cassie was pacing the family waiting room at the hospital. The question that kept revolving through her thoughts: would her grandmother's unconscious face disappearing behind a curtain in resus be Cassie's last sight of her alive?

Seeing the registrar striding down the corridor towards her, Cassie felt dread envelop her like a cold fog. She had to resist the urge to grab her by the arm.

'How is she?'

'She's conscious and aware.'

Thank God. Cassie realised she had just crossed herself. 'What did her bloods say?'

'As we suspected, it was a TIA, which means—'

'Transient ischaemic attack.' *A mini-stroke.* 'Can she talk?'

'Her speech appears to be unaffected. She's still suffering some weakness down her left side but we're hopeful that will pass, too.'

Cassie followed the doctor to the curtained alcove. In the bed lay a wizened doll-like figure propped up on a stack of pillows, eyes closed, barely recognisable as her indomitable grandmother.

'Babcia! How are you?' Cassie took one wrinkled hand in hers and chafed it. 'You're so cold!'

'I'm fine.' Her voice sounded faint, like it was coming over a phone line from Siberia.

'Listen, the doctors say you're going to be OK,' Cassie pulled the blanket up over her skinny chest. 'You'll probably need to take blood-thinning drugs, and you're going to have to take it easy for a while.'

One of her eyes opened a crack, 'No more skydiving?'

Relief washed over Cassie. 'Is there anything you need? Are you thirsty?'

She shook her head, then opened both eyes. 'There is something I must tell you, Cassandra.'

'Can't it wait until you're feeling better?' Cassie already had enough to deal with, trying to absorb the idea of her grandmother dying, or worse, left in some mentally altered state.

'No.' A hint of her usual determination came to the surface. Pushing herself a little higher on the bank of pillows she sought Cassie's eyes. 'It's about your mother and father.'

'Not now, Babcia . . .'

The old lady brought a hand from under the blanket and set it on top of Cassie's. 'It has to be now, *tygrysek*. I should have told you long ago. I cannot risk going to my grave without you knowing the truth.' Her voice grew a little stronger. 'Cassandra, your parents didn't die in a motor car accident.' She scanned Cassie's face. 'I have to tell you that your father, he . . . he murdered your mother.'

It was as if Cassie's entire being had been jerked up and out of her body, to be left hanging in mid-air.

'I'm so sorry to have to tell you such a dreadful thing.' She managed to squeeze Cassie's hand, which brought her back to herself with a jolt. 'I have had more than twenty years to become accustomed to it – as if such a thing were ever possible.'

The old lady's eyes closed, and she fell silent for so long that Cassie started to panic. 'Babcia?'

They opened again.

'Can you tell me . . . how it happened?'

'Not long after you were born, the marriage went bad and your father took to drink. One time I found your mama with a black eye – she made up some story, but I knew it was just to protect him. Then he got it into his head that my Katherine was having an affair. That sweet, loyal child! One night he followed her and beat her to death in a drunken rage.'

Cassie stared down at her grandmother's hand, mottled and lumpy with veins, against her own pale smooth one. 'What happened to him?'

'He went to prison.'

'What? Are you saying he's still alive?' Everything twisted and lurched: all the years she'd spent thinking her parents died together in the crash – had even viewed it as a romantic ending of sorts. Now she understood why her mother was buried alone in Camden Cemetery: not, as Babcia had always claimed, because her father's family insisted he be buried in Ireland.

'Yes. And five years ago, they released him!' Cold fury strengthened her voice. 'For years I dreaded him turning up on the doorstep, but I thank the Lord he never did.' She sketched a cross over her chest. 'The parole people told me he went to live in Northern Ireland, where his family was from.'

Cassie stared out of the window at the heartless blue sky, gripped by the knowledge that nothing would ever be the same again. The dad of her imagination was shattered: no longer the handsome Jack the Lad with the ready smile – a bit of a rebel, like her – but a jealous, violent man. A man who had brutally murdered her mum.

Cassie's childhood memory of him came rushing back, newly vivid: her dad's dark curly head bent over the bowl of food in front of her, his expression intent, as if hunting for something. A sweet, tomatoey smell in the air. All of a sudden, she remembered. The bowl had held alphabetti spaghetti, one of her favourite foods, but for some long-forgotten reason she wouldn't eat the Xs. So her dad would track them down and pick them out, one by one.

How to reconcile the father prepared do that for his child with the man who would go on to beat his wife to death?

'When I saw the news about that animal they let out of prison to rape another woman, it made me fearful, Cassandra.' Babcia sounded agitated. 'I realised that if I died and he decided to track you down, you needed to know what he did to your mama, what kind of man he really is.'

'But Gran, why would be come looking for me after all these years – after what he did?'

'He denied it, of course, so he might have tried to persuade you. But the police told me it was an open-and-shut case.' A nod of grim satisfaction. 'And at his trial the jury was unanimous.'

Cassie didn't know what to say, still struggling to adjust to the monumental shift in her world-view.

'Losing my Katherine broke my heart. But I know it left a scar on you, too, *tygrysek*.' She squeezed Cassie's hand. 'I think perhaps that's why you find it hard to make a lasting relationship with a boy. Or a girl.'

Cassie shot her grandmother a shocked look. *So, the old fox had known all along.*

'Maybe that is what makes you walk away from people, before they walk away from you.'

Complicated feelings churned in Cassie's stomach. Seeing her grandmother about to say more, she said, 'Babcia, you were my mother *and* my father. I didn't need anyone else. Now, you get some sleep. I'm going to pop home to pick up some things for you.'

With a final squeeze of the warm and bony hand, Cassie pulled the coverlet up to her grandmother's chin and watched her drift off.

Her father's crime explained so much at a single stroke: the mysterious absence of photos of him, the barbed comments – and silences – she'd found so confusing over these past twenty-one years. The revelation had already launched a hundred questions buzzing through her mind – but finding the answers would have to wait until Babcia was back to her old self.

After taking the bus back to the high street, Cassie took the canal towpath towards her grandmother's place.

Although the sun had already set the sky was still light, silhouetting the canal bridge fifty metres up ahead where she had fought for her life a week earlier.

Seeing a woman in a red coat striding across the bridge, Cassie slowed. The woman paused and turned to look at her. Her face was shrouded in darkness, backlit by the evening sky, but the voice in Cassie's ear was so clear it might have come from an arm's length away.

Life's too short, Cassandra, to spend it with the dead.

And with that, Mrs E walked off the bridge, her dark head disappearing down the stairs.

With a stab of regret so fierce it caused a sharp in-breath, Cassie knew that she would never see her again.

Acknowledgements

Creating Cassie Raven and her world wouldn't have been possible without the input and advice of a bunch of smart and generous people.

My greatest debt of gratitude is to Barbara Peters, the award-winning anatomical pathology technician with whom I have spent many a happy hour discussing life, death and evisceration. Her knowledge, not just of working with the dead but also the emotional pressures of dealing with those they leave behind, has been invaluable.

Others who have patiently endured a bunch of dumb questions about dead bodies include pathologists Neil Shepherd, Dominic Chambers and Mike Heath. I am also indebted to toxicologist Joanna Hockenhull and the world-renowned toxicology team at Charing Cross Hospital headed by Sue Paterson. As ever, DI Paula James has been a no-nonsense font of knowledge about police matters. And on the legal front, I am grateful to all the lawyers who have lent me their legal nous – Maggie Morrissey, Neil White and Phil Hill – as well as to the delightful coroner-turned-sheep-farmer Alison Thompson. Any errors are mine alone.

For helping me turn an idea into a novel and launch it into the world, heartfelt thanks to my legendary agent, Jane Gregory, and the team at David Higham Associates, including Sara Langham, and especially Stephanie Glencross.

I was also lucky enough to receive five star feedback and cheerleading from the brilliant Isabelle Grey, and the support and scabrous humour of my fellow criminal types in crime writing's 'Fight Club' – they know who they are . . .

Finally, a huge thank you to the team at Zaffre, including Ciara Corrigan, and above all to my talented editor and friend Katherine Armstrong for her enthusiasm and sure-handed direction – I couldn't have had a better midwife for the series.

Further reading

Forensics – The Anatomy of Crime by Val McDermid
Unnatural Causes by Dr Richard Shepherd
All That Remains: A Life in Death by Prof Sue Black
Down Among the Dead Men by Michelle Williams
Past Mortems by Carla Valentine